The Opportunist

J Rowland Broughton

 New Generation Publishing

This Book is dedicated to my wife Karen and to my two children, Alison and Stuart, in the hope that in some way it compensates for all of those times that I was not there.

Author's note:

It should be noted that the events described in this book took place before the era of paid elected councillors was started and the only payment for lost time at work through council activities was a simple £10 per day which was paid to Committee Chairmen for attending meetings with Chief Officers.

The boast of heraldry, the pomp of power,
And all the beauty that wealth ere gave,
Waits like the inevitable hour,
The paths of glory lead but to the grave.

Introduction

Most people believe that politics is a dirty business, and that those who enter the field at any level should be aware of that fact before they commit themselves to the 'game'. In many respects it is, nothing more than a game that elected people get the chance to play, but the beauty of it all is that they are always playing it with other people's lives and other people's money.

The reality is that there are many who have a genuine belief that they can actually do something about the conditions in which they, their families, friends, and relatives live. It is 'the system', the traditions, and the pointless process of opposing something for the sake of presenting 'an opposition' that really gets in the way of good government.

This is a story about one such man and his election to local office, and the way in which he was treated by those around him, those whose motives turned out to be opposite to what he had expected. The plot and the characters are purely in the mind of the author, and any resemblance to anyone living or dead is purely coincidental.

The City of Hainton does not exist it is a complete fabrication, and the various officers and councillors in all of their words, deeds, and actions are pure fantasy. The dates that are given are arbitrary, and do not relate to any specific year or period of Government or to any particular individuals in any party. The views expressed are my own, and do not refer to the policies of any government either past or present.

Clearly there has to be some foundation on which an author builds such a story, and in this case the writer draws on some of his own experiences of being a member of council, for a short period, in his home town.

The lives and the occupations of all of the people were constructed to show how the actions of one set of individuals can affect the lives of the people around them, and how people can be manipulated, elevated and eventually destroyed, simply to preserve the vested interests of a few people who control the certain aspects of the lives of others.

This is not a story that is intended to evoke some sort of sympathy or empathy towards those who set out to try to enter the corridors of power. It is more a cautionary tale to warn others that no matter how much you think that you control what you are doing there are always others who are in positions that allow them to think that they can dictate the direction that the lives of other people might take.

All of the events described in this tale are the product of the writers imagination and do not relate to any person or persons either living or dead.

J Rowland Broughton 2005.

1

Monday

The rain battered down with sufficient force to make the droplets rebound from the pavement, and the bitterly cold wind buffeted the lone walker as he battled to make his way along the road. 'No one should turn a night out on a dog like this.' He muttered to himself, still able to joke about himself despite the weather, and to be frank there was no one else listening anyway.

He put his head down and pressed onwards, despite that inner feeling that there would be no one daft enough to want to attend a meeting of the local Tenants Association at this time of year, and if the inclement weather factor was added to the equation, then the chances of more than two other people being there were pretty remote. Another blast from the North-east smashed the rain through his trousers, and he could feel the water running down his legs and into his socks. Once the water had forced its way through the cloth, the cold wind quickly adapted the same route for its own purposes.

The Colly Farm Estate had been built in the late 1950's, to plans that had been laid down before the start of the Second World War. The original land was a series of sandy tracts that extended over four or five, hilly, medium sized, farms that were for the most-part devoid of trees. But the worst aspect of this was in winter when the wind blew from the north and east, and there was no shelter to be found anywhere on the whole estate. The houses were generally of good quality, but the amenities of the area were poor and the bus services into the city or to the nearest shopping centre were infrequent, and very unreliable.

It was nice of those thirties reformers to think that everybody in the world really wanted to live out in the country, but the people here were towns-people and did not want vast open spaces and fresh country air, even when they had no choice in the matter.

As he climbed towards the top of Chestnut Crescent John Robertson muttered to himself. 'Is there nowhere on this bloody estate that does not involve climbing hills, or vast flights of concrete stairs?' He'd asked himself that question many times before without coming to a reasoned conclusion. He turned through the gate of the house where he was expecting to attend a meeting, and climbed the twenty steps that led up to the concrete path the leading to the front door of the house. 'They've put old people out here to improve their quality of life'. The thought rippled through his head like a joke that had gone seriously wrong before the first houses had been occupied. Clearly no one from the Planning or Housing Committees had ever ventured out into this neck of the woods to find out what it would be like to live here. The people could go nowhere without having to climb a series of hills or catching a bus into the town centre about five miles away.

He knocked at the door, and it was opened quickly. "Get yourself inside lad. What a bloody awful night." Martin Smith stated in a dull monotone voice that belied the intelligence that lurked behind his rugged features.

"You're the first here." He continued, as he took the soaked coat from him. "Chances are that you'll be the only one here if the weather's anything to go by. I'll bet you could use a nip of the hard stuff for purely medicinal purposes of course."

"That would be just right." John answered as they moved in to the long lounge. The house was a typical three bed roomed council house of the early sixties; the type that had a through lounge and a kitchen downstairs, with a minuscule hall at the front and an even smaller access room against the back door; two medium sized bedrooms, a small 8' x 6' room, a bathroom, and toilet upstairs. The sum total of which was that all of the members of the family were for ever in each-others way. Children trying to do their home-work had nowhere to work other than in the lounge, and while they tried to work the rest of the family could not watch TV or listen to a radio or play music.

Martin and Jenny had two daughters and a son, and living conditions were cramped even when there were no visitors to the house. Martin drove buses for the local City Council, and was the Transport and General Workers Union representative at his Depot. His life was a round of work and meetings. Added to all of this he was an active member of the Constituency Labour Party. His was the now old fashioned, left wing, Socialism, the same as his fathers had been before him, and he was proud of it.

The two of them sat down against the open fire. They were complete opposites who respected each-others political beliefs and aspirations, but here they were united in their attempts to extract better living conditions and local amenities for Local Tenants and Residents from a City Council that appeared to have lost all sense of community care and amenity. The fact that its current make-up gave the Labour majority an overwhelming control was of little consequence to either of them. Their aims were simply to represent the people of their area in the best way that they could.

"How's Kathryn?" Martin asked seriously.

"She's no better, and it looks as though she will have to spend some more time in hospital."

John took out his handkerchief to wipe some of the

11

rain from his forehead."

"Would you like a towel to dry yourself off lad?" Martin asked beginning to rise to his feet.

"No thanks I'll be OK in a minute or two." said John indicating to Martin that he should remain in his chair. "I think that you and I should have a quiet word or two before the others get here. Did you hear that there was another accident down on the relief road last evening?"

"Yes I heard it on the local news," said Martin seriously, "The whole thing's getting beyond the point where we can delay any longer. We have to get a controlled crossing down there before we have someone else killed or injured."

"What's the Transportation Committees budget position for new traffic light controlled crossings?" asked John.

"I put the matter to our Ward Councillors at the Branch Meeting last Friday, and they said that there was no provision for additional crossings in this area in the current years allocation, and there would be nothing for next year either because of the spending constraints that were being applied by National Government."

"Good God!" John groaned. "Won't any of them ever learn?"

"It's all right for you, your lot hardly have a say in it." Martin was apologetic. "My lot on the other hand, have the means to make a difference, but will not grasp the nettle or make a decision either at National or Local Government level." Martin was clearly embarrassed by his Parties inability to find resources for what he and many others felt were essential road safety measures.

At this point the door- bell rang and another dripping wet member of the Tenants & Residents Association gratefully entered the warmth of the house. Of the eight person executive committee only three had managed to attend what had been a well- publicised meeting. As usual it was the three most regular attendees who were present when the meeting finally got underway.   John Robertson, Martin Smith, and Molly Bacon, the stalwarts of the Association There was little wonder that a Council (of any Political persuasion) could get away with half-baked schemes, and still ignore those needs that they believed had no political muscle, when the only resistance to their policies was this small band of people.

The meeting was an informal affair due to the fact that there were only three people in attendance. It was Martin's turn to chair the meeting and he had drawn up an agenda which they followed closely, and the regular business of the meeting was concluded in about thirty minutes.

It was when they reach that point in the meeting where they were asked if there was any other business that there was a sudden rush of enthusiasm. It was clear that all three of them wanted to raise questions about the road accident that had taken place the previous night but Molly got the question in first.

"The latest accident on the relief road is now a fatality," She spoke slowly. "Can we take any action to put pressure on the Council to force them into installing a traffic light controlled crossing at the junction of Williamson Street and the Relief Road?" She was clearly very distressed about the death. "You do know that Betsy was my niece, and that the accident has been a terrible blow to all of us, don't you?"

There was a stunned silence, but after a few minutes John said, "We didn't know that Betsy was a close relative of yours, and we are deeply sorry for you and the rest of the family. Please convey to them our deepest sympathy in their loss."

"I have already raised the question with the two

councillors for this Ward, and have received negative responses." apologised Martin. "I cannot believe that any council which purports to represent the people can dismiss, without investigation, a state of affairs that is costing our young people their lives." He paused, held his face in his hands. "How can they be so cruel, so blind".

"Perhaps we need to approach the opposition." John suggested. "After all there are Council Elections coming up in May this year, and all of the Parties will be looking for local issues on which to base their election programs. I know that will be of little comfort to the Browns at this time, but we must press at all levels to get some response from the main groups. Now we all know that each of us is affiliated to a different Political Party, so we all have a chance to do something that looks after the interests of the Tenants and Residents of this area. We must force our local politicians to do something for the area that they claim to represent and if they don't commit themselves to the improvement of amenities and Road Safety, then it will be the responsibility of this Committee to inform the people of their reluctance".

"My God" Martin interrupted. "That will put the cat amongst the pigeons. Can you imagine the situation where all of the parties are trying to out-do each other, and all on the same local issue?

That is what I call a stroke of real genius." He laughed. "Let's go for it?"

"Yes, I must say it has a rather sadistic appeal to me too." Molly smiled and had that rather 'far-away' look in her eye that some people have when they can visualise the out-come of a train of events before they happen. "Do I take it that we will all take the same appeal to our respective parties, and watch while the pot boils?" John asked quietly.

"Oh, yes please" Giggled Molly for the first time since she had heard of the death of her niece.

"I wouldn't miss this for the world." smiled Martin

"And neither would I." said John quietly.

And so it was they set off on their individual journeys into the political game reserve...

2

Tuesday

Edward Mayer, the local Conservative Party Agent was not the usual 'run of the mill' Conservative. He was a professional agent, and the general consensus of local opinion was that the party should not have had recourse to employ a person who cost them money, when there were those among them who thought that they could do the job equally as well he, if not better, On a purely voluntary basis.

In truth the Conservative Federation for the City had believed when they employed him that if they, at any time, blundered on any matter , they could point the finger in the general direct of the Agent, and he would absorb the blame, and absolve them from any wrong doing. After all was said and done, he was the professional, and as amateurs they were not really to blame for anything. John did not share the general opinion. Whenever he had needed advice on political or electoral matters Edward had always given him his best attention and advice. John had known that he would be working into the evening at the Party Office, so he 'dropped in' to have an informal chat.

He tapped at the office door, and a voice from within called, "OK it's open". And as he pushed at the door it continued, "Hello John, what can I do for you?" The man in front of him was pounding away at an ancient type writer, and he looked for all the world like an old time explorer or mad professor. He had a mop of rampant white hair, wore thick rimless spectacles over a pair of icy blue eyes, and to finalise the picture he was dressed in a suit of neatly pressed khaki drill.

Hardly what one would expect to find a Political Agent dressed in. 'What?' Except of course the ones that the opposition employed.

"Well it's like this Ted." John started to tell his tale. The listener, if indeed he was listening at all continued to hammer away at the keys of his typewriter. "Our Branch Association at Colly Farm will soon be meeting to select our candidates for the City Council Elections in May, and we were asked to look out for items that would be of interest to the prospective candidates.

You know that I am a founder Member of the Colly Farm Tenants and Residents Association, and at our meeting last night we heard reports of a fatal accident that took place on the main access road to the Estate on Friday of last week. This is the fourth fatal accident at the same spot in under two years, and in addition to this there has been a high number of accidents that have resulted in serious injury mainly to young people and small children.

The Labour controlled Council have tried to put off the idea of carrying out a traffic census and an analysis of pedestrian flows on the basis that they do not have the staff available to carry out the research that is necessary, and even if a case was made, they cannot install a controlled pedestrian crossing, because they do not have any cash in the current year's budget to get the work done. Nor do they have any allowance in next year's budget either."

He stopped typing. "Can you run that past me again" He stroked his chin thoughtfully as John repeated what he had said. "Hmmmm!" He emitted. "What do you intend to do about it?" He swung round to stare John full in the face.

"That's what I came to see you for. If I knew what to do I would be doing it now." John played a forehand volley straight back on to his backhand.

"Perhaps we should leave it to the Labour Party to trip over during the election campaign." Ted pondered. "If we kick up a fuss, win the election, and then can't find the funds to do it either, then we will be at fault. Where-as if we leave them to fry as, 'the none-caring', 'out of touch' party, the people will accept what-ever we do as a bonus."

"That's not an option." John pushed himself out of the chair. "That's just the sort of treatment that the people in this area are beginning to fight against. If we sit back and do nothing we will build a wall of resentment that it will take years to remove."

"Hold on, hold on, old son." Ted was suddenly all peace and tranquillity. "There's a lot more to this than I'm appreciating isn't there?"

"There certainly is." said John, calmer now. "The fact is Ted for the first time since the Estate was built the Conservative Party stands a real chance of winning both of the Colly Farm Seats.

The two Labour Councillors have done very little in the area, and the fact that the Council has refused to support a Controlled Road Crossing for the children has been the final straw. Even their prospective candidate has taken the unusual step of asking both us and the Lib-Dems to approach our members to see if we can get anything done."

"That puts a totally different slant on this whole problem." Ted was now all ears. "Can we get together with your Tenants and Residents to carry-out a full survey of traffic and pedestrian movement during peak travelling times, on each working day in the next week?"

"I reckon that we can just about cover the evening peak," John paused. "But the mornings are going to present us with some problems. Most of the women work during the day, that is until about three-o-clock in the afternoon."

"Well if your people can cover the evening, I'll get cover for the morning rush hour, even if I have to go out there and cover the thing myself." He burst into a fit of laughter that was as infectious as it was maniacal. "God I can't remember when I last did a survey like this. John it's good to be at the grass-roots of politics again. This is just the type of problem that will decide whether we win the next General Election or not."

"You don't really believe that do you Ted" John had dropped back into serious mode.

"Too damned right I do, and if you don't, then you should look after the job that you've got, and forget about politics. Anyway give me a call tomorrow, and let me know if you've got any gaps in your schedule for next week, and then we can swap oddments to make certain that we have full coverage. Now I want to change the subject for a minute. I've had Charles Brown round here tonight asking a load of questions about you. I'll bet you didn't know that!"

"What the devil does he want" John was puzzled.

Ted lowered his voice. "Now I did not tell you this OK? but Charles is not the most liked man in our camp, but he's looking around for some of the new candidates (Soon to be Members) to give support to his continued leadership of the Conservative Group on the Council. He thinks that you will make a good Chairman of a Committee, and he's asked that you attend the next meeting of the Tory Group to be held before the next meeting of Council. Now take a word of advice, if this guy shakes your hand, make sure that you count your fingers when he lets go.

Don't commit yourself to anything with him unless you're absolutely certain of what it is all about.

Do you understand what I'm saying?"

"Yes I understand perfectly." John said, but he was

already in auto-drive.

"Well I hope that you do, because if you get caught up with him your career in politics will be a meteoric, but short one. Before too long, he will get caught, and when he does all hell will be let loose." Ted shrugged his shoulders and then added. "Make sure that you keep both your hands and your feet clean." He paused and then returned to the business in hand. "You know, just thinking about this survey for a minute, perhaps it wouldn't be a bad idea to have a meeting here on Friday, so that we can tell every-body what we intend to do, and why the survey will help us." He thought for a moment. "Shall we say seven thirty in the small meeting room?"

"Yes!" said John. "That's great. That will really show that we are at least trying to do something about it."

Ted looked at John without saying a word for almost a minute, and then said, "You do know that you will not be allowed to stand for the Colly Farm, seat don't you John?"

"Don't be silly Ted, the nomination is mine for the taking." John retorted.

"I'm not being silly John, but your seat will be decided without anybody consulting the Ward committee. In fact I think that the seat that you will fight has probably already been decided."

He put his finger to his mouth, shook his head, and then continued. "It would be best for me if you forgot that I just told you that. All I want to say is that I think that you have the potential be a very good national politician, if the petty minded, and totally corrupt are kept away from you.

The trouble at this stage in your career is that you have not yet got your aeroplane off the ground, and yet you are attracted by the towering clouds, and you can hardly wait to be up there amongst the stars. So be careful John. Be very careful."

3

Wednesday

Martin was the first to show up at John's house, just before half-past-six in the evening.

"Come on in Marty," John greeted him. "You're a bit early for the meeting aren't you?"

"I wanted to have a word or two with you, before any of the others turned up." He looked troubled. "There's something I've got to tell you." John tried to intervene, but Martin said, "No, let me carry on. The Local Party has asked me to fight the Central Ward in the City Council Elections, and I don't know whether to or not. It means that I would let a lot of people down in this Ward. The whole of the Party's ward executive voted for me to be their candidate. But I know how things are going at this end of the City, and to be frank I don't think that I would win this seat anyway. I don't think that we will get a majority in the Council. I've waited a long time for this opportunity, and I feel that if there is a better chance elsewhere then I will move elsewhere, what do you think John? Am I letting my friends and neighbours down?"

"Jesus, Martin, what a question to put on me." John looked at him and smiled. "Damn it all man I'm the opposition. I'm the hated Tory Fat Cat, you know, the guy who bleeds all of the workers dry, tosses them out onto the pavement, and then goes home to chuckle over the deeds of the day. I'm likely to be a candidate who will oppose you, and here you are asking me if I think you are letting the people down."

"I know that I'll get it straight from the shoulder from you John." He smiled at the idea that his Tory friend should be so concerned for him. "I also know that you are probably the last person on earth I should be asking this question. But I need a straight answer, without any frills, and you are about the only person who will give me that sort of answer."

"I'll tell you what I do think," John continued from where he had left off. "I think that it is the Labour Party who are letting the people down, but you Martin, no, you're not letting anybody down but yourself. You feel that just because this is the area in which you have lived and worked for the past ten years you are in some way obligated to stand here. Well the fact is that you're not, and neither am I. What people expect is that because you have fought their battles for years, in many cases both of us have wet nursed them, because they were too tied up in their own little worlds to do it for themselves and now they believe that we are obligated to continue to look after them until they decide that they no longer want us. It is always a one way trade, and at the slightest sign of trouble. they will kick you over the edge of the bridge and into the water; And within a week they would not even remember yours or anyone else's name. You and I are political animals and we will have to find our way on our own, and if you can get yourself a safe Labour seat then more power to your elbow."

"Do you really mean that John?" Martin was clearly surprised.

"You bet you bloody boots I mean it my old friend," John offered his hand, "We have always managed to work together without allowing our different political points of view to spoil our friendship, and I do count you as one of my closest friends. We have always been honest with each other, and I hope that we can continue to be so."

"There is just one point though," Martin was almost

apologetic. "I have not yet had the opportunity to tell my Ward Association that I will not be a candidate in this area, so I would be obliged if you would keep it under your hat for a while."

"That's no problem," said John reassuringly, "I won't tell a soul. I think that what you want to do with your political life is your private decision and your decision alone. You must always do what you consider is the best option for you, your family and your beliefs."

"God I wish the rest of the mob were going to be as understanding as you have been." Martin was clearly apprehensive about the change in his and his parties plans for the election.

They shook hands on it and the conversation was finish, but only just in time for no sooner had they moved out of the hall than the doorbell rang, the others were turning out to hear what their 'fledgling' representatives had done for them.

The meeting had been called by John and Martin to allow all of the people who had raised questions about Road Safety and the provision of Controlled Crossings with their various contacts in other organisations, Political Parties and Departments of Council.

Because Martin was a member of the Majority Party in Council he was asked to speak first.

Martin was clearly apprehensive about speaking at all "I'm afraid that I have very little to say."

He spoke in a very subdued voice. "I must admit that the Members of Council in my Party do not place a very high priority on Road Safety in this area, and there is no provision in the Budget for the current year, and there will be no money available next year either.

Bearing in mind that both of the Councillors for this Ward are members of the Transport Committee, the committee that finances Road Safety in the City, they have demonstrated no awareness that a problem even exists, and until I raised the matter with the Chairman of the Committee, no one has mentioned the rising tide of accidents that are occurring at the bottom end of the estate. A consequence of which is that the Budget for next year has been finalised and there is no allocation of funds for the provision of a Controlled Crossing and Traffic Calming Measures for at least another 18 months." Martin sat down in total silence.

Everybody was clearly stunned at the response that had been elicited from the City Council. John stepped in to prevent there being a series of questions asked that no one in the meeting had the facility to answer. " I can only reiterate what Martin has just told us, but there is a way in which we can get together the necessary data or information, call it what you like, to allow us to take the matter a step further than the City Council seems to be prepared to do." He paused for a moment to arrange his thoughts. " As you are no doubt aware, the City Council are only the Agents of the County Council who under the Town & Country Planning Act 1971, are responsible for Transportation and Road Safety within the County. I asked the same questions at County Council, and got virtually the same answers that Martin got."

"What's the point in continuing?" Molly spoke in a voice that was half- strangled with tearful emotion. "Our young children count for nothing. They die, and nobody gives a damn outside this community. The fact is that nobody really wants to know about us."

"That simply isn't true." John raised his voice to make himself heard above the mutterings of the other eight people in the room. "Martin and I have spent time and effort trying to find out what other people are doing, and the fact that they are doing nothing, only serves to prove that if we can't get help to cure the problem, then we must help ourselves. You've always said that this community would get up and fight if it had a cause to fight for. Well now you have one of the best causes that any community can have that is the 'Safety of Our Children'. If the powers that be, want a fight, then let's give it to them. Let's take our fight to them and supply them with the facts that they say they need to reach a reasonable conclusion. After all when I asked them what was the problem, the answer was the usual stock excuse that they had not received their full allocation from Central Government and so this year's funds had been allocated on the basis of known criteria. This means that any Scheme that requires Surveys or Research will not be considered simple because there is not the staff available to gather all of the data to allow them to make a considered judgement. It is a vicious circle and the only way to break it is to carry out the Surveys and Research ourselves."

"It's easy for you to speak," Trevor Calley stood and spoke with a passion that rarely entered his daily round of Bookies and Pubs. "None of us has the money to go galavanting around Council and Party Offices, and if we did, we would get what we always get; Lame excuses from snotty bureaucrats who think that they can control the riff-raff only by treating them with contempt and sending them running about all over the place until they get fed-up and pack it all in as a bad job. They don't listen to us, and it doesn't matter whether we speak to them as a group or individually, not does it matter what the politicians say either. Civil servants always know in the backs of their minds that "Politicians come, and politicians go, but the Civil Servants go on forever" you might not like what I'm saying, but I've stood in the Town Hall Tavern and heard them say it, and I'm not talking about two bit clerks either. I'm talking about Senior Officers of this

City.

"That maybe the case," John spoke to return to the point of the meeting. "but what we really need to do is to survey the volume of traffic using the Relief Road and Williamson Street, as one operation, and to count the number of people crossing the Relief Road as a separate operation."

"Oh!" Martin interrupted. "Here's a point that I think we all should write to the Government about. Do you know that in all of the figures that are collated in respect of peoples movements, the movement of children to and from school are deducted, because they are not part of the criteria necessary for judging whether Controls are required or not."

"What set of idiots laid down the rules for that?" Molly Bacon asked incredulously. "I would have thought that they would have formed the core of all safety in any area of the country."

"That I can't tell you," Martin assured them, "but I got my information from a scientist at the Road Transport Research Laboratories".

"So whatever we supply to them, they are going to apply some nationally agreed figure to, and then deduct all of the children travelling to or from school." Molly cupped her hands over her ears and said, "There is nothing in the world that can make sense of an arbitrary decision like that. Do we have any idea where that idea came from?"

"Well I do know where it came from," John interrupted, "but I would prefer not to say."

"Why does it go against your Conservative principles?" Molly interjected sarcastically."

"Well I will tell you if that's what you want me to do," John was playing to the gallery now, "but I can assure you that you won't like it, and that applies particularly to you Molly."

"Come on man, tell us and hang the consequences," Tim Colby the other member of the Lib-Dem Party in the Group called out, "then we will all know where to lay the blame."

"I don't think that you will like it either Tim." John had now discarded all attempts to save the face of the few, for the enjoyment of the many. "It was proposed by Lord Jolly, as part of the findings that arose from his commission on a series of crashes in fog three or four winters ago."

The room erupted into a series of hoots and hilarious laughter. Lord Jolly was the Chairman of the Liberal Democratic Party and a former Minister of Transport. Molly and Tim left the meeting with faces glowing red. Their departure was followed by a brief discussion in which it was agreed that the Association would participate, with other organisations in a Survey to be carried out with the intention of supplying the details required by the City and County Councils for them to reach a decision on the need for a Controlled Crossing at the danger point.

They agreed that the survey should be carried out over a period of five days during the next week, and a rota of people available to assist was begun. The response was almost unanimous.

All of the details were finalised, and a group of four people were selected o attend the Friday evening meeting at the Conservative group office.

After a very successful meeting the committee members drifted off in the general direction of the pub feeling as though they had at least made a start towards solving the problem.

At 10 o'clock the night ended as it had started with John and Martin, sitting alone, talking about politics.

"What do you think the Government will do about the next General Election Martin?" John asked

"If they've got any sense at all they'll avoid it for as long as possible." Martin smiled into the fire.

"What I really want to know is what are you going to do, John. You're not really a Conservative, you do know that don't you? You're a right wing Socialist, and if you continue with your lot they'll nail your coffin lid down before you get anywhere. I wish that you would listen to me, because the Labour Leader on the Council has asked me to talk to you, to see if I can persuade you to join us. He thinks that you're a confused socialist as well. What do you say?"

"There isn't anything to say Marti." John paused. "and don't think that I don't appreciate what you are saying, because I do, but there is so much that I could not agree with in the Labour Party that it would be a waste of my time and yours. I am a Conservative, not a Blue Nosed Tory, but a Conservative, and anyone who cannot tell the difference, should not be in politics.

But I rather think that if the Press cannot tell the difference, the chances of the General Public being able to make an informed observation are remote."

"Are you still in the Union John?" Martin asked the question with a broad grin on his face.

"Of course I am, why do you ask?

"A couple of the blokes asked me last week at the meeting of the Trades Council, and I didn't know." He was embarrassed.

"There's nothing wrong with the Trades Union Movement that a withdrawal from Politics wouldn't cure." John laughed as the subject got round to one that they had hammered into the ground on so many occasions that they each knew the others arguments so well that it was pointless to continue, "but I'm sure that you've heard it all before. Changing the subject for a moment, when will you know that you will be a candidate for the Central Ward?"

"It's all signed and settled now, and all I have to do is let my Ward Party know that I will not be standing for them." Martin was clearly uncomfortable about the idea. "That will all take place tomorrow, and I do not relish the idea of having to tell them. But it has to be done, and the sooner I get it over and done with, the better I will feel."

"It's my Association meeting tomorrow night as well." John changed the subject again, but only slightly. "I have the feeling that there is something going on in the back-ground that I am not party-too. I have had one or two very broad hints dropped to me and I will admit to being bemused by it."

4

Thursday

John stepped softly round the door of the bedroom to find Kath sitting up in bed reading one of her romantic novels. "I'm just off to the Branch meeting to see if I can chase up some activity on the question of road safety at the bottom of the estate near the Relief Road. It's getting really bad down there."

"I heard. Molly had a chat with me on the phone yesterday." Kath clearly was not up to talking much, but she pressed him. "Are you going to be able to do anything?" She asked seriously.

"You do know that it could have been one of our kids involved in that collision."

"Yes!" He replied. "I'm only too aware of the dangers that are involved in our own children coming home from school and going down to the youth club. To be perfectly frank.it scares the knickers off me every time they go out at night."

"Do what you can Johnny." She placed her hand on his arm. "If for no one else, do it for your own two children."

"I will. I will." He said quietly, but with a venom that she had rarely heard before. "I should be back at about half-nine he called as he moved out of the bedroom.

"Yes I've heard that one before, as well." She replied with an air of complete resignation. She knew then that he would get into a conversation that would make him lose all sense of time, and he would crawl back full of apologises and beer in the early hours of the morning.

But he didn't chase other women and he looked after her, despite all of her problems, and the children adored him because he was as soft as grease with them.

It was raining again, and the wind was whipping in from the east, "Looks like we could have some snow before the nights out." He said inwardly.

Unlike the majority of his colleagues at the Branch Meeting of the Colly Farm Estate Conservative Association John did not have a car. What is more to the point John could not afford a car and was not nearly as affluent as most of the other people in the party. What he lacked in ability to hand over sheaves of cash he adequately made up in time and effort on behalf of his chosen political party. This he pondered as he made his way through the pouring rain towards the bus stop and the bus that would drop him outside the constituency office. He had one rule, and that was that he would always make his own way to meetings. That is he would not rely on anyone who promised to 'give him a lift'. He had it in his mind that if he did so he would somehow become beholden to them, and that was against his own principles. So he got himself cold and wet merely to protect his own integrity.

He was pleased to make the warmth of the office. He could hear the usual sort of chatter that preceded a meeting, as he removed his coat and hung it in the cloak-room area just inside the main door. He removed the papers he needed for the meeting, from his brief-case and then strolled into the main hall through the double doors that were standing open. He paused for a moment just inside the doors to drink-in the scenery, and to see who was present and who was missing.

"Hello there John." a voice from behind him called. "I'm glad the you're here this evening, because I need to talk to you."

He turned to find himself face to face with the

leader of the Conservative Group on the City Council. "Hello Charles!" He said with an element of surprise. "What are you doing here at a lowly Branch Meeting?"

"Well we do like to get down to the grass-roots of the Party when we can, and tonight we can."

Charles Brown was a big man, he stood over six feet tall, a factor that belied the fact that he had spent the war years in Midget Submarines, and as he had grown older his weight had increased to the point where he was now grossly overweight. "I have been watching your progress," He continued. "and I would like you to put yourself forward as a candidate for the Council Elections on the sixth of May. Now before you dismiss it out of hand, I want you to know that we will win this time, and I need young men like you to take on some of the seats where we have retiring councillors who are sitting on safe seats. What I want to hear from you is whether you are prepared to put your name forward as a candidate?"

"Well Yes!" John stammered. "But I'd rather thought that I should get some experience in tough Labour held seats."

"Good God what for?" He exploded.

"Well the fact is that I've half-promised to fight the Colly Farm Seat, and that's why I came here to-night." John was still surprised.

"There's no benefit to be gained from that Lad!" Charles stated. "Can't plan my Committees on the basis of people who might not get elected, I want you to be a member of the next City Council, and if you follow my advice you will be. Now as far as to-night's meeting goes I want you to follow my lead, bearing in mind that I will be the first speaker in respect of candidates and after that there will be no doubt in anyone's mind that you are going to fight the New Park seat."

"Well if that's what you want Charles. I will be

pleased to follow your lead." John said without any apprehension.

"Good. That's settled then." And without any further comment he turned and strolled into the meeting.

The meeting was the usual dour business, which slid over John rather like a play in which he was a member of the audience. For most of the time his mind was in turmoil, he hadn't really considered the prospect of being elected to council at his first attempt. Or how would all of this affect his work? What would his family and friends think? It was all a puzzle to him.

It was when the meeting got around to the selection of candidates for the Election that Charles Brown rose to his feet and began to speak. "Before we get into the problem of Candidates, I have a few things that I would like to say. Firstly, because of the way that the Socialists have run this city for the past twelve years there is little doubt in my mind that the next Council will be Conservative controlled." He waited while the smattering of applause subsided.

"We currently have only eleven members, and six of those intend to retire at the end of April.

That leaves us needing some very good candidate to fill their places. I know that you have all-but selected your two preferred candidates, but on the question of John Robertson I'm afraid that you will have to think again." Questioning glances shot round the table. John could almost feel the accusations in their eyes. "Before you hang the poor fellow without a trial, I want you to know that he will be one of my right-hand men in the new council, and for that reason, I want to be absolutely sure that he will win the seat he contests with a clear and thumping majority.

For that reason, he has been chosen to take one of the seats vacated by a retiring member, so I will be obliged if you will remove him from your list of candidates and select someone else. That is all that I have to say on the matter, so unless you have anything that you wish to raise with me, I'll leave you to it."

As he walked out of the room he paused long enough to say to John. "I'll be in the Club next door. When you've finished with the meeting I'd like to see you."

The removal of one of their candidates created some turmoil, but in the end they decided on asking the Area office for a list of candidates and going through a formal selection procedure.

When it came round to 'any other business', John raised the question of Road Safety, and question of Controlled Crossings in the Ward. a great deal of interest was shown, and it was finally decided that the members of the Association would assist the Tenants and Residents Association to carry-out a traffic and movement census at the crossings of Williamson Street and the Relief Road during the course of the next week. They also agreed to send three people to the meeting to finalise the rotas and to cover the sessions for a whole week

The detailed results of the surveys, along with a record of accidents over the course of the past three years would be sent to the Transportation Department of the County Council who were the Highway Authority.

The meeting ended at about ten minutes past nine. But everybody wanted to speak to John and to prevent have to repeat himself, he spoke to whole room. "I just want to let you know that until Charles Brown walked into this room tonight I had no idea of the arrangements that he had made in respect of the forthcoming elections. He spoke to me as we came into the meeting and asked me if I was a candidate for the elections and

I said that I was. He then told me that I was to be a candidate in another Ward, and that he would make an announcement here this evening.

I want to assure you all that I knew nothing of this when I arrived here tonight. Now if you will excuse me, he has told me that he wants to see me before I leave here tonight. So I'd best get going."

John collected his papers, and walked out aware of the disgruntled mutterings that were going on around him. He knew that the actions taken by Charles had created considerable bad feeling in the Ward, but he felt that most of it was sour grapes anyway.

John wandered round into the Conservative Club and looked around to find Charles, but could not see him in the bar. He got himself a drink and walked off down the corridor looking in each room to see if he could see him. He found him in the sitting room leafing through a pile of letters and committee papers.

"Ah! There you are John. I'd almost given you up. I see you've got a drink so come here and sit down." He paused for a moment while John sat down and positioned his case and drink, and then he continued. "Well I guess that there are one or two people in there who think that I have been a bit high handed and interfering in Ward business, and I suppose that they are right. They will also think that you are a traitor before too long, but don't let it worry you. They're a lot of silly old farts really, but they do raise the money, so we have to put up with them and smile benevolently when they come up with an idea that they think is brilliant, but has been tried and found wanting many times before."

"I suppose that you are right, but in a way I feel as though I've let them down." John searched for a response, but there was nothing there.

"What I really want to do is tell you about the

selection meeting on Tuesday of next week where you will be adopted as the candidate for the New Park Ward." Charles spoke as though it were all cut and dried. "I can see that you are surprised, well don't be. The chairman has agreed that you will be their candidate, and there will be enough of your supporters there to take care of any problems that may arise."

"I wasn't aware that I had any supporters in the Ward yet." John was perplexed.

"Take my word for it, you will win all of the ballots that may be taken on the night. "His voice was soft and reassuring. "What I wanted to talk about is the question of what you must read up on, and the actions that you must take to get you in the public eye. Now transport is a great bone of contention at the moment, and our spokesman on transport is also a barrister, so most of his time is spent in court, and he hasn't really given us much joy on the matter. I want you to concentrate your effort on raising matters relating to transport. If you can get the information together pass on to Jean in the Party Office and she will arrange to type it, and pass it on to the relevant Newspapers and Agencies. Have you got something in mind?"

"Oh! Yes." He replied. "There have been a number of fatal accidents at major cross-roads around the city, and I have been pressing for additional traffic-light controlled crossing in an attempt to reduce the danger."

"Excellent!" Charles beamed. "There's a Council Meeting a week on Monday, get me some information together, and I will question the Leader of Council on the matter. I must have the details on Thursday of next week do you think that you can manage that?"

"Yes, but not being a member of Council makes it difficult for me to get the necessary accident statistics. I've been waiting over a month for then at this time." John added.

"I see.... Charles pondered. "This is what to do. Contact Andrew Trimble at County Hall, and tell him what you want. I will tell him that you are researching something for me. If you haven't got what you want by Tuesday ring me at home in the afternoon."

"Thanks Charles that will help me a lot."

"That's enough for now. Come on, I'll give you a lift home, it's on my way." Brown stood up and made for the door. John left his drink, grabbed his coat and brief-case, all most ran to keep up with the man who was forty years his senior.

His car was a big, ancient, well- polished Rover with beautiful leather seats. It started first time, and the engine purred like a well satisfied cat.

Charles set off without being told where to go, he clearly knew exactly where John lived; a factor that he found surprising to say the least. "How's that young wife of yours progressing?"

The question came right out of the blue.

"She's not too bad at the moment, but she won't be properly right until she's had the necessary surgery. We are waiting for her to go into hospital at the moment." John poured out the answer without thinking. "Well we'd better get it over and done with as soon as possible." He responded. "I'll call you and let you know when she's going in tomorrow.

Is it OK if I ring you at the office?

"Well yes! But the Doctor told us that it would be about three months." John could hardly believe his ears.

"I can't have you worrying about your wife when you've an election to fight." He was adamant.

"Let's get it over and done with so that you can concentrate on more important matters. Not that I don't think that a wife and family are important, because I do, it's just that I want to be able to ease the way for the two of you. It will give you peace of mind, and allow you to enjoy electioneering."

They arrived outside Robertson's House "Thanks for the lift Charles, it was a great help. And thanks for all that you've done for me to night."

John was searching for the right words but they would not come.

"While we are sitting here John I wondered if I might ask you a personal question" Charles was suddenly very serious. I wonder if you might consider moving into the ward that you will soon represent. I do know that you have been looking at houses elsewhere."

"Houses in New Park are a little out of my price range." John confessed.

"Not if you can get a mortgage through the City Council." He answered rather too quickly. But John did not appear to notice. He continued. "There is a nice three bed roomed house in Arundell Avenue that you would be able to get for around £100,000. You would be able to move in while Kathy was in hospital. I say this because the people in New Park will turn out in droves to elect someone who lives in the community." The edge to his voice was almost hypnotic.

"I'll talk to Kathy about it in the morning and let you know" John already knew what the answer would be, but he let it ride.

"Good!" Charles beamed like a Cheshire Cat in the darkness of the car. It was good the have putty to manipulate again. "Well. Good Night and we'll talk again tomorrow."

John climbed out of the car, waved good-night and disappeared down the garden path. Charles Brown pondered the night, smiled, and inwardly congratulated himself on a good-nights work.

He had got one chicken in the coop, now for the

rest.

John hooked himself round the door."Blast these Chicken Coops" he thought to himself. "Hello Kath it's me," he called up the stairs.

"This is a funny half-past nine." She said with mock severity. "Whose car brought you home tonight?"

"Charles Brown brought me home and boy have I got some news for you. You will not believe the night that I've had." He was full of it, but he didn't know where to start.

"Now simmer down." said Kathy taking his hand as he walked to the side of the bed." Now tell me about it slowly so that I can hear what you are saying."

He told her slowly what had happened at the meeting, and the about the talk in the Conservative Club. He followed this with the details of the discussion in the car, about her operation and the house. She listened with the patience of a mother listening to a small child, and when he had finished she said "Why?"

"Does it matter?" He asked. "All we ever wanted, is about to come true, and all that you can say is "Why?"

"Why should he do all of this for you? It's not as though he knows either you or me. He appears to know everything about us, and yet we know very little about him. I would really like to look at the house, and I'm over the moon about you getting the New Park seat, but what I can't understand is why should he do this for us? Be very careful Johnny nobody does this type of thing without a purpose."

"But he and I have the same political goals." John stammered. "Surely he isn't playing some petty little game with me."

"I don't know Johnny all I'm saying is be very careful with everything that you do. You must cover yourself at all times. Please don't think that I'm trying to put a damper on everything."

She looked him straight in the face. "You know that people who give in this way are just as capable of taking away all that they have given."

As John laid in bed that night his brain far too active to sleep, he pondered the night's events. He had always wanted to be a politician, a Conservative Politician, but had always refrained from putting himself forward because he had no vast supply of money to draw on. Unlike most of the others in his wider political circle, he had to work for a living, and if he didn't work, his family didn't eat. He had a good job as an engineer, with good prospects within the company.

Progress might be slow, but the future would be all right if, he kept his nose clean he would have a job until the day that he retired. The prospect of all of this made him uncomfortable, the idea that he would be a company man and patiently wait for his older colleagues to die filled him full apprehension. Johnny Robertson would not sit around and wait for things to happen, he wanted to make things happen as a result of his own efforts. Kath was being over cautious, she was a nice girl, a good mother and his house was always spotless, but he didn't think that she knew enough about the world outside to make much of a contribution to the political side of his life. He would let things run their course, and if that meant jumping on the band waggon, then he would jump.

5

Friday

As most of the people involved in the running of the Party disappeared into the hinterland at weekends there were very few meetings held on Friday evenings. John had arranged to pay two or three house calls during the early evening to sort out problems that the tenants had been unable to fathom for themselves. He had walked out towards the eastern side of Colly Farm Estate to sort out a repair problem, and at about eight o'clock he found himself near to Arundell Avenue on the edge of the New Park Ward.

On the spur of the moment he decided to have a walk past the house that Charles had spoken of, and he found himself looking at a detached house standing in larger gardens than he had anticipated. He could not see much in the dark, but it was clear that the house was empty, and he had a very good inner feeling about it. "Kathy would like this" he thought.

His solitary musing was suddenly brought to an end. "Hello there, are you viewing the house?"

The question came from a middle-aged lady who had appeared as if from nowhere.

"Yes!" He replied. "I'd heard that there was a house here that was for sale and thought that I'd have a preliminary look before I brought my wife here to have a proper viewing."

It's a nice house, but it needs some work doing on it. Old Mrs McQueen was virtually bed-ridden for the last two years that she was here, so there not been a lot done for perhaps three or four years." She smiled. My name's Sarah Beecham, I live at number seven. Do you have a family?" She asked and then continued without waiting for a reply. "It would be nice to have some young people on the Avenue again after so many years without them."

"Yes, we do have children," John answered the question. "A boy age ten and a girl aged thirteen. But I haven't made an offer for the house as yet. This really is my first look at the place.

You are right. I get the feeling that it is a nice house and I'm sure that my wife will like it."

"It is a very quiet little Cul-de sac." Mrs Beecham said. "With a very nice group of people, who are very friendly without being too intrusive I'm sure that you will know what I mean. We don't neighbour like they do in many of this type of small road, but if anything goes wrong, we all pull together."

"Yes I understand what you are saying," John said. "We are, that is my wife and I, of the same opinion. You can be friendly, but without becoming too close to your neighbours."

"Yes that is exactly what I mean." She replied. "I had better leave you to continue your initial survey." And with that she walked up the slight incline and into her garden gate

John quietly strolled around the garden, trying to get some idea of the size of the house, but it was difficult to make a judgement from the outside.

It was an early 1930's house, very well built and from what he could see, there were no tell-tale signs of mining subsidence, a real problem in the areas surrounding the city. His impression was that it was just the type of place that they would need now that the children were beginning to grow up.

But he would now have to hurry, to get to the meeting at the Conservative Office, it had taken up much more of his time than he had anticipated.

By the time that he arrived, all of the people who had been invited to the meeting were seated, and the Party Agent was pacing impatiently up and down outside the hall, in the main entrance.

"Where the hell have you been John?" Ted was clearly angry. "I got tied up with an old lady who has an access problem at her house, and I couldn't get away from her." John lied.

"It's been all that I could do to keep some of these people here." He explained. "You know what our lot are like about Friday night meetings. Most of them think that the working week ends at about two o'clock on Friday afternoon, and usually by this time they are into a nice meal and a bottle of wine somewhere out in the sticks."

"Yes Ted, I am sorry." John emphasised. "But I had to work until Five, and then I have such a large list of house calls to make this week-end, I decided to try and fit two or three in this evening so that I might get some free time on Sunday."

Ted smiled.

"What's so funny?" John enquired

"Oh! It's you young man." He almost whispered, as he put his hand on his shoulder. "It's you, and your enthusiasm about what you do. I've been around politics for about thirty years, and I had quite forgotten what it is like to be fighting the forces of socialism at the very roots of our society. And I saw in you something of the spirit that I know is necessary to put this party of ours back into Government. So come on, let's get started."

They walked into the room together, the young man full of enthusiasm and promise, and the aging cynic, full of knowledge and carefully developed caustic responses. Martin walked towards them.

It was strange for John to see the two portions of

political life together for the first time, The Tenants and Residents Association and the Colly Farm Conservative Association. They were two very differing groups of people politically, the Conservatives were, for the most part, comprised of home owners from in and around the Colly Farm Estate, and the Tenant were all Council Tenants on the Estate. But the significant factor was that with the general exception of John Robertson, all of the Tenants were Labour or Lib-Dem Supporters or Members. For them to be sitting in a Conservative Party Office was, in itself a bit of a miracle. All that John, Martin, and Ted had to do was to get them to work together in a common cause.

"Ted, I would like you to meet Martin Smith" John started but was cut off before he could complete the introduction.

"It's all right John." Martin stated bluntly. "Ted and I are well known to each other. He used to be a friend of my father's many years ago."

"In that case we had better get under way." John was equally blunt. It was clear that this was not going to be easy for any of them.

"Just a minute, you two" John fired at the two of them. "I don't know what's gone off between you two in the past, but we are here to do one job, get the information that we need, and that's it. So can we call a truce for the duration of this survey?"

They both agreed and the meeting got under-way. In all they had accumulated about forty names for their listings, and by the time that they had taken details of all of the times that people were available they could just about cover the whole of the time zones necessary for their purpose.

It was a hard nights work, and it all went surprisingly swiftly and smoothly considering the diversity of interests that were represented in the mixed groups. In the end they had designed the form that they needed to collect the right sort of information, and had trained the survey members to fill them in correctly. The last item was to call a meeting for all of the people involved in the survey to let them know the outcome, and when it was all done they went off into the night each to their own form of relaxation. Ted, Martin and John found their way to the Old Hen Pub and indulged their thirsts with a pint of cold bitter in quiet and peaceful surroundings. As they sat talking the question of Martin and Ted's previous encounter soon became clear.

"I suppose that your parents are both retired by now." Ted began.

"My dad never got to retiring age." Martin stated openly. "He collapsed and died one night about ten years ago and Ma now lives out at Apton near my sisters place."

"I'm sorry to hear about you father." Ted admitted. "I really liked him, he was a man of principle, and there are precious few of them about these days."

"His defeat in that bye-election was about the worst thing that ever happened to him." Martin said reflectively. "To lose a rock solid Labour seat to a Conservative, just about broke his heart, and it was the last time that the party ever gave him the opportunity."

"I can remember it all as if it were yesterday." Ted mused. "I was the agent who over-turned a twenty-three thousand Labour Majority, and returned a candidate to Parliament with a majority of three thousand. Nobody has ever bettered that, and I still get no satisfaction from that result, because Harry and I had been such good friends."

"Ma still won't talk about it." Martin reflected. "She still thinks that the miners were bribed by the party not to turn out and vote because dad had such extreme views."

"I know, old son." Ted recalled sadly. "I know, but you and I must keep in touch Martin, we must."

"I'm sure that John here won't let us forget now that he is in the know."

Martin's attitude was much changed from earlier in the evening. "Any way it is time that we forgot the whole sorry business, and tried harder to improve the lot of the masses."

"I get the distinct feeling that I've heard all of this before somewhere." Ted said bursting into laughter for the first time that night.

That's a lot better." John decided "It's about time some-one got another round in."

It is strange how one's past meetings and acquaintances could popped out of the woodwork to cloud issues years after the original happen, John mused to himself as he walked home with Martin later that night. 'I wonder what really happened to make both Ted and Martin react to each other in the way that they did. Ted was not a local man, he came from Sussex. There was more to this than met the eye.'

When John arrived home Kath was sitting up in bed waiting for him to come in from his meeting.

"I had a phone call while you were out." She stated coyishly.

"What was that about?" He enquired.

"It was from the hospital. I am being admitted on Sunday, in preparation for my operation on Monday." She added. "It looks as though your friend Charles Brown has already started do what he said that he would do. I don't know whether to feel glad or not. Now that the time has arrived, I feel really nervous about the whole thing. Whilst it was something in the distant future I could cope with the issue, perhaps because it was too far away to get excited about it. Now that it is actually going to happen, it fills me with a peculiar kind of dread."

"It will be a good thing for you and what is more you know that it will be." John started to console her.

"I know that it is silly of me." She began to cry. "But what will happen to all of you if anything goes wrong with it all?"

"Well that's just the point that you've got to consider." John joked as he slipped his arm around her. "It's either a fit you, or your mother running us all around, and perhaps even my mother getting her hands on your children so that she can 'bring them up properly'."

Oh! my God." She exploded with laughter. "All right governor you've convinced me."

"There is one thing that we must do before you go into Hospital," John changed the subject.

"We must take you round to have a look at the house in Arundell Avenue, just to make sure that you like the prospect of moving there, before you go into hospital. I know you won't be able to see the inside of the house. but at least you will get some sort of feel for the place. It seems as though I'm rushing you, but if everything goes to plan, we should be able to move house before the election campaign starts. To do this I will need to get the buying process underway before you leave Hospital."

"Don't worry about it luv," Kathy explained. "From what I've heard, it is a very nice house in a quiet Cul de Sac.

"Oh! So you've had the spies our have you?" John was surprised.

"No it was the bush telegraph." She smiled. "Actually it was Sarah Parkin who phoned me this morning to see how I was. And during the course of the conversation she just happened to mention the fact that she had heard that we were in the market to buy a house just round the corner from where she and Mike lived."

"What did she have to say on the matter?" John asked.

"Well. all that she really said was that it was a very nice house with a large garden that had been neglected because of the long illness of the previous owner." She shrugged. "But she did add that it was Mike who had told her that we were going to move into the New Park Area."

"Yes, I suppose that I had better get in touch with Mike," John spoke his thought out aloud "And ask him to act for us in this case; Perhaps that is what this really was a reminder that he is our solicitor, and that he could use the business."

"You really are an old sceptic John Robertson." Kathy commented. "I don't suppose that the question even entered Sarah's mind."

"No, I'll bet it didn't." John smiled to himself. "Anyway I'll see if we can borrow Martin's car to take you round to have a quick look at the place in the morning."

"If Sarah say's that it's OK then you can bet you life it is." Kathy remarked. "She is about the fussiest person that I know. So if she says it is a nice place, then it will be a nice place."

"And we will still go down and give the place the 'once over' before we start the legal processes." John concluded.

6

Tuesday

Charles Brown had been as good as his word, Kathy was admitted to hospital on the Sunday evening and by Tuesday evening she was sitting up in bed looking like a new woman following surgery. She had streams of visitors, dozens of 'Get well Cards', flowers from John, and Martin but most of all she had a visit from Councillor Charles Brown who was also the Chairman of the Hospital Board of Trustees.

He arrived in the Hospital Ward followed by the Hospital Administrator, and an assistant who carried a huge bouquet and an equally huge box of chocolates.

"Hello Kathryn." He beamed. "I just thought I'd drop in and see if you are comfortable, and that you have everything that you need. We can't have you worrying whilst you're in here, can we?"

"Thank you Councillor Brown." She replied. It was very kind of you to get things moving for me."

"What is all of this Councillor Brown business?" He snapped back. "How many times must I tell you to call me Charles? Your husband is one of my most talented protégées. By the way, this is Robert Harrington who is the Hospital Administrator, and this young fellow is Richard Clarke my P.A. If you need anything at all, and you can't get hold of me, just let the staff know and they will contact one of us. I understand that John has been in to see you, and is now away working busily on his report on the safety of road crossings in the city." He continued without giving anyone the chance to interrupt his flow. "Are you feeling any better?"

"Yes thank you Charles." Kath had decided to play

his game.

"I must say that for someone who had major surgery yesterday, you look a picture of health."

He paused.

"Well, all of my pain is gone, and for the first time in almost two years I feel free." Kath explained.

"That's wonderful!" Charles boomed. "Ah well, I'd better get off and do some work. I'll see you again tomorrow." And with that he turn and swept out of the Ward with something of the air of a Lancelot Spratt in his hey-day.

Kathy had wanted to giggle, but the presence of other patients caused her to restrain herself.

But she was brought back to reality by the lady in the next bed who muttered just loudly enough for her to hear. "Gawd I'm in a bed next to some politician's tart". Katy came down to earth with a bump.

The Staff Nurse came bustling around, "Now Mrs Robertson, you didn't tell us you were a close friend of the Chairman, or that he would come and visit you. And just look at the state of your bed and area. I'll never live this down you know. Our Mr Harrington is not at all amused.

In fact he is so annoyed that he said that I have got to move you to one of the side rooms away from the big ears of other people in the ward." She motioned over her shoulder to the lady in the next bed and then continued. "Your husband rang to see how you were this morning, and said that he would come in and see you on the way home from the office. Your children rang to ask the same question and said that they were OK at your mothers. But I had to tell them that they could not see you for at least another two days.

That's Doctors orders. I think that we can move you into the Side Ward now, so if you relax I'll wheel the bed in and the Auxiliary will bring in your locker and notes later." Without more ado she wheeled the bed in slow state down the centre aisle towards a small room near the Ward Sisters Office.

The old lady was still prattling on but her venom gradually faded into the back-ground noise of the busy hospital, and she was soon forgotten in the routine of the day. Kath could now sit and listen to the radio in peace without constant interference from people around her. But despite all of this apparent freedom within a few minutes she had fallen into a deep sleep.

***

The estate agent was gushing. Yes, he did have a property in New Park, but he already had a number of inquiries and they had arranged to start the viewing processes tomorrow.

"This is very awkward" Said John "My wife is in hospital, and I can't make arrangements the look at the property until the weekend."

"That really is unfortunate Mr Robertson." He sneered. "As you probably know we do operate on a first come first served basis, and I'm afraid that if you do not agree a price before your competitors, they will have the priority."

John agreed to see the house the following day, and took all of the details so that he could show them to Kath. But he had little time in his lunch hour to be able to go into his bank to make arrangements for a mortgage.

He didn't think that he would have any bother, but it would be best to find out what price he could go up to. He dashed across the Market place to catch a bus back to his office.

It was ten minutes past two when John finally got into the office. His long-time friend and work mate,

Harry Richards was looking out for him when he walked through the door.

"John, the old man wants to see you straight away. He's been pacing up and down in his office since two." He pulled a face and added. "I don't think that he's in the best of moods, so watch out."

"Thanks for the warning Harry, this is just what I need this week." John mumbled to his friend and set off in the direction of the MD's office. He knocked and walked in.

"John, it's not like you to be late." He began.

"No, I'm sorry but I had to slip into town on business." He interjected.

"How are things?" Conrad Barnes continued.

"Not too good at the moment," John explained. "Kath is in hospital, she had her op. yesterday, so I'm chief cook and bottle washer at home for the next few days. If you add onto that the fact that the house that we have been waiting for is finally on the market, then things are hectic to say the least."

"Are you sure that is all that is bothering you at this time" He paused for effect "because a little birdie told me last night that you were going to be the Conservative Candidate for the New Park Ward in the forthcoming city council elections. Is this true?"

"Well yes it is." John admitted. "I had intended to tell you after I was sure that I had been selected.

"That is awfully good of you young man!" Barnes was livid. "What the hell does a young fellow like you want in the mish- mash of politics, and local politics at that?" He walked over to the window and stood looking out, with his hands rammed deep into his trouser pockets, and suddenly spun round, head forward, pointing his finger directly at John's chest.

"I want you to know that I will support you in your endeavours to enter politics, and I will allow you a

53

reasonable amount of time off during the week, that is as long as it does not impede any of the work of the company. But you will log every hour you spent on Council Business and you will make up the time during evenings and weekends. This is a grave mistake you're making, because from now on I cannot consider you for any major contract, any promotion, or any advancement within the company. I want you to think about this very carefully before you make your final choice, and if you want my advice, if I were you I would run-away from this pile of Bull-Shit and concentrate on your real career."

"I've already committed myself to fighting the New Park seat, and I don't wish to retract my candidature." John stated in a clear and confident voice."

"I knew that you would say that." Barnes smiled with an air of resignation. "and I wish you the best of luck, you know that I support the same party as you, but still I think that you would be better off staying in the profession for which you are trained, and for which you have a natural flair. But that's the end of it. In view of all of the commitments that you have at the moment, I will have to send Harry to Germany on Friday of next week, so can you brief him and bring him up to press? God I hope you know what you are doing. Do you know what a complete and utter bastard Charles Brown is? Lad, he eats people like you for breakfast, he's scoundrel and that's only if he's not a crook. Be careful, that's the only advice that I can give to you.

"Thanks Conrad, I knew that you would understand." John turned and left the office.

Conrad Barnes sat still for a few moments, and then dropped his head into his hands. "Christ what a waste." He spoke to the silence. "What a bloody awful waste!"

John strolled back to his desk in the open plan office and sat down.

Harry could hardly contain himself. "Did he tell you John? He's sending me to Germany next week. I thought that he would be sending you, after all you speak German, and I don't"

"Well it's because Kath's in Hospital, and the house has come up at last." John lied, because he knew deep inside that this would be the first of many trips that would be passed on to others.

"I need to spend some time with the family getting things ready for Kath to come home, and organising everything for a possible move to a new house."

"Well thanks for giving me an opportunity to prove myself." He enthused "I always pictured myself flitting around the world to new and exotic places."

"Germany is not either new or exotic." John smiled.

"It might not be for you, because you're used to travelling around," He pronounced, "but for me, it's like having the shackles removed."

"Get away with you, you poor hard done to slave." John laughed as he threw a sweet paper at him.

John turned back to his desk in thoughtful mood, the whole structure of his life was changing about him. He felt confident that he was making the decisions that were right for his family and yet everyone was telling him to beware of the very people that he had got to work with to achieve those goals that he had set himself. He could see nothing wrong with his self-elected mentor. Charles Brown had done nothing other than to ease his way into the political arena.

Why did everybody distrust him so much, when all that he appeared to be doing was to set him on the right pathway to allow him to attain his life-times ambition? The truth was that John Robertson would make his own decisions, he would trust his own judgement, and make his own way in the political world.

7

Wednesday

On the way home, as he crossed the Market Square, John diverted into the Town Hall. He asked for Councillor Brown at the reception desk.

"Do you have an appointment to see him?" The receptionist asked.

"No but he asked me to bring these confidential papers here to him today." He replied. "I will need to see him to explain some of the conclusions."

"Just a minute," she said, "I'll see if he is available."

John looked around him. He had never been inside this hallowed place, even though he had lived in the city all of his life. It had that hushed almost reverential hollowness of a cathedral, and was much more ornate than he would ever have imagined.

"Mr Robertson. Mr Robertson!" The receptionist broke into his reverie.

"Councillor Brown will see you now. Do you know where his office is?

"No I'm afraid that I don't." He responded.

"Well!" she started. "If you go up to the top of the stairs, turn right towards the Lord Mayor's office and right again, you will see a corridor of Oak Panels in front of you. Walk down there and Councillor Brown's office is the third door on the left. All right."

"Yes thank you, that's fine." John set off on his journey of exploration.

The receptionist turned to her working partner and said, "What a shame, that one seems a lot brighter than all of the others."

John found the office without a problem and

knocked on the door. "Come in." A female voice called from within. Inside he found a bright-eyed blonde girl of about twenty-two sitting behind a stout polished desk.

"My name is .....

"Yes I know, you're John Robertson, and you have some papers for Councillor Brown." She smiled. "I'm Barbara Stokes, I'm Charles secretary, and I did the research on your back-ground for him, so I know all about you. "If you would wait for a moment I'll see if he's ready for you yet. Please take a seat."

She slipped through a door into an adjoining office, closing it silently behind her, and returned a few second later. "If you would go in to see Charles now"

It was a double seal door, one opening outwards, one opening inwards, so that there would be little possibility of ever being able to eavesdrop, even if the delectable Barbara were not there.

"Come in John, would you like a drink?" Charles was all charm and sophistication. "Do come and sit down. Scotch or Scotch?" he asked with a flourish.

"I think I'll have the Scotch." John agreed.

"Now let's have a look at what you've got here." He was immediately immersed in the paper-work of John's Report. He read steadily through it sometimes reading rapidly forward and then search backwards to confirm or retrieve a lost figure or detail and after about 20 minutes he put down the final sheets and turned to John and said. "I know that you are some-what bewildered by my sudden interest in you, but when I see research and presentation like this I know that I am right to concentrate my efforts on you. This is not the first report of yours that has finished up on my desk John."

"It is the only one that I've ever handed to you Charles." He was puzzled.

"Well two years ago you did an analysis of traffic

flows in the city to try to establish which routes in and out of the city were the most congested." Charles grinned sheepishly . "That report was commissioned by the Taxi Associations in an attempt to discover easier routes in and out of the City at peak travelling times. A copy of that report found its way onto the desk of the General Manager of the City Transport Department, and using your basic analysis his staff were able to calculate all of the points in their bus network that could be conveniently re-routed to provide a more efficient service. When I found out that you were a member of the Party at Croft Farm Estate I did not know whether to offer you a full time job, or wait to see if would rise through the ranks, and seek elected office."

"I'm astounded my company think that I'm a run of the mill sort of chap, who will be OK with about ten more years of experience." John sighed audibly.

"What's the matter John?" Charles was quick to spot the sigh.

"I've been working for the same company since I finished university." He paused to look around the office and then continued. "Today I was taken into my MD's office, and told in no uncertain terms that if I decided to go into politics, I could kiss any chances of promotion good-bye, and I would have to cover all of the time that I spent on Council affairs at the week-ends, or after normal hours. I'm not certain whether or not I should jeopardise the well-being of my family simply because I enjoy politics."

"So Conrad Barnes really did try to get to you?" Brown laughed. "He said that he would do. But I didn't think that the old bastard would go as far as putting a hold on any promotion that might come your way. Can't you see what he's trying to do? He simply can't live with the fact that he's made four or five attempts to become a City Councillor and each time he was beaten in the attempt. I did think that he might give you some help, but it seems that I was wrong."

"Well in the mean time I have to work for him, and if he applies the rules in the way that he says he will then I am in for a rough time." John stared at his own feet and fell into silence.

"I think that you might have to leave your job, if you want to make your way to Parliament."

Brown trotted out in a monotone regular voice that made him sound rather like a robot.

"No!" said John, "I can't do that I would have nothing to live on. My wife would batter me to death. No! It is not an option."

"I don't mean right away John." Charles tried to explain. "It's simply that if you are to become a

Chairman of a Major Committee then the amount of time that it takes up makes it almost impossible to do anything else during the course of a normal working day. I'm lucky I have staff who work for me in my business and in politics. They are like me now they can hardly detect the boundaries between the two. So when the time comes you may have forgo the job, and simply administer your council department."

"I can't see my way to buying a new house, and not working, because unlike you I'm only just setting out on my Political career, and I do not have a private income." John felt that he was not listening to him.

"You are a graduate engineer" Charles interrupted him. "And from what I hear you are a good engineer who is being held back because he is working for a company that is slow and out of date. "If you were to set yourself up in a small consultancy there would be quite a volume of work that would come to you from surrounding companies who need the short term services of a good design engineer. Just think about it.

Carry on as you are for now and we will discuss this at some date after the election.

Have you ever been round the Town Hall John?"

"No!" He answered enthusiastically. "I've lived most of my adult life in the city, but today is the first time that I've ever put a foot inside the place."

"Come on then," He said, getting out of his chair, "I'll give you the half- crown tour."

The tour took about half an hour, and by the time that they got back to the main stair-case, there were groups of people making their way into the main Ballroom..

"There's a Civic Reception starting in about ten minutes." Charles announced. "It's for a group of French and German Engineers who are attending a conference at the University, why don't you come in with me and see how it's all done? " It should be right up your street and you will be able to speak to them in their own language, which is more than most of us can do. You're fluent in German aren't you? And I understand that your French is pretty good too."

"Well yes," He stammered, surprised at the fact that Charles Brown knew so much about him.

"But these people will be academics and I am used to speaking on technical matters. Standard German is a different kettle of fish."

"We'll see." Brown smiled as he ushered John into the centre of the Ballroom. There were about sixty people scattered about in groups talking and drinking, and as they stopped in the middle of the room, a waiter came to them and passed a drink to Charles. He then turned to John and asked, "What would you like to drink Mr Robertson?"

John was bemused, was there no one in the building who didn't know who he was?

"I'll have a Gin and Bitter Lemon please." He

replied softly.

"Just one moment, I'll get you one right away." He was gone and back before John could think of anything to say to Charles. It was a very large drink and the amount of Lemon did nothing to disguise the fact. The alcohol coursed down into John's system, and he could feel it reaching down into his empty stomach. He would have to be very careful of the amount he had to drink because he'd had nothing to eat since breakfast, and he did not like drinking without having eaten. Apart from that he had to go to the Hospital to see Kath when he had finished here, and it wouldn't do for him to turn up there in an inebriated state. He couldn't stay here for too long, because visiting hours finished at eight.

"John!" Charles called him over to join him. "I want you to meet Brian Eve our Transport Spokesman on County Council, and I know that you have already met Michael Parkin who is our leader there. Brian, this is John Robertson who will be one of our main speakers on Transport in the City when we take control in May."

Charles obviously didn't know that there was the small problem of having to win a seat before anything so bold as being a spokesman could take place.

Brian Eve was about the same age as John, and he had already been a Councillor in the City before winning the seat on the County Council. They shook hands, and he launched into a rather lengthy diatribe with Charles on the question of some new legislation that was being processed through Parliament.

Mike Parkin besides being and old friend was also John's family solicitor. "I understand that you are in the market to buy a house John," He began. "Will you be wanting me to act for you in the matter."

"But of course." John stammered. "I was going to ring you in the morning to get things underway. The problem is that I know the house that I want, but Kath is in hospital at the moment, and she hasn't seen the inside of the house as yet. I've got the finance set up, but until we have viewed the house properly together I don't want to make a move."

"Who is the agent?" Mike enquired.

"Monk and Company, just round the corner from your office."

"Give me the details now," Mike said, "And I'll have a word with Terry Monk in the morning.

Did he give you his usual spiel about there being another client who was about to make an offer?"

"Yes," John admitted, "He said that I should make an offer straight away, because he operated on a first-come first served basis."

"I thought that he would." Mike smiled. "He always does that to try to put you in a position where you think that you will have to rush the purchase and thus prevent others from beating you to it. Have you got the details with you?"

John passed him the details, which Mike quickly leafed though, made a few notes on a scrap of paper that he pulled from his pocket, and then he passed them back to John.

"I'll have words with him in the morning, and get him to hold the property for you, until Kath is fit to go and have a look at it. It's in a nice spot, just round the corner from my house as a matter of fact. But just a word, don't let 'Old Monk' get you to sign anything yet. He's a bit of a Hustler at the best of times. Let me deal with him. I shall start all of the usual searches straight away, just to reduce the time you will have to wait after you have decided with Kathy whether or not you will be taking the place. I'm sure that Kath will like it. Don't bother to come and see me, I'll call you if there are any problems, other than that I will wait until you give me the go-ahead."

"That will save me a lot of problems." John said with relief. "I figured that I would have to wait at least a week for an appointment."

"And so you would in normal circumstances, but now that you are going to become my City Councillor, I think that a bit of preferential treatment will not be out of place. It will be hectic enough for you in the next few weeks, and time will be at a premium for you. Especially as you have Kath in the hospital. When she's fit again both of you must come in for a meal with Sarah and I." He paused. "Are you visiting Kath to night?"

"Yes, I must get on my way in a few minutes." John replied.

At this point they were re-joined by Charles. "Are you going down to the General Hospital John?"

"Yes Charles! I was just saying that I would have to be away in a few minutes."

"There's no hurry," He added, "I'm going down there too, there's some minor problem that they want me to attend to, so I'll give you a lift if you can wait for a few minutes."

It was about half past six when they finally left the town hall for the short journey to the General Hospital. Charles had picked up a folder of paper at the reception on the way out, which he promptly handed to John saying: "Here you are you'd better get used to having a vast amount of paperwork to deal with on a daily basis. These are the Committee Papers for the next meeting of the County Council's Transportation Committee. Mike Griffin has made arrangements for all future papers to be sent to your home address and you had better send a copy of your CV to the Chairman of the New Park Ward Association so that he can pave the way for your adoption as their Candidate. There is a meeting of the

Conservative Group on City Council that you will have to attend next Tuesday Evening starting at 6.30.pm in the large committee room and I want you to read the City Council Meeting agenda and voice any of the things that you want said at the next meeting of Council. You will be expected to attend all of the group meetings that will be held before the Elections." He continued talking through-out the journey.

"As you can see there will be a tremendous amount of reading and preparation required so that you will be ready to take up your position as Chairman of Transport in the City when you are elected. I will be holding a Chairman's Meeting just as soon as I have completed my listing of prospective Committee Chairmen. I want you to be fully aware that we will win this election, and you will play a major part in the new City Administration. So you had better prepare yourself for a fairly hectic time. Mike also told me that he was going to get everything ready for the purchase of the new house so that you will be able to move in time to get your new address on all of the election documentation. So the sooner you can persuade Kathy that the house is the right one for you the better."

During all of this time John had spent sitting and listening to Charles as he peeled off all of the details. He had not appreciated that Charles would expect him to move home before the election. "That only gives me about eight weeks to complete the sale, and get moved in. If there is any delay I'm going to be meeting myself coming back."

"We are doing all that we can to help you," Charles interjected. "But if you think that it is too much, you should see it when we are really busy".

"I'm not complaining, but I do think that we should allow ourselves just a little bit of lea way all the same."

By this time they had arrived at the Hospital and

Charles drove his car into the parking spot reserved for the chairman.

"This is all going to be a question of timing" Charles responded, "You really should be living in the Ward at the time of the election to gain maximum response from the people. They really like their Councillors to live in the Ward, and you will be jeopardising your chances if you cannot move before you start your campaign. Take my word for it. You need to move as soon as possible. From my point of view I will assist you in any way that I can, so there is no need to make a major production out of this."

"I hear what you are saying Charles. OK I will try to get the move completed in the quickest time possible." John really wanted to get a little breathing space so that he could work out a plan of action. But every time he thought that he could sit and work everything out, there was another commitment that took priority over his life and his time.

They strolled into the Hospital through the Main Entrance together, and John was surprised to see Robert Harrington waiting for them in the Main Reception Area.

"Good Evening Chairman, and to you too Mr Robertson," He was always the well dressed, well mannered, and helpful to the point where it could be a little over-bearing at times. "The people are assembled in the small Lecture Theatre on the first floor Chairman, but I haven't made arrangements for Mr Robertson to attend the meeting." His voice trailed off.

"That's all right Mr Harrington," John tried to put him at ease. "I'm just coming in to visit my wife on the way home from the office." And he left them standing talking to make his way to the Surgical Ward where his wife was a patient.

He found Kathy surrounded by flowers and cards

and books from all sorts of friends and neighbours. She looked remarkably well. "I'd almost given you up today" she smiled as he leaned over and kissed her on the cheek.

"Yes I got kind of tangled up at the Town Hall on the way through, then I met Charles to discuss the paper that I've produced for him." He sighed heavily as he sat down in the chair at the side of the bed.

"That's just typical of a man," she joked, "Stick the little woman in a side ward in the local hospital, and then go galavanting all over the place while she's out of the way."

"I'm sorry love, but you know how it is." He said apologetically. "But everything seems to happening all at one time, I'm finding it difficult to keep pace with it all."

He told her about the visit to the Town Hall, of his meeting with Michael, of the arrangements that he had made, but she seemed unimpressed.

"Don't let Charles rush you into anything that you don't want do." She said emphatically. "We will decide on the house, we will decide when we move, and Michael will advise us on when and how things can be safely completed." She suddenly changed subjects. "I'm really feeling much better today, better in fact than I have felt for a long time. And I've had streams of visitors, Sarah came in to see me, and told me that Michael had heard that we were looking for another house, and guess what, she told me about the house in Arundell Avenue and about what a nice place it was.

Apparently she knew the lady who lived in the house until about three months ago, and has visited the place many times. She thinks that I will like it, and having heard that from her I can't wait to see the place.

Anyway the Professor came into see me today, and he said that I was making tremendous progress, and that if I behaved myself, he might consider letting me come home after they have removed the stitches on Saturday. So I might get to see the 'Dream House' this coming weekend."

"Hey baby, you're going to have to take it easy for a while when you get out of here." John said firmly. "But I don't think the a drive round to the house will tax you too much. Any way Michael said that he would get the agent to hold it for us, but it looked OK from the outside, and it has a big garden that will keep you busy while I'm looking after my Department.

The way Charles Brown is talking, the election has already been decided."

"There is just something that bothers me about that man." The smile disappeared from Kathy's face. "There is something that just doesn't ring true. I would try to keep him at arms- length if I were you John. You always said that if you went into politics you would be your own man, I think that you would be well advised to be just that."

"I still think that you are barking up the wrong tree love," John tried to push his own doubts to the back of his mind. "He has been true to his word so far, and I can't find anything to fault him on. If there is one thing that he seems intent upon it is to get me into the Chairmanship of the Transport Department so that I can implement my own ideas on how we should improve the services without increasing the costs to the travelling public. There is nothing wrong with that."

"You're missing the point darling." Kathy insisted. "All of the things that he is doing for us will put us in the position of being beholden to him. Sooner or later he will want his pound of flesh, and then there may be some conflict, if your ideas don't coincide with his. He is the type of person who expects each of his little seeds to eventually come to fruition. So be careful John. You may not wish to parley the price that he will ask.

"Alright, if it makes you feel better," he relented, " I will start to watch my back even before I get elected."

They exchanged gossip on what was going on in the ward, and what was happening at John's office, but he left out the details of why Harry was off to Germany, and his discussion with Conrad Barnes generally. The visitors bell sounded to let everybody know that the visiting hours were now over, and the long trail back to houses in far flung reaches of the City began for those like John, who relied on Public Trans port to travel around the City.

One of the surprising things about the siting of the Great Modern Hospital in the city had been the fact that if you lived in any suburb it was necessary to catch at least two buses to reach it, and if you had the misfortune to live in some of the more distant villages, it was impossible to catch a bus home after the evening rush hour. This made it nearly impossible for people without their own transport to visit their family when they were hospitalised.

It was after nine when John finally got home, by which time he was very tired, but no sooner had he turned on the light, than there was a knock on the door. It was Martin.

John invited him in and turned on the gas fire to put a little heat into the lounge.

"I've only just this moment got home from the Hospital, and I'm wacked."

He said. "Yes I know, I saw you get off the bus." He answered, but he was not his usual self.

"How's Kathy getting on, is she OK?"

"To be perfectly honest, she looks a picture of health, I can't believe how well she looks." He said half to himself. "Is there a problem Martin?"

"Well yes and no." He mumbled. "A little bird has

just told me, that not only are you not standing for election in this ward, but that you will also be moving home before the City Council Elections."

"Oh where did you get that from?" John was suddenly alert.

"I got it from a very good source at the Labour Party Office in town." The answer was too swift to be made up. "In fact I was told that at the next meeting of the New Park Ward Conservative Association you will be adopted as their candidate. Now look John you and I have been friends for a long time..."

"Yes, and we will continue to be friends if we trust each other." John's riposte was swift. "The truth of the matter is this, Kathy and I have been looking for a bigger house, and we don't qualify for one under the rules that govern the allocation of houses through the council, so we have been looking for a suitable house to buy. It is true that in the last few days we have found one that we both like, and we are now trying to raise the finance to buy it. So that answers one of your questions. The question of where I will stand as a candidate has been decided for me.

The committee that decide who will sit where, have proposed that I contest the New Park Ward. The fact that the house that we are trying to buy is also in the New Park Ward is purely coincidental. Neither of the two proposals have been confirmed, but what has been stated quite firmly is that I will not be contesting the Colly Farm Ward. That is where the situation stands at the moment. Does that answer your question?"

Martin was clearly still agitated. "I decided that I would not stand in this ward because I knew that you would win it 'Hands Down', and now you're telling me that you are not standing here. I thought that when we were speaking the other night on this subject, you would be standing here, and I knew that we would be able to carry on the work that we've been doing for the past six or seven years. Now you tell me that is not the case. I feel a bit let down I thought that you would be able to trust me enough to keep what was happening to my-self."

"Martin. Martin." John was surprised to say the least. "I haven't tried to deceive you. All of this happened at the time that Kath was going into have her op., and to be honest, I haven't told anybody yet, not even the family. It all came out of the blue when I went to what I thought was my adoption meeting, and Charles Brown came in and altered the whole ball game. Since then my feet have hardly touched the ground. What with Kath being in the General, and the kids being at the Mother-in-Laws, I haven't had a second to call me own."

"Well John, I just thought that you would have let me know, but now you've explained the situation, of course I understand." Martin was still clearly upset or annoyed, and it was difficult for John to know whether it was Martin being annoyed with John, or Martin being annoyed with Martin.

"That's all that there is to say then," he said in an off-handed fashion. "Neither of us will be a councillor for this ward. But there is another thing, the fact that both of us are standing in other areas of the city is now common gossip amongst our Committee Members and both of us are no longer the flavour of the month on this Estate. Our names are mud, and the usual trouble makers are having a field day. Not the least of those is Molly Bacon, who is standing in this area, and she's putting it about that because we didn't think that we stood a chance against her and the Lib.Dem's, so now we've both run to other Wards to make sure that we would get a seat on Council."

"Well I suppose that she has to make hay while the

sun shines," said John, "for it is certain that she will have it all on to do anything in this area, even if our two parties make a total cock-up of the campaign."

For the first time since he came in Martin smiled. "I knew there would be a reasonable explanation, but I couldn't quite see how it could have happened. But it just goes to show, no one of can spit in this town without everybody knowing about it."

"You're damned right there." agreed John. "If I wasn't so bloody hungry I'd take you down to the Pub for a pint, but I haven't had a bite to eat since breakfast, and I'm blood starving. Do you fancy a walk down to the Chippy?"

"Yes, why not" The war was over and the two of them bundled out into the cold night air in search of some quick hot food.

8

Thursday

The letter box rattled, and the post hit the floor with a thud. John was awake. "Christ what's the time." He muttered to himself. "Half-past Bloody seven. Christ I'm going to be late for work. I must have forgotten to set the alarm." He scrambled off towards the Bathroom and washed his face in cold water to wake him-self up. Martin hadn't left until after midnight and by the time that he'd done a few urgent jobs about the house it had been past one. John hated being rushed in the morning, and he slowly made his way down to the kitchen to get his injection of hot coffee. The place still reeked of their fish and chip supper of the night before, and it most certainly did not smell as appetising as it had done while they were eating it. He liked to be in the office early so that he could take his usual stroll around the assembly shop before he settled into the routine of the day.

He poked his head round the kitchen curtain. "Oh Christ It's bloody raining again; just the thing to put you in the right frame of mind when you've over-slept." He moaned to himself.

He poked some bread into the toaster, and started opening the mountain of post that had wakened him as it fell through the door. A stack of Committee Papers from both the City and the County, and he wasn't even elected yet. "A sixty page agenda for a sub-committee meeting and look at all that bloody detail. Man this is going to take more time than I ever imagined."

John spoke out aloud even though he was on his own in the house.

He arrived at work just in time to prevent himself from being late. He did not like being late for anything, in fact he usually arrived well before the allotted time for any appointment. His father had always been a person who would not be rushed into anything, and if ever the family had a bus or a train to catch, it was certain that they would finish up have to run for it.

Times without number they were too late, and finished up waiting around for hours for the next one. It had he knew that his family constantly joke about the amount of time that he would allow to get to an appointment on time and insistence on always bing at the prescribed place at the prescribed time.

Even the staff in the Convellium offices who were aware that he was always on or before time were just beginning to think that he wasn't going to be in the office. Conrad Barnes was already in his 'Goldfish Bowl' (The commonly used name for his all glass office). He looked up as John walked through the door and indicated that he needed to speak to him, so John walked straight in to his office.

"You're a bit later than usual this morning John." He was baiting him. "What's the matter is your alarm clock in the hospital?"

"You could be right there, in a round-a-bout sort of way, of course," he paused for a moment, "but I would never admit, even to you, that I could not look after myself when the lady of the house is away. And I'm certain that you wouldn't admit the same to me either."

"I really just wanted to know how Kathryn was progressing, and if there was any help that you needed." Conrad appeared to be genuinely concerned about her.

"To be honest when I saw her last night she looked a picture of health." John confessed. "I can't believe that it's the same person who gave me so much trouble over course of the past four years. The morning after her op. she looked a picture of health. It's as though the moment that they took away the cause of the trouble her body said 'that's better', and all of the tensions that had built up over the months simply slipped away. She looks great."

"That really is good news, and I'm glad that Kath seems to be on the mend at last." He was having difficulty making this sort of conversation and it was the first time that John had noticed this sort of trait in him. "I've been giving your election campaign some thought, and have come to the conclusion that if you are going to stand, you might just as well have the best agent that you can get. So if you will accept me, I'll be your agent, always assuming that you are adopted as one of the candidates for the Ward at the Adoption Meeting tomorrow."

Inwardly John was astounded, after all of the arguments and his trying to persuade him not to stand, John could not believe that this offer was real. But he heard himself saying, "I cannot think of anyone who I would sooner have as my agent, than you Conrad. Thank you very much.

I accept your offer with humility. But will you answer me one question, why did you so vehemently oppose my nomination when you had every intent of asking if you could lead the team when I was selected?"

"It's like this," He said with his eyes lightly closed, "when you go into politics, you never know just what you are letting yourself in for, so when a close friend or working colleague has indicated the they would like to enter the field of politics I have always tried as hard as I can to dissuade them from embarking on such a career. Not out of envy or out spite because of my failures in the past, but because I wanted them to be fully aware of what they were letting themselves in for. You are all that I said you were, but you will make a good leader John, given the right sort of guidance you will be in the House of Commons within ten years. Of that I have no doubt, but I wanted you to know that there are sacrifices that you will have to make along the way. You will have to sit and watch lesser people rise in the work place because you have commitments elsewhere.

This is a factor that you will have to learn to cope with." He handed John a set of papers.

"These are the contracts for the Schellenberg contract, I want you to go through them with Harry, right down to the finest detail. Harry has not your ability to think on his feet, but I must send him to Germany because you will have too much to do here, and I am relying on you to get him through his first visit. I cannot stress enough the importance of our gaining this contract, without it, we will be making people here redundant before the next two months are through. It is really your baby, and Doktor Linz is aware of this fact, and he will not be at all happy if there is any problem. I have told him that you are going into politics, and I think that he understands the differences between politics in Germany and politic here. Stay on top of this one, and everything should be all right."

"I understand the situation Conrad," John remarked. "And I will do all that I can to make certain that everything is set out for Harry's visit." "I know that you will." Conrad responded. "Now about you adoption meeting tomorrow night, there will be no formal selection, because we have decided that you and Malcolm Griffin will be the two candidates for that Ward. All that will take place is that there will be a meeting of all of the Conservative Party Members in

75

the Ward, and they will be asked to adopt the pair of you. There will be a need for you to prepare a short address to introduce yourself to the members and then I will ask for them to adopt you as candidate on a show of hands. There is not usually any bother in this type of ward, they rely on the skill and experience of their officers to out the two people who they think will represent the best interest of the people in the ward. We have never had a problem in all the years that I have been the Ward Chairman. So I don't expect any last minute problems." He paused for just a moment, and then continued.

"If I am your Agent, I want you to understand that you will not make any decisions about the conduct of the election without my expressed approval. You will not deal with any payments of any kind, and you will refer to me, anybody who tries to hand to you, anything in the form of a gift. You will not buy anyone who is a voter who lives in the ward, as much as a glass of lemonade, or anything that may be construed as an inducement. If we go into a Public House I will purchase all of the drinks, and we will settle the matter at the end of the day. I cannot stress enough the importance of this for you to appreciate the fine print of the Representation of the People Act, and the lengths that some people will go to compromise your Candidacy. Once you are adopted as a candidate I am the only person who can make payments on your behalf, and I am a stickler in that respect. I wish you well and will do all that I can to ensure that you are properly elected. Do you understand that?"

Yes Conrad and thank you again for all of your wishes and assistance." John was duly impressed, and they shook hands to seal the arrangement.

9

The Adoption Meeting

Conrad Barnes tapped the gavel on the table and called above the chatter of voices, "Ladies and Gentlemen." He paused whilst the chatter subsided. "It is now seven-thirty, and we should get this Adoption Meeting under-way."

There was the usual scrapping of chairs as the seventy or so people made their way to their seats.

"Are we all settled?" He called, and then he commenced speaking. "as you are all aware there are to be District Council Election on the sixth of May, and at the last meeting of the Ward Executive Committee it was announce that both of our sitting City Councillors would not be seeking re-election. We therefore found ourselves in the position of having to find two suitable candidates to contest the two seats in this ward. Let me pause here to thank our retiring councillors for their service during the past fourteen years, I'm sure that you will all join me in a round of applause for the absolutely first class job that they have both done. George Hynd, and Arthur Broadbent."

He paused while a great volume of clapping drowned all other sounds in the hall. "At that same meeting it was decided that we would not go through a formal selection routine, but that along with the other members of the executive we would try to find two suitable candidates for this Ward. Firstly we have living in the Ward Malcolm Griffin, who you all know, and who has represented the Carlbury Ward for the past two years following a bye election, I asked him if he would stand for us given the opportunity, and as he was 'One of our own' I have asked him to attend this meeting, and I will present him to you in a few minutes. He is, of course, well versed in Conservative Politics. His father is the current MP for the Heverston Constituency, and his mother is the secretary of our own constituency party. His pedigree is therefore an excellent one." He paused and took a sip from the glass of water on the table in front of him. "So finding one candidate was not a problem. We did not want to have to go through the labourious process of selecting from a huge list of candidates because of the time factor, but the second candidate was presenting some difficulties for us. It was only a couple of weeks ago that I learned that a young man who works in my own office at Convellium, was on the list of candidates seeking a seat for the coming elections. Not only did he work for me, but he was in the process of buying a house in the New Park Ward. John Robertson is an excellent engineer, but add on to this the fact that he has been beavering away, forming a new party organisation in the Colly Farm area of the City, and the fact that he has also formulated the Conservative policy on transport for the forthcoming election, and you will start to appreciate the quality of the man.

When I approached him he was reluctant to stand, believing that his loyalty should lay with the Party organisation that he was instrumental in setting up in the Colly Farm Ward. But help was at hand, Charles Brown, who had also earmarked John as one of his key experts for the campaign, stepped into the fray, and asked John to stand for this area. He has agreed to do that, and what is more pleasing is that he will be moving into Arundell Avenue sometime next week, so by the time that the election arrives he will also be 'one of our own' as well. Ladies and Gentlemen may I present to you the two young men whom the executive believe, should be our candidates, Malcolm Griffin and John Robertson."

John and Malcolm, who had been waiting outside the rear doors of the Hall, strolled into together to a warm round of applause.

Conrad waited until they had seated themselves, one at each end of the table, and then continued, "Before we ask you to formally select these two young men as candidates, I will ask them to speak to you for a few minutes. First of all may I present to you Malcolm Griffin."

Malcolm, who John knew vaguely, was an accomplished speaker. He was public school educated and he was everything that John was not, that is within John's perception of what the average Conservative voter sought in a Conservative Candidate. The truth is not always synonymous with the individual perception.

"Good Evening Ladies and Gentlemen," the dulcet tones smoothed his way into his brief message. "I would just like to say a few words on the subject of Council Taxes. We are all aware that our local taxes have risen rapidly over the course of the past few years under Socialist control, and the standard of service has significantly declined. In any-bodies language that is an unacceptable state of affairs. As Conservatives we expect to pay a reasonable price for the services that we receive, but are we to sit silently by as the prices rocket, and the standard of service declines? We expect to pay for our services, but we also expect to receive 'Value For Money'. That is to say , service at a price, but not service at any price. The current level of Council Tax is far too high, and the standard of service is far too low,. As your Councillors John and I will strive to ensure that you receive Value for what is after all your money. John and I have only met for the first time this evening, but I feel that we will make a good team.

John is expert in the fields of Transport and Housing, and I specialise in the areas of Finance and Planning. So with your support the two of us can offer the New Park Ward a comprehensive team with which to meet the challenges that lies before us."

He sat down to rapturous applause from the audience that was comprised mainly of rather elderly but well -dressed ladies, plus a smaller number of equally elderly men.

Conrad again rose to his feet, "And now Ladies and Gentlemen, with the exception of one or two of you, John Robertson is unknown to you, so I would like to give him a friendly New Park welcome. Ladies and Gentlemen Mr John Robertson" The ensuing applause was equally ecstatic. John rose slowly and some-what reluctantly to his feet. "Ladies and Gentlemen" He paused mainly for effect, but it also gave him an opportunity to cast a glance around the room.

"First and fore-most I want to thank you for your friendly welcome here this evening. In my previous Ward we were such a small group, that we were all known to each other, a situation that I hope I will soon achieve here. But please give me a little time. I thought that I would tell a little about myself. I am thirty-eight years old, I'm married to Kathryn who owing to having been in hospital for surgery is unable to be with us this evening. We have two children, the eldest a girl called Anne aged thirteen and a boy called Jason who is ten years old. They will both attend schools within the ward, after the end of this current term. Conrad has told you that I am an Engineer, and Malcolm has already informed you that my areas of interest are Transport and Housing, and unless there are other areas that you would wish me to take on board, it is my intention to continue with my two specialties. Unlike Malcolm I have no experience of elections, for the past few years I have been a 'Backroom Boy', and a electoral agent, but I've never been a candidate before. Malcolm has told you that we have met for the first time this evening, but like him, I feel that we will make a good team. We achieved an immediate rapport that augers well for the coming weeks and years in New Park Ward. If you select me to be your candidate I will do all that I can for the people of this area and this City.

Thank you for at least considering me as a candidate."

With that John sat down. He had used an approach that didn't take it for granted that he would be accepted, and Malcolm had taken the approach that he was taking the vacancy as of right.

The whole process of selecting candidates in the party was in a state of flux. Some believed that each Ward Party and each Constituency Party were completely autonomous and could act in what -ever way they liked when it came to the selection of candidates. Others believed that there should be a single well established process for the selection of Candidates.

There were many arguments, at all levels, on this very contentious issue. Clearly the New Park Ward Committee were of the former opinion for this evening they had presented the Party Membership in the Ward with a fait accompli and without more ado Conrad Barnes asked, "Now Ladies and Gentlemen can I have a show of hands for those in favour of adopting first of all Malcolm Griffin as a Candidate in the New Park Ward for the forthcoming District Council Elections. All those in favour" Conrad paused. "Are there any against?" There were none. "So the adoption of Malcolm Griffin is carried unanimously. We now move straight away to John Robertson, on a show of hands, all those in favour of adopting John Robertson as our second candidate for the forthcoming District Council Elections, indicate now. Is there anyone against? So the adoption of John Robertson was also carried unanimously. "There was a round of spontaneous applause from the floor and the two adopted candidates walked to the front of the stage to meet their supporters.

The rest of the evening was spent chatting to the people who really counted at this and at all levels of political life, that is to say the people who devoted their time and money to the maintenance of the party machine. These were the people who did all of the leg work at Election time . These were the people who raised the money to pay for them by holding all sorts of small functions in homes and halls all over the area. Without their support the Party would not exist. Anybody who turned away this group of people did so at their own and the Parties peril.

When , at last, the meeting came to an end and last of the Members had left the hall. John, Malcolm, and Conrad had a brief meeting to decide when they would plan their election campaign. What the main issues for the Ward were to be; when they could meet with the existing Group on City Council, and many other peripheral matters. It was approaching eleven o'clock when John finally made it home. The house was still empty because Kath would not return home until the following day, and he felt that sense of isolation that all men feel when they have become used to being greeted on arrival at home, no matter what the time, night or day, and when there is no one to greet them.

He was hungry, and it was far too late for him to venture out to obtain a 'Take Away' meal. In this area of the city everything closed down at ten thirty, and by eleven o'clock the streets were deserted. He sorted absently through the pile of post that had been stacked behind his door since the morning, and then wondered into the kitchen to find him-self some form of quick and easy meal. He really wanted to settle down and go to sleep, and would have done so if it hadn't been for the hollowness of his stomach. Eggs and bacon seemed the quickest answer to his problem, and so he set about the cooking of it with enthusiasm.

"The political lark is taking up a lot more time than I thought it would." He thought to himself.

"At this rate I'll soon be getting no sleep at all. Come to think of it I still haven't dealt with yesterday's post yet, and not there's another lot to add to it. If I leave it tonight, by the time I get to it tomorrow there will be three days mail to contend with. So I'd best sort it out tonight before I go to bed." So it was that for the fourth night running John Robertson did not get to bed before two thirty in the morning, and even when he did get there he could not sleep. His ever active mind was churning away at new and revised ideas. He always said that if this ever became the case he could stop there and then, and leave it all behind. There is, however, more to this than he could fathom. The whole process had a hypnotic effect, and he could feel himself being gradually drawn into the centre of the web. All of the detail that was contained in the letters, and Committee Papers, and requests to visit here or there and speak on this matter or present prizes, became a jumbled night mare and when he finally woke in the morning, he was sweating and still as tired as when he fell into bed the night before .

10

The Election Campaign

Photographers are a funny breed. Funny, because they try to give the impression that they have an artistic temperament, when in fact they are usually morose, and practical in the extreme.

Dennis Earl was not an exception to this rule. He had been a photographer for almost fifty years, and he was not about to change his modus operandi now. John Robertson was not an easy subject. First and foremost he was about as rigid as a person could get and still be alive.

Second he was not used to posing, and that only made matters worse.

"Now look John." Dennis spoke to him as he would do to a small child. "You must relax and talk to me, just as if I were one of you colleagues on Council, and while you're doing that I will wander around and take a few shots for your Electoral Address."

John felt ill at ease he could have found many better pursuits on which to invest his day's holiday. He did not like the idea of having photographs taken by a professional photographer, but Conrad and Charles were adamant on the matter. "Why can't I do what I do when I want a new passport? Its a lot cheaper, and I don't have to spend all of this time being hassalled by this silly little man." The thoughts ran through John mind, but he was obliged to continue with this portion of discomfort. He would rather be doing anything other than this. But he knew in his own mind that if he went to the Party Offices with anything other than a set of Professionally Worked Publicity Photographs he would only have to go through the whole process again. So he made the best of a bad situation. After about ninety minutes he finally escaped from the over-powering warmth of the studio with it's banks of spotlights and coloured filters, with its air of deception, and the ever-present idea that lured in the back of John's mind that the sexual proclivity of the man with the cameras would not place any of the sparkling gallery of maidenly virtue in any sort of danger.

He was pleased to be away from it all, and even though it was only ten forty-five in the morning, he felt the need to have a good stiff drink simply to purge his system of the thought that the world was sullied by that particular type of human.

The Three Bells presented him with a welcoming open door. It is always a surprise for the majority of people to find that there are pubs which are full even at the most unlikely of times.

John was suitably surprised to find that not only was the place rather crowded, and that the crowd included Conrad Barnes, Charles Brown, and Malcolm Griffin, who were in deep conversation at the far end of the bar.

"Is this a private conversation," John interrupted their obviously intent conversation, "or can anybody join in?"

It was clear that they were all very surprised to see him in there, but Charles Brown was the first to recover. "John we didn't expect to see you here this morning." They had been caught out.

"We were under the impression that you were having you publicity shots done this morning."

"I was, and I have done that one, and having spent the past two hours in the delightful company of our dear friend Mr Earl," He paused for breath. "I felt in the need of a sharp drink, the type that would set me on my way after such an enlightening experience." They

85

understood the sentiment.

"Well from our reaction when you came in it must be clear to you that we were talking about you." Conrad Barnes made no attempt to disguise what they were doing. "You walking in here rather made it look to us as though you have arrived more by design than by accident."

"Well as it happens," John tried to explain. "I was in Earls Studio by nine-thirty this morning, and by the time that I came out I was in dire need of a drink, and as this is the nearest pub, here I am. If you are going to talk about somebody, and you don't want him to drop in while your talking, then perhaps it would be advisable to hold your little get-togethers at a place that is not close to where he's going to spend the day."

"We were not discussing anything that was detrimental." Charles Brown started to say.

"Like Bloody Hell you weren't."John laughed ironically. "None of you could have looked more surprised if the Pope had walked through the door and ordered a Creme de Menthe shandy.

What-ever it was that you were saying I certainly was not going to be a party to it either now, nor I believe at any time in the future, and yet I know it was about me. Now you can make of that, and that means all of you, anything that you bloody well like." He looked down the bar at the Landlord, and said, "A large whisky and dry please Eddie, but the drink was already standing on the bar.

"That one's on the house, John." The land lord had heard it all. "It's nice to see you about in town again."

"Thanks Eddie" he replied. "It's good to be about again. How's Maureen?"

"She's OK thanks."He moved off to serve but called over his shoulder, "She'll be down in a few minutes. She'll be pleased to see you again."

"Well now that you're here you'd better come and hear what we've been talking about." It was

Malcolm speaking from his seat at the end of the bar "We have been trying to predict who is going to win seats for us on the sixth of May, and the reason for the attempted prophecy is that we need to know who is going to be available to take on the committee chairman's jobs."

Charles Brown took up the lead. "As it stands we need eight are Chairman to lead the major committees, and at the present time we only have seven suitable candidates, and that is assuming that they all get elected." He was clearly at a loss for words.

Conrad Barnes took up the baton. "What this really boils down to is the fact that Charles is going to have to throw you in at the deep-end, and make you the chairman of Transport right from the start. He had hoped to give you a couple of months to get used to being a councillor before he moved you up the ladder. But the previous spokesman on transport has been asked to lead in a Case that is going to run for about six months, and he has declined the Chairmanship."

"I'm sorry John." This was the first time that John had heard Charles Brown apologise to anybody. "But I have no choice in this matter. The rest of the new candidates look as though they are pure voting fodder. So you will be straight into the Chairmanship as soon as you've won your seat."

He turned to the others, "I have to be careful with this young man, I can't quite make out whether he's got a short fuse, or if his sense of humour is so dry that there are times when I don't spot if he's joking or not."

"You'll know when he's not joking." This was Conrad. "I've never seen anybody loose their temper in quite way that John does. When John starts talking very quietly, and very precisely; when all of the colour start to drain from John's face, take my advice, leave quietly through the back door. Do not pass 'go' and do not collect two hundred pounds, because John is about to go ballistic, and that is not a pretty sight. I've only seen it happen once; once is quite sufficient for anybody other than a complete idiot to get the whole picture. To say that John doesn't suffer fools gladly is an understatement." Conrad concluded.

"Then the rest of the party on the City Council had better be kept away from him, not to mention the Officers." Malcolm added to the general air of 'taking the piss out of John'.

From there onwards the conversation gradually turned to the progress of the campaign, and Charles was pleased to announce that all of the seats would be contested by a Conservative Candidate, even those where if Labour fielded a pig wearing a red rosette it would win. The three trained agents in the City had already drafted a general message to the voters in the area of the city, and all that the candidates for each ward had to do was to agree a joint message to their voters.

In the New Park Ward, because they had a large number of willing helpers it was decided that they would have three deliveries to each house in the Ward. The first would be a card with the names and photographs of the two candidates; the second would be the election address complete with a general outline of Conservative Party Policy; and the third would be an eve of poll reminder that the election was due to take place on the following day.

This was a great difference here to electioneering in Colly Farm Estate, where because of the small numbers of helpers there was only ever time for them to get an election address into each house.

Charles had lapsed into silence, and so had John.

"Are you thinking what I'm thinking Charles?"

John asked quietly across the table.

"I blood hope so lad." He replied. "Because if we don't take one or two seats from them where they think that they're strong, then there is a possibility that we may get a 'Hung Council' and that won't do any of us any good at all." He sighed.

"Isn't it time that we got ourselves properly organised?" John demanded. "We have wards like New Park, where they have so many workers that they don't know where to put them all, and at the other end of the spectrum we have wards like Colly Farm, and Fordham where they are lucky if they can get an election address into each house in the Ward before Election day. If we can get all of the drops done quickly in the Wards where we have a large number of helpers, then we should have some mobile groups to help those who do not have the resources to make deliveries."

"Then we are thinking on the same lines then." Charles boomed across the table. "I think that if we can get the ladies to do most of the deliveries in New Park during daylight hours, we can zoom some of the fit young men into Fordham and Colly Farm to help them with their deliveries. If we do that John do you think that we will be able to get two deliveries into each house in the North of the City?"

"It depends on just how many people we can get to help." John pondered. "One of the biggest problems is that the Colly Farm Estate is scattered over some of the hilliest terrain in the area, but I don't see why we couldn't make their deliveries for them a matter of three day with about ten elpers at most."

"Let's go for it then." said Malcolm. "We need a meeting to try to twin each Ward in the City that has a delivery problem, with a Ward in the City that has a surplus of helpers. That way we will maximize our effort."

"The real point about all of this is not that we will maximize our effort, but the opposition will see that we have strength on the ground." Conrad was seeing the beauty of duplicating the effort.

"They are demoralized before they start the campaign, just imagine what the affect of seeing twice the number of people working for us that they are usually used to seeing. My view is that we will only need to use them once or twice to blow the Socialists right out of some wards. I know that Charles was concerned about pulling John out of Colly Farm, but the Labour Party have pulled one of their strongest candidates out of Colly Farm too, and this because they are not certain that they are going to win that seat either."

"Charles was watching them all intently and smiling to himself "You know what, I think that the Labour Party are running scared. They know that they are going to loose this election, and they are trying desperately to carry out a damage limitation exercise. If the four of us get together with the three full-time party agents in the City, I think that we can almost reverse the situation that prevails on council today."

John sat and thought about that for a moment, and whilst it would be a very nice position for the party to be in, there was the added problem of all the politically immature people that would need to be carried for at least the first few months of a New Council.

The well organised machine in the New Park Ward began the process of canvassing their support. This meant that a party worker had to call at each house in the area and try to establish which party each of the voters in the house would vote for. The information from the canvas eturns were then marked onto a set of Electoral Registers which would form the basis of the information for supplying Transport to the polls for Conservative Voters.

This initial stage, plus the first delivery was normally completed by Election Day minus 21 days.

The Main delivery was normally completed ten days before the Poll, and then there was the final reminder on the last night before the poll. During the last two week-ends and the last week after six o'clock in the evening the two candidates with three or four helpers walked down each road in the ward, and tried to answer to questions and queries of their voters. In this way the two candidates could visit all of the roads in the Ward between the two of them. Nothing was left to chance, even the most innocuous inquiry was run by one of the candidates, and where there was not an immediate answer the addresses were revisited before a problem became a major issue.

11

Exchanging Contracts

John did not have a very good opinion of Estate Agents at the best of time, but when the phone rang one day whilst he was in the office, and he found Mr. Monk from the Estate Agents on the line.

"I thought that I'd better ring and tell you that the vendor is considering another offer for the house in Arundell Avenue so that now the asking price has been increased by one thousand Five Hundred Pounds." He was very matter of fact about it, he was now twisting John's arm for a further one and a half grand.

John was having none of it. "I'll tell you what Mr Monk, you go to your vendor and you tell him that if he has not agreed to the price at which the house was advertised within the next ten minutes, and you have phoned me to indicate his acceptance, I am informing you that I will instruct my solicitor to withdraw from the sale, and I will look for a house elsewhere. That is ten minutes from now." At which point John put down the phone.

Nine minutes elapsed, and the phone rang. "Hello Mr Robertson?"

"Yes Mr Monk! Do you have an answer for me?" John was sounding very stern.

"Yes!" Monk replied. "My client has agreed to the price as advertised."

"Good, then you'd better get onto my solicitor, because I've just told him to tear-up all of the papers and send me the bill."John added.

"Please excuse me Mr Robertson." Monk was almost screeching down the phone, "But I must make an urgent dash to Mike Parkin's office."

Less than Fifteen minutes elapsed and Mike was on the phone. "I've just had Old Monk in here n a terrible state, he said that you had instructed me to withdraw your name from the sale of the house."

"Yeah ! That's right." John laughed. "The old bastard tried to gazump me for another one and a half grand, about fifteen minutes ago, so I thought that I might start to play hard ball with him and he didn't seem to under-stand the rules."

"Well you can relax now, tomorrow we are going to exchange contracts.

How does that suit you.?" Mike was happy about it all. John knew that Kath would be pleased that the move was, at last getting under way, and that she could start to plan exactly what she wanted for the new house.

"Do you need me to be there Mike?" John enquired.

"No this is just a notice of intention, and when the searches have been completed then we can sign all of the necessary papers." He paused for a moment and then continued. "By the look of things, we should be able tofinalise everything next Monday, and you should be able to move in on the Friday or Saturday, because there is no one else involved. So you can phone Kath and tell her to start packing."

"That's very good news for us." John was pleased that it was moving without any problem.

"Don't give me any credit." Mike laughed. "Old Monk decided that he wanted to get this sale over and done with before you had time to change your mind. He told me that it was a good job that all of his customers weren't like you, or he would never make a penny out of selling houses.

You must have really put the wind up the old twister."

"I guess that I did, but what I don't like is people

93

who try to make money out of others, when they are in a vulnerable position." John said seriously. "And that old bastard knew that I wanted the house, and saw an opportunity to grab a few more pounds from some one who was under a bit of stress. What no body told him was the fact that when I'm under pressure I am a really tough cookie."

"I think that I will commit that to memory for the future." Mike Laughed.

"But Old Monk is not too bad really, when you get to know him. By the way how is Kathryn?

Is she on the road to recovery?"

"Yes she looks fine." John replied. "In fact she looks better now than she has done for years.

It's almost as if the operation took away all of her pain, and her body was finally in a position where it could function properly. She has recovered so well that I will be fetching her out of the Hospital later on today, and taking her home. Of course she will still have to take things very gently for a few weeks yet, but all being well the operation seems to have cured the problem."

"I'm very pleased to hear that." Mike said. "I know that it has been a serious problem for the past two or three years, and to know that it is over and done with must be a great relief to you."

"It is I can assure you," John said. "It will be good to be able to get together as a family again.

The Children have been at Kath's mothers since she went into the General."

That business concluded John worked for the rest of the morning, and then left the office to prepare things for Kathryn homecoming. So it was that at about two thirty in the afternoon Kathryn Robertson was discharged into the care of her husband, and they set off aboard a Local Authority ambulance to their home in the Colly Farm Estate.

As John tried to open the door, he was met by Jason and Anne, and his mother-in-law, who had beaten them to the house.

Kathy had been given strict instructions to go straight to bed when she arrived home, so the ambulance men took her straight up the stairs and tucked her up in bed before the children could overwhelm her. The whole process had taken less than an hour, and the family were now together again in their home.

"You cannot know how good it feels to be back at home." She confided to John. "I know that I had a private room all to myself in the Hospital, but there is nothing that can compare with being in your own bed, in your own house."

"Well the truth is, my love, that this will not be our home for many more days now." John smiled. "I spoke with Mike this morning, and it looks as though we will be moving into our new home at the end of next week."

"I will never be ready." Kath raised herself from the bed. "There is nothing packed and nothing prepared or ordered. We can't do it in that short time."

"You're very right there." John answered. "You will not be ready, nor will you be fit enough to participate. Except in a supervisory capacity, that is. I have arranged for a company of specialist removers to come along and do all of the hard work for you, all that you will need to do is sit and tell them what you want and how you want it doing. I have discussed it all with the children, and we are in total agreement. You are not to do any of the lifting and moving. So sit back, and watch us all tear our hair out. Everything is under control."

12

Group Meeting

The meeting of the existing Conservative Group on the City Council took place usually on the Thursday evening before a full Council Meeting. The Full Council Meeting usually took place on the first Monday in the month, unless it coincided with a Public Holiday, in which case it was moved to the second Monday. John had been invited to attend the last meeting of the Group before the May Elections. There were only eleven Conservative members on the existing Council, and only seven of them were going to stand at the forthcoming District Council Election. None of the retiring members attended the Group meeting, which indicated to John that there were probably some divisions within the Group. The meeting was held in one of the large committee rooms in the Town Hall, and commenced at seven thirty in the evening. Charles Brown and Mike Parkin sat at the head of the table, and the rest of the members were distributed around a 'U' shaped committee table. The rest of the visitors were invited to fill the gaps.

The object of the meeting had been unclear to John up to this point, but it soon became clear to him that they were going to go through the Agenda for the Council Meeting and decide how they were going to vote on each issue, and who was going to speak in the debate. In normal circumstances the Chairman of the Committee directly responsible for the action would speak on behalf of the controlling party and the shadow spokesman would respond. Where there was an issue of real contention then the whips were applied and a recorded vote would be asked for and taken. The process of Whipping would be fully applied at this the last meeting before the Election.

Charles Brown opened the meeting on the dot of seven thirty. "I would like to welcome you all to this extended Group Meeting. For obvious reasons we will need to give some of our incoming recruits some experience because after this meeting we will be reduced to only seven experienced members, and that is including my-self. So I will begin by asking each of the invited prospective members of council to introduce them-selves and to tell us a little about them-selves.

We will start on my left and work around the table in a clockwise direction."

This whole process took about thirty minutes, and all of the new attendees were constantly interrupted by a stream, of what appeared on the surface, to be a whole host of pointless questions. The Agenda for the next meeting of council was rather a timid affair, for most of the people who would speak in the debates were either not attending this meeting or would not be attending the Council Meeting. The whole process appeared to be a bit of a fiasco to John, for despite numerous attempts by both Charles Brown and Michael Parkin to liven up the proceedings, none of the Councillors seemed to have any fight left in them. Thinking about it though, John realised that they had been in opposition for almost twelve years, and during that time the strength of the Conservative Group had gradually declined. So perhaps it was just as well that a defeated and disillusioned group was being, for the most-part replaced with younger and fresher candidates, who would not be weighed down with the disappointments of the past.

The whole process was one of preparing a united front to the people of the City on the eve of an Election.

Charles Brown presented John's blue print for Transport in the City, and the elected members debated the advantages and disadvantages of the policy. The main objective was to move away from the current Governments Policy of Subsidising all forms of Passenger Transport, and the suppression of private car in the centres of city's. The intention was to create a subsidy free, financially self-supporting, passenger transport undertaking within a period of three years.

All of the people in the room were aware that John had prepared the documentation and had done all of the research and had formulated all of the policies that were required to make this function in it's totality. The fact that he was only at the meeting as an observer was quickly swept under the table, and all of the questions that were raised in respect of the Policy were directed at him.

Even so, he discovered that when he had finished his explanation of the policy, the majority of those present did not understand the intricate details of the subject matter. In spite of John's attempt to soften the detail to allow for better understanding the majority of those there could not comprehend the potential of the program that he had devised. John was blissfully unaware of this until Councillor Maltern, who had once been a Chairman of Transport, whispered down the table, "Do you want us to vote Yes or No John?"

The fact that no one seemed to be able to grasp the fundamental points of his policy did not fill him with any great hope for the future. If this lot could not understand even the simplest of strategies, it was going to be Bloody Hard Work getting the rest of the councillors to vote on Policy matters.

By the end of the meeting his policy had been adopted as the declared policy of the group for the Whole City for the election, and then to be carried by the New Conservative Chairman of Transport in to the Council.

Charles terminated the meeting promptly at nine thirty, so that all of us could wander down to the leaders office where there was to be a small party for those members who were retiring from active politics.

It was almost as if it did not matter what the excuse, there was a drinking session after every meeting that was held in the Town Hall. Perhaps it was nothing more than a big boys drinking club, with politics given as an excuse for getting together in the first place. "No it can't be that simple."

He answered his inner voice. "I'm jumping to conclusions, it's really because they're near the end of a term of office, and they've run out of steam. Yes that's what it will be."

13

Moving House

The process of moving house was a new thing to both John and Kathy. Before they moved into their house on the Colly Farm Estate they had lived in a four roomed furnished flat over a Doctors surgery, so all of their personal possessions were easily packed into a single small van. This move was omething different. Now there were four of them, and a house full, almost beyond its capacity. That plus the fact that John could now move all of his beloved books from his mothers house, because in the new house he had at last got a study all to himself, and it was fitted with floor to ceiling bookshelves along two walls sufficient to house his nearly four thousand strong book collection. Without those books he still had close on four hundred that he had gradually collected during their time at Colly Farm.

They jointly agreed that Friday would be the best day to move, simply because it would allow them three days including the weekend, to set out those items of furniture that they were keeping. Kathy had done as much packing as her state of health would allow, but the Removals Company had said that they would deal with all of the packing, and they arrived in two large vans at seven-thirty in the morning to commence operations.

Kathy, along with Jason and Anne, their two children set off with Kathy's brother Kenneth driving, to take them to the new house. The two children were excited, for although they had seen photographs of the house it was the first time that they had been to the place.

It is surprising just how difficult it is the get out of a house, that which seemed to go into the place with relative ease when you moved it in. But the four men carrying out the operation seemed to accept each difficulty with resignation. There was nothing here that they had not tackled before.

The upper floor of the house was cleared first, and all of the bedroom furnishings disappeared down the road in the first lorry at about ten-thirty.The remaining down stairs furnishing were rapidly loaded, and at about eleven thirty the second lorry set off on it's short journey. John was then left to contemplate the empty shell of the house whilst he was waiting for the Gas and Electricity Metre readers to come and take the final readings.

It hadn't been a bad sort of a place really they'd had some hard times here, particularly when John had spent months laying flat on his back following a spinal injury. He had enjoyed being involved in local affairs having spent much of his spare time involved with the Tenants and Residents Association and had eventually become it's Chairman. From there he had moved into the political arena, but being a Conservative in a staunchly Socialist area was not an easy brief.

The metre readers came and went, leaving the supplies either locked off or removing the metre and John was left to take one last look round the empty shell that had been their home for almost ten years. He turned off the water supply; made certain that all of the windows were securely fastened; locked and bolted the back door for the last time; removed all of the keys from his key ring, and put both sets onto the ring that he would hand into the Council before the Housing Office closed at four-thirty. He looked vacantly out of the rear window of the lounge, and smiled as he saw the sand pit that he had made for the children when they were small recalling the time when along with a colleague from the office he had called in at the house one summers afternoon to find hoards of children running about all over the place. The colleague had gasped, "Christ are all of these kids yours? God I bet you don't get much time for watching Television."

The truth was that Kath loved working with children, and all of the local kids came to play in the sand and on the swings out in the garden and she loved it.

He moved round to look through the front window, over looking its brief patch of garden and privet hedge, across the Close, with it's parking bays at the top. There were some good people here he thought, but now was the time to move on.

So it was they moved out of the house that had been their home for more than ten years. It had served it's purpose and although they had never felt that this would be their permanent home, there were some elements of regret at leaving the place where all their friends and neighbours had shared the same mode of life. They had made all of the usual promises to keep in touch, that everyone makes at such partings, and their new house was less than three miles away from the old, but in their hearts they all knew that as the days progressed all of them would strike up new relationships, new friendships and the old would gradually slip into the past.

He walked down the road saying his good-byes to those of his friends and neighbours who had seen him preparing to leave, turned the corner at the bottom, and walked away from the close forever. He knew that he would never return.

As he waited at the bus stop Martin walked up, on his way to start his afternoon shift. "You've got it all done then?" He said with an air of disappointment."

"Yes I'm just off to hand my keys in at the Housing Department." John was equally morose.

"God I'm sorry to see you go John." He was almost in tears. "I thought that the two of us would really get something done up here, and I know that we've started things moving, but I thought that we would be mates for many years past today."

"This doesn't change anything." John protested. "We can still get together and argue all night long, I'm not moving to the moon you know. It's only three miles away."

"But it's not just round the corner either." He responded. "I won't be able to amble round to your house in me slippers at two-o-clock in the morning just to have a cup of tea and a natter. You're the first bloke that I've really been able to talk to, did you know that?

"No I didn't!" John was surprised.

"You are the only one who never smacked down any of my ideas, no matter how much you disagreed with them." He smiled. "That meant more to me than any of the politics, more than anything that money could buy."

The bus came along, and they sat together in silence for all of the twenty minute journey into the City, each of them thinking over their years of fighting against City Hall, each of them knowing that soon they would be part of City Hall themselves.

They shook hands and parted without further words, each knowing that their paths would be moving in different directions in the days ahead.

John handed in his keys at the Housing Department, and gave them the details of his new address. He walked back across the square, and boarded the bus for New Park. Their new life started here.

By the time that he arrived at Arundell Avenue the

Removal men had done their job and left. All of the furnishings were in their allotted room, and just needed positioning in the way that Kathy wanted them. The electricity, gas and water had been turned on and the children had already started to organise their new and bigger bedrooms.

As he entered the door he could hear the sound of voices from the dinning room at the rear of the house, and walked through to find Sarah Beecham and another lady in conversation with Kathy. This room was ready for use, the carpets on the ground floor had all been left and were in very good condition. The dining room furniture had been set out in the way that Kathy had wanted. Clearly Sarah Beecham and her other helper had taken instruction. But more to point from John's point of view there was food on the table.

Kathy turned. "Just look what they've done for us John."She said gratefully. "They've made up all of this food just for us, aren't they kind?"

He knew at this point, that come what may, this was the right thing to do.Their new neighbours came in to welcome them, each bringing a bottle of wine and staying just long enough for them to have a drink and by eight-o-clock they still hadn't unpacked any of their clothing. So they began by getting out the bedding and making up the beds, so that when they felt like it, they would be able to drop into them and sleep.

The only room that was empty was the lounge because it was so big they had to completely refurnish it that is with the exception of the carpets. Clearly the previous owner had an eye for quality for the carpets were of very good quality and in excellent condition. It was also a practical decision to leave the lounge without the main items of furniture so that the room could be used as their committee room during then forthcoming election. There was two great advantages of this house over their old house, this one was centrally heated, and it had a separate bath and shower.

By ten-o'clock that night they were all exhausted, so they locked up, and went to bed in their own house for the first time.

14

Election Day May 6th

The alarm rang at 6 am.and John stirred, leaned over and pulled back the curtain. "Well at least it looks as though we are going to get a fine day for it." He mused. Even though he was still half asleep, and he could hardly see the outside because of the posters that decorated the outside of each pane. He hauled himself out of bed, and shuffled his way round the boxes that they had not had the time to unpack, and made his way down to the kitchen. This took a couple of attempts due to the fact that he was still on auto-pilot, and that meant that he was trying to carry-out the functions that pertained in the old house. On the way he gazed into the lounge, with its trestle tables set out for use during the coming day, this was to be his Main Committee Room. The canvas cards were laid out neatly a card for each road marked with those on each who had pledges their vote to him, and as the day progressed the returns from each Polling Station would come in every hour so that those who had voted could be marked off. It was also the control room for all of the cars that picked up the old and, the infirmed to carry them to voted. As the day progressed, so the activity here would increase until in the last couple of hours the pace would be almost frantic.

Perhaps it was just as well they had decided not to have the lounge furnishings delivered until the week-end. There would have been no room for it anyway. The Party had a well tried and tested format for all of this, and the Party Faithful all turned out to do their bit. John was well versed in this whole process, for in the past he had played his part at all levels of Election Organisation from being a teller at a Station to being an Agent for a Candidate. All good experience if you are ever going to be a Candidate yourself.

"Well today is crunch day, old son." The inner voice mused. "every thing now depends on two things, the first is 'will the locals turn out and vote for the two of you, and will the Party Organisation manage to get the Conservative Core to the Polls in sufficient numbers for you to win? It was too late now if they'd overlooked anything now.

He made coffee for himself, and tea for Kathy who was still snoring gently in bed when he returned. He could hear the children stirring, they would be helping out in the house during the course of the day, as goffers, and Thomas Wilken's, a Young Conservative and Student in Accountancy would be running the Committee Room. John and Malcolm would be touring around the Polling Stations and generally showing themselves in the Ward for most of the day. The bulk of the work would be carried out by a team of ladies who had been 'doing this sort of thing for years'. It was something of a novelty for John to have such hoards of helpers. In previous years he had worked in those areas of the city that were traditional Labour strong-holds, and the numbers of helpers could usually be counted on one hand. That meant that the Agent usually had to do all of the work himself, simply to allow all of the others to use their cars to ferry people too and from the Polling Stations. This was something different. This was the way that it should be done.

"Kath, Kath! Here's a cup of tea for you." He woke her from her half-sleep. "Come on Baby, the big day is here and the helpers will be arriving at about seven fifteen."

Kath lifted herself into the sitting position.

107

"Thanks!" She yawned as she took the cup. "What time did you say that they'd be arriving?"

"About seven fifteen." John repeated the time.

."What the hell do they want to be here at that time for?" She muttered past the hand that she still had to her mouth. "The polls don't open until eight-o-clock, and the first returns will not be here until after nine."

"All of the troops are meeting here to get their rosettes and telling sheets" John explained. "They will arrive at least the first group will arrive at half past seven; so young Tom has arranged to be here when they arrive. You know what these YC's are like. Full of energy and enthusiasm."

"I thought that I would be able to have a bit of a lie-in this morning." Kath stated with some hint of face pulling.

"Well that is something that I wanted to talk to you about." John was serious. "I don't want you to over-do it today. Let the others do all of the spade work, and if you feel like having a rest, then come up here away from it all. I don't want you to knock yourself up when there are ample bodies to do the work for you. This will not be like the elections we've done together in the past, here there are plenty of helpers, and you can have an easy day simply playing a support role. But don't do to much."

"Listen to the Doctor!" she joked. "The truth is that I don't feel like doing too much. I can't get going at all."

"You'll have to learn to take your time for a while." John replied. "The doctor said that you will have to gradually increase the amount of work that you do, he told me that it could take up to a year for you tocompletely recover. So don't rush things, everybody knows what the situation is, and these mature ladies will not let you do a thing, mark my words."

At least the bathroom was in full working order, even if the rest of the house was in turmoil, and John relaxed by having a shower. This was real luxury compared with the cramped bathroom at the old house. There wasn't even room for a shower to be fitted in that rabbit hutch. The day gradually got underway, the children were down in the kitchen getting their breakfast, and John was now getting dressed to face his public.

Tom arrived on the dot at seven fifteen, and immediately set about getting things arranged to suit his method of operation. By seven thirty there were six cars parked outside the house, and tellers were being detail to their various Polling Stations.

Malcolm arrived at about eight-o-clock, and he and John set off to take John to vote in his old Ward. They stopped while Malcolm cast his vote at the New Park East Polling Station, and then went on to Colly Farm Central, where John tried to speak to Sheila Jones who was acting as a teller for the Party, but she turned her back on him and refused to even take his Register Number.

"I say, that was a bit off" Malcolm commented, "Whatever have you done to her, old man?"

"They haven't taken kindly to my sitting and moving to another Ward" Sighed John. "They think that I'm a bit of a traitor, because they thought that I would be sitting here."

"Oh it's like that is it?" he responded. "Do you think that you could have won this seat then?"

"Yes, but only this time around." John explained. "In a normal year we wouldn't stand a snowballs chance in Hell of winning it. It's usually rock solid Socialist, of the extreme Left Wing sort, at that. We had been planning to move out of the area anyway. Long before I decided that I would stand, and the fact that the house that we found was in the Park Ward was purely coincidental. The Lib.Dem candidate was the first to start shouting 'traitor', and the Labour boys had a field day. But they've had their chance over the last twelve years, and they did nothing to improve the quality of life out here, so my thinking is that it will be a close run thing between the Liberals and us at the end of the day. The canvas returns looked very good, but there aren't enough workers on our side to really maximise the effort, chances are that we will loose out simply because we will not get the old folk to the Poll."

They drove back to New Park, and started their round of visiting Polling Stations to make sure that they had got full cover, and making sure that there were no difficulties for the Staff who were conducting the Pole. By lunch time they had completed their round and returned to the Committee Room to find the place a hive of industry. About ten ladies of varying ages were busy making up the Tellers Cards, and drivers were coming and going to pick-up voters to go their polling station. The fine weather had resulted in a good turnout during the morning, and everyone was in high spirits. During the course of the morning the Area Chairman, Lord Rooke, had visited the Committee Room, and Tom, who didn't know who he was, had thrust a name and address for a pick-up into his hand and told him to get out on the streets where he could do something useful. He promptly returned to his Rolls Royce and did just that. Much to everybody else's amusement, but he didn't come back to do another. The children, who did know who hewas, found this incident highly amusing and told everybody who came into the house, what had happened. The story was repeated at all meetings of Conservatives through-out the day.

Charles Brown, accompanied by Conrad Barnes, dropped in at about two-o-clock to let them know that the turn-out through-out the city was very high for a local election he was full of it.

"We are going to annihilate them today John me boy, and by the time that we get to the victory party tonight there will hardly be a Socialist to be seen on the City Council. Just a quite word for a moment," he said in a whisper "I've had a word or two with Conrad, and he's said that he will support you as much as possible, but he can't cover all of the work that you do, so it looks as though you will be burning the midnight oil a bit in our first few weeks. Of course it will settle down after the first month or so. You'll just have to do what you can." Having said his piece he and Conrad disappeared into the sunny afternoon.

The afternoon was very slow, most of the voters would be at work, and they all took the opportunity to get something to eat, and take a breather, before the late rush. From about four-thirty the tempo gradually increased until by eight-o-clock it was a complete mad house. The last rush to get those last few votes that might make the difference proved beyond doubt that the careful planning was paying off. Malcolm who had spent the afternoon driving people from the Old Peoples Homes to the Pole arrived at about eight-thirty, and along with John they made their way to the Federation Office where there were many of the Fifty-five Candidates each preparing to go to their Ward Counts.

John and Malcolm's count was to be held in the main hall of the local school, and they were allowed four observers for each candidate. To be able to attend a count it is necessary to have documentation that is signed by the electoral returning officer for the area. Only those who have the papers can attend the count. It had been arranged that those who had the accreditation would meet at the School at Nine-o-clock.

From the out-set the count was very smooth, the observers for each Candidate, spread around the tables and monitored the sorting and separation of the Ballot Papers. Once they had been separated the papers for each Candidate were counted into bundles of a hundred papers per bundle, and placed in rows on a table at the end of the room again one table for each Candidate's votes. The piles of votes for John and Malcolm grew at a faster rate than all of the other candidates, and by the time that the count was nearing completion it was clear that they would have a very large majority.

Finally the Returning Officer passed the result for each Candidate to see along with the list of spoilt voting papers. This being agreed all of the Candidates, along with the Returning Officer moved onto the stage at the end of the Hall and the result was declared.

"I Frederick Harper being the returning office for the New Park Ward here-by declare that the number of votes cast for each candidate are as follows:-

Arthur Brown	Labour	1693 votes
Anthea Mary Colby	Liberal	802 votes
Harvey Henry Dalton	Liberal	724 votes
Malcolm Anthony Griffin	Conservative	3671 votes
Mary Roberts Mullins	Labour	1872 votes
John Marcus Robertson	Conservative	4032 votes

And I therefore declare that the said Malcolm Griffin and John Robertson are duly elected to serve as Councillors for the said Ward and I call upon Councillor Robertson to say a few words.

John was completely unprepared, but he stepped forward, "I would like to thank all of the people who have conducted this election, for the calm and professional way in which they have carried out their duties. My thanks also go to the Police for making sure that everything was secure, and that the Ballot Boxes were delivered to the right places at the right time" A brief ripple of laughter ran round the hall. "the people of the New Park Ward have made their choice, and this has resulted in a huge majority for the Conservative Party. From my point of view, I will represent the best interests of the Ward in Council, and I thank the voters of the Ward for the trust that have shown in me. Thank you."

There was a huge cheer from all concerned, and then Mary Mullins stepped forward and spoke as follows:-"The people of this Ward have made a huge mistake, one that they will soon come to regret. The Labour Party have always had the interests of the people at heart, and will continue to do so in the future. I will however echo the words of Councillor Robertson in thanking all of the workers who have made this count and the conduct of the election so easy to follow."

John and Malcolm walked round and thanked all of the people, both official, and from the party, for their hard work, and then they made their way to the awaiting car, and were driven to the Party at the Conservative Office.

"How have you faired?" was the first question that they asked. We won with a very large majority."

"Both of you?"

"Yes both of us, with around a two thousand majority each." John replied.

"How are we doing in the rest of the city?"

"Well we look as though we are going to have an

overall majority, but there are still only about half of the results in, but we are making gains all over the place." This was the Federation Chairman speaking. "Your old Ward has been split between us and the Lib.Dems, but the Labour party only just failed to hold one of the seats. There are a couple of re-counts underway, but we will have to wait and see. Come on and get yourselves a drink and a sandwich."

A huge board had been placed at one end of the room and the results were being marked in as they became known. As each Conservative victory was announced another phase for cheering and dancing was started. It looked as though some of the people there had been celebrating since early afternoon. As the night progressed it became clear that the period of Socialist control in the city had finally come to end.

At half-past-one in the morning Charles Brown appeared amid scenes of jubilation, with one exception, which was going to a third recount, the Party had forty three of the fifty-five seats on the City Council, Labour had Nine, and the Lib.Dems had one.

Charles was over the moon when he spoke to John, "There you are young man, you're now a Councillor, but not only that you are to be the new Chairman of the City Transport Committee. I want you to see me at ten in the morning, at the Town Hall. The Chief Executive will be there, and you will have to sign your declaration and list any interests that you may have that could affect any decisions that we will have to take. You know the type of thing. Then you have a meeting arranged at the Transport Department, to meet all of the senior staff, the General Manager and Deputy, the Chief Engineer and all of the heads of Department. They usually have a bit of a buffet, and tour round all of the depots. It will take about a couple of hours or so. You'd better get off and see how Kathy is, I'll bet she hasn't seen or heard from you since late this afternoon."

Molly Bacon after years of trying had finally made it on to City Council, and Martin, John's old friend was also an elected Councillor for the Labour Party in the Central Ward.

The revelling went on into the small hours, but John and Malcolm left to seek the comfort of theirs respective beds, it had been a long day.

Kath was sitting up in bed when he arrived home, looking tired, but happy.

"Congratulations darling." She held out he arms to hug him. "You really deserve it. The children are absolutely thrilled about your result, and when they heard that you were to be the New Chairman of Transport they were astounded."

"Yes I suppose that we should have prepared them for that." He paused. "Anyway how did you know that I was to be the Chairman, I never told you either."

"No it was your friend Charles Brown," She smiled. "He told me when he visited me in hospital that if the Party had a majority after the election, you would be in charge of Transport."

"So the old bastard had you in his pocket all of the time." He glowered at her. "I don't recall you having told me that he visited you."

"Ah well," she said, "A girl has to have some secrets just to maintain her mysterious charm."

15

First Meeting of Council

7th June

After all of the pomp and ceremony that surrounds the making of a Lord Mayor, and the Civil Church Service, that is followed by a party given by the Mayor in the Town Hall, John was at last relieved to get down to the real business of Council. He had never attended a Council Meeting so the whole process was new to him. He knew where his seat as Chairman of Transport was, but as to the proceedings he had no idea. He had the Minutes of the previous meeting and a copy of the agenda, along with sheaves of paper that had been handed to him by the Transport General Manager (Peter Church) as he entered the Chamber and that was all.

The agenda included an item that read 'Questions to Chairmen of Committees, and he was aware that he had three questions to answer, but the rest of the proceedings outlined were a mystery to him. The first item was simple enough, it was to approve the minutes of the last meeting, and as there were only about eight of the previous Council now sitting as members, the minutes were accepted on a straight vote, and that was unanimous.

The Chief Executive who acted as Clerk to the Council then announced"Item two, Questions to Chairmen of Committees. Questions to the Chairmen of Transport:- Councillor Smith."

If John was nervous, then Martin, who was asking

two questions was a gibbering wreck.

"Could the Chairman of Transport please inform me why the number 44 bus service has been re-routed down Middlemas Lane?"

John had a very good knowledge of the service routes in the city, but couldn't place Middlemas Lane along the route of the 44 service. He glanced at the proposed reply given by the General Manager but this did not coincide with the details of the question. He looked at the next question which was also from Martin and realised that in his highly nervous state he had mixed the details of the two questions. There was nothing for it he had to make a reply:-

"As far as I am aware the number 44 bus does not travel along Middlemas Lane on any part of its route, and this service has not been diverted or re-routed for over twenty years. Are we living in the same City Councillor Smith?" There was a ripple of laughter across the chamber.

"The Chairman knows exactly what I mean My Lord Mayor." Martin stammered.

John rose to his feet again. "I can only answer the question that I am given in this Chamber My Lord Mayor, but if the Councillor cares to see me after the meeting so that I decipher what he does mean I will give him a written answer."

If the first question had made him nervous, then the second almost reduced Martin to tears:- Could the Chairman of Transport confirm or deny that late night buses on the 37 route will no longer travel past the Market Place in Fordham?" Martin realised at this stage that he had transposed the two route numbers, but he'd already asked the question so he knew what was coming before he sat down.

"I must confess" John began, "To being a little bemused by this question, because the 37 route does not go through Fordham Market Place, and I'm afraid that I will have to ask the Councillor to give me some time to get my bearings, perhaps it's me who doesn't live in this City."

"Supplementary Lord Mayor" Alan Nichol's the leader of the Labour Group sprang to his feet.

"Good God," thought John, "What's a supplementary Question.

But Nichol's was going on, "The 37 service has been re-routed My Lord Mayor, so could the Chairman please inform Council of the details that made the re-routing necessary?"

John replied reading from the typed script that the General Manager had handed to him. "This is a temporary measure made necessary by the relaying of sewerage pipes down the centre of the Main Street in Fordham, and whilst I agree that the current route is unsatisfactory, it is only a temporary measure, and the service will return to it's well established route just as soon as the pipe laying is completed and the road is satisfactorily reinstated." John sat down.

But the Chief Executive had not finished. "Question to the Chairman of Transport :- Councillor Needham."

"Could the chairman of Transport please inform council on the current status of bus orders from the Babbington Bus Corporation?"

John did not need to refer to any papers for an answer to this question. "The current status is that orders from this Company are current running approximately five years late, but if the Councillor will bear with me, I do intend to present a Report on this matter at the next meeting of Council when I will be able to elaborate more on this matter."

John sat down, and the Chief Executive intoned, "Question to the Chairman of the Policy Committee." John discovered that he was sweating profusely, and the Chairman of Arts and Recreation said out of the side of his mouth "You did all right there John, not bad for a first timer." Ernest Fisher had been a member of Council for almost forty years and knew all of the ropes. This was not bad coming from him for he was not in the habit of commenting on anybodies actions.

The meeting droned on until there was some discussion on the detail of a proposal, when one of the New Councillor's got up and made a short speech on the subject. He said what he had to say, and everybody in the Chamber applauded as he sat down.

"What was the applause for?" John asked of Councillor Fisher.

"He's just made his maiden speech, and it is the custom to applaud it whether it was good or bad." He replied.

"I just made my maiden speech, but nobody applauded me." John smiled.

"That's true," It was Fishers turn to smile, "But you are a Chairman of Committee and therefore you do not fall into the category of a 'rookie' councillor. You have to sink or swim with the rest of us old timers."

Well I'm damned thought John, I don't even get a look in, even though it's me who has a bucket full of work to do, it's all of these plebs who get the plaudits for it all. A sort of crude justice I suppose.

The meeting ground to its close at about half-past-four, and everyone trouped out to beer and sandwiches, It hadn't been as bad as he had anticipated, but the pause didn't last, one of the messengers sought him John out and informed him that he was required in the Leaders Office.

There was food and drink laid out in the secretary's office and all of the Chairmen were in with Charles laughing and joking.

"Ah there you are John." It was Charles, glass in

one hand, and half eaten cake in the other. "It is usual for Chairmen to come in here after the Council Meeting for a bit of a chin-wag, and to talk over what has happened in the Meeting. I suddenly thought that perhaps you didn't know about it."

"No Charles I didn't, but I expect that I'll get used to these little traditions as I go along."John was feeling particularly narked about the whole thing.

How was a person to get to know that these sort of things if no one told them?

"I just wanted to tell you how well you performed in there today." He beamed out his praise. "You handled the whole 'balls up' in just the right way. You don't have to give these Socialist any more information than they ask for. They've treated us like rubbish for the past twelve years, and it did my heart good to see you make them squirm a bit today. While you were speaking I looked round the Chamber, and all of the old hands were smiling into their papers. By the way, I thought Smith was a friend of yours."

"Yes, I think that 'was' is the operative word there." John replied. "I don't think that we will be having a quiet pint together for some time to come."

"Well he is the opposition when all is said and done, and it is better for you to recognise that fact early in your political career, than learn to regret the fact at some later date."Charles spoke as though he had experience in this area."Anyway we all think that you had a very good first meeting don't we everybody?"

There were murmurs of agreement from around the room.They all may feel smug, thought John, but inside he still felt as though he had betrayed and injured a friend of many years simply to gain a little short term kudos for himself. This little party within a party was gathered round it's leader, drinking to excess, sheltered from the real world outside, and John began to wonder if this was the state of play at all levels of the political life. If it was, then the time was not too far distant when the people in that real world would ask them to repay the cost. The feeling did not leave him as he made his way towards the bus to go home, by then it was early evening, and the whole day had been a revelation to him. The party in the leade'rs office had been in full swing when John slipped away.

He'd had enough of the plastic friendship and the bonhomie, one slip and they would round on you and destroy you simply to advance their own careers. What he really wanted was a quiet night at home with his wife and family.

He arrived home to find Kathy curled up in a chair in the lounge reading, looking very relaxed. "Hello" She called dreamily. "I didn't expect you home for a while yet. I thought that you would all be full of yourselves, drinking and generally celebrating the fact that you were now in control of the city.

He kissed her on the forehead and said, "They are, but I didn't find it very interesting at all, all they appeared to want to do was to drink and heap self praise on each other."

"Oh ,by the way, She interrupted "Martin rang about half-an-hour ago he wanted to have a word with you."

"Yes I'm sure he did." John almost snapped back.

"Oooo, that sounds a bit ominous." Kathy was surprised by the harsh response. "What has he done to you?"

"It's not what he's done to me," John sighed. "It's what I've done to him. He had put down two questions to ask me in the meeting this afternoon, and when he got up to ask them he was so nervous that he scrambled details of the two questions and it made it sound as though he didn't even know the bus routes that ran though his own Ward. Well instead of answering the question that I knew he had wanted to ask, I made out that I didn't know what he was talking about, and made great play of the fact that the services didn't run down the roads that he had mentioned in his questions. The whole chamber, including the members on his own benches laughed, and when I stopped to consider it was a cheap trick to play on a man, who despite our differing political views, has been a staunch friend for a number of years."

"That is so unlike you John," Kathy said seriously, "don't let all of this change you because I still want you to be the man that I married for his good humour and his friendship to everyone who came in contact with him. Now go and telephone Martin, while I get you something to eat, and you apologise to him before you both do something that you will regret for the rest of your lives."

The phone was answered on its first ring. "Hello Martin it's me." John said tentatively.

"Oh Hello mate, thanks for calling me back," He spoke as though nothing had happened, "you know those question that I asked you this afternoon, I wondered if you could spare me a few minutes tomorrow night so that I can explain the real problem to you? The only problem is that I'm on evenings so I won't finish until about ten."

"I've got a short meeting that starts at six-thirty." John mused. "I should be home by about half-past eight."

"My shift finishes at the Park Depot, so I could walk round to your place before I go home, if that will be OK?"

"Yes that's fine." said John with relief. "I want to apologise for this afternoon Martin, I should have given you the opportunity to correct your questions before I gave my answer."

"Don't think about it, I would have done the same thing to you if it had been the other way round, and what's more you know it." He sounded quite cheerful. "I made a 'pig's ear' of the whole thing and you played it for what it was worth. The trouble with you is that you think too much, and you often feel bad about things that other people accept without a thought. You should attend a few Labour Party and Union Meetings if you really want to see people tearing each other apart. I'm quite used to that sort of thing, so just forget about it, mate."

"OK I'll see you tomorrow night then, and we can sort things out between ourselves." And with that John put down the phone and returned to the lounge. Kathy had anticipated that John would be hungry, so she had made up some sandwiches and coffee on a tray for when he arrived home. So that by the time that John sat down the tray and the coffee were on the small coffee table against his chair.

16

Tuesday 8th June

John's desk was piled high with unanswered enquires and drawings that had been sent to him for approval, when he arrived in the office early in the morning. Harry was away in Germany and Conrad Barnes had started his two weeks holiday, so it was up to John to hold the fort.

He had decided that he would get into the office before the works started simply to give him-self time to clear all of the essentials before the streams of enquiries and problems started to come from the assembly shops. This meant that if he left home a little before six am perhaps he might be able to get an uninterrupted day, that is uninterrupted by Council business.

But that wish was soon quashed. The phone rang a little after seven-thirty, it was the Transport Department Chief Engineer Ian Mackay, "I'm sorry to interrupt your day Chairman, but one of our vehicles has been involved in a fatal accident and that the General Manager has requested that you be called to visit the scene. There is a car on it's way to pick you up right now. I don't want to say too much now, but it is imperative that you be here as soon as possible."

"Are you sure that I'm needed?" John was annoyed.

"Oh yes Chairman." He replied. "There are certain aspects of the accident that you will need to know. But as I have said, it would be unwise for me speak at the moment, because of the circumstances."

"All right then I'm on my way." He slammed the phone down and grabbed his coat just as the loading bay charge-hand burst into his office to tell him that there was an official car waiting for him down in the car park.

"OK, thanks" John called to him. "I say Paul, would you let reception know that I've been called out, and ask them to re-route my calls to the Transport Department if they're urgent?"

"OK John will do," He called from the corridor. "What's up, can't they do anything for themselves? I thought that these local council workers were paid enough to make them responsible, at least that's what the Government keep telling us." He disappeared down the stairs and through the door into the works.

"Tell me about it." John murmured to the empty office has he made his way towards the car park.

The bus had crashed into the front of a newspaper shop at the bottom of Market Hill, a customer in the shop had been killed out-right, and the shop owner had been seriously injured. The Police and the Fire Brigade were still in attendance, and the bus was still firmly wedged into the front wall of the building when John arrived. The whole of the traffic flows around the city centre had ground to a halt, and the situation was so bad that John and his driver had to park the car and finish the journey on foot. The Press and TV were out in force, and as soon as he was spotted John was surrounded by people wanting a statement.

John was quite calm about it all and said, "I have just arrived on the scene, I do not as yet have any of the details of the accident, and as soon as I have collected all of the information that is available, I will give you a statement. Until then I'm afraid that you will have to wait."

Ian Mackay spotted him " Thank goodness you're here Chairman," His usually sombre features were emphasised by the fact that he was obviously in a state of shock. "These are the facts, as I know them. Vehicle number 3261 was stolen from the central depot at sometime after seven-o-clock this morning, and was driven by some person, as yet unknown, and parked half way down Market Hill. As far as we can ascertain it was left without it's brakes on. It was seen by one of our duty inspectors, but before he could enter the bus, began to roll down the hill, and when it reach the bottom it careered across the road and ran into the shop. There was no one in the vehicle and the side doors were open. There were two people in the shop, one an as yet unidentified customer, and the owner. The customer has died, and is his body is still trapped under the front of the bus. The shop owner has been extracted from the rubble and is currently on his way to the General Hospital. That is all that I have for the moment Chairman."

"Thank you Ian, for giving me the details without trying to gloss them over." John looked at him and then continued. "I think that you should walk down to the Town Hall and get yourself a good strong cup of tea, and two minutes peace and quiet. I'll find out what I can from the Police and Fire Brigade, and then join you as soon as I can."

"Thank you Chairman," he said with relief, I could do with a breather."

"Oh, just before you go Ian," John added as an after thought, "Where is the General Manager, and why wasn't he available to attend this accident?"

"He had a long standing appointment to speak at a meeting of the Omnibus Society in Birmingham today Chairman. So when I called him to tell him about the situation he told me to call you out." He was visibly uncomfortable. "I hope that I've done the right thing!"

"Surely the next in line should be the Deputy GM." John added. "Why wasn't he called out?"

"Mr Watkin is off sick Chairman." He answered.

"He has been for nearly three months now."

"All right Ian, I get the picture."

He realised that there was a real problem, and nobody really wanted to know, so this poor sod was left holding the baby John thought, as he watched as Ian Mackay walked off towards Town Hall.

Accidents are a magnet to all observers of City life, and this was no exception. John had to push his way through the increasing circle of on-lookers. The bus was firmly wedged into the structure of the building and it looked as though it would be a major job to extract it. There were a number of inspectors from the department, in discussion with a Fire Brigade Officer, and a Chief Superintendent of Police. John approached them and called out "Good Morning Gentlemen, what have we here?"

They turned and muttered their 'Good Mornings'. The policeman spoke first. "Are you aware of the details so far Councillor?"

"Yes thank you Superintendent, but perhaps you can bring me up to date on the situation." John replied.

"I think that Station Officer Gorman will be the best to do that at the moment Sir." The Policeman clearly thought that there were other priorities.

Station Officer Gorman was a fairly young man, but was clearly in control of things. "Well Councillor we are in some difficulty, there is the body of a man trapped under the front end of the bus, and we are trying to extracate him. When the bus hit the front of the building it pushed the joist that supports the upper levels of the building through the wall, and into the front of the shop. So we have a situation where the only thing that is holding up the front of the building is the bus. If we remove the bus the whole of the front of the building may collapse and that would cause a major hazard. I would like to remove the body, but to do it I would have to move the bus, or cut away part of the structure of the bus. That would mean that the whole bus would be a right-off, and with that in mind the Transport Chief Engineer could not authorise the eventual destruction of the bus. That is the immediate problem." He concluded.

"Cut away the front of the bus, and extract the body." John instructed. "That is on my say so, and I will sign any authorisation that you require.

That is of course subject to any forensic examination that you might need to carry-out superintendent."John said turning the Officer.

"Judging by the state of the cab and front access doors there won't be any chance of getting much from what's left, I don't think." He pondered stroking his chin. "I think that we can go ahead and remove the body."

He turned and looked at John. "However I do think that you and I should have a brief meeting somewhere away from here, so that we can agree on exactly what has taken place here."

"Yes I think that would be a good idea." John agreed "Where shall we go, to the Police Station or the Town Hall?" They agreed that it would probably be best if they went to the Police Station.

They picked up Ian Mackay from the Town Hall, and proceeded to the Central Police Station.

The interview room was dimly lit, it had no windows and the only furnishings were a heavy duty table and four assorted chairs, which were at least comfortable.

Superintendent Potter opened the proceedings. "The simple facts are that a bus was stolen from the Main Depot at or around seven-o-clock this morning, it was driven from there by a route that is as yet unknown to a place on Market Hill where it was parked. We believe that it was parked without the brakes being applied, and left unattended with the doors open. It was spotted by Inspector Graves, but before he could get to it the bus it began to roll down Market Hill, it crossed Bridge Street, and crashed into the front of number 61 Bridge Street, a News Agents Shop, severely injuring the proprietor, a Mr Oldknow, and killing a customer who has yet to be identified. The shop is badly damaged, the bus is probably a right off, and the traffic in the City Centre will have to diverted for perhaps two or three days." He paused to take a drink of water. "If it transpires that the bus was stolen, and we have yet to prove that fact, and if it was parked in the manner that has been described, then clearly there has been an act that has resulted in the death of an innocent member of the public.

I should say here. that if this is the case then who- ever parked that bus, did so knowing that he or she had left it in a dangerous position on a hill without applying the brakes. When we find out who has done this, he will be facing a charge of Manslaughter. That is the position from my point of view." He concluded.

Ian Mackay decided that this was the point where he should have his say, "Fleet No 3162 was parked in the Central Depot after it had completed it's service at approximately eleven-forty-five pm last night. It was due for a tyre change during the course of today, and was not scheduled to go out on service until early tomorrow morning. It was seen by the garage foreman at around seven this morning, but when he asked one of his crew to move the bus into position for it to have it's tyres changed, it was discovered that the bus had been removed from the garage. The foreman went to the radio room and put out a call for the bus to be returned to the garage, believing that someone had mistakenly used the bus to go out on service.There was no response from the drivers, but inspector Graves said that he had seen the bus parked on Market Hill, and that he would go back and investigate. Before he could get back to the vehicle, it had started to roll down the hill, and despite an attempt to get onto the bus, in which he was injured, the bus went down the hill and crashed into the Newspaper Shop. That is all that I can say at this time."

John had listened closely to what had been said and began, "All that I can say is to repeat what you have all ready told me. If this bus was stolen, did any body notice who the driver was? How can a Bus be taken from a supposedly secure garage, and be driven along city streets, and none of the officials be aware that the bus had been taken? What sort of maniac would do this type of thing? What can I tell the wives and families of the dead and injured." What do I release to the Media?"

At this point they were interrupted by the Chief Executive and the City Secretary and Solicitor. The Chief Executive began, "What is going on here?"

"We are merely exchanging points of information to try to clarify the events leading up to a bus running into a News Agents Shop in Market Hill." John answered his rather curt question.

"We have reason to believe" Potter stated "That a number of offences have been committed."

"And who do you believe committed those offences?" He continued in the same vein. "Because if there is an inference that the Transport Department is in anyway involved or implicated in those crimes, then the Councillor and the Chief Engineer are not qualified, by statute, to make statements or give information without the express authority of either the Leader of Council, Myself or the City Secretary and Solicitor."

"Let me assure you that we are not taking statements, we are not making accusations against the

130

City, we are merely trying to piece together a series of events that led to a bus being park on Market Hill." Supt. Potter was emphatic. "We came here to avoid the attentions of the press and to compare notes."

The two legal officers of the City visibly relaxed. Michael Fox the City Secretary said "We were told that the two of you had been taken away by the Police, and we thought that you had been arrested." They all laughed and when Potter played the recording of the conversation that had been held, they settled for a cup of tea, and a stroll back to the Town Hall.

The Media were there all waiting, with very little patience, for a statement from all concerned. The Chief Executive briefly stated the facts as indicated in the recording in which they had participated.

The Superintendent stated "That investigations were in a very early stage, and as soon as there was something more to tell them there would be a press release."

John was questioned about the security of the Central Depot and he replied "That there was to be an internal investigation carried out and that when the findings were known all of those steps necessary to ensure the security of the Central Depot and Garage, and indeed all of the transport depots, would be made."

They all declined to answer further question because there was nothing else to say at this time.

17

Return From the Front

John arrived back at work to find that the time was One-o-clock lunch time. But there were a whole pile of enquiries including one from Harry over in Seigburg, Germany were an hour ahead of GMT so John dialled the number. The reply came very quickly "Firma Stellenburg. guten Tag."

"Guten tag. Ich mochte bitter Mr Harry Richards sprechen."

"Wie ist Ihr Name, bitte?"

"Hier Spricht John Robertson von das Firma Convellium im England."

"Ah Hello John how are you?" He knew the receptionist very well.

"I'm fine Stella. How are you?" He said, pleased that she had recognised him.

"I'm not too bad." She replied. "But you know how it is out here."

"Is Harry about anywhere, he left me a message to call him?"He asked.

"Yes he's with the Herr Doktor at the moment. Shall I interrupt them?" she enquired.

"I think that you had better put me through to Wolfgang's office." He was now very concerned. Stellenburg's were one of their biggest customers and if anything went wrong there, it would spell disaster for Convellium.

The mechanical voice intoned, "Bitte warten", and he waited. It chimed again 'Bitte warten' and a very nervous voice nearly whispered "Hello!"

It was Harry. "Hello there Harry," John tried to

sound casual.

"Oh thank Christ you've called," He sounded almost at his wits-end. "God I'm in the most awful mess here. How the hell have you managed to keep them sweet for so long?"

"What's the problem?"He was curious. Wolfgang was the most pleasant of people.

"Well I quoted them the figures for the China Project, and they went ape.They began chattering in German amongst them-selves. Then Doktor Linz told me that the prices were far too high. I told him that this was the best price that we could offer him, and he said that if that was the best that we could do, then he would take his business elsewhere. Frankly I don't know what to do?"

"How did you quote the figures, in pounds or in Euros?" John enquired.

"As we always do, in Euros." he replied.

"Give me the figures for some of the machines in Euros and I will compare them with our Sterling price." John demanded.

The prices were past and John looked at the current estimated price of the machines in Sterling, and then calculated the prices in euros. The figures did not compare. It looked as though all of the prices had been calculated using the wrong conversion figure.

He returned to the phone. "Harry it looks as though all of the figures in the estimate have been based on the wrong conversion factor, making all of the prices about 15% too high."

"John you are a life saver," Harry commented with relief. "Never mind that Harry," John continued. " put Wolfgang on the line, and let me speak to him."

"Hello John. How are you?" The accent was very strong.

"I'm fine Wolfgang, and how are you?" He replied

"Sehr gut, danke." He reverted to German.

"There has been a mistake in our estimates," He began, "and Harry Richards did not pick it up before he presented you with the total costs Wolfgang. The wrong conversion factor has been used, so all of the figures need to be reduces by at least 15%. Do you understand that?"

"Ach! I knew there would be a simple explanation." Linz sounded relieved. "You have, how do you call it 'Sent a boy to do the work of a man' Ja?"

"Well I've been fairly busy here in England, so Harry has had to do some of the running about for me." John offered by way of explanation.

"Yes I hear that you now have two jobs, one as an Engineer, and one as a politician. In Germany we do not have such problems. We pay our politicians enough to let them carry out their work on a full time basis. Doing it that way we make sure that they can do their work properly. The trouble with you English is that you rely on people like you who will do the job for expenses only. That makes it very difficult for all of you to have a good service from your local politicians, and you ruin their professional and family lives into the bargain. You see I have tried to understand why you cannot be away from your City as much as you have been in the past. But you must ensure that your junior staff are fully trained to look at all aspects of negotiations and that they are capable of sorting out problems when they arise."

"Yes. Thank You for being so understanding Wolfgang." John grovelled a bit.

"I would not normally do this sort of thing." He returned. "But you are not only a supplier, you are our friend, and in Germany we try not to forget our friends. You have spent many hours of your own time working with our engineers, and you did it without being asked, and without being paid. For that we now try to return what you call 'the compliment'."

"That is very good of you and your staff. Thank you!" John felt very humble. "I will get the proposals re-typed, and faxed through to you as soon as possible."

"That will not be necessary, we will make the changes here, on the basis of what you have told us and Mr Richards will bring the revised documents back to England when he returns. The figures minus the 15% are now acceptable to us, and we will sign all of the necessary papers for him, and you can go ahead and start manufacture." Linz was clearly very happy with the revised costings. "I will look forward to seeing you when I am next in England, then you can show me round your massive Transport Department. Auf weidersehen." With that he was gone.

Linz was clearly not impressed with Harry. He clearly did not like the idea of dealing with someone who did not understand the German language, and who was making no effort to address the problem. It was perhaps fortunate that Conrad was away on holiday, because he would have torn Harry into little pieces and thrown him out of the back door. Let's hope that he doesn't find out about it. It is one thing to make a mistake, but not to be able to sort it out on the spot, when it arose, was quite a different matter. Harry Richards was not the man for this type of work, he was the guy who worked at the back of the office, who was good at his job, and his job was producing good designs. In this he excelled.

John made a mental note, that the next time that he was in England Herr Doktor Linz would get the full City and Company treatment. Yes he would see the whole of John's massive Transport Department.

John ploughed through problems that had accumulated during the morning, visited the Assembly and Machine Shops to resolve the errors and various annoyances that arose in a normal working day and by half-past-six he was just settling down to finish off a report that was required by the Directors, when the Cleaner came in and told him to get off home.

That was her way of telling him that she couldn't do her job properly if he was in the way. It was like being at home really. So that's where he went.

Kathy had dinner waiting for him when he arrived home. "Who's had a busy day then" She giggled. "The children were absolutely amazed when they saw your face on the National News."

"It wasn't, was it?"He was surprised.

"Oh yes it was!" Jason called from the lounge. "It was on the Regional News as well." He added. "Oh there's a dispatch box from the Transport Department in the Study."Kathy remarked casually. "And there's a pile of post about two feet high as well. At this rate you'll need a full time secretary."

"Well I'd thought that my best girl would assist me with that after she's done her homework. of course." He winked at Kathy across the table.

"In your dreams Dad" The anticipated reply came from Anne who up to now had remained silent.

He finished his dinner and then retired to his half unpacked study to plough through yet another pile of Council Papers and correspondence.

He was still working when Martin arrived just after ten.

"I didn't know whether I'd find you in." Martin said as he opened the door. "There's been all hell let loose down the Central Depot."

"Come in mate" John said motioning towards the lounge.

"Ay, this is a bit nice John." Martin spoke as he turned round looking the hall and staircase. "It's a bit bigger that the place you've left, and no mistake. Mind you I'll bet you got a mortgage as long as your arm."

"No it's not too bad at all." John confided. "The fact is that we got it for a song really. They wanted to get a quick sale and we were the first there."

The two of them walked into the lounge where Kath was sitting curled up with a book. as usual.

"You've got a real nice place here Kath." he smiled, "I wish that I'd seen it first."

"We were lucky," She admitted, "someone told us about it before it had been properly advertised, we made an offer and they accepted it straight away. Would you like a drink and a sandwiched Martin? I know that you've just finished your shift."

"I could murder a mug of sweet tea." he replied.

She left them to it.

"I don't know what to make of this supposed bus theft," he volunteered, "but the word in the depots is that one of the garage hands must have left the keys in the bus, or that one of them took the bus out, and saw what had happened and decided to play it clever."

"What do you think?" John asked

"Well this is strictly off the record," he confided, "but I think that someone in the Department took the bus, because it's virtually impossible for a member of the public to walk into the duty office, get hold of a set of keys, and know where the bus for that set of keys would be standing."

"There is another problem Martin" John interrupted. "I was called out because the General Manager was going to speak to some Bus Society in Birmingham, and he thought that his speech was more important than the operation of his department and his assistant is off sick, and has been for the past three months."

"Yes they are a real problem the pair of them." Martin said thoughtfully,

"The trouble is that once they get up to that level, and all Senior Officers are the same, they are virtually impossible to move. So the truth is that they just about please themselves most of the time."

"So you are telling me that I have a sickly Deputy General Manager, and a General Manager who shows up in his office when he feels like it."

"Yeah, that's about right." He leaned foreword. "Now this is strictly off the record, but last year the Chief Executive tried to get rid of the pair of them, and he ordered a check to be kept on the number of days that the GM spent out of the City, and in 13 weeks he only appeared in the office on seventeen working days. He wasn't sick, he was just out of the city at meetings that relate to the department and his hobby. Now I don't know how many of the days were taken up on authorised business, but that is the extent of the days that he is not in the department."

"What about the Deputy?" John was astounded.

"Well I have a little sympathy with Watkin the deputy, he's good bloke really." Martin was still speaking in a whisper, " I think that he's had a nervous break down, by trying to do the two jobs on his own, plus the fact that his wife ran off with a bloke in the village where he lives and he's been left with a year old baby to contend with.

"Thanks for the information Martin," John paused for a moment. "It just goes to show that one half doesn't know what's happening half of the time. By the way that is just between you and me, OK? Now you'd better tell me what the problems are on the 37 and 44 routes."

"Didn't I make a bloody mess of those two questions? I could have crawled into a fire bucket and died. Our group were not quite as polite as you were when we got to our leaders office after the meeting.

Alan Nichol's blasted me into space, and then said out of the blue "That he knew that you and I were mates and that you weren't too bad, as Tories go, so that if I got the opportunity I should have a word with you on the QT. But I'd already decided that I would do that anyway. Nichol's reckons that you are all right and that you won't stand for any crap from the likes of Charlie Barnes and company, apparently he's had a word with some of the blokes who knew you when you were a union representative. You never told me that you once took all of your blokes out on strike for three weeks.Anyway the problem is one of safety, not that of the drivers, but that of the pedestrians. When buses turn off Main Street into Belton Street at the start of the diversion, because of the positioning of some bollards in the centre of Main Street it is impossible to turn a bus into Belton Street without running on to the pavement, and using nearly the full width of the pavement at that. We told Mr Church about this before the road works were started, but nothing has been done, and now the drivers are saying that unless some thing is done in the next couple of days or so, they are going to refuse to drive on the 44 route. They really think that some one is going to be killed before too long." Martin concluded.

"Why didn't you or the TGW Secretary simply give me a phone call?" John enquired.

"The fact is that we were a bit strapped for questions to ask, and Alan Nichol's thought that this would show the Unions that we were up to press on all of the things that were affecting the City's workers." Martin was almost apologetic. "All it has achieved is that it has delayed any action being taken for five days."

"I'll have a word with the Traffic Manager in the morning," John offered, "and we will see what can be done. What do you think is the best way of getting round the problem?"

"There are two different approaches the first is simply to remove the offending bollards." He was in his element. "That would take about half an hour in an off peak period, and then we would replace them once the pipe works are finished. The second is to divert the traffic through Beatrice Street along Charles Street, and then back along Edward Street. The first is the easiest; the second would require a temporary parking ban along the three streets involved that would take at least ten days to put into operation."

"What about the 37 route?" John had accepted his conclusions. "What's the problem there?"

"There have been a lot of problems lately at night with attacks on drivers and passengers, by boozed up lads." He paused. "I know that it's true, because I've had problems a couple of times myself. It was agreed over a month ago at a meeting with the former Chairman, the GM, and the Union Branch Chairmen, but still nothing has been done. You could have a serious problem if this matter is not resolved quickly, and it won't be one route that will stop, they're talking about stopping the whole system after nine-o'clock during the week, and after six-o'clock on Fridays and Saturdays. In the past six months we have had seven drivers hospitalised for a week or more, and one of those will never drive again. We have had three others who have had limbs broken, and five who have slashed with Stanley knives. The last one was just over a week ago."

"I'll tell you what, I will be in my office at the Central Depot at seven-o'clock tomorrow morning, and I would like to see the Branch Chairmen when they are available." John was becoming increasingly annoyed about the way things were left to drift, little items of communication that could bring about major disruption if they were left to fester. The stupidity of the situation was that they were being left to fester. "I cannot allow simple matters of communication jeopardise the efficient running of my, no, of our Department. Do you think that they will turn up to see me at an unofficial meeting?"

"There is no such thing as an unofficial meeting in the TGWU, as soon as there are four officials there it is an emergency meeting called at your request to discuss attacks on drivers." Martin pealed off the reel like the Union Man that he was. "If you like I'll phone the Union Secretary now and tell him."

"Yes, do that now." The decision was made.

He dialled the number. "Hello Harry, this is Martin Smith speaking." He paused and then said,"Yes I'm fine, but I'm with Councillor Robertson, and he has requested a meeting with Branch Chairmen to discuss the problems of attacks on drivers." He paused again. "Tomorrow morning any time after seven-thirty, in the Chairman's Office in the Central Depot"Martin put his hand over the receiver, and said to John he say's that they will all be in your office at seven-thirty tomorrow morning and he would like a word with you." John nodded and took the handset.

"Good evening Harry," John smiled into the phone as he spoke, "A long time no seeold friend"

"So it is young John Robertson." Harry Bolton was just confirming his own observations. "It seems centuries since we used to run about on your grandfathers farm. They were good days, people used to help each other then, and you've certainly at least started to help me and Martin out of a hole. The tear-aways have already got their posters printed, because nobody would listen, they were intending to go on strike tomorrow night, with or without union backing. My lot will be there John, and so will the GM, this time. I'll make certain they are, with a bit of good will we can nip this in the bud. I'd best get on with it, I've ten or eleven telephone calls to make. See you in the morning." and he was gone.

"How the hell do you come to know Harry?" Martin demanded.

"His father used to be my grandfathers herdsman when we lived out in Lincolnshire, when I was boy." John tried hard to make it sound casual.

"So if I hadn't come and seen you, he would have come round to see you himself, because he's known you longer that I have. And you never mentioned it to me." Martin was getting quite heated over this. "You're turning out to be a bit of a dark-horse Mr Robertson. Is there anybody in this bloody City who you don't know?"

"Just a few." John laughed. "Just a few."

18

People do the Strangest Things

The outcome of the 'Stolen Bus Episode' came charging back with a vengance, when the Agenda for the next Finance Committee was circulated. The costs of the damage to the vehicle and the claim for the repairs to the property were enormous, even without the claim that would be made for loss of business, the death of two people, and all of the peripheral claims that arose from an accident of this type.

The question of 'Who did steal the Bus?' and ' Has there been any success finding the culprit?' suddenly took on a whole new meaning to many of the people who had let the matter slip from their minds.

An internal enquiry carried out by the Chief Executives Office failed to discover whether the incident was the work of some one in the Transport Department, or that of a casual interloper who gained access by simply walking through from one periferal road to the other. The Police in their attempts to find the culprit came upon a 'Wall of Silence' that is common in this kind of case. Everybody in the department kept their own council on the matter. The Unions advised that no one should jeopardise the work of their 'brothers', so it was the silence remained.

Josh Catton had worked for the Transport Department from the day that he had left school; First as an apprentice, and then as an engine fitter in the garage. Now 45 years later he was taking early retirement, and there was a Departmental Party and presentation to mark the event. As it was a departmental affair, the General Manager was in charge of the proceeding. In the main Politicians shied away from this sort of 'Close-knit' group event. John Robertson was no exception to this rule, and he stayed in his office while the Transport Department said 'Good-Bye' to one of its own.

Catton was a remote, loner, who had never married, and he still lived in the house that his mother and father had bought when they got married. Even his hobbies of walking, bird-watching and gardening, he did alone, and very few of his colleagues had ever managed to get even near to him.

This did not mean that he could not communicate, for when it came to explaining how things should be done to the young men who came to him as part of their training, he had a natural talent for the job, and could explain thing in an acceptable and structured way. Many of the engine fitters now working in the Undertaking had reason to thank Josh for his patience and skill.

The Monday following his retirement Josh set off for Malaya, to visit some of the places that he had seen when he had served there briefly during his National Service. It was the only time in his life that he had managed to get away from the ropes that bound him tightly to a grasping family.

For a month, his retirement holiday allowed him to live the life of a Colonial, frequenting all of the plush Bars and hotels that he had seen only from the outside all of those years ago. And when all of the money that he had allotted for the trip had been spent, he returned to England. Returned to his small house with its out-moded furnishings and decorations; Returned to the life that he had despised for so many years he could no longer recall what had been the initiator of his hatred. So he sat down and drank the bottle of whisky that he brought at the 'Duty Free' Shop. He placed a neatly written envelope on the mantle peice, where it would be quickly seen. He then sat calmly down and placed a 'draw-string' type plastic bag over his head, and pulled the strings tightly apart. So it was that Josh Catton died.

The Police brought the letter to John Robertson while he was doing his daily stint in his office in the Transport Departments Central Depot.

The officer asked. "When did you last see Mr Catton alive, Councillor?"

"To be frank" John replied. "I can't remember having ever met Mr Catton" John told them after they had given a brief description of the circumstances. "I knew that he retired about a month ago, but those sort of events are strictly insider events, and as a politician I was considered to be an outsider, so I contributed to the collection, and I signed his 'farewell' card, but I stayed away from the presentation and the party because that is the General Managers province, if you get my meaning!"

"Yes I understand the position perfectly Councillor." The Police Sergeant replied with a smile. "But this letter is addressed to you, and we really need what he says in the letter so that we can inform the Coroner."

John took a paper knife and slit the envelope oped, and extracted a single sheet from the envelope, which he passed back to the officer. "You may need that for Forensic Examination" John stated as he opened the sheet and began to read:-

"Dear Chairman,

I want you to know that it was me who took that bus from the Depot and left it parked in Market Hill. So it was me who caused all of that damage to the shops, and killed two innocent people. All I did was to borrow the bus to go and pay my Council Tax, and when I got back the bus was at the bottom of the hill. So I decided that I would walk back to the Central Depot.

The deaths of those two people have played on my mind and I can see no way of being able to stop it from hurting, and now that I am finished at the Department, there really is nothing to live for. So I planned all of this during the past two months and by the time that you are reading this I will be dead.

I am sorry for all of the trouble that I have cause both you and the department, and I am ashamed for all of my friends, because it was the only place where people accepted me for what I am. Please forgive me.

Yours Faithfully

Joshiah Catton"

"I think that you had better read this Sergeant!" John passed him the letter. "It certainly clears up a mystery that has been causing both of our organisations a headache."

The Sergeant read, and then re-read the letter, just to make certain that there was no doubt in the matter. He looked up, "I think that is fairly clear Sir!" He remarked as he placed the letter in the desk. "I think that the Coroners Sergeant might need a short statement from you in due course, but as far as I am concerned that is all that there is to it for the moment."

So ended the 'Mystery of the Stolen Bus', but a few months after the events outlined above, John Robertson recieved a letter from Mike Parkin asking John to drop in and see him at some convenient time. John did so, to find the Solicitor was all smiles, and said. "I think that I may have a bit of a surprise for you John! Can you remember a fellow called Josiah Catton?"

"Why Yes!" John answered. "He was a Transport Department employee who committed suicide about three months ago. What has he got to do with me?"

"I thought that you might to be able to answer that question!" He replied. "His solicitors have been on the line to me to ask if I was still your family lawyer, and I have assumed that I am. They have informed me that you are the sole beneficiary under the terms of his will. So what have you to say to that?"

"I'm absolutely flabberghasted!" John declared. "I've never met the man. All that I have done is to contribute to the man's retirement present from the Department."

"His will has been processed through probate, so there is no doubting its contents" Mike smiled.He's left you every thing, including the house. But the will has stipulated that all of his belonging were to be sold, and the accrued money was to be ceded to you."

"I don't know what to say." John shook his head in disbelief.

"Well now come's the real shock!" Mike laughed. "The value of the estate after all of the fees and his bills have been paid is One Hundred and Eight Thousand, Two Hundred and Forthy-Five Pounds. Wait for a moment. That is the cash value, excluding the values of the house, and I think that will be worth about Two Hundred and Thirty Thousand Pounds."

"That's a hell of a lot of bread Mike." John gasped. "Why?" He asked. "Why?"

"That is something that only Mr Catton will know!" Mike Shrugged. "But as you well know, he is dead, and I think that you might be in need of a large whisky."

"How right you are." John agreed. "I'll bet that you will put the cost of it on my bill anyway."

"You're damned right I do." He answered. "Anybody who has just inherited in excess of Two

Hundred and thirty grand after the payment of all dues, can afford it too."

"This is really strange, don't you think, Mike?" John was still bemused by the whole thing.

"I've heard of much stranger bequests than that." Mike informed him. "I have handled a case where a great-grandfather had placed in Trust a number of stocks and shares in companies at the start of the twentieth century, for his heirs and successors to benefit from in the year 1990.

By that time two of the companies had gone Bankrupt, but the third had had grown into an International Conglomerate, and the value of the shares was over two million pounds.

"Well let me make a toast." John raised his glass. "Here's good wishes and God speed to Josh Catton where ever he may be."

19

Meeting with Trade Union Branch Chairmen

At half past seven in the morning the offices of any transport undertaking is a hive of industry. Any organisation that provides services for an average of nineteen hours in every twenty four has to provide management back-up to those services. So despite the fact that John thought that he would catch them all napping, they, by working their normal day, simply demonstrated that they were quite used to working at this time in the morning.

Of course many of the offices were empty, and would be until nine o'clock when the clerical staff commenced their day. There is a certain air of expectancy that one feels when walking through an area that is normally buzzing with energy, in that brief space of time when it is empty. It's almost as if there are some elements of latent energy that remain some-how suspended in the air of the place in anticipation of the hour to come.

The Chairman's office was not a grand affair like that of the General Manager. It was a simple desk set in a carpeted room, without all of the trappings that one would associate with the office of a dynamic manager. This was a room full of after thoughts, there was nothing here that was of use to anybody who wanted to play an active part in the daily life of the undertaking. It was here merely to placate 'The Chairman', to give him a place in which to sit and talk to anybody and everybody that no one else wanted to see anything that would keep him out of the way of those who 'really knew' how to operate a Transport Department. It was large, and it had a conference table, of sorts. But other than that it was bare, it was hollow, and most of all it told everybody who came into it, just how contemptuously the senior managers here viewed those who tried to interfere with their closeted little world.

The current General Manager was Mr Peter Church who had been with the undertaking for almost thirty years. Robertson had only met him twice, once at a Civic Reception at Town Hall, and briefly before the first meeting of Council, when Church had thrust the suggested answers to the questions that were being asked of him as Chairmen of Transport. On that occasion the GM had scurried away, without explanation, like some cat that was afraid of having it arse kicked.

John spent the short time before the start of the meeting simply looking around his office, trying to get a feel for the place, but as is usually the case where there is rapid turn-over of political incumbents, and a management that has developed it's own sense of infallibility there is little character to syphon off into the structures.

About seven-twenty five John was joined by three drivers who were also chairmen of their respective branches. "Is this where the meeting is going to be held mate?" One of them asked as they invaded his office without even knocking on the door.

"Yes!" John replied preferring the anonymity.

"Has the Chairman arrived yet?" The same man asked.

"Yes!" John regarded the driver, who must have been about his own age.

"I wonder what the old bastard will have to say about us going on strike."

The driver was inflating his own self esteem.

"You know the Chairman then?" John asked innocently

"Only by reputation," the driver replied. "My name is George Pike."

"And just what is this reputation" John enquired. "So that I can be pre-warned of it" But he was not destined to find out because the door opened and the next man to come in was of West Indian extraction, who stood about six and a half feet in height. He muttered "Good Mornin" and sat down grumpily at the far end of the table. After this there was a steady flow of men coming into the office, none of whom introduced them-selves, and all of whom seemed to be content with their own company.

Just before seven-thirty Peter Church entered the office, and sauntered up to John. "It is normal practice for the General Manager to arrange meetings between the Undertaking and the Unions, Mister Chairman."

"It is normal practice for a General Manager to be available, in the case of an emergency, Mister General Manager." John's answer was in monotone and he deliberately did not look into the face of the GM. "What is more to the point, is this, that if these people are prepared to assist us in providing the City with an efficient Bus Service, then the least we can do is to take the trouble to listen to them when they and by inference we, have a serious problem."

"Chairman, I wish to record my objection to your sitting in on this meeting." Church in his quiet but insistent way was trying to undermine John's position. "I have already informed the Chief Executive that you are making unreasonable demands on the management of this Undertaking." His voice petered out as John slowly turned to face him. "Mr Church," John's voice was very low, and very slow. The whole room was now silent. "Mr Church, I think that we had better get one thing very clear. I am the Chairman of this undertaking, and if anything goes wrong, I am the one who will take all, I repeat all, of the brick-bats. It has been my practice in the past, when faced with situations like this, to give all the orders, and take all of the flak. I can see no reason what-so-ever to change that practice, and if you, or for that matter anybody else in the Undertaking cannot live with that, then you are perfectly at liberty to leave and leave now.

Now my understanding of the situation is, that I am the Chairman, and you are my General Manager, so if I decide on a course of action, which in this case is to call an urgently required meeting, then regardless of whether you like it or not I will hold that meeting and you can go and inform God Almighty if you like, but I will still hold the meeting. Do I make myself clear?"

"I wasn't trying to undermine your authority Chairman." He bleated.

"Then what the hell are you bleating about? John was trying to maintain control over his rapidly rising blood pressure.

"I just wanted you to know that it was the usual practice for my office to call meetings with the Unions." He still trying to excuse his lack of cooperation with John, by inferring that precedence ruled, in all that was transacted in the Department?

At this point Martin and Harry came into the meeting with profuse apologies for their being late. "We got caught in the traffic on the way into town." Harry offered by way of excuse.

John took the lead, "Gentlemen could you all find a chair please." They all moved to the conference table, and in a few seconds they were all seated. "I would first of all like to welcome you to this informal meeting here in my office, and hope that this is the first of many that we will hold simply to make sure that the views of all employees in the Undertaking are heard. I ask for this meeting to be called following a disturbing conversation I had with Harry Bolton and Martin Smith, and in the absence of the General Manager, and due to the urgent nature of the situation I decided that it was necessary to deviate from the usual procedure and call a meeting at short notice. That is how we came to be sitting here today." And then looking straight at his first antagonist he continued, "And this 'Old Bastard' is here to listen, and not to pronounce, upon anything that you care to raise here."

There was a ripple of laughter from those who had heard the earlier pronouncement from George Pike, who joined in with the laughter totally unabashed at his bragging.

"There are, I believe, two real problems that we need to solve." John had their attention. "The first is the question of the turning circle that is necessary to safely turn off Main Street Fordham in to Belton Street I have been to have a look at this problem with the traffic manager and the Road Safety Officer from County Council, and it has been agreed that the set of bollards that are causing the problem, will be removed during course of this morning. Are there any questions on that problem." Mr Church was clearly only in the meeting in body his mind was clearly somewhere else.

George Pike stood. "First of all Chairman may I say that I am sorry about my bragging earlier this morning, and then on the question of this diversion, our Martin Smith has looked at this and from what he was saying there should be a diversion that follows a route on the other side of Main Street."

"I understand what you are saying George," John replied. "But to get all of the road traffic orders to allow that to take place would take almost a month, so in the interests of getting the job over and done-with in the least time, we've arranged for the bollards to be removed."

Harry Belton chipped into the discussion. "If I tell you that the Chairman was so concerned about this problem that he arranged for a meeting at his own home after ten o'clock last night you will agree that he has not been hanging about on this issue. We've always complained that we haven't had sufficient voice in the solving of this type issue, now that we have a Chairman who is ready and willing to help us. We may think that he is a member of the wrong Party, but we can't fault him on this issue, and I think that we should agree to let this go ahead. If anything goes wrong we can always raise the issue again."

There was a murmur of agreement from all around the table.Martin was the next to speak,

"There have been a number of serious assaults on the drivers of late night buses, mainly at week ends, and these have now become so bad that drivers at the outer Depots are threatening to go out on strike unless something is done about it." He paused to manipulate his papers. "During our discussion the Chairman indicated that he would contact the Police and see if there was anything that could be done to guard against these attacks taking place. I know that he has not had time to carry-out our request, mainly because he has been here since about seven this morning."

"It is true that I have not been able to contact the Police as yet." John spoke above a rising tide of conversations being held round the table. But the more I think about it, the more that I am inclined to believe that it may necessary for our drivers to refuse to drive buses after eight-thirty on Friday, Saturday, and Sunday Nights."

Church was on his feet straight away. "Mr Chairman, you can't propose that our drivers go on strike!"

"Why not" John was adamant. "The service that we provide is for the use of the general public, and it is a portion of the General Public who initiate the attacks, and the rest just sit and watch. If we withdraw our services until further notice, perhaps the General Public will be a little more help-full when it comes to the identification of some of the culprits. I will not be a party to trying to force our employees to work in situations that put them in physical danger. My feeling is that we notify the Press and the Media, that we will withdraw our services on each Friday, Saturday, and Sunday night, commencing at eight o'clock on Friday next, and until further notice."

This statement was met with surprise applause, and general agreement. The meeting had only been called to attend to the problems surrounding attacks on bus crews, and that matter had been satisfactorily concluded.

This being the case Harry Belton moved to finish the meeting, but the towering West Indian, whose name turned out to be Jimmy Newham did not think that a good opportunity should be lost, and tried to raise the issue of the Inspectors Pay.

John did not know about the problem, and asked for a brief adjournment so that he could be briefed on the matter.

Jimmy was not in the mood to be put off by what he thought was a hostile action by the chairman. "You are trying to put the matter off." He insisted. "My members want an answer now, you can cure all of the problems of the drivers in the sweep of an arm, and as soon as it comes to something that the inspectorate need you start inventing excuses."

With each sentence Jimmies voice was getting louder, and despite the fact that all of his colleagues were trying to calm him down, he was clearly going to shout until the rest of the room listened. They had not reckoned with John Robertson. "Mr Newham" He shouted above all of the rest, "I want you to know that I do not agree with the philosophy that dictates that he who shouts loudest will be first to be heard. This being the case, no matter how loud you shout, I will ignore you, until you recognise that the chair rules the meeting, not the biggest nor the loudest person present. Now I will say this once, and once only, I do not know the details surrounding the Undertakings dispute with its Inspectorate, but if you will give me a few days to apprise myself of the problem, I will then arrange a meeting with you to discuss the resolution of the problem."

Harry Belton got to his feet. "Now all of you can go back to your respective depots, and tell your members that you now have a Chairman to whom you all can talk and you know that he will listen to you. There is no need for private or irresponsible action to get a fair and reasonable decision. Go back and tell them to use the established channels to air their grievances. We cannot run a Public Service using blackmail and threat as a means of getting our own way. The new Chairman will try to hear all of our complaints, but it will take him time to get to know the intricacies of all of the problems in the Undertaking, please give him a chance, after all he's only been in politics for one week." On that note the meeting broke up. George Pike walked round the table towards John. "Can you tell me Chairman, why you, are a Union Member, and a member of the Tory Party?"

"Well it's very simple really." John smiled. "I looked for a party that had the highest percentage of what I believed in, in its manifesto. That turned out to be the Conservatives.

20

Meeting with General Manager and Staff

So far John was less than impressed by the actions of the General Manager. He could not be found when there was a serious accident, and when he was found there were more pressing events outside the Undertaking that required his attention. There had been no formal tour of the Transport Department, and what was more disturbing, none of the staff had been informed that the New Chairman would be adopting a 'Hands On' approach to the running of the Undertaking.

After the meeting with the Unions Church had scurried back to his Office before John had chance to speak to him, so being tenacious by nature he followed him back to his office. He entered without knocking. to find Church in the process of putting on his hat and coat.

"Well Mr. Church!" He began, "Perhaps you could tell me exactly where you are going today."

"I thought that as we had completed our business." He stuttered, "I would go home and finish some of the paperwork that has accumulated in respect of the Omnibus Society."

"Well I think that I might be in need of your assistance here in the office today." John spoke with restraint but the edge on his voice left Church in no doubt that he would be remaining in the office for the rest of the day.

"When I speak to my fellow Committee Chairmen, I find that they have all been given a tour of their respective Departments. They have all met their second and third tier officers, and have all been given access to secretarial services. I have found you reluctant to supply even the most elementary information and your attendance in your office is the butt of numerous jokes around the city. I cannot continue in this way." John found that he had to be very careful not to breech the strict code of employment ethics that surrounded the employment of senior officers in council. "I demand to meet the officers and staff in this department. I demand to be informed of the day to day problems that make it difficult to run a department that is as far reaching and complicated as this. If you do not inform me, then how can I support you in your endeavours?"

"My last Chairman" He began apologetically. "did not come into the department from one years end to the next. As you have no doubt found out, the Chairman's Office has not been used these last ten years." He seemed to be lost for words, but John could not tell whether it was all show or not. "I have been used to doing more or less as I liked. I sit on a number of national committees in respect of transportation and of passenger transport in particular, and these involve me being away from the city and the department for about ten working days per month. No one has ever questioned my involvement before."

"Mr Church," John spoke with great patience, "I am not questioning your integrity, nor am I questioning your capability for the job, but I am going to ask questions when you are not available in an emergency, when your deputy is not available in your absence, and your Chief Engineer is not afforded full authority in the absence of both you and your deputy."

The phone rang, "Hello! John Robertson speaking." there was a pause at the other end of the line.

"Hello John." It was Charles. "I'm here with the

Chief Executive, and I wonder if you could pop across to the Town Hall and see us?"

"What now?" John was surprised.

"Yes if it is possible." He sounded peeved. "There is a bit of a problem with the Transport Department that we need to clear up right away, if possible."

"OK then." John replied, "I'm on my way, I should be there in about ten minutes." He turned to Peter Church. "It looks as though this matter will have to wait for a while. I must go to the Town Hall."

What the hell did he want? John thought as he pulled his coat on. He strolled down the hill from the Central Depot to the Town Hall, and breezed through the doors and up to the reception desk.

"Ah! Councillor Robertson, the Chief Executive is with Councillor Brown in the small Committee Room, and they ask you to join them there." The duty receptionist smiled. You didn't even have to ask a question here before they gave you the answer.

"Thanks, Sheila" He called as he turned to move towards the Committee Room. What the devil was so important that they would want to drag him away from his office? He strolled through the door, to find Brown and Harvey relaxing with coffee and biscuits.

"Thanks for coming down so quickly John." Charles was over playing it a bit. "The fact of the matter is that your General Manager has reported you to the Chief Executive for making what he describes as 'An unusual request'." Brown seemed lost for words.

Harvey took over "What Church has said is that you have requested copies of all out-going correspondence, is that correct? He glowered at John, who glowered back in return.

"Yes, that is correct?" John decided to play it all by ear..

Harvey continued the cross examination. "Can you

tell me why you have made that request?"

"Oh! Yes the reason is quite simple really." John answered. "My General Manager is hardly ever in the department, and the Deputy has been off sick since before I became Chairman. With little or no contact with my department, I decided to look for an easy method of keeping myself abreast of the operational situation, and I found that by reading all of the in coming and out going mail I could find my way around most of the problems that were eventually referred to me."

"There you are!" said Charles, "There is no ulterior motive involved at all. The trouble with you Harvey is that you see trouble where no trouble exists."

"I wouldn't say that there is no trouble in the Transport Department." John interjected. "I find it difficult to find anything out even when I ask Church for information he is either reluctant or otherwise involved. But the real problem is that he is hardly ever in the Office."

Harvey leaned forward conspiratorially, "I would not wish this to go any further at this juncture, but we have been having attendance problems with Mr Church for the past three years. The previous Chairman raised the question of how many outside bodies he had contact with, and we were asked to keep an eye on him. Many of the bodies for which he has committee status, are not sanctioned as official. He therefore attends many of them not as the GM but as a private individual, and his days away are therefore technically listed as absences. It is very difficult, because he is a member of the Management Team, and we are constantly having to badger him for ordinary run-of-the-mill reports. Frankly I would like to see him take early retirement. But we are very limited in what we can do, and he is a very sharp individual when it comes to his own rights."

"What about this report then?" John was inwardly furious that Church hadn't the gumption to question the request himself. "Why the bloody hell didn't he ask me, my office is two doors down the corridor from his?"

"What is your opinion of the GM so far John?" Charles Brown cut into the conversation. "Is he any good?"

"I think the man is too frightened to do anything. He expects others to make his decisions for him, and in the absence of others he dithers on the brink but in the final analysis, he makes no mistakes, because he cannot make up his mind one way or the other." John was in no doubt about what to do with the GM.

"Does that answer your question?" Charles asked Harvey.

"I've known the answer to that question for a long time." Harvey stated uncomfortably. "The problem is, what can we do about it.? As for young John here he makes what amounts to a simple request to reduce the amount of enquires that he will have to make and Church tries to make out that he's collecting evidence to get him the sack."

"What are we going to do about him and for that matter, what are we going to do about Watkins the Deputy?" Charles was clearly well informed "I've had words with the DGM, and he can see no point in coming back to work if the GM is going to carry on in the way that he has been for the past two years." Harvey held his head in his hands. "I often think that it might be better if I retired and left them all to it, because I'm certain that they will all out live me."

"I had intended to go out and see if there was anything that I could do to help Watkins," John ventured "but it must be something in the genes of Transport Managers, I couldn't find him in that last couple of times that I called at his house."

"I think that it might be best if you left all of that to Personnel." Harvey suggested. "He might start getting as jumpy as his GM if the Chairmen starts calling at his house. I can't see any harm in John having copies of correspondence, can you Charles?"

"No! I think that it's a damned good idea" Charles boomed. "I wish that I'd thought of it myself."

That was the end of it. Church would have to sort out his own paranoia, and he would still have to provide John with his copies despite all of his back-door dealings. What John couldn't get over was the fact that Church was such an innocuous sort of individual on the outside he looked as though he was an innocent in the wild. The softly spoken, move as quietly as a mouse, I wouldn't hurt a fly sort of individual, who held an ice-cream in one hand, and a stiletto in the other. John would have to watch this deadly Chameleon very closel, so far there was not a single person who had a good word to say about him.

John strolled purposefully back to the Transport Department, gradually letting off the head of steam that had developed during the course of the day. By the time that he had climbed the hill, all thoughts of murder and bloody revenge had seeped away, which was just as well, because by the time that he arrived back, the General Manager had decided that perhaps it might be better for him to work at home after all.

"Oh you can bet your boots it is!" John shouted out a loud, "You can bet your Bloody Boots it is."

The GM's secretary poked her head round the door. "Was there something that you wanted chairman?"

"No I don't think so." He replied, trying desperately to stop the blushing from showing,

"I'm sorry" She said, "but I though that I heard someone call me."

She left, and as she went John thought that perhaps

this was her way of keeping sane. Perhaps she was part of some gigantic conspiracy to drive all politicians mad.

John walked down the main stair case and into the foyer of the Central Depot, and looked around the drab, and colourless displays that were used to advertise their range of services. They were still done inside the department using techniques that were archaic by all modern standards.

It was a strange world, this world of local government, where little dictators ruled their little realms without fear of wrath from above, and with little possibility of being sacked, no matter how little they did, or how incompetent they were. The standard of the publicity shots was appalling. The city had a modern and very efficient Publicity Department, and yet this haven of Victoriana still tried to produce half the volume required at twice the cost. But no one would say a word to them, because it was not the done thing to criticise the motives, let alone the abilities of a fellow officer.

"How the hell can one break down the tremendous barriers that have been constructed over hundreds of years?" John posed the question to himself. It was all in the mind really; politicians thought that they controlled all aspects of policy, and Officers knew that they could do a much better job, but if only they could get rid of all of the politicians. It was all a question of control, all a question of power, but when it was all poured into the melting pot who was in control, and what were they in control of?

It was the end of the first full day that John had spent in his Department, and it had been marred by petty squabbles and childish attempts at manipulation. Robertson felt pretty useless there was nothing that he could do without the support and assistance of his officer. But they were off on some wild campaign that in his humble estimation, could only lead to failure. He headed off home walking the short distance to the City Centre Terminus of the New Park Bus Service. As is usual when one has to wait at a bus stop, it had started to rain. John looked across the small church yard of the Holy Trinity Church, in the centre of the small square, to where the queues for the buses up to Colly Farm was forming. He could see Martin waiting and waved across to him, and they mutually decided that they needed to talk to each other and strolled to the northern end of the square, and stood under the cover of the shop awning to speak.

"I expect that you're just about ready to start yet another campaign to get rid of the GM?" Martin smiled that long slow smile that indicated that he was in possession of all of the facts, even though he was supposed to know nothing. "You will learn that there is nothing that you can do without your actions being circulated around the whole Council. The fact is that the Chief Executive has been trying to get rid of our friend Mr Church for the past seven years, and so far without success. As soon as you were called to the Town Hall, the spies were put into operation, and the subject matter of your meeting with Messrs Brown and Harvey was being passed around to all levels before you had even got back to the Central Depot, that is why when you got back to the office you found that he'd gone home. That's what he always does when he finds out that they're going to try and shell him again."

"Why don't you just brief me on what's happened at the end of each day, that way I won't even have to go into the office." John smiled, but only to hide the disappointment that he felt, knowing as he did that all that bluster about local politics was all hogwash, because it could all be summed up as a few rather pathetic individuals playing futile games with each other, and all the public got was the dubious pleasure of having to pay for it all.

"Well you can take some credit for having averted a strike on the buses this coming weekend." Martin was looking quite pleased with himself. "The Union Branch Chairmen were all very impressed with you at the meeting this morning and what's more Harry and I got a vote of thanks for having got you to talk to us so quickly."

"I can't believe the volume of petty tensions that are allowed to cloud fairly simple issues." John was letting the day get to him. "Why didn't the previous Chairman speak to the Unions, who were after all, supporters of the same political party? What the hell is the General Manager up to, because I cannot understand the actions of the man?"

"All that I can say John is that you must take your time; find out all of the details and then draw your own conclusions." Martin was trying to be totally detached from the problem, "All that I can do is to warn you that the whole set-up is a time bomb, and that if you can avoid getting involved do so."

"What is it with these Local Government Officers?" John was clearly not impressed. "Have they recognised that they are a dying breed, and cannot change to meet the new demands of a new age? Are they about to commit public Hari-Kari on the altars of everlasting conformity?"

"I don't know about all that." He put his hand on John's shoulder. "But I do know that you have made an impressive start in the eyes of the Unions, and they will now be looking to you to carry on in the same vein."

"Hey there's my bus!" John suddenly noticed that the New Park bus had just arrived.

"Trust the drivers to get the Chairman's bus into the

square first."Martin laughed. "And that's another thing that they like about you, you actually use the bus service, and not just occasionally either you use it everyday. They notice these little things."

"I'd best get across there." John insisted.

"You'll be OK" Martin assured him, "The terminus inspector is just over there, and he is already aware that you will be catching the bus that's at the terminus. It will wait for you."

"Is there some sort of secret signalling device that we mere mortals do not know about?" John was amazed.

"Well the word went out about you some months ago." Martin informed him. "You know when you were doing that secret report for the Conservative Party about traffic flows and that sort of stuff. The feed-back was good from the crews that is, they said that you were alright, and that even though you were a Tory you knew what you were talking about because you used the services."

"Anyway I'll see you Martin." And John moved off across the square to get on his bus.

The bus was only half full, and the driver spoke as John stepped onto the bus. "Good evening Chairman how are you?"

"I'm fine thank you driver." John put his hand into his pocket to find the fare.

"No! That's not necessary Chairman." The driver held out a pass to him. "The duty Inspector asked me to pass this to you when you got on the bus. The chairman doesn't have to pay for travelling on his own buses, at least not on this bus, he doesn't."

"Thank you!" John felt rather humble at that simple tribute. But he couldn't help wondering why the inspector had not handed the past to him himself, "It couldn't be something to do with the fact that the inspectors were in dispute with the Council over their rates of pay, and the erosion of differentials, could it now?" They just never give up do they?

He couldn't travel anywhere on the system now, without being recognised by all and sundry, and there was always the fact that any of the people who were employed by the undertaking could 'meet' him 'by chance' of course, and pour out their problems to him. There were advantages, but there were also many disadvantages. The days were gone when he could walk about without being recognised.

He arrived home to discover that they had visitors. "Is that you John?" Kath called from the lounge.

"Yes love." He called back as he removed his coat. "Who have we here?" He asked as he moved in to the room. "Ah! Mr Harrison, Let me remember now, yes the Colby Advertiser right?" John was always good at remembering people from years back.

"James Harrison," he said rising from the chair, "But I now work for the Fordham Gazette. It's good to see you again John and I don't say that to many politicians." They shook hands.

"What can I do for you Jamie?" John sat down and helped himself to a biscuit and a cup of tea.

"Well I understand that you held a series of meetings today," Harrison was well informed, "with both the management and the unions, to discuss the problems surrounding bus services in the Fordham area?"

"Yes there have been some problems concerning certain aspects of safety in and around the Market Place in Fordham." John admitted.

"Would it be in order for me to say that the question of the safety of pedestrians has now been solved by your intervention in what was rapidly becoming a stoppage of work situation" Harrison was going to the heart of the problem. "By that I mean that the Unions were about to take strike action on this matter."

"I think that there was talk of action" John admitted. "But the necessity did not arise, after an examination of the situation, and a brief call to the highway authority and the matter was quickly solved."

"Good that checks with what I had from the Unions." Harrison was pleased with himself. "Now I understand that in the interests if the safety of your crews, you have agreed to suspend some of the late night services in and around the city."

"Yes that is correct." John really wanted to get this across in the right way.

"The real problem is that we have had a number of drivers seriously injured following attacks by groups of drunken youths mainly at weekends, and frankly I do not believe that it is right for the drivers to be put at risk for the entertainment of a few drunks. I hope that the General Public will understand that it is the actions of a few louts who have caused the suspension of their late night services on Fridays, Saturdays, and Sundays."

"Do you think that this is punishing the whole population for the actions of a few, Chairman?" Harrison asked obviously trying to draw out more of the thinking behind the proposal.

"It may appear to be that on the surface," John confessed. "But the facts of the matter are simply this:- That when drivers are injured in this type of attack it is the City who have to pay for the injuries. I do not know whether you are aware of this or not, but the City is it's own insurer, and consequently it is the city who has to pay for the damages when they occur. So however we look at it the people of the city end up paying the price for the actions of the criminal element on the buses. I do not believe that the majority of people will object to bus services being curtailed early if the action will prevent drivers from being attacked."

"The Unions have voiced their concerns about some of your policies." Harrison knew that he was now on unsure ground. "In the area of the rationalisation of services and the clearing away of termini in the City and Township Centres, Can you let us know how your revision of the services will affect Fordham?"

"The policies to which you refer are not at a stage where they can be fully explained." John was surprised that any of these suggestions had got out. "Because of the interlocking nature of the existing local services it will be difficult to formulate a comprehensive program until all of the analysis has taken place. This is not a ploy to avoid having to answer the questions now it is simply that until all of the analysis has taken place the whole problem cannot be fully appreciated. It is all rather a like a jig-saw puzzle where you cannot see the full picture until the last piece has been put in place. Is that sufficient for you Jamie?"

"Yes thank you John." Jamie rose to his feet. "I intend to do two articles on the subject of Public Transport. The first is on current services and how Councils try to protect both the public and their staff. I will stress the hardship factor but only from the point of view of how the actions of a few yobs can affect the services of the many. The other article will be on how transport will be changing over the next few years, and what councils are doing to try to improve the services that we have and you have provided me with information in both areas. Thanks John, and now I'll let you get your dinner." With that Harrison left to wend is way back to the Gazettes Offices.

John wandered into the dining room to find Kathy where she was sitting watching TV on the set that overlooked the Dinner table. "Hi! Babe."

His usual greeting was not evoking the usual

response. "Is there some thing wrong?" he enquired, and all that Kathy did was to turn and stare straight him straight in the eye.

"There have been a lot of telephone calls during the course of today." She began her tale. "Most of them have been from people making enquiries about transport services, and some of them have been from your office."

Again she looked him straight in the face. "By your office, I mean your real office, you know, the one where you are supposed to earn your living." She paused again. "But that's not the problem there have been five or six really bad calls, where they have used bad language and threats to the children. I really don't want Anne to have to listen to that type of filth."

"I didn't expect my wife to have to listen to that type of filth." John was appalled. "How long has this been going on?"

"We used to get the odd one or two when we were at Colly Farm," She smiled through her tears, "But they were nut cases who didn't know any better, but these are vicious, and calculating, and I want you to do something about them."

"I never realised that this sort of thing went on in real life, I though it was something that writers made up simply to pad out a short but boring section of prose." He paused to reflect on what he had just said. "I will get in touch with the police and the telephone company in the morning, and get the number changed, and then keep it as an Ex directory number. God Darling I feel terrible about this, but I really did not think that it would happen."

"The caller is always a man," She spoke as though she were listening to him speak, "And he knew all of our names, even the childrens. He knew when and where they go to school, and he uses the most awful

170

language. Every other word is a swear word."

He sat down beside her, and wrapped his arm around her shoulders, "Why didn't you tell about this before?" He spoke very softly. "I could have had the number changed before now."

"You have been so busy this past few months," She looked round at him. I didn't want to put any additional burden on to you in the circumstances. It all seemed so petty to start with, but now I'm getting scared, and I don't like it one bit."

John picked up the phone and dialled a number. "Could I speak to Inspector Edwards please."

"Who is calling please?" The operator enquired.

"Councillor John Robertson," He replied. He was put through.

"Hello John!" Edwards sounded in a good mood. "What's all this I hear about you plunging into the realms of Politics God I thought that you had more sense than that."

"Yes, it true." John replied. "In fact it is on that very subject that I wish to make a complaint about."

"Sorry mate but we cannot arrest all of the opposition members." He joked.

"I just wanted to report that we have been receiving threatening phone calls for about two weeks." John interrupted him.

"I take it that it is a bloke, who always calls when you're not there?" He was spot on. "Well you are not alone in your new intake of Councillors there are at least four who are in the same boat as you. Some pathetic little twit with an inadequacy stripe down his back as broad as the M1, I shouldn't wonder." Clearly there was not a lot that they could do about it."I can't put a man outside your door, but I will get your phone number changed first thing in the morning and put a tracer on the calls to let us know where the calls are

171

coming from. Other than that there is not a lot that we can do." He said apologetically. "I thought that you had more sense than to join that rat race John."

"Unfortunately I'm not the one who keeps getting the calls." John protested. "Kath is not scared to

answer the phone, but if Anne or Jason answer the there will be all hell to pay."

"Yes! I understand your feelings, and I will do what I can. Sir" John knew that he had just offended an old friend but where his family were concerned he had no friends.

He went back to Kath. "They will get our number changed first thing in the morning, and it will be kept as an ex directory number from now on. We will not give it to anyone other than members of the family and close personal friends. The police are going to put a tracer on the old number and try to catch the guy who has been doing this."

"You don't look very happy about something luv." Kathy looked across to him.

"I think that I have just lost an old friend." He smiled. "It's something that I'm getting quite used to these days. I spoke to Mike Edwards at Haverbury Police Station, and he thinks that I was being a bit officious. Probably thinks that I was throwing my new weight around a bit." He paused. "Well to be perfectly honest, I was, and I was doing it in what I believe was a good cause, my family."

"You are not as bad as I thought you were." Kathy smiled. "But I think that you would get quite a shock if you heard what your two children had said to our foul-mouthed caller."

"You mean that they have already spoken to this Kook?" He asked.

"Oh Yes!" She laughed. "Jason called him a 'Fucking Pervert', and told him to get stuffed, and

Anne told him that he was in need of psychiatric care, and neither of them turned a hair they both treated it as an every day occurrence. So I don't think that you need loose too much sleep about it really. It's just that I thought you should know about him, I mean that he has become a regular caller, so the police will have no bother finding out where he is."

21

Calling the Tune

"Good Morning John Robertson speaking." The telephone had been rattling away since he first got out of bed, just after six-thirty. This time it was Peter Church the General Manager. "I'm sorry to disturb you at this hour Chairman, but I thought that you should know as soon as possible, that late yesterday afternoon one of our vehicles was involved in an accident in which a man in his late forties was killed. We have now been informed that a second person has died following the accident." We have been informed that the driver of the bus was allegedly well over the legal alcohol limit when tested at the scene.

"So now we face the possiblility of a double manslaughter charge arising out of the incident." John responded. "But more to the point have we been able to speak to anyone who knows the either of the victims?"

"We have full details relating to the man who died at the scene Chairman! But we only have a name and address for the person who died this morning." Church informed him. "So far there does not appear to be anyone who would rank as a next of kin Chairman. The Police are still continuing to try to find some one who qualifies to deal with the problem."

"Before we both rush off to work through our separate doorways," John was searching for the right sort of wording to avoid causing problems." I think that we need to stop and consider all of the possible alternative ways that yesterday's accident could have been prevented. I think that you and I need to get together along with the Union People and the DGM to

174

devise a means by which we can spot the signs of drivers who are given to drinking whilst on duty and why they do it."

"John Watkin is still off sick." Church was quick to inform.

"Yes!" John smiled. "I know he is, but perhaps this sort of problem is of the type that might well tempt him back to work. But what ever it is we need a full team in operation in the department, and I would like to see him back here playing a full part in the running of the Undertaking."

"Right you are, Chairman!" He sighed heavily. "I'll get a car to go out and pick him up, because if we try to phone there is a chance that he won't answer."

"Whatever it takes, but we want him back into the department." John demanded. "I think that we should aim to have the meeting at around eleven this morning."

"Very well Chairman!" Peter Church answered heavily clearly he was not a happy man.

There was a buzz around the Transport Department. People were beginning to feel that they were a part of a unit that meant something at last. They hadn't really grasped the significance of the movement, but they had the distinct feeling that no one could hurl abuse at the department without getting the immediate response of the Chairman and the General Manager. So the rest of the employees fastened on to this and their confidence grew.

John Robertson's management team met as arranged at eleven o'clock, and the DGM was there, looking nervous and very pale.

They had a few minutes of informal chat before they settled down to the job in hand. The meeting took the form of an open discussion, the object of which was to suggest as many possible ways in which the driver involved in the previous days fatalities could have been prevented from drinking when he should have known that to do so was against all of the provisions set down in his terms of employment and why his obvious problem had not been spotted by those who worked with him and those who supervised him. Mackay told them the history of the man and the vehicle up to it finishing service on the night prior to the incident. The vehicle had been in service for almost seven years, and was due for a tyre change on the morning that it had erroneously been allowed out onto the road.There was only a period of about thirty minutes when it appeared there was a gap in the supervision of the vehicle, and it was not clear why the driver had selected a vehicle that was due for inspection to take out onto the road, having said that it was unusual in a garage that had a total compliment of around Four Hundred and twenty vehicles that one should be taken from the wrong place.

John asked. "Can you tell me if anyone had seen the driver as he progressed from the duty room to the point where he picked-up his vehicle?"

John Watkin explained. "When a driver finishes the last run on a route, he first of all radio's to the Control to tell them that the vehicle with fleet number what-ever, has left the terminus, and gives a destination. The bus may be going to start a series of services on another route or alternatively as in this case, they are in transit to a depot. The operator will log them off the route, and then off the road when they arrive in the garage. The position of the bus by bay number and position from the end of the bay is then entered into the control computer. In this case the bus was parked in the Service Bay because it was to be the first bus on the ramp for a tyre change on the morning of the incident. In fact it was the tyre change that prompted the search for the vehicle." Watkin paused for breath and to get a drink and then continued. "The process for getting a bus out on to the road is that the driver goes to the control room to pick-up two things:- First of all he needs his route sheet . He then needs a vehicle that is refuelled and ready to go out onto service. The controller or traffic manager then hands the driver a log sheet that relates to a bus by its fleet number, and indicates where the vehicle is parked in the depot. The dispatcher will then issue the keys for the vehicle. All buses are parked in the garage with their doors open. This is for a number of reasons the least of which is access for the cleaners to clear the bus after a day in the road and for rapid access in the event of a fire in the garage.

I fail to see how this could have been done in error unless the keys to the bus had been left in the vehicle. There is nothing to stop a driver from walking through garage, but one would need to know where to go and what to do to get hold of a set of keys.

"What do you think Mr Church?" John asked.

"I tend to think that the driver took this bus in error because the keys had been left in the ignition." He added thoughtfully.

"Mr Mackay?" John looked to see if he had anything to add.

"I don't think that it was a member of the garage staff who left the keys in the bus. It was either the driver of the vehicle from the night before or the driver was given the wrong vehicle to take out on the road." He scratched the back of his head, and looked around the room. "All I conclude from all of this is that there seems to have been a series of errors that led to a man who was probably unfit to drive a bus of any kind being issued instructions to take a bus that was not fit to be on the road."

"The real problem here is going to be the police investigation." John observed. "There are two deaths here, and the coroner has already been informed. There has to be an internal investigation by the department to try to minimise the possibilities of a similar incident happening again.

As an Undertaking we are going to be liable for all of the damage and the deaths, plus the cost of a replacement vehicle. I think that you, John should look after the security aspects of the depots, because I believe that we should consider this to be a Department wide problem. And that you should get onto this as soon as possible, so that when the awkward questions start popping through the air we are seen to be already tackling the problem as quickly as we can."

"Yes Chairman I agree." Peter Church leapt in to support John's campaign for getting the DGM back to work.

Watkin oblivious to what was going on added "Right I'll get in to that straight away."

The meeting broke up with all of them having specific tasks to perform within various time constrains. The GM was the first to leave the office and Ian Mackay set off to visit the Newham Depot, so Robertson took the opportunity to speak to John Watkin the Deputy General Manager.

"I'm pleased that we have a chance for a chat John." My opening gambit was a bit obvious. "I just wanted you to know that I would like my team here to be frank about their problems, whether those problems happen to be personal, departmental, or indeed political. I know that you have been through a very difficult period John, and that there has been considerable pressure on you, when you were ill-equipped to cope with it. That I can understand but now you need to start anew. Put the past behind you, and do what you can to make you career and your family secure in spite of what has happened. From my point of view I will give you all the support that I can, but in return I want a Deputy General Manager who is fit and ready to take over at a moments notice."

"I am ready Chairman." He smiled. "But I don't want to be placed in a position where I have to do two jobs simply because the GM is not here from one weeks end to the next. I like my job, but now that my wife has left I also have my daughter to consider and I cannot suddenly leave her on her own in the middle of the night, because Mr Church has decided that he cannot come out."

"I hear what you are saying." John replied. "But surely there is a rota for the call out of Senior Officers!"

"There used to be." Watkin answered. "But of late, because there are only two of us with a general authority to act in circumstances where capital expenditure is required on an immediate basis, it boils down to the fact that when the GM is out of town I am on permanent call out. That is unless you are readily available to sanction expenditure on an emergency footing."

"Then it is time that we spread the load a little." Robertson replied. "I will propose a change to top and bottom limits of current authorisation structure, so that we can include the Chief Engineer, and the Traffic Manager in the emergency procedures. Can I leave it to you John to get in touch with the Secretary and Solicitors Department to get the necessary documentation prepared for the February meeting of the Transportation Committee, and for the March Meeting of the City Council?"

"Yes I can do that Chairman." He seemed almost eager to get on with the job. "And I would like to thank you Chairman, for giving me a second chance."

"Let me get this across to you, so that you

understand what I am about." Robertson was firm but not unfriendly. "I judge people on how they are when I meet or work with them. I will take you as I find you, warts and all. I will form my own opinion about you, and not read into any assessment of you, anything that other people care to say. I expect you to give me straight answers to straight questions, and if I am saying some thing that is not correct I expect you to tell me. I expect answers to come from the shoulder, not disguised in any way. Give me an answer to the question that I ask, not an answer that you think that I would like to hear.Answer the question, and I will decide what the action will be. That way only I will be responsible results."

"Thank you Chairman." Watkin replied. "I am returning to work as of now, and I hope that I can live up to your expectations."

22

Transport Committee

The Transport Committee was one of eight major committees that made up the administration of the City Of Hainton. It was made up of twelve elected members and four officers of the District Council.After the Election Day success of the Conservative Party the Political make-up of the parties was Eight Conservatives, Three Labour and One Liberal. The Chairman was Councillor John Robertson and the Vice Chairman Councillor Frank Jamieson, both of whom were Conservatives.

The General Manager and the deputy General Manager of the Undertaking sat on the committee ex officio, as did the Committee Clerk, who was normally a member of the Chief Executives staff, in addition to this there was a member of the City Treasurers Staff who sat as a permanent member of the committee.

In normal circumstances the Committee met on the second Tuesday in each month, and the sub-committee's on Hackney Carriages, Private Hire Licensing, and the Road Safety Committee met on the third and fourth Tuesdays in each month respectively.

Following the normal practice of the Council, the Vice Chairman chaired the Hackney Carriage Committee, and the Chairman ran the Road Safety Committee. In addition to this the Chairman was ex officio a member of the Policy and Resources Committee, and The Finance Committee. The Chairman was also an elected Member of the Appeals and Disciplinary Committee, and was also a member of the Highways Sub-committee of the Planning

Committee. In addition to all of this the Chairman was a Member of the National Committee and the Transport Committee of the Association of District Councils, and a Member of the National and Area Boards of the Confederation of Passenger Transport, not to mention various Government, Local Government and Agency bodies that demanded time. All of these Committees met on a monthly basis, and when all of the matters were taken into consideration there twenty five monthly meeting to attend, without regard for Party or Sub-committee considerations.

The required volume of reading required tobe knowledgeable in the interest of the affairs of all of the committees and organisation was considerable, and this did not take into account the amount of post that was routed through the individual's homes.

In a normal day, it could be anticipated that there would be around fifty items of post, and the Department would also send a dispatch case with at least an additional eighty items at about four-thirty each evening, so that it was essential to clear as many of the items on a daily basis merely to prevent a serious bottle-neck in information and reply.

To make sure that the various political groupings followed their party lines, it was usual for them to hold a 'pre-agenda meeting' at which they went through the agenda of the next meeting of the committee or Council, at which it was decided, the way they would vote, who would speak on each agenda item, and who would either keep their mouths shut, or not be available when a vote was taken.

Each committee had its share of people who would not, for various reasons, toe the party line, and it was up to the Chairman, and the Whip for that committee to make certain that Keynote Policies were passed without delay or embarrassment.

John Robertson was considered to be a good Chairman by a majority of the people involved. He was fair in his facility to allow all of the points of view to be heard, he was competent at getting those aspects of policy passed, that were demanded by his parties manifesto, and his rapport with the officers was at all times calm and succinct. He had the ability to control meetings in a fair and unbiased way, and when it came to dealings with the work force his abilities were exceptional.

The Chairman, General Manager, Committee Clerk, and the Chief Executive usually decided on the Agenda for the Committee Meetings, and the Reports that would accompany the papers and other documents that were to be circulated to members.

The papers were distributed to Committee Members at least seven days before the meeting was due to be held, although sometimes papers for individual items were delayed and sent at a later time.

All of this John Robertson discovered after he had agreed to take the position of Chairman and without any warning from those members with wide experience of City Affairs. The main factor was that the City was also the Highways Agent for the County Council also involve the Chairman with Traffic Policy and Highways Maintenance Costs with the County Council were additional responsibilities not mentioned before the person was in office. He was also expected to attend Transportation Committee Meetings of the County Council also held once a month.

The second Monday in the month quickly came around, and at seven thirty in the evening John Robertson called the meeting to order.

"Come on now Ladies and gentlemen, let's all get this over and done with so that we can get off to our cool pint." He called above the chatter, and slowly the noise subsided. " All right let's have a look at Item 1., the minutes of the last meeting. Are we agreed that this is a true record of that meeting? Are there any objections to any of the details set out in the minutes?" There was no response to his questions. "OK Frank you propose and Peter you second in the meeting."

John looked round the table. They were all concentrating on their papers.

He continued "Item Two relates to the revenue for the passed month, any problems? No? OK you propose Edith and you second Derrick!"

"On the question of Item 3 Chairman," Colin Brailsford asked. "Has there been any conclusion to the police enquiries about the bus, and are we going to have to wait months to get the newsagents back into operation."

"This is a sticky at the moment Colin," John answered. "The Chief Executive will be at the meeting tomorrow, and I think that he will exclude both the Press and the Public from the discussions on this item.

Now I do know that the family involved are from your Ward, but until the Police have finished their investigation of the crime that led to this accident, we will have to play this one very carefully. So I have no objections to you asking the questions, but at the same time I think that from a legal and judicial point of view we may be restricted as to what we can do at this time. Has anybody else anything to say on this one? I'm sure that the Chief Executive will ask for any action on this matter to be deferred until after the criminal investigation." He paused. "On the Chief Executives request Frank will propose, and Tony will you second? Thanks."

And so the process went on through each item, nailing down what the group were going to do and who would make the proposals, and who would second each item. Very little was left to chance. Very little was left that would allow any of the members to think for themselves. That was the policy of the Leader of the group and that is what the Committee Chairmen took down to their respective Committees.

23

The Association of District Councils

The meetings of the national Executive of Association of District Councils took place on the second Thursday of each month at the Associations offices in Buckingham Gate in London commencing at 10-00.am. There were two types of Members of this Executive, Political and First Tier Officers. It was normal for the Leaders of Council and the Chief Executives to take these two places. In the case of Hainton however the meetings alway coincided with the monthly meeting of the Policy and Resources Committee of which the leader of council was the Chairman, and the Chief Executive was the Committee Secretary.

John Robertson was a Member of the Association National Bus Operators Committee, which met on the second Thursday of each month in the afternoon commencing at 1-30pm. John was asked to deputise for Charles Brown soon after being elected to Council, and therefore had a very full day of meetings in and around Buckingham Gate. It was also the normal procedure that when the Chief Executive required a deputy, the City Treasurer filled the position.

In order to be at Buckingham Gate for a ten o'clock start it was necessary for the attendees to leave Hainton on the six-fifteen train in the morning. There are a lot of things that the general public do not know about local government, but one of them is that first tier officers are given the right to travel in First Class Accommodation. Elected Members are not.

But in this instance, where it was always necessary to hold a briefing meeting, in order to let this take place both people would have to travel in the same level of accommodation. Officers would not step down, so it became necessary for John to travel in First Class Carriages simply to be able to have a meeting with the appointed officer on the way to the meeting. John Robertson was of the opinion that if you could not attend the meetings of Committees of which you were an ex officio member the only thing that you could do was to relinquish the position and appoint a permanent member to take your place. That is point some one with all of the right and powers to take your place. In the case of the Association of District Councils, Charles Brown had no intention of giving up his right to sit on the committee, instead he deputised John to go down to the meetings and tell them what Charles Brown thought on the range of subjects under discussion. This alright if the views of the two people were in harmony, but where they were not, there was a conflict of opinion.

On the day before the meeting John would meet with Charles Brown and together they would go through the Agenda for the meeting and Charles would decide what he wanted said for the City.

The early start meant that John had to be out of the house to catch the five-thirty bus to the station, and this combined with the fact that he would not get back to Hainton in time to slip home before his Ward Meeting in the evening. So his day would last from about four o'clock in the morning, and he would be lucky to get home before ten thirty in the evening.

John slipped out of bed at the first buzz of the alarm, and staggered off to the bathroom. He was not looking forward to attending his first meeting of the Association of District Councils.

He hated having to express views with which he disagreed, but to which he was committed to resenting.

He left the house, and strolled down the road

towards the bus stop, and not surprisingly he was the only person there. The bus was on time, and the driver recognised him before he displayed his pass. "Good Morning Chairman!" He called cheerfully as John got on the bus. "Couldn't you sleep Sir?"

"Good Morning Driver Ball!" John recognised one of the Union Branch Reps. "No, I'm off down to London for a series of meetings, and the first one starts at ten o'clock."

"There's no rest for the wicked." He smiled. "What times the train then Chairman?"

"Oh is not until six fifteen." John answered.

"Even so this is the only bus that you could catch." He remarked. "But then again you always catch buses and so do the rest of your family. Your daughter often catches my bus in the morning when she's off to school. She is a nice girl and it's good to know that at least someone on the management side uses the services that we provide, and can comment, first hand, on how we present it to the public. Now you know from first hand what the bus services are like. You don't have a car do you Mr Robertson?"

"No I don't" John responded. "The simple reason being that I live close to a fairly regular bus service makes it un-necessary to have one. When we need a car we can hire one or get hold of a taxi. Most people are just lazy they get in their cars to drive a hundred yards down to the local newspaper shop to buy a paper. That is ridiculous in anybodies language."

"We were talking about you at the last Branch meeting." The driver remarked. "They said that even though you were a Tory you understood more than the members of the Labour Party, when it came to buses, because you not only used them, you talked to the people who provided the service. The labour Councillors never bothered to get on a bus, and never

188

showed their faces down at the Depots. You are always dropping in at the Central Depot and you use your office down there, so if there is a reason for one of the staff to consult the Chairman, there are times when you are in your office and people get to know when you are available. I like that."

"Ah well! Here's the Station coming up." John picked up his bag from the front seat. "Suppose that I'd better get underway." "Have a safe trip Chairman." The driver waved him off.

"Who's he then?" asked the only other passenger on the bus.

"He's the boss." The driver replied. "He's the Chairman of the Transport Department."

"What's he doing travelling on a bus at this time in the morning?" He sounded amazed. "If I was in his position, I'm damned if I would be out at this time, and I certainly wouldn't be riding on a bus."

The driver did not comment, but he thought, 'that's the difference between you and him, and that's why the roads are getting blocked with traffic every day'.

John walked into the ticket hall of the station, which was pretty deserted, which was no surprise. He already had his tickets so he walked straight through, and down the corridor that led to the platforms. He branched off towards platform 3a, and went down the stairs to the platform. He was surprised to find that the station Buffet was open. He stepped inside into the steamy heat that always seems to be associated with station buffets, put his brief case down against a table, and strolled up to the counter.

"A cup of coffee, and a packet of biscuits please." He asked as he sorted through the money he had taken from his pocket.

"Aren't you going to say hello to an old friend then John?" The blonde behind the counter asked.

189

"Good Lord! It's Maureen Shaw." He was very surprised. "I haven't seen you for more than fifteen years. How are you? It is good to see you."

"I thought for a minute that you were not going to remember one of your old friends." She smiled. "Some people don't you know. It's amazing what a little bit of position can do to a persons memory."

"I was looking at the money in my hand." John spoke apologetically. "I know that it's a bad habit, but I didn't really look at you when I was making the order."

"It's all right John." She laughed. "I was only pulling your leg. I knew that you would speak as soon as you knew who it was. I saw what you were doing and decided to have a joke with you." She served his coffee and passed it to him with the biscuits, and he turned and went to where he had left his case.

No sooner was he seated, and the door opened to reveal the City Treasurer Alf Blick. Alf was an unlikely character for an accountant. He had a round beaming face, and a very pleasant personality; was a lover of the local football team, and liked his pint of bitter at lunch. He dressed in a very dapper manner, and was given to wearing very loud ties. He strolled up to the table and said" Hello there John. I thought that I'd find you in here. Didn't they tell you that you'd be getting breakfast with me in the train?"

"To be honest Alf they didn't tell me anything at all." John answered. "For all I know, you could have gone down last night, seen United's match, and gone on to the meeting this morning."

"Old Charlie wouldn't have any of it." Alf moaned. "He wants me to wet nurse you through this meeting and give you chapter and verse on the way down."

"Well if he wants to be absolutely certain of what is going to be said at this meeting this morning he should bloody well go and say it himself." John snapped.

"I thought that was how you might feel on the subject." Alf warmed to the day. "Chances are that the rest of the Committee will feel to same way too. I think that Mr Brown may well be chancing his arm a bit with you young man. I don't think that you are the 'Yes Man' that he seems to think you are, and I am not alone amongst the City's Management Team who think so either, and that includes your General Manager.

On the QT he thinks that you are the best thing that has happened to the Transport Department in the past forty years. I haven't seen old Church looking so enthusiastic since I first started with the City. He's actually spending more time in the office now that he has a Chairman who wants to play a part in the running of the Undertaking."

"I think that we'd better get out onto the platform." John prompted him."The train is coming into the station now."

They strolled out onto the platform and boarded the train to sort out their reserved seats, and having done that they walked through to the dining car and ordered their breakfast for as soon as possible after the train had got under way. At six-fifteen on the dot, the train slowly moved out of the station on its one stop run into London St Pancreas. The ETA was quarter past nine leaving just enough time to get across to Buckingham Gate without having to rush too much. The two of them sat down in the dining car, and the waiter began to serve them breakfast. They slowly ploughed through the papers for the morning meeting, as they ate and there was little that differed on. The question on which Charles wanted John to speak, was one of the sale of council owned houses and other properties. Charles wanted to be able to dispose of all of the City Councils Housing Stock, a point on which he and John had a difference of opinion.

191

Alf knew that this would be the case, and asked, "How are you going to able to register your disapproval without causing yourself serious problems back home?"

"There has to be a way round this one." John sighed. "And I will find it before I have to speak on the matter."

The train arrived in London just a few minutes late, and they hopped into a cab to get across the city to the meeting. The were joined in the cab by Albert Henson the leader of the County Council, who was in turn the leader of the Conservative Group in Coltby District, an adjoining District Council to Hainton who had unbeknown to them, travelled down on the same train. Perhaps it was fortunate that they hadn't got together for Bert was well-known for his feats of alcoholic athleticism, and it did not matter what time of day it was.

It was nine-forty-five when the three of them arrived at the Associations offices, and most of the committee members were already present, and were indulging in a little circulation and introduction exercise. Many of the people there were attending this set of meeting for the first time, and some of the more experienced members were trying to get the various new delegates to relax and join in the spirit. Alf Blick being an officer of long standing was quite used to all of this, but went off in search of other City Treasurers to talk Shop, and no doubt laugh at the antics of the elected members whom they had to serve.

Bert Henson too, had been around a long time, and disappeared into the mass of strange faces,

"It really looks like a Rugby Scrum, doesn't it?" A cultured voice spoke from the right.

"Yes it does rather." John answered.

"I'm Douglas Clamp" He introduced himself. "the

leader of the Vale of the White Horse District Council."

"My name is John Robertson." He offered his hand. "I'm from Hainton City Council."

"Ah Yes!" He admitted. "You are the young man who is deputising for Charles Brown. We've all been wondering what you would be like. Come on let me introduce you to one or two of the long serving members." He moved further into the committee room, followed by Robertson.

He stopped, and said "John I would like meet James Vickery the Leader of the City of Bristol Council. Jim this is John Robertson who will be deputising for Charles Brown."

"Hello Admiral. How are you?" Vickery asked, and then turning to John said. "You have my deepest sympathy, but I'm sure that you will have appreciated that we are from opposing parties. I hope that you will enjoy the experience." He promptly turned round and walked off into the melee.

"My advice is do not take a lot of notice of these chaps here or of the parties that they claim to be members of. Many of the Conservatives are more Left Wing than some of the Socialist, and some of the Socialist are a little to the right of Ghengis Khan." He laughed. "Anyway we had better get this show underway."

Douglas Clamp turned out to be Vice-Admiral Sir Douglas Clamp the Chairman of the Association of District Councils, and the Conservative Leader of the Vale of the White Horse District Council. The various representatives with their officers close at hand were distributed around a large oval conference table, but Alf Blick was not at hand, he seemed to be enjoying a private conversation with another Treasurer, on some matter that had no bearing on that under discussion, and was hidden away in the far corner of the meeting.

Most of the subject matter was of no importance to John, or to the Transport Undertaking, but he made copious notes so that he could brief Charles Brown on the detail of the meeting. As the morning droned on, and the agenda item relating to Housing Stocks came closer and closer, so John's nervousness increased.

Suddenly Alf was behind him "Are you OK John?"

"Yes! I think so." The reply was firm.

Admiral Clamp looked around the table, and said "We now come to the Governments statement on the Privatisation of the Housing Stock of District Councils, and the Right of Sitting Tenants to Buy Policy the Houses that they have rented for a minimum of two years." He continued. "We would, as an opening, like to hear what the major Councils have to say on the matter. Firstly what have you to say on the matter Councillor Vickery from Bristol?"

Jim Vickery had clearly expected this, "Thank you Chairman, I had rather anticipated that Bristol being a Labour Controlled Council would be placed in the position of having to lead the opposition to the Governments policy of getting rid of the Housing Stocks of Councils across the length and breadth of the country. My view on this particular policy is that there are enough Private Houses available for those who want to own their own house, without having to put the whole of the Properties that are available for rental at reasonable prices into the melting pot. There are still many hundreds of thousands of people who cannot afford to pay the prices offered by private landlords, and these people will look to Local Councils to provide them with accommodation. One of the stupidities of these proposals is the fact that where people are declared 'Homeless', it will still remain the duty of the District Council to provide them with accommodation. How will we do this, if we do not have a controllable stock of suitable housing? In Bristol we have about 400,000 habitable premises, and in Hainton they have about 270,000 premises. In both cases this represents about 60% of the total available housing. In many of our large city's the only real hope of obtaining decent living conditions is via the Council Housing System, and if we are to gradually erode the quality and the quantity via a 'Right to Buy' process then one of the most envied systems of providing housing for the masses will gradually die out due to the erosion of Council House Stocks. This will be brought about by the fact that all of the best and most desirable housing will be snapped up by people who could just as well move to private housing that is readily available. We cannot in anyway support the 'Right to Buy Police of the Tory Government' and move that this Association do all in its power to prevent the proposals from becoming law."

As the details of Jim Vickery's statement unfolded, it suddenly dawned on John, exactly what Charles Brown had done. He had not really wanted to have to make a statement at National Level that might put him in conflict with the Parties National Policy. As it was he had little fear of that, because he was going to implement the parties policy, but he again did not want to be involved in making the decision, and if the matter was raised at some time in the future he could in all honesty say that he was not involved in the process, and if he had been he would have made different arrangements. But now the crunch was at hand, and Clamp was now going through the process of introducing the delegate from Hainton. John smiled inwardly as the Old Admiral spoke, for in announcing him as a delegate he had offered him a route away from all of this. The delegate is delegated to tell what he has been told to tell. On the other hand the representative, can give a view that is entirely his own, and argue that his view is representative of what his group would have wanted him to say.

As this was not a speech, John remained seated, and began "I am instructed to tell you, that in the opinion of the Leader of Hainton City Council, the sitting tenants right to buy should be encompassed in law, and that the City will, within the next four weeks commence the right to buy process, and attempt to reduce the City's Housing Stock by up to 60% during the course of this Parliament in accordance with Government Policy. This is the declared intent of this Authority, and we move that the Association of District Councils adopt this Policy as part of their program of support for the duration of this Parliament."

There was a full hour of heated discussion on the matter, and at the end it was moved to a vote in which the Governments Policy came out a narrow winner. Had John voted with his heart the matter would not have been carried.

Alf Blick was all smiles, "You passed the buck back to Charles Brown quite admirably there John. You left the meeting in no doubt that the point of view that you had given, was not in accord with your own point of view, and you actually had people there believing that your view was that Council Housing was a good thing. But the most important thing was that you made it clear that it was not necessarily your point of view that was being expressed. I'm beginning to find you a very interesting prospect." He said with a broad grin.

The meeting gradually came to an end, and returned to the form of a crowd of people discussing the weather and other diverse things, but nothing as important as politics. Jim Vickery made his way over to John, "

"You managed to get yourself around that one quite nicely lad, but you do realise that Charles Brown is not going to be deceived by that, no matter what Alf Blick has told you. Never forget that he is Charles Browns man down to that last corpuscle, and he will report the detail back to him."

"But not before I do." John insisted. "I do not like being put in this sort of situation, and I will continue to express my opinion, when and where I consider it necessary. You are the second person today who has discovered that I am my own man, and although from time to time I will be asked to express other peoples views, when it comes round to my opinions only I will state what they are, and if I fall because of them it will be because of what I have said and no one else."

"I'm glad that you feel that way lad." Vickery agreed. "But you do know that you're in the wrong party, don't you?"

John and Alf went together across the road to the Grenadier Guard Public House and for a small fortune bought a modest lunch and a pint of bitter which they consumed in a few minutes whilst standing in a passageway against a window sill. This was not at all the type of lunch that John had assumed that they would get. Within half an hour John was back in yet another committee room attending a meeting of the Association of District Councils Transportation Committee. The only people that he knew were the Admiral and Bert Henson, and the meeting was really a very routine affair that was over and done with by four o'clock. John knew that there was a train back to Hainton from St Pancreas at four-thirty so he rapidly collected his papers and ran for the door. His first visit to big meetings in London had left him singularly unimpressed.

If there was one thing that John enjoyed about London, it was the availability of cabs, no sooner had he put up his hand than a cab swept into pick him up.

He was at the station in a little under ten minutes, and he found the train sitting on the platform in readiness to depart. There was one real problem here that Alf had warned John about. Bert Henson had a nasty habit of rounding up all of the people on the train who had attended the meetings that day, and inviting them for a drink in the trains bar. The idea was that it was best to wait until the next train, but that did not arrive in Hainton until after eight o'clock, and John had a meeting that started at seven thirty. John hid, but he didn't hide well enough, because Bert found him, and there was no escaping the spirited charms of Bert Henson. "Ah! there you are John, Alf told me that you were catching this train back home." He was like a little boy. "The trouble with these afternoon trains is that they never have enough Whisky to last us the whole journey. So I went into the Dining Car and bought the whole stock."

"What do you mean you bought the whole stock? John was bemused

"Well they only have those small bottles, the ones like you get on aircraft and they only had one box of those, so I bought the lot." He grinned like a Cheshire Cat.

"How many of those bottles are there in a box Bert?" John asked simply to pass the time along.

"It's not too bad lad." He studied his face. There are only forty-eight of them in a box. It should just about last us until we get into Hainton, don't you think?" He slid the box through the door, and was on the third bottle when the train finally slid out of the station.

Fortunately Bert Henson was not a noisy drinker. In fact he was quite lucid, and rattled on about politics and local affairs around Hainton.

John could always drink, and rarely if ever exceeded his limit. Kathy could not remember the last time when he had come home the worse for wear, so bearing in mind that he had been in some fairly heavy company he was not prepared for this. In fact John only drank about eight of the small bottles as far as he could remember, and by the time that the train slowly ran along the platform of Hainton Midland he felt rather pleased with himself. He stood up and started to get his case from the rack, and Bert said to him "God I'm glad that you're here, I don't seem able to get up off the seat."

"Stop messing about Bert." John grinned at him sheepishly. "If course you can get up off the seat. All you have to do, is to put your foot down, and press hard."

Bert tried to do this, and he simply fell forward into the corridor. John was perplexed. He could hardly leave him where he was and let the train take him on to the next station. So he opened the window and called for a porter. A West Indian gentleman came ambling down the platform with a large trolley. "Is it Bert?"He asked casually.

"Well yes!" John replied some-what astounded by the fact that this chap knew him.

"I thought it was this week that he went down to London for his meetings. Have you travelled with him all of the way?" he asked without rancour.

"Yes!" John proffered.

"In that case you have done extremely well, if you don't mind my saying so." He laughed. "It's usually Bert who has to have them transported to the outside world."

"You mean that he's always like this?" John asked.

"Yes! We usually put him on the trolley, and take him up the lift to the top level," He giggled. "and then we put him in a cab and send him home. It's usually his drinking partners that we have the trouble with. We know Bert, and we know where to send him, but we don't always know who he has been drinking with, so it's difficult to know where to send them."

"Oh my God" John muttered. "How the other side live, or more to the point, how the other side see us."

"You don't have to worry your head about it Mister." The genial Porter said. "We get all sorts of people here, and we get used to all sorts of tempers and types. You are a quiet man, and that is unusual for friends of Bert's. You leave him to me Sir I'll see that he gets home all right."

"Thank you very much." John said thankfully. "Best get a cab myself or I'll be late for my next meeting." And with that John departed into the night leaving the porter to his job.

24

The Babbington Bus Builders (BBB)

Babbington Bus Builders are the largest manufacturers of buses in the British Isles and most of the English Bus Undertakings have purchased their vehicles from them for a number of years. One of the problems with there being only one manufacturer is the fact that whilst everybody would like to buy from a home manufacturer, it does make it very difficult when it comes to deliveries of new vehicles.

John rapidly discovered that the fleet of vehicles in the city was aging rapidly, and that maintenance costs were rising. He decided that he should discuss the matter with the General Manager. A meeting was duly arranged and provision was made for a meeting to be held in the large Committee Room at the Town Hall. The General Manager was asked to present a report on the matter.

The meeting had one item on the agenda that was:-

To discuss the volume of outstanding and overdue Bus orders from Babbington Bus Builders, and decide on a revised program for continuing with the orders.

John was in the chair, and the meeting comprised three officers, and four members of council including the chairman.

Mr Church the General Manager rose to speak when the chairman requested him to present his report. "The City, have sixty-four buses on order from Babbington Bus Builders at the present time, these are made up of five separate orders each placed at different times." Church was clearly uncomfortable with the detail of his report. He was speaking in a very low, in fact hardly audible voice and he was very slow in his delivery, John, who was sitting only a few feet away from him, was finding it very difficult to hear what he was saying.

"Mr Church, could you please speak a little louder please!" John requested. "I can hardly hear what you are saying, so I am certain that others here cannot hear at all."

"I'm sorry Chairman," He looked perplexed. "I'll try to project my voice a little further."

He continued, but there was great improvement in the volume of sound. "The first of the orders for sixteen buses was recommended by the Transport Committee on 12th of September 1989 and approved by City Council at its October meeting in the same year. The vehicles were priced at £12,000 each, that is to say that in accordance with the terms of the contract BBB would supply us with the chassis and the engines and a City style body would be fitted in our works at Fordham. The original cost of the contract in this case was for £352,600, and these vehicles were to be delivered one every week to reach completion of the contract by the 30th of March 1991. How-ever, before the end of the Contract Term, and in accordance with the terms of the Contract, there were two increases in the costs of the vehicles that raised the price per vehicle to £24,000.

In addition to that, and because of the fact that the BBB have been unable to supply the vehicles up to the present day, there have been annual rises in the costs of the vehicles on the outstanding order that have raised the total price to £42,500 per vehicle. This has resulted in an increase in cost of £438,000, and the Total cost is now £780,000."

John was astounded by this and he interrupted the General Manager. "Are you telling us, that because they have been unable to carry out the terms of this contract we are being asked to pay an increase of more that 100% on the original price of the contract?"

"Yes Chairman." Church admitted, shuffling his papers nervously."Shall I continue?"

"Yes I suppose that you'd better." John muttered with growing impatience.

Church droned on. "There were additional orders placed in the following five years totalling some 64 vehicles all of which should have been delivered before the start of this current financial year. The total value of the outstanding vehicles in terms of contract price is £3,820,000. We have not as yet received any letters of intent to start delivery of those vehicle ordered in 1989, and seven years on we are facing increasing maintenance cost, and the distinct possibility that we may have to reduce the size of our fleet, simply because we cannot obtain new buses from our preferred supplier and thecurrent stock is deteriorating rapidly. That is the current situation Chairman." The General Manager sat down in a stunned silence.

John broke the silence. "Mr Church, please help me to understand what you have just said. Am I correct in saying that because BBB have not delivered the buses to time, they are entitled, under the terms of the contract that this city has signed and agreed to, to increase their costs and charges to us, and there is nothing that we can do about it?"

"Yes that is the case Mr Chairman." He mumbled.

"Who the hell negotiated this contract? It's incredible." John could not disguise amazement.

"Oh that is a standard form of local authority contract Chairman." The man from the Chief Executives Office explained.

"Then it is high time that we started to change the Standard Format of Local Authority Contracts." John exploded. "It pays large companies not to complete their Local Authority contracts on time because they can make more money out of them by being late than if they supply them on time.. If this is the case then the later the better for BBB."

There was a stunned silence, no one could believe the facts that they had just had placed before them. John briefly discussed the legal implications with the City Secretaries Representative, and then turned back to the meeting,

"In the light of what we have just heard," John started. "I have decided to adjourn this meeting to an as yet unspecified date. This will enable the General Manager and I to arrange a meeting with the representatives of BBB, to try to extract some delivery dates from them. Until we have done this there is nothing to add to the Report presented by the General Manager, which I think speaks for itself."

Mr Church was not at all amused, for when all of the other had left and he and John were left alone in the Committee Room he challenged John to explain exactly what he was trying to do.

John's answer was simple, "We are not here playing some wonderful game for half grown men. We are trying to run a Municipal Transport Undertaking, and we can't do that on the basis of promises from our main suppliers. Their deliveries are seven years behind schedule, and I wouldn't mind if their prices were held as of the date of order, but they have increased more than one hundred per cent, and you seem to think that by questioning the ethics of it all, I am about to commit a major crime."

"If we start to create about this we will certainly run into problems." The GM was certainly no poker player. "BBB will delay even further, and we will run into difficulties providing even the most elementary of services."

"Look here Mr Church...... The GM interrupted him.

"Chairman, if it's all right with you when we are alone I don't mind if you call me by my Christian name..... its Peter."

This simple act seemed to be a great problem to him. It was as if he didn't want anybody to get to close to him just in case they found yet another weakness in him. "I just find it difficult to communicate my ideas, and so try to keep people at a distance".

"Look Peter I'll make a pact with you."John offered him his hand. "This is what we will do, you give me a hand to solve the growing problems that face the Undertaking Politically, and I will offer to support you where ever I can in committee. I'll tell you what I want from you..... When I ask you a question I want the facts as they exist. I do not want the answer that you think that I would like to hear, I really do want to hear it as it is. No frills, no attempts to disguise the true horror of it all, what I expect from you is the unvarnished truth. There will be no repercussions from me."

"But what about ideas......."

"Yes I want those, and anything else that you want to put in. The idea is to put forward all types of suggestions and then tear them to bits, in an effort to find out what is the best way forward for this undertaking, to do that I need you and your deputy working here in the office as a team.

Now I have heard all sorts of rumour and innuendo since I took this job, and I want both of you to know that I try to form my own opinions of people, and up to now I haven't been given the opportunity to find out about either of you. I require you to rectify that as soon as it is possible. In respect of your deputy, I understand that he has a problem, if he cannot talk to you, perhaps there is something that we can do as a department to assist him. I want you to get him to come here so that we can have an informal meeting to try to help him resolve his problems. This is not a disciplinary affair this is an attempt by two friends and colleagues to try to assist a friend who has a problem. Do you think that it will work for him?"

"I don't know John," Peter smiled. "But it is the Christian thing to do, so I suggest that we give it a try."

"OK! John said with relief. "Now what are we going to do with BBB problem?"

"I have been reluctant to do anything because of the last Chairman's insistence that we must source all our new buses Britain, and that restricts us to buying from BBB." It was all flowing out now. "I can buy buses direct from companies like Scandia, and have them delivered here within a month, and at 75% of BBB prices, and that is fitted out in our livery and ready for the road."

"Let's cross our bridges one at a time." John was soothing the way. "Let's see if we can get one of BBB's senior sales people down here next week and see what they have to offer. Who do you think will be the right man for us to talk to?"

"I think that the right man will be a fellow called Terry Straw, who is their senior sales manager in this country," Church paused for a moment. "The trouble is that he will also be the hardest of their people to deal with. He was the guy who negotiated the first of the orders that I mentioned in my report and he will stand to loose quite a lot of face if we cancel these contracts. And it must be added that BBB have had a very tough last six months because of cancelled orders."

"Their production problems are now beginning to influence our business." John emphasised this point. "And when that begins to bite into our facility to operate what are our basic services, then we can no longer afford to trade with them, and the contracts that we have outstanding have been broken by their inability to supply us to time. Anybody in private industry would laugh at the naivety of the terms of the standard local authority contract. The whole relationship of supplier and customer is turned on its head in this situation, and I for one will not be held to ransome in this way."

"But this will mean changing the trading methods that have been applied by this council for decades, Chairman." Peter Church was clearly amazed that anyone should even question the procedures by which the lives of beavering local government officers had been ruled for so many years.

"The Chief Executive will have a baby, just you wait and see."

"I would imagine that they will all view the proceedings, with more than a little scepticism Peter." Robertson was at last beginning to enjoy himself. "I think that it is high time that we started to stir the pot a little. So go ahead, and arrange the meeting with Mr Straw, let's see if there are any cracks in their structure, to compare with the ones that they are inflicting on us."

There is, of course, no method of preventing an officer who is in fear of loosing his job, from buttering his bread on both sides. John was aware that the first call that would go out from Peter's office would be a sign to the Chief Executive, that his Chairman was about to declare war on one of the biggest manufacturers in the British Isles.

The Chief Executive would in turn phone the Leader of Council to warn him that one of his

Chairmen was about to take an action that may or may not involve the Council in Legal Expenditure. Charles Brown would call a meeting of all parties involved, and from that they would decide on the make-up of the deputation that would meet the representatives of BBB, when the meeting was arranged. It all followed what was becoming a familiar and predictable process. The question arose about the viability of it all in a modern and more accountable world. Would the people continue to follow these well ploughed furrows simply because that was the way that they'd always been done, or would they relish a newer more open approach that allowed officers the scope to search for a better albeit short term solutions to what were in essence perennial problems?

The anticipated re-actions all took place, and in due time a meeting was called at the Town Hall to 'Investigate the situation in respect of Outstanding Bus Orders'. Charles Brown as the leader of Council, and the Chairman of the Policy and Resources Committee was in the chair. All of the 'Interested Parties' were represented and it turned out to be a dower, all afternoon affair, that really got no further forward than John and Peter had done at the brief meeting, except , of course that it had taken another three weeks, and a myriad of papers to do it. The outcome was that it was now a City investigation, as opposed to it being a Transport Committee investigation, and instead of there being seven people involved there were now thirty-two. This meant that even the large committee room was not big enough to house all of the required attendee's, and allow members of the public to attend as spectators. So the meeting had to held in the Main Council Chamber.

The whole affair was turned inside-out, and it was finally agreed that the City would invite BBB's Mr Straw to a meeting at the Central Depot, on a date that was to be decided between all of the parties who would be needed to put the Cities case. John couldn't help feeling that he had done all of this before.

The day of the all important meeting arrived, and John arrived in his office in the Central Depot before eight-o'clock in the morning. Martin was obviously informed of his arrival, because John had only just taken off his jacket, when there was a knock at the door.

Martin strolled in "Hi John, how are you this morning?" He seemed very chirpy.

"I'm OK thanks," He replied. "How's your-self?"

Martin did not answer his question but went straight into the reason for wanting to see him before the meeting. "I've been asked to set up a meeting between you and Terry Straw, before the main meeting, and strictly on the QT. Do you understand what I'm saying?"

This was a new slant on the man whom he had thought that he knew well. "I think that what you are saying is the it might be in my best interests to meet Mr Straw, and agree a course of action before the start of the real meeting." John was way ahead of Martin, and Martin was aware that John knew that he was uncomfortable about what he was proposing. John continued. "Can I deduce from this that your interest might prefer it if I made an agreement before certain other external interests were fully aware of what was happening?"

"I think that is what I'm trying to say. But my instructions on the matter were rather vague." Martin was being used here, and he wanted John to know that he was being used.

"Is there a venue for this meeting?" John asked of his friend.

"Yes!" Martin stared straight at him. "If you go into the GM's office at ten minutes past ten this morning Mr Straw will be there to meet you.

There will only be the two of you there, and he wants to make you an offer that may be of advantage to both the City and BBB." Martin remained stone faced.

"Shall I tell my lot that you will be there?"

John thought for a moment. "Yes, you may tell them that I will be there."

"Now there is one more thing," Martin said relieved that the initial and most important part of the business was over. "How do you and Kath feel like going out for a beer and a natter tomorrow night?"

"Do you know that's the first sensible suggestion that anyone's made since we were both elected to Council." John smiled. "I'll have to check with my secretary, of course," He spoke with mock severity. "But I do think that I might have a window in my diary sometime tomorrow. I'll have my girl call your girl to make the final arrangements."

"Where abouts shall we meet, assuming of course that your girl and my girl can agree to a meeting?" Martin continued the slide into stupidity.

"How about the "Oxford Crew' at about eight or eight-thirty."

"That sounds good to me." John agreed.

At five minutes past ten John moved out of his office and walked along the corridor to the GM's office. He did not knock. He simply pressed the handle and walked in, and was confronted by a man who was considerably younger than he had expected.

"Are you John Robertson?" His voice had a rich deep sound to it that implied a maturity that was not written into the face.

"Yes I'm Robertson." John was intentionally short in his reply.

"What is your problem Mr Robertson," Straw was abrupt.

"Oh, I don't have a problem, Mr Straw." John emitted all warmth and light. "It's you and your company that have the problem."

"I don't quite understand what you mean by that

210

remark." Straw was continuing to play the game of cat and mouse. "Perhaps you will tell me what this is all about."

"Let me put my cards on the table Mr Straw." John insisted, "I came to this meeting at your request, and that to me implies that you have some sort of suggestion to make to me. If you have, would you please get on with it, and if you haven't then I will go back to my office."

"So you are a straight talker!" He paused to light a cigarette. "I like that. I understand that you, as the Chairman of this undertaking, are contemplating cancelling all of you outstanding orders for new buses with my Company?"

"Yes that is so." John admitted,

"I must warn you," Straw pointed his finger at John. "that if you cancel the orders there are significant cancellation charges that will be made against your undertaking,"

"I don't think so, Mr Straw." John responded.

"I can assure that BBB will sue you for significant cancellation charges if you go ahead and cancel the orders." Straw was still trying to control the situation.

"Mr Straw" John began speaking very slowly, "I will put my case to you in very simple terms:- If you think that you can make a case for your company from the fact that you are more than seven years late in the supplying of an order; and if you think that you can stand all of the adverse publicity surrounding the fact that whilst you are seven years behind in your deliveries your prices have increased by 120%, and you still cannot give me a date on which you can supply my immediate needs. If you sincerely believe that we have not demonstrated a degree of patience that would have long been exhausted in a commercial enterprise, then go ahead and sue."

"I have been instructed by the company to make you an offer. The offer is of a single payment, to be made to you, or to anyone whom you nominate, and into any bank account in any country where you may want it paid, the sum of £250,000 by way of a gift. This, you will understand, is not a bribe or inducement, but is by way of a payment for services rendered to the Company." He smiled, and waited for the reply.

John was astounded, and he now understood the embarrassment that Martin had felt when he came to tell him of the secret meeting. This was an attempt to bribe, a straight forward illegal payment of a vast sum of money to a politician, so that Straws Company would retain the contracts for the supply of the these buses.

"I cannot, and will not listen to any more of this." John rose to his feet. "To be brutally frank, you have just offered me just about the most horrifying insult that I feel that one human being can offer to another.You have the gall to stand there and believe that I am in this business to make money, and to make money illegally. You think that I can be bought. Well I can tell you now that you are wrong. In fact you couldn't be more wrong than you are right now. I am not a rich man, and by your standards I do not want to be rich. Any chance that you and your company had of supplying vehicles to this city, went out of the window the moment that you started to believe that I could be paid to do just what you wanted me to do."

He was surprised. This evidently was the point at which he could normally relax and have a cigarette with his new won friend. It would seem that this was the first time that this ploy hadn't worked for him, and he was dumb-founded.

"I'm sorry, Mr Robertson" He put up his hand to indicate that he wanted John, who had started to move towards the door, to stay. "I understood that you were a career politician, who had not as yet found yourself a backer and this was to be your fighting fund.........."

"Mr Straw," John interrupted him. "I don't know who has put you up to this, and I don't really care, but let me get one thing straight, I am not in the market to be purchased by your company, or indeed any company. I will make my own way in politics, using my own resources and if I fail that will be my fault. I have one stubbornly resolute intention, and that is I am, and will remain essentially my own man. I will not be bought, suborned or bribed into doing anything that I don't want to do, and right now you haven't got a snow-balls chance in hell of retaining any of the contracts that you have outstanding with this city."

"Then we will sue you."He was now seriously annoyed.

"That being the case," John stated categorically. "I will see you in court."

There was nothing further to discuss, and John left Straw sitting in the General Managers office to return to his own. Once there, John pondered the possible outcome of his action, an action taken more in anger that Straw would even think that he was open to bribery of that kind, than of consideration of the affect on the running of the Undertaking.

About ten minutes elapsed, and there was a knock at the door, and the door opened to reveal Straw looking more downcast than aggressive.

"May I come in?" He asked.

"Certainly" John replied gesturing him to a chair.

"I have had words with the production side at our plant." He began. "and they have told me that we will not be able to provide any of your outstanding orders until later on this year. In view of your requirement for immediate delivery, which we cannot meet, I discussed the matter with our Managing Director, and unless we can reach some compromise at the meeting later today, I have been instructed to inform you that we will, in these special circumstances, be prepared to let you cancel the outstanding orders without any cancellation charges."

"Thank you!" John was inwardly sure that this would be the end of the matter. "I just wanted to add that unlike many people in politics today, I am not open to receiving any thing that may constitute an inducement of any kind. And I do not know where you obtained the information that I might be, but you can tell them from me that I was raised to believe that if any-body received such a payment at the beginning of a process then by the end of it you finish up paying out yourself like a fool. I may be a fool, but I am my own fool, and I will stand or fall on my own merit, and nobody else's."

"Well I was told that you would be open to such an inducement, and I must tell you that you are one of the few who have declined such a payment in my experience." He held out his hand, and John took it. "I trust that this will be the end of the matter, because if you tried to take the matter any further I would be placed in the embarrassing situation of have to reveal my source. That would cause me and my company great problems."

"I would not dream of taking this matter any further," John admitted "I would have extreme difficulty in even proving that our conversation had taken place, and what is more, I am sure that any embarrassment that you may experience by my taking any such action would be of small shrift compared with the problems that it might raise in this Authority. There will therefore be no repercussions unless of course you try to pressure me into taking any action that I regard as detrimental to the functioning of this Undertaking."

"I understand what you are saying," Straw replied, "and I feel that there will be little point in my remaining to attend the meeting. BBB accept that due to our production difficulties we have been unable to give you the standard of service that you most urgently require and we will therefore write to you and let you know that we will withdraw from the contracts."

"Then there is nothing left to say." John concluded. "I will await your letter, and will inform the meeting that you have had to return to your company on urgent business, if that is all right with you?"

"Yes that will be fine." He replied. "All there is to say is good-bye, and I hope that the next time that we meet we will be able to have a drink together having put this sorry matter to bed once and for all."

With that he left the office, and a few minutes later John saw through the window of his office that Straw was being seen off the premises by the General Manager.

Peter Church wasted no time in getting back to John's Office. He burst through the door with more energy than John had seen in him from the day that he took over the Chairmanship.

"I say John!" He said with enthusiasm. "Terry Straw has just admitted to me that they can't meet our delivery requirements and should we wish to cancel the outstanding orders that they will allow us to do so without any cancellation charges."

"Yes he's just been in my office and told me much the same as you." John decided to keep to himself the details of the conversations that he had held with Straw. "Whilst he was here he received a call to tell him to return to BBB as soon as possible. But he did confirm the details of the possible cancellation with his MD whilst he was here in this office."

"I don't know what you've said to him Chairman, but it certainly worked." Church was almost rubbing his hands with glee.

"There is just one thing that we must do before the meeting Peter." John was serious. "We must get some projected figures and delivery dates from other suppliers so that we have a clearly defined course of action to present to the meeting."

He came back without a pause. "I knew that you would want that sort of information to hand, so I took the liberty of getting some quotes from the other major suppliers and there will be a recommendation with you in about ten or fifteen minutes. The Deputy and I have been working on it since you indicated that you might go for cancellation. But he will do that after this meeting is over and done with."

With that off his chest he was out of the door, clearly with a new spring in his step, but he had hardly closed the door when Martin slipped round the door.

"How did the meeting with Straw go?" He clearly had his orders to get the latest information to his Union colleagues as quickly as possible.

"How did you expect it to go?" John threw the ball straight back at him.

"I thought that he would try to buy you off." He countered.

"Well he did, and I didn't buy it." John responded. "We need new buses as soon as we can get them, and they cannot meet the schedule that we require. That was all that I could and would consider."

"I bloody well knew that you wouldn't." He was elated. "I've won money on that. I'll bet that you didn't know that there was a book being run on it and they were betting that you would take the money and keep BBB as our main supplier."

"Then you were on a sure thing then." John added

"Because you knew me better than that."

"I'll tell you what." He replied. "When I had to tell you that Straw was in the GM's office, I thought that you'd been got at! Now we will be able to get some decent buses at a reasonable price from any of the other suppliers. The GM will be as pleased as punch, when he get's to know."

"He already knows." John said quietly. "And what is more, out friend Mr Straw is on his way back to BBB and will not be attending the meeting later today. As far as I'm concerned the matter is over and done with, and there will be an interim proposal put to the meeting today, that will be approved at the next meeting of the Transport Committee."

"I'd better go and let Harry know." He smiled. "He's been pacing up and down like an expectant father ever since he heard that you were having a secret meeting with Straw. I'll buy you more than a couple of drinks tonight my old friend." With that he was gone.

The meeting was an anti-climax. The sudden withdrawal of BBB from the equation changed everything, and the proposals tabled by the General Manager were given the go-ahead, subject to the approval of the full Transport Committee.

Charles Brown was not as happy as the rest of the participants, he appeared to be distracted by something, and left the meeting at the end of the deliberations without any comment to John.

John made his way back to his office at Convellium, spent the rest of the day trying to catch up on some of the details that had been left in abeyance during the turmoil that had surrounded the supply of buses to the City. It was a strange feeling to be back in the position of having to do the spade work for his self after have and entire Department at his beck and call.

25

A Night at the Pub

Kath was ready to go out when John arrived home from work, but she hadn't really expected that he would be at home as early as he was.

"Have you had an easy day them love?" she asked as he came through the front door.

"No not really. It's been one of those funny sort of days, where you expect there to be endless trouble, but in the end it all melts away without any real problem arising." He spoke as though there was still something nagging at the back of his mind.

"What about the bother over purchase of buses?" She dropped the question out casually.

"What do you know of the Transports Departments bother over the purchase of Buses?" He was surprised that she asked, mainly because he didn't really discuss the problems with her in any great detail.

"It's been on all of the local radio programs about the big meeting that you've been holding with BBB, and how you've cancelled millions of pounds worth of bus orders."

"I haven't said a word to anybody about it, and the meetings were supposed to be secret." He said with a frown on his face.

"Well Charles Brown has been on both radio and TV telling everybody how you've save the city about four million pounds, by cancelling contracts with BBB because they had not been able to fulfill their contracts." She informed him. "Martin rang to say that you had gone right up in the estimation of the work force and the Unions, and Harry, what his name, made a statement to the press that said you had done the city a great service."

"Isn't it just like the press to talk to everybody but the bloke who actually performed the miracle?" He winked as he said it, and kissed her lightly on the cheek.

"The press have been trying to find you all day. The phones never stopped ringing. I've just told them that I didn't know where you were." She said innocently. "Which was true in a way, but it's mainly because I didn't want you to get all tied up and not be able to go out tonight. You need a night's relaxation once in a while, that's why Jenny and I decided that you and Martin could do with a night away from it all."

"You crafty little minx" He said, pinching her bottom. "I'll bet that Martin still believes that the idea was all his."

"Well we had to apply the 'Ways and Means Act' to make it work." She laughed. "If we didn't the pair of you would forget that we both exist."

John showered, and they ate a light dinner before they dressed to go out for the evening. It was to be a casual get-together of themselves and their friends Martin and Jenny at the 'Oxford Boat' a fairly large pub where they were all known.

The pub stood on the corner of one of the main arterial roads, just round the corner from one of the Transport Department Depots, and as such it was frequented by many of the drivers and Inspectorate of the Department.

It was a warm and friendly place, one of those, so typical of English pubs, where there were no barriers of any kind, and it was expected that there would be all sorts of friendly badinage.

The beauty of the place was that both couples could stroll from their respective homes, and not have to take cars or buses to get there or back home at the end of the evening.

John and Kathryn walked into the place at about eight o'clock, to find that the afternoon shift from the depot were still there in some numbers, and as they were strolling through to the large lounge area John was ribbed about the deal that he had completed that day. Martin and Jenny were already seated when they arrived, and their drinks were ready waiting for them when they sat down. They all said their 'Hello's' and Jenny and Kath started to talk about their families, whilst John and Martin sat quietly drinking and smoking to relax from the cares of the day.

Martin had wanted to speak to John on the subject of Pedestrian Crossing, and launched into it without thinking. "I've had a few words with the Highways boys at County Council, and they are now trying to bring forward the introduction of some of the proposals that we made to them after the survey up on Colly Farm." He reached into his pocket to bring out a document that he received from them. "As you can see on the map, they will be placing the new crossing fairly close to the traffic lights, and this may cause us some difficulty. I wondered if you or the GM could raise with them the question of the proximity of bus stops, and the dangers that can arise from havingthem too close together?"

"I don't see why not, let me have a copy of the papers and I'll see what I can do." John replied, having casually glanced at the papers.

"You can have these John." He responded. "I copied them before I left the depot this evening."

John stuffed the papers into his pocket, and tried to change the subject. "Do you still find time to have a game of darts now and again?" He asked.

"Yes, but not as often as I used to. Martin was a

very good player on his night. "I did slip my arrows into my pocket, on the off chance that we might get a game in tonight, while Jenny and Kath have a natter. At least that way we will keep off council business."

They wandered off to make their mark in readiness for a game, and were lucky enough to get straight into a foursome on the basis that John scored for the first game. As a pair they fared quite well, for what John lacked Martin easily made up with his steady hand and very good eye. John was not a good player, but had flashed of brilliance that were usual followed by flashes of really poor play, and after the forth game they were well and truly beaten, and decided to return to the table.

The place had been fairly well packed when they arrived, but this was a popular place where people usually called in at the end of a days work for a pint of bitter before they set off home, so within a short space of time the crowd began to thin out a little.

They sat down and chatted about all sorts of things and the drinks came and went, they had been there for about an hour, when a group of rowdy young men came into the lounge, and took up station around the table where they were sitting. It soon became clear that this was not a casual positioning, because they started to make loud and pointed comments about the bus services.

John was not going to be drawn, but as he picked up his pint to take a drink one of the group hit him in the back with his knee and said very loudly "What are you doing with our fucking bus services then?" The blow was not sufficient to cause John any trouble so he ignored the incident. But the man was intent upon creating a disturbance.

"Are you fucking deaf as well as daft? He shouted. "I said what are you doing with our fucking bus services?"

221

"And I ignored you on the basis that I don't discuss politics in pubs with drunks." John replied.

"Oh you're a clever bastard into the bargain as well are you?" He said as he pushed his knee into John's back again.

The whole pub had gone very quiet, and Martin had got up to his feet. John said "Sit down Martin this is not the place for you and I to get involved in a fracas." He turned to face the four antagonists who were edging closer to the table. "I said that I don't discuss politics in pubs with drunks, I'm here to have a quiet drink, and that is all."

"You've stopped our bloody buses at the weekends and I want to know why." He insisted.

"Then write a letter to me at my office." John returned to his drink.

"You're here now, so how about you earning your bloody money for once?" The youth was persistent.

There had been a quiet movement of people away from the lounge, but there was also a gradual movement of men wearing Transport Department uniforms, and they were beginning to make a circle around the group.

"If you don't get up and answer me," The youth continued, "I'll have you off that stool, and make you answer me."

At this point Eddie the landlord came up to the table and said, "Is there any trouble John?"

John turned to him and smiled. "I think that you'd better ask these young gentlemen to leave Eddie, because there is no trouble at the moment, but just look." He turned to indicate that there were about forty men in uniform standing in a circle around them. "I don't think that these drivers are taking very kindly to the fact that their Chairman is being harassed by people when he's out for a quiet drink."

Eddie eyed the growing crowd, and spurred on by the fact that one of them said out loud, "Are you OK John?" He decided that he would tell them to leave in the interests of their own safety. They were escorted from the premises by a group of very determined bus drivers and garage hands.

"Wow! I thought that we were in for it there." Martin exclaimed. "You can't get away from the job anywhere these days."

Kath was visibly shaking. "Is that what you have to put up with all of the time when you go out?"

"No, calm down love, that was just a yob trying to show off in front of his mates." John said soothingly. "You just don't have to let it get to you. But you can see why we usually drink in places where the general public can't get to us. They think that you have to pander to their wishes all of the time, but if you asked them to do anything at all in their own time they would refuse point blank."

Jenny said. "I was surprised that you even spoke to them at all."

"Normally I wouldn't have done, but the guy was driving his knee into my back." John explained "and if I hadn't been cocky about it, he would have taken it as a sign of weakness, and would have been so sure of himself that he would have had a go at me, straight away. So I played for time."

"There was half the bloody afternoon shift standing there by the time that Eddie got here." Martin informed her. "And this man," he said pointing to John, "Has done more for the crews in a few short weeks, than the rest of the Council has in the past ten years. They were ready to murder them, and just bear in mind that they are probably some of the bastards who have been kicking our crews about at the weekends."

By this time the Police had arrived, and an inspector

came into the lounge with the landlord. "I understand that you've had a bit of trouble Councillor!" He said with a smile on his face. "They must be out of their minds, fancy trying to tackle the Chairman of Transport in a pub full of bus drivers. I can't understand where some of them get their brains from. Anyway we've taken them into custody, they're well on their way to being drunk and they've caused a problem in a Public House so we'll charge them with a Breach of the Peace. Have a good night." He turned and left.

"It's not always going to be like this is it?" Kathy enquired.

"No love the majority of the people are good people." John assured her. "We will probably never have another night quite as exciting as this will we Martin?" He laughed.

They were joined by the Landlord and his wife Maureen, who arrived at the table clutching a bottle of Champagne, and the rest of the night turned out to be quite a party in itself.

They strolled home through the streets of the suburbs, it was a warm night, and it had been a long time since they had done this.

"I don't think that I am going to like this life very much if it makes it difficult for us to have a separate life outside of politics." Kathy stated as they walked. "It is difficult enough, without having to choose where you go to avoid that sort of intrusion into our lives."

"I don't think that what we've experienced to night will be a common occurrence." John commented. "That was just pure opportunism on behalf of a group of yobs who thought that they would be clever. It won't happen again."

The real problem here was that in his heart John knew that it would happen again, it was one of the realities of Public life that there would always be those people who would react violently to decisions taken by others. But more to the point there would always be that element of society that would go out of its way to confront those people in public life whom they felt were in some way restricting the way in which they thought that they could live their lives, even when their actions were outside the bounds of the law. The reality was that their actions usually involved people who had not participated in the decision making process. John pondered all of this as they strolled home.

26

Committees

Anyone who has been involved at any level of Government be it local, regional, or national will be aware that they generate committee upon committee. Each committee is then split into a whole range of sub-committees, which in turn are broken up into working parties, and so on.

There are, in addition to elected members, various officers, and departmental managers who report to the committees, and supply the members with all of the necessary documentation that is required for them to make a reasoned judgement of a topic, and to ultimately decide what is the course of action that best reflects the interests of the people.

In most cases officers supply the necessary information, and analyse the various options that are available, and the costs that are involved. Some go even further, and recommend their favoured course of action. The seasoned member, regardless of political persuasion, can usually work out for himself or herself what course of action will best suit the policies of their party. John was not a seasoned member, and he found it difficult at times to reconcile his own thinking with the decisions that were taken by the administration in which he was a serving member.

In his own area of responsibility he was quite clear, because he had been instrumental in defining the Conservative Policy on Transport in the City, and having an interest in the whole infra-structure of both regional and national transport, he was well read on the subject. He could therefore guide the Conservative members in a direction that culminated in them following the 'Party Line to the outsider, the whole process might have appeared to be cumbersome, but so that themembers of each party were aware of how they were expected to vote, each Committee Meeting, and Sub-committee Meeting is normally preceded by what is loosely described as a 'Pre-Agenda Meeting', held separately by each party group, at which the responses to all of the business would be decided.

John Robertson found that being a Chairman of Committee was also to be a member of the' inner circle' of the ruling group, and this entailed much more involvement than he had originally expected. The first he knew of the extent of his involvement was when the list of Committee membership were published. He knew that he was to be Chairman of Transport, but his membership of Policy and Resources, Finance, and Planning Committees came as a complete shock to him. Nobody had taken the trouble to explain at the out-set that all Chairmen were members of the Policy & Resources Committee, and the Finance Committee, or that because of the inherent Planning implications, the Chairman of Transport also sat on the Planning Committee. When he stopped and thought about it John could see the logic of it all but all of this was presented after the event. By the time that all of the Committees , sub-committees, working parties, membership of outside bodies, School Governorships, and liaison committees etc., had been allocated, he found that if there were no emergency meetings, disasters, or world wars he was committed to attend a minimum of thirty-five meetings per month, four of which were held in London. This did not take into consideration any of the meetings that he held with the various Unions or groups of workers at any of the six functioning depots, two repair shops, and one body shop all integral parts of the undertaking.

Because of his experience in trade union organisation John was also made the Vice-Chairman of the Appeals and Disciplinary Committee, and was also the vice-chairman of the Magistrates Liaison Committee.

In three short weeks the whole of his life had changed, from his being a full time Engineer in a medium sized manufacturing company, to being an attender of meetings, a reader of Committee Papers, a researcher into all aspect of local government, and a very occasional attendee in the office from which he was supposed to derive his income.Many of his late nights attending Party Functions, and invites to speak at Engineering, Business and Local Action Group Functions. The prospect seemed never-ending, and he loved it all. He was hooked, drawn into this banquet of debate, decisions and intrigue, that tested all of his instincts, that diverted his thoughts from all that made him the man that he had been into a new being that was developing by the day.

As the weeks progressed, so the volume of work and involvement grew. He was elected the area Chairmen of the Conservative Regional Trades Union Committee, and this gave him a seat on the Area Executive Committee. But in addition to all of that he was now a member of the National Union of the Conservative Party thus increasing his need for travelling to London at least twice a month. The applications for his time and energy seemed endless.

His main committee was, of course, the Transport Committee, and this regulated the City's Municpal Bus Undertaking. It also dealt with such peripheral as the licensing of Taxis, both Hackney Carriage and Private Hire. Because of the large commitment to equipement for the repair and servicing of buses the transport department also carried out the maintenance of all of the Local Area Health Authority Ambulances, and liaised with the County Council on all matters that related to Highways and Road Safety.

The Transport Committee was comprised of twelve members, a committee clerk, a representative of the Chief Executives Office, the General Manager and the Deputy GM plus the Chief Engineer. Because of the balance of council theirwere seven members of the Conservative Party, four members of the Labour Party, and one Liberal Democrat. Martin Smith, and Molly Bacon, both members from his days in the Colly Farm area were also members of this committee. There were two permanent Sub-Committees, one for Hackney Carriage Matters, and one for Private Hire Vehicle Licensing.

One of John's first duties was to appoint his Vice Chairman. This was not as easy as it first seemed, because there was a considerable amount of jockeying for position, and the appointment had to be approved by the Leader of Council. It was finally decided that the best person for the job would be Councillor Frank Jamieson, and John went to see Charles Brown to seek his approval.

When he told Charles of his decision he was obviously surprised, "Why the hell have you selected him?" He ranted. "He is a pretty useless sort of individual at the best of times."

"That was probably the real reason for my selecting him." John responded. "I don't think that he will be able to cope with all of the documentation, and plot behind my back to try and have me removed so that he can take over from me."

"Well there is that to it." Charles was placated, but not a lot. "He does have quite a basis for support, with his daughter and his son-in-law, both sitting as members from the west side of the city."

"Yes but when I approached him on the matter he was as pleased as punch" John added. "He doesn't seem to have much idea about how the whole process comes together, but then again none of the rest of the committee do either."

"Yes!" Charles agreed. "That is one of the problems that we have all round, and one that we will just have to live with until we see just what the calibre of the new Councillors is like." Brown pondered this for a moment. "OK go ahead with Jamieson, but if you find that there is a problem get rid of him. If I were you I'd let him Chair one of the Sub-Committees, but that doesn't preclude you from sitting as an ordinary member of that Sub-Committee. Whilst you're here there are a couple of matters that we need to discuss, firstly I am a member of the Association of District Councils National Committee, but their meetings always coincide with the meetings of the Finance Committee, so I have nominated you to be my deputy. The reason is simple their meetings always take place on the same day as the meetings of the Confederation of Passenger Transport, in meets in the afternoon and the other in the morning both in London so you will halve the costs of both of us going down. They meet once a month, by the way. The second point is that there will have to be an urgent meeting of the Appeals Committee to discuss the dismissal of a member of staff in the treasury. I propose that to take place in two days from now. Clarence Booth will not be available to Chair the meeting so that you as his Vice-Chairman will have to do the honours in his place. Do you think that you will be able to cope with that, bearing in mind that you have not yet attended one of the Committee's meetings?"

"I should think so!" John said, but without a great

deal of confidence in his voice. "I will just have to read up on the procedures during the next two days."

"It is pretty straight forward." Charles added. "The man was convicted of theft from the Council and has just completed a short prison sentence and is applying to be re-employed in the same department.

The Unions are trying to establish a precedent in this case, so tread carefully. The City Secretary and Solicitor will brief you on the law before the meeting, and will attend the meeting as the officer member of the committee. So you will have all the help and advice that you may need close at hand." They parted with that last statement.

The tactic here seemed to be quite clear to John Robertson; Charles Brown was trying to create a bad atmosphere between John and the Unions. There was no need to set a precedent here. There really was no need for this to come up on appeal at all. The man concerned had been convicted on a charge of stealing as servant, and there was no set of laws anywhere that could force an employer to re-employ someone who had be so convicted, in the same position of trust. There was an ulterior motive here, some reason for Charles Brown to place Robertson in a position where his judgement could be questioned.

Robertson requested all of the records that were available on the person in question, he read all of the reports and notes on all of the interviews that had taken place prior to the charges being made.There appeared to be nothing that could form the basis for a reinstatement of the man. The final papers came through on the next day, and the basis of the appeal was a straight forward one "That the man had served his sentence for the crime that he had committed, and the case was that he had paid the price for his crime and should therefore be considered for resuming his career with the Local Authority."

The whole case hinged on the fact that he had served his sentence, had paid the price for his crime and therefore his record had been wiped clean. The case was heard in camera with only the necessary officers and committee members present. All of the evidence was presented by the mans Trade Union Representative, and in the end when the vote was taken on whether they should reinstate the man, the vote was tied, four in favour, four against. This was the situation that Brown knew would arise from the make-up of the Committee. The City Secretary and Solicitor asked if there was a need for an adjournment. "No!" said John. "That will not be necessary, I have given such a situation considerable thought over the past two days, and in this case I will use my casting vote against reinstatement." There was a sudden outburst in the room but John continued. "my reason for doing so are quite simple really. If this were a case of selecting a person for a job that requires trust and integrity I would apply the same principles that I am applying here. This person has a record that displays openly his weakness when it comes to handling other people's money. He has been charged, tried, and found guilty, and he has paid the penalty that was fixed by the law. We are not here to comment on that matter but we are here not as individuals, but to assess whether or not this man is of the right calibre to carry out a job that is a position of public trust. We have a duty of care when it comes to Public Funds and we have to try to reflect on what would be the public perception of our actions, if we knowingly re-employed a convicted felon in a position where he has already demonstrated that he is open to temptation.

If this were a question of choice between this man, and a person of good character, I think that all of you here would choose the man who does not have a doubt against his name. It is on that basic principle that I must use my casting vote to refuse this appeal. The appeal says that this man has paid the price for his crime, and I must reiterate that he has served the sentence required by the Law, but it is only now, in retrospect, that he will fully appreciate what the price of his action really is."

The Union Representative stood up and spoke. "I understand what you are saying Mr Chairman, but this is a matter for which we believe a precedent should be set, and I give notice that this matter will be submitted to ACAS in the hope that it will be heard by an Industrial Court."

"I appreciate the point that you are trying to make." John replied. "But that factor will not change my view in this matter. The Appeal is Refused Good Morning that is all." John walked out of the Committee Room, and made his way to Charles Browns office. "Good Morning Sheila!" He said cheerfully, "Is Charles available?"

"Yes Councillor Robertson, he's been expecting you." She smiled. "Go straight in."

"Hello John!" He said without enthusiasm. "How did the Appeal go?"

"Pretty well as I expected that it would" John replied. "The vote on the matter was tied, and I had to apply the casting vote."

"And how did you cast your vote?" He asked eagerly.

"I voted to Refuse the Appeal." John answered flatly.

"Was there any backlash from that?" Charles was now all attention.

"Oh yes!" John smiled. "The Union is going to raise the matter with ACAS with a view to getting a hearing in the Industrial Courts."

"What did you answer when he said that?" Charles asked.

"I said that it did not change my view on the matter." John repeated.

"I then reiterated that the Appeal was refused, and I ended the Hearing. I had given my reasons for the decision, and I based them on what the Public Perception would be of reinstating the man. I said that we had a duty of care when it came to handling Public Funds, and if we had a choice of employing this man, or a man without a record, most people would expect us to choose the latter. That is all that there is to it really."

"What did the City Secretary and Solicitor have to say on the matter?" Brown asked.

"Not a lot really!" John answered. "I don't think that there was very much to say. The case was not one that should have got this far, and for what it is worth I don't think that ACAS will allow the case to waste their Courts time. All courts take a very dim view of 'theft as servant' and when it comes to Public Service they are really hard on it. This chap was convicted of theft, and they will not find in favour of him. "

"Are you certain of that?" Brown questioned.

"I took the precaution of looking up one or two other cases of this type." John stated. "And in all of them they found in favour of the Appeals Committee. This chap has had a fair hearing, and his former employers have refused to re-employ him, that is a basic right."

"I was told that you were good at this sort of thing." Brown admitted. "That is why I arranged for the Chairman to be away. He holds the view that if it comes down to a Chairman having a casting vote, then one should always vote in favour of accepting the appeal on the grounds that there is a reasonable doubt in the minds of the members of the committee members."

"That is not always logical, and certainly wasn't here." John explained. "This was an attempt by the Unions to establish a precedent, and the Socialists voted on a Political Point that did not form part of what we were there to hear. My point was based on what had happened, and not on what a particular faction thought should happen. I'm quite happy with the way that it went."

"So am I John! So am I." Brown gloated. "The chief Executive will be over the moon as well. He had visions of having to reinstate about ten others who have been involved in the same type of thing."

27

Party Conference

It was Saturday and for once John was lying in bed after six-thirty while Kath made the coffee. He heard the letter box rattle, and Kath called, "OK I'll get it." And she staggered upstairs with the large pile of mail that had recently become the norm. "Just the usual" She announced with a shrug as she dropped the pile on the bed. "I think that you are keeping at least one paper mill in business all on your own. I wonder where they manage to get all of the topics from to keep up this barrage of paper."

"I know", John mumbled sleepily, "I reckon there's a general conspiracy that involves driving me mad, by constantly changing the position of the goal-posts." He sat up and started the process of opening the mail and giving the contents of each a cursory glance. He arranged each group of letters and reports in neat piles in front of him, whilst drinking his coffee and trying to get his brain to function.

He suddenly sat up straight, "Hey love!" He turned to Kathy. "We've got an invite to the Conservative Party Conference in Brighton"

"What do you mean WE?" Kathy said, "I don't normally go with you on Party or Council affairs."

"Well it's definitely for the two of us," He responded, "It's from Sir John Allen the Secretary to the National Committee, he is asking us to confirm the booking that he's made for the two of us at the Metropole Hotel in Brighton for the week commencing Monday the forth of October. He say that as a Member of the National Committee and the Parties Trades

Union National Advisory Committee I will be expected to take a place on the platform with senior members of the Parliamentary Party."

"You're joking." Kathy said as she took the first page of the letter from him. Oh! My god you're right. I didn't know that you were that high in Party circles." She commented. "Are we going to go then?"

"Well we won't be able to get a holiday this year." He said thoughtfully. "So I suppose that this will be a good opportunity to spend a few days away together."

"Well you are a famous old thing then, after all I've joked about it." She purred affectionately."Who would have though that we would be spending a week away at the Conservative Party Conference in the autumn two urchins from the back-streets of a council estate."

"It just goes to prove that if you put your mind to it there's very little that a non-entity achieve in a short time." But even he was stunned, because all that he'd done so far was to attend a few meetings.

So they decided that they would spend that week in Brighton, purely for the experience. But it soon became apparent that they would not be spending too much time together. John's time would be very much taken up with the various aspects of Conference that affect his two main interests, whilst Kathy was to join the ladies in a series of events that would take them all over the south coast area of the country. There were to be a number of events in the evenings where they would be together, for most of the time John would be in and around the Conference Centre.

Questions of security had never really been a problem for John, and when he received a request for details of how he intended to travel to the conference and on which train he intended to arrive, he never gave it a thought other than to think that the Hotel would arrange to meet them at Brighton railway station.

When the day finally arrived they set off from home leaving Kathryn's mother in charge, and enjoyed an uneventful journey down to the South Coast. The train arrived on the time shown in their travel arrangements, but as was to be expected it was raining.

As they reached the ticket barrier at the station they were approached by a young man who asked, "Are you Councillor John Robertson?"

"Yes that is me." John replied.

The man showed his warrant card and continued. "I'm Inspector Ian Francis of Special Branch, and we have a car waiting for you outside, if you would follow me Sir."

A porter came forward and took their cases, and they followed the man towards the front of the Station.

"What's all this about?" Kathy enquired.

"I'm damned if I know!" John answered with a puzzled look on his face.

Once at the car John paid off the porter, and Francis turned to them and said "I have been assigned to you for the whole of this week, and will make all of the arrangements for your travel too and from the conference. So if you could let me have some idea of what and when you will be doing other things, it will make it a lot easier for us all."

John had an urge to burst out laughing, but instead remarked, "I suppose that you have a hand-gun tucked away under your coat."

"We find it better not to advertise the fact Sir!" The reply was both curt and straight faced. "There is a terrorist campaign running in these Islands, of which you no doubt are aware, and Party Conferences are a certain target. The security of this Conference is to be very tight, and no one will be admitted to the Conference Hall without the formal identification card.

I will give you yours when we arrive at the

Metropole Hotel. Please make sure that you carry it with you to all of your meetings."

The drive to the Hotel was a short one, and once they had booked in, and had their luggage taken up to their rooms Ian Francis asked then to come down to a small room just off the main reception area, which they did.

"As you can see," He began, "There is a huge security operation here.

Each Member of the Government and each member of the National Committee are regarded as being targets for the IRA, and have therefore been allotted an officer from the Security Services. I have been allotted to you Councillor Robertson, and will be available to you at any time day or night, should you finds it necessary to travel anywhere from your Hotel. As I said in the car, it will be easier for us all if you could give me some idea of your itinerary before your first visit to the conference. As for you Mrs Robertson, I have seen the list of events that are being held for the ladies and we have allocated one officer to attend at each function."

"What you are saying is that you will be in sight of me each time that I leave the Hotel." John wanted to be sure what was expected of him.

"Yes that is so." Francis replied. "I must stress that it is my job to look after you, but not Mrs Robertson, but whilst you are together obviously I will perform both functions, and arrangements have been made for those times that you are apart. Do you intend to attend the opening session of the conference this afternoon?"

"Yes, but I will only be there for the opening speeches I will then be leaving to go to the Royal Pavilion for a meeting that starts there at three o'clock. Can you advise me on the time that I should leave to get there for the start?"

"Yes I will have a car waiting for you outside the

Conference Hall at two-forty-five that should get you to the Royal Pavilion with about five minutes to spare." He was very well organised John thought. "Will Mrs Robertson be attending the wives get-together at the Hotel?"

"Yes, and she will wait there for my return. We will be eating in the Hotel this evening, and the attending the welcome party that is being held in the ballroom."

"In that case I might get to watch the football on TV tonight." He smiled. "But should you make any changes to your plans, if you will let the office in the reception area know we will assign someone to you."

Their rooms were on the second floor of the hotel, and did not have a view of the sea, but that did not bother Kathy, she was living a dream, and nothing could dampen her spirits. There were sheaves of papers and advertising for a whole range of events that were to take place during the week. They were fortunate in that the Conference Centre where the main Sessions of the Conference were to be held was only about a hundred yards down the road. It seemed almost pointless to have a car to take John to the session, nut having discussed the matter with Inspector Francis they agreed that perhaps his way would be better. As he explained, "If you go by car you do not have to run the gauntlet of all of the reporters and TV crews who will grab at the smallest straw to get a different view of a subject. The beauty of doing it this way was that they could go to the rear of the Centre and enter through a security door that was reserved for those with Special Branch Officers, That suited John down to the ground, because there was nothing he hated more than being jostled to give an opinion when he would rather keep his opinions to himself. It worked like a dream, apart from the two officers assigned to the door, who both new Francis, they saw no one as they entered.

The opening speech was made by the party chairman and lasted for about ten minutes, and as preparations were made to start the first debate, John rose from his seat in the second row of the auditorium, and made his way towards the rear door. Inspector Francis detached himself from a small group of his colleagues, and joined John as he walked to the door. A voice called out, "I say there you aren't by any chance going to the do at the Pavilion are you." They both turned to see Sir Reginald Reevesby standing there with his Special Branch man. Reevesby had been a member of the cabinet, but had opposed the Prime Minister for the Leadership of the party and had lost, he had subsequently been dropped from the Cabinet, and was now supposed to be in the Political wilderness that all people who have the temerity to opposed the leader find themselves when they loose the crucial vote.

"I don't suppose that I could grab a lift with you, could I?" He asked seriously.

"But of course Sir Reginald, be my guest." John answered cheerfully. "My name is John Robertson, by the way." John turned to Francis and confirmed. "Is that OK?" Francis nodded agreement.

They all clambered into the car, and it shot off at a high rate of knots.

Reevseby seemed to be in an agitated sort of mood. "To be frank John I didn't tell my 'nurse-maid' that I was going to this affair at the Royal Pavilion in the hope that I could loose him somewhere on the way. Poor old Bella, that's my wife, hates having them around, so we've made it a habit to try and loose them when we are at do's like this.

Do you have them on your tail all of the time?"

"Good Lord No!" John stammered." We live way from London so we don't normally have a 'nurse maid' as you put it."

"I suppose that they are there to look after us," He muttered accusingly, "but they are an infernal nuisance when one wants to prepare a surprise for one of the family. Are you at the Metropole?"

"Yes, in 206." John replied.

"Are you really?" Reevesby exclaimed "Now that is a bit of good fortune because Bella and I are in 204, which is right next door to you. We must get together and have a few drinks. Is your wife here?"

"Yes, but she's gone off on some trip or other, with the rest of the ladies."John answered.

They arrived at the Royal Pavilion and slowly wandered into the meeting together, getting acquainted, as they strolled through to the front of the hall. They took seats on the front row, had coffee together at the intervals, and arranged to travel back to the Metropole together when the meeting was over.

At about five o'clock they walked down the corridor to their rooms and as they opened their doors Reg exclaimed "I say John, I think that your Kathryn is here." So it was that John and Kathryn became the close friends of Sir Reginald and Bella Reevesby. They dined together, and the two men argued incessantly, whilst the ladies sat and smiled at each other because they knew that they were enjoying themselves. John and Reg moved to and from the Conference together, sharing transport, but going their own way when they arrived. The two ladies enjoyed each other company, and went as friends on the arranged trips and visits during the week. But all of the time they were shadowed by the two members of the Special Branch.

By the time that the Thursday arrived, both pairs were utterly sick and fed up of seeing the 'two goons' as Reevesby had christened them, following them around.

"I don't know how you can put up with it all, of the

time." Kathryn remarked to Bella.

"It's not too bad really, but it does restrict us a little bit." Lady Reevesby replied. "And we can't decide to shoot off somewhere on the spur of the moment, because we have to make three or four phone calls before hand, and wait whilst it is decides who will 'Cover us', and that all seems to knock the spontaneity from it all."

"Yes I see the point." Kathryn agreed.

"Fortunately we don't have children to contend with now." Bella added. "If we had, that would cause me all sorts of problems."

"Why is that?" Kathryn enquired.

"You have children, don't you?" Bella shrugged. "Well the truth of the matter is that if ever anyone really wants to get to you or John, it will be the children who they will go for. Special Branch have all sorts of problems with the families of Cabinet Ministers and senior party members, because their children are the most difficult to contend with."

"I don't think John has ever considered that aspect of politics." Kathryn thought out aloud.

"No, and neither does Reggie," Bella agreed "They are too wrapped up in their silly little games to notice the changes that have taken place in their daily lives. They cannot see that their notoriety is a form of restriction on the liberty of their families. That is one of the reasons why we must keep in touch after this conference is finished."

While Bella and Kathryn talked of practical difficulties, John and Reg were inclined to talk of the theoretical, but late on Thursday afternoon Reg asked John "What are you and Kath doing tonight?"

"We really hadn't thought about it so far." John replied. "We've run about all over the place this week, I was hoping that we'd spend the night in the Hotel."

243

"Well Marius Clarke, John Barker, and I," He spoke secretively. " along with our wives of course, are going to slip out of the Kitchen Door of the Hotel this evening , and go to a little Pub I know in the Lanes, to have a quiet pint of Pedigree, and a game of Darts. We just want one night free of the KGB. The point is that we need a forth to make a match so I'd rather hoped that you would make up the four. I'm sure that Kath will come along too."

It was all arranged with one of the cooks, he would show us out of the kitchen door, and nobody would know the difference.

The whole show got underway just after seven-o'clock when Reggie dressed casually in sweater and trousers, knocked on the door as whispered, "Are you ready? Then follow me."

They crept down the back stairs, giggling like naughty school-children, and went along numerous passages that the average visitor never got to see and then through the Kitchen, and out into the staff car park, and away into the back streets of the Town. They were met just outside the hotel by Sir Marius Clarke MP and Lady Clarke, and Sir John and Lady Barker who were joint Secretaries of the National Committee.

The Pub was just as Reg had promised a quiet little place that served a range of good beers, and had three dart boards that were available to all who wanted to play. They ordered their first round of drinks, and as John turned from the bar, his attention was drawn to the face of Inspector Ian Francis, who was drinking quietly against the door of the pub. He looked up and smiled as John's eyes found him, and tapping the side of his nose with his fore-finger as the smile crept across his face. Robertson decided that he would not mention the fact that there four members of Special Branch drinking in the foyer.

It was never -the-less, a very good night. John and Reg slaughtered the opposition, and Marcus accused Reg of importing a professional to make sure that he was on the winning team. Sir John

Barker proved to be a quiet man, with a very serious approach to all things. He was a very good Darts player, but Clarke had extreme difficulty in landing his arrows in the same room as the board.

They staggered back towards the Hotel, strong in the belief that they had at last managed to get away from the shadows. They ate Fish and Chips with lashings of salt and vinegar, and wandered complete with their feeling of freedom, along street where they would not be recognised. John knew their shadows had been aware of their plans, and had been waiting to see if they changed from the normal routine of these rascally knights.

It was long after mid-night when they finally settled down. Kathy was full of it "Do you know I felt right out of it tonight"She pouted. "I was the only woman there who wasn't a Lady."

"You're always a lady." John's speech was slightly slurred.

"You know what I mean," she said. "I've been sitting in a pub tonight with Sir John, Sir Marcus, and Sir Reginald, I wish your mother could have seen us, she would have called us a right toffee-nose lot."

"Yes you're right." John paused for a minute. "That is the first time that it has occurred to me this evening, and what's more we've had a very good night."

Tomorrow was the last day of the conference, with the prime ministers speech, with all of the traditional clapping and the singing of 'Land of Hope and Glory', and this was followed at the night-time by the Ball for all of the delegates. Kathryn turned to say something to John, but he was already asleep.

They breakfasted early with Reg and Bella. They had a table in one of the bay windows that formed the front of the hotel, and were for the most-part silent, each of the four being engrossed in the process of getting breakfast, and watching the sea, as each wave lazily distributed itself across a wide expanse of sand; the waiters silently slipping around each of his charges with an ease that disguised the amount of work that they accomplished.

Tomorrow they would all be going back to their differing ways of life, and this was a quiet interlude that bridged the two. Bella and Kathryn had decided that they would spend the day shopping in the Lanes, both almost eager to avoid the political nature of their visit. John and Reg would have to attend the final session of the conference, knowing that it would be a case of the preacher preaching to the converted. But it was good theatre, and they both would enjoy the blatant nationalism that would be mixed into the entire session. But now, they each in their own way contemplated the end of a week where all had extracted their own interpretation of a good time.

John was surprised at the volume of work that he had managed to fit in between the sessions and the parties and the drinking sessions. The daily post had continued, and the dispatch boxes had been sent down by rail from his department. All of this had meant that he had spent up to two hours per day clearing the basic needs of his department. Reg was also burdened with a vast amount of post, so as the week progressed they had taken to sorting and reading their letters whilst consuming a large number of cups of coffee, and seeking each others opinion on the differing types of enquiry that was make of each of them.It became clear, as the week progressed, that Reg had not given up his desire to become the leader of the party, and on this last morning as they sorted their post he said as much.

"I know that you are a committed member of the Party John," Reg began. "But do you intend to seek a seat in Parliament? I could really use someone whom I could trust to help me, both in the House and in the day to day planning of my political and industrial life. The fact is that every-body has written me off, but there is life in the old dog yet, as they say."

John put his letter to one side. "I've only just been elected to the Council back at home." He thought for just a moment. "I suppose that it is my ultimate aim, but I need to get some experience before I start trying for the House of Commons."

"The fact that you've gone straight into the Chairmanship of a major department, I think, qualifies you for having the necessary experience." Reg deduced. "If a wyly old bird like Charles Brown thinks that your'e good enough, then my conclusion is that you have enough natural ability to get you through."

"Oh! Do you know Charles then?" John asked trying to sound casual.

"Oh yes, there are not many in the party who have not had to deal with friend Charles at one time or another." Reg imparted studiously. "The trouble with Charles is that he will hold grudges, and that does not pay in politics. It doesn't matter how bad the hand is that you are dealt, you have to smile sweetly, and simply wait. That is wait for an opportunity to try to push for what you want. It is not a bad thing for a potential politician to have an ultimate gaol, but some matter of national significance is a good spur to gaining what you need to achieve it."

"That is one of the problems that I have." John admitted. "I haven't been in the arena for long enough to have developed a sense of what would be a good strategy for even gaining the nomination for a seat."

"What nonsense!" Reevesby Laughed. "Why only last night you were out playing darts with the Secretary of the National Union of the Party and the Chairman of the Candidates Selection Committee. There you have two of the most influential men in the party, here you are saying that you don't know how to go about becoming a Candidate."

"I knew that John was the Secretary to the National Union." John confessed, "but I thought that Marius was just another long serving member of the House of Commons."

"Well I can tell you now," Reevesby smiled, "that if you were to put your name forward, as a prospective candidate, you would no doubt be accepted for the Central Office List of Preferred Candidates. Both John and Marius were very impressed with the pair of you. But they liked Kath much better than they liked you." He laughed. "So if you are intending to move towards a Parliamentary Career, now is the time to do it. You must strike whilst the iron is hot, fate has presented you with a unique opportunity, so take it John. Take it." He pointed his finger at him,

"And when you get your nomination, as I am sure you will, Bella and I will come and canvas for you. Mark my words, this week you have made a lot of friends."

"I can't understand what I've done to gain such popularity." John mused.

"Perhaps it's that you are personable young man," Reg suggested "or it could be that you have managed to fit in with some of the hierarchy without it having a pronounced affect on the way that you act. In simple terms, you have remained essentially unchanged by all of the attitudes and the chaos around you. At the same time you are conscientious enough to have continued to receive and process all of the documentation that has been piled upon you during the week. We have been very impressed with you young man, very impressed indeed. If I hadn't been I would not be sitting here telling you what I have just told you."

"Well I must admit that I've thoroughly enjoyed the whole week" John said eagerly, "I wasn't really bothered about coming to Conference, but Kath persuaded me that I could do with a little time away from home. You know what I mean a change of view that would allow me to get things in perspective."

"Yes I can understand that." Reevesby remarked. "You have a very fine lady in your wife, and I'm sure that she would support you all of the way, but the main point that I must make is that I've never seen Bella take to anyone as she has done to Kathryn, and that tells me a lot. Anyway you think about it, but don't take too long about it."

It was soon time for them to set off for the final session of the conference, for they wanted to be in place in time to hear the Prime Ministers speech that would mark the end of the Party Conference. Their two watch-dogs had arranged things so that there would be one of them at the Hotel, and one at the conference centre. It all worked with smooth precision, and Francis met them at the front reception and marched them through into the hall. It was still only half full, and so Reevesby was asked to take a seat on the platform behind the members of the cabinet. "Will you look after Bella for me John" He called as he was led off into the depths of the auditorium.

"Would you come this way Lady Reevesby?" One of the stewards asked.

"Not without my two friends." She replied sweetly.

"You will have a seat on the front row, and that is reserved for Senior members of the Party." The man replied."Councillor Robertson is a member of the

National Committee." She responded. "And as such is a very senior member of the party."

"Oh! Yes! His name is on my list" He turned to John. "I'm sorry that I didn't recognise you, but there are so many people trying to get on to the front rows, we have to be very careful. I'm sure that you understand."

So they were shown to their front row seats and left to wait for the session to begin. It was all that John had expected, a speech from the Prime Minister full of tradition, preparation for the coming General Election, and assurances to the Party that they would win handsomely, that was followed by a full five minutes of applause and the singing of 'Land of Hope and Glory'. The Prime Minister then walked through the auditorium shaking hands with the party faithful.

All of this took until just after mid-day, and the hall gradually started to empty, but there were groups of people chatting and catching up with old friends. Reg and Bella were known by simply hundreds of the representatives, and a large group gathered around them. Reg was in full flood, and at every touch and turn he took John into the conversations that railed back and forth over various aspects of Conservative Policy. It took about half and hour for the majority of them to clear, but it became obvious that one man was going to remain until the rest had departed.

Marius Clarke wandered up, and opened a conversation with John. "Reg tells me that you are wanting to start out on the nomination trail, and I wanted to let you know that if you send me your CV, I will start the process of getting your name added to the Central Office List as soon as possible."

"Thank you, Marius," John replied, but that will take about a week because I haven't as yet even prepared one."

"We do know most of the details that we need to know." Marius said thoughtfully, "But it will be best if you make a formal request through Central Office, and to be frank, the sooner that you can get it to us the better."

"Right, then that is what I will do." John asserted.

All of this time Kathy had remained at his side, listening intently to the conversation, knowing that this was probably very important to John, and just a little concerned that he had not spoken to her about any of this.

"And what do you think of the idea of John here becoming a Member of Parliament then Kathryn?" He asked his accent betraying his Yorkshire roots.

"I think that he will make a good MP." She purred back at him. "But surely he needs more experience before he tries to get into the House of Commons?"

"No I don't think that is always the right way." Marius was now very much the politician. "The House is not anything like the process of sitting in a local council, and the best place for getting experience is by sitting on the Back Benches, and drinking in the ambience of the place."

Bella and Reg, accompanied by the fellow who no one seemed to know but Reg, had now joined in the group.

"Marius is right you know John." Reevesby cut into the discussion "The best thing for you to do is get on the list, and then your name will be circulated to all constituencies that will need a new candidate at the next election. That is why Horace Parker here is bending my ear he wants to know the names of a few people so that he can make a recommendation to his Selection Committee. Come round here Horace." He has singled out John."This is the young man who I was telling you about, his name is John Robertson and he will be a hot property when it comes round to selection time. John, Horace is the Chairman of Handlebury Constituency, whose Member is not seeking re-election next time."

"Hello Mr Parker." John was taken unaware at this turn of events.

"John," He replied "I just wanted to give you my card, and ask you to write to me before the end of next week, and I will arrange for you to come down and visit the Constituency so that you can have a look round and perhaps meet a few people. Reevesby has told me all about you and your wife, and we have always supported him when it has come to National Party votes. My committee back home asked me to look out for a young man who would continue that support on our behalf, in the House of Commons. I understand that you fall into that group."

"Yes that is true." John stuttered. "But you do understand that I have not yet been vetted as a candidate,"

"Now don't you worry about that." Parker patted his shoulder. "Central Office cannot over-ride the wishes of a Constituency Party, much as they would like to be able to do it sometimes. I have spoken to Sir John Barker and to Marius here and they assure me that you are of the right calibre, so contact me, and we will make the arrangements for you to come down and visit us."

John and Horace exchanged cards, and they all decided that it was time for lunch, which was taken at 'Wheelers' the cost being met by Reg and Bella.

They all strolled slowly back to the Hotel along the promenade, chattering away, laughing and joking about all sorts of things, just as if they had been friends for years.

It had been a full week for both John and Kath, and

they slumped back onto their beds.

"Don't you think that this is all going a bit too fast, love?" Kath asked. "I must say that I was quite surprised by the conversation about you becoming a Parliamentary Candidate. Usually we talk about these thingsbut this time you haven't said a word."

"The fact is my love," John knew that this would come, "Reg didn't even mention it until this morning, and I thought that he would at least give me some time to talk about it to you. But you saw what happened."

"Bella told me that he wanted you to stand while we were talking on Wednesday morning." Kath whispered in his ear. "I can't believe that you know so many people, you sly old thing."

"Well I thought that I wouldn't stand a chance at the next General." John was thinking out loud. "I figured that I might get a shot at some Socialist stronghold, if I was lucky. But this is moving along at a fair old rate of knots and Handlebury, well that's a rock-solid Conservative Area hardly the sort of seat that a raggy-arsed kid from the back-streets of Hainton could even hope to get."

"I know all about it, Bella has been giving me a running commentary on it all week." Kathy stated in a mater of fact sort of way. "It appears that Reg thinks that you are the sort of candidate that the Party ought to be selecting if they want to remain the party of the middle classes. My only doubt is that we may not be able to finance your being a candidate, now that we've bought the house, and with the children growing up, we could find ourselves really stretched in the next few months."

"That's my only doubt too." John remarked. "But this would be too good-a chance to pass up, if anything comes of it."

"I know that if you get such a chance, then you

should take it." Kath put her arms around him. "But I thought that you'd taken the decision without talking to me, and that is not really like you. It seems however that I was the one in the know, and you were the innocent in the wild for a change."

"Yeah! Just like a woman to keep her man in the dark." He teased.

They both drifted off into a light sleep, and were awakened by a porter bringing in a dispatch box from the Transport Department. It was just after seven o'clock, and they went into panic routine to get ready for dinner and then the Conference Ball.

They ate with Reg, Bella, and Horace Parker in the main dining room of the Hotel, and then walked into the Ballroom at abou't eight-thirty. The place was packed even at this early hour, and everyone who was anyone was there, with the exception of the Prime Minister, who would make a Grand Entrance at about nine o'clock. A table suddenly became available for them, and the group began to grow almost straight away. Marcus and Mavis Clarke were the first to join them, and they were quickly followed by John and Mary Barker, but after that, the comings and goings were such that it was impossible to keep tags on them all. But the core group remained intact through-out the evening. They dance and jived, exchanging partners, they drank, and talked incessantly, with the exception of the period that was set aside for the PM to do his tour. He came to the table and spoke briefly with Reevesby and Clarke, and shock hands formally with all who were there, and then he was gone.

Marius asked Kathy "What do you think of John seeking a seat in the House of Commons, and how will it affect you?"

"I have some reservations about it to be honest." She replied. "I suppose that it is a sort of fear of stepping into the unknown really. But the most important factor is that we are not wealthy, and we need to have a sound financial base before we can really commit ourselves fully."

"You are quite right my dear." Marius agreed. "But the fact is this that if half of the people who now sit in the House had waited until they were financially sound, then most of us would have never got there, and that does include me and Reg. When we started out we were as poor as church mice. That's why he would make a very good Prime Minister." He whispered. "But don't tell him that I told you so. Now I want you to make all of the people of my age jealous by dancing with me." And off they went into the throng.

"Have you discussed that matter with Kathryn?" Bella asked John.

"Yes, but I feel that I should have seen it coming sooner that I did. The penny didn't drop at all until Reg spoke to me on the matter this morning, and by then it was too late to talk to Kath about it. I felt rather badly about the whole thing, particularly as she was there when Marius started to tell me how to go about getting my name on the list, And then to top it all Horace being introduced into the equation, that really put the cat amongst the pigeons."

"You need have no fear at all John," Bella assured him. "Kathryn will support you through hell and high-water. She is immensely proud of you, and she will make a good MP's wife. Now are you going to concentrate on the dancing?"

"Most certainly Bella" And they too tripped out onto the floor.

The whole party was now out on the floor, just as it became an 'Excuse Me Waltz'. John had started the dance with Bella, but the Prime Minister tapped him on the shoulder and took over his partner. The PM was in jovial mood, "Now who was that bright young man who you were dancing with Bella?" he asked. "It's not like you to have a young man in tow."

"That is John Robertson," Bella Looked after him as he went and excused Reg so that he could dance with his own wife for a change," he's the Chairman of Transport on Hainton City Council, and Reg thinks that he has great potential."

"Does he really!" The PM said thoughtfully, "then we'd better get him out of there before Charles Brown ruins him. Marius had better get him set up on the Central Office list as soon as possible."

"I think that it is all set up Prime Minister," Bella was treading carefully, "I know that they've all had a chat with him, that is Reg, Marius, and John Barker. I've sounded out his wife, and Horace Parker has already invited him down to Handlebury. You know Horace 'Just to have a look around, and get to know a few faces'. John is a modest man, who loves his wife and family, and from what we hear he is an excellent engineer."

"I must admit to knowing a little more than I've told you." The PM said in that annoying way that people have when they have been trying to catch someone out and failed. "His dispatch box from Hainton Transport was delivered to my suite in error, so I asked the security boys to do a check on him. He's clean, so don't look alarmed, and I think that Reg is right, there is one other factor that you haven't found out" the PM whispered. "He speaks German like a native, and has many contacts in the business community in Western Germany. Yes I think that Mr Robertson could be one of our men for the future."

The dance finished and the PM escorted Bella back to the table, they arrived there at the same time as Kathryn and John. "Now who are these two young people?" He enquired. Marius did the honours." Prime Minister I would like to present Mr and Mrs John Robertson from the City of Hainton. That is John and Kathryn."

"I have been hearing some very nice things about you John," The PM was stuffily formal all of the time. "I'm particularly interested in a policy paper that you presented to the City & County Councils and I would be obliged if you could send a copy to Number Ten, mark it for the attention of Sir Richard Caulton, and it will find me."

"Yes Prime Minister," He answered with a look of amazement on his face. "I'll Post a copy to you as soon as I return home."

"May I give you some advice?" The PM smiled. "Listen to what these three good chaps tell you, for they will give you the benefit of their years of experience, and get your application into Central Office as soon as you can. And now that the music has started can I ask you for the next dance. Kathryn?"

Kath had stood next to John, in stunned amazement, whilst the whole conversation had taken place, and when the PM asked her for a dance she was astounded. The two of them simply waltzed off into the crowd of dancers, and he said "I've always liked to dance, but I get so little opportunity these days, that I always take advantage of the Party Conference to hone my skills. You are a good dancer Kathryn, and I noted that John was too. Bella Reevesby doesn't dance with clog dancers, and they've had two or three dances this evening."

"I like dancing too, Sir" Kathryn finally found her voice, but like you I don't get the chance very often either."

"That husband of yours, "He looked into her face. "Is he a good man?"

"Yes he is Prime Minister." She answered with far-away look that enters the eyes of women when they speak of the one that they truly love. "Yes he is a good husband and father, and we all love him very much."

"You have children Kathryn?" He was genuinely surprised at the revelation.

"Oh yes we have a girl who is thirteen years old, and boy who is ten years old," She told him.

Whilst they had been dancing there had been huge speculation about who was the young woman dancing with the widowed PM, and cameras were clicking as they danced around the floor, a factor that neither of them seemed to notice. When the dance came to an end, again the PM escorted his partner back to the table. Where he surprised her by saying, "It might be a good idea for you to bring them to have a look round Number Ten, the Cabinet Office, and we could spend Sunday at Chequers do you think that they would like that?"

"I think that they would both find it very interesting, Prime Minister." Even she was getting into the swing of things now.

"Good, I'll let you know some dates." The PM confided. "and we can arrange a visit one weekend for you all. I have no relatives of my own and it is a long time since I had the pleasure of children's company."

Suddenly Kathryn felt a great sadness, here he was, the most powerful man in the country, and he was desperately lonely.

"Yes please do, we will all enjoy it." She heard herself saying.

With that achieved the PM said good night, and walked back to his ring of security men, but now he had a spring in his step.

"You've made a real conquest there." Bella laughed. "I've never seen him dance outside of a very strictly controlled group of partners before."

"I know." Kathryn whispered with amazement. "But what is more he's invited our family to spend a weekend at Number Ten with him, and that includes the children."

"What did you say Kath?" It was John who had just returned to the table.

"The PM has invited you, me, and the children, to spend the weekend with him at Number Ten, and at Chequers."

"Are you sure about this Kath?" John asked.

"Just about as sure as I can be" She smiled at John. "He's a lonely man, who is trapped in a security ring that will not allow him to meet the people that he would like to meet."

"Well I'm damned" Reg uttered aloud. "The old bastard is trying to hi-Jack you John."

They partied on until the small hours of the morning thinking that they would not meet again this way, until the next Party Conference. New friendships had been forged, and they were reluctant to go their separate ways. For John and Kathryn it had all been rather like a dream. They had been rocketed into the realms of high politics and had mixed with the leaders of their country, and had been accepted for themselves, and now they had to return to their normal everyday sort of existence.

They had accepted that there were some set-backs to this process; the ever present Inspector Francis, and the chore of having to plan everything in advance. But as the week had progressed even he became part of the accepted procedure. The Reevesbys had been fantastic, and being with them as part of their entourage, had open many doors that they would not have normally been able to approach and all of this from the fact that they were fortunate enough to get the next room to them in the hotel. They all said their farewells in the corridors outside their rooms and went to bed strong in the knowledge that they would all meet again.

They were out of bed early on Saturday morning to pack their cases and get off to the station and wend their way home. They had breakfast alone in an almost deserted dining room, had their case brought down, paid their bill, and went out through the front door to meet the day. Ian Francis had their car waiting for them, but they had to run the gauntlet of reporters and TV crews all eager to find some morsel to fill the ever-growing News Industry. As they opened the door it began. "Is it true Mr Robertson that you are to be offered a new Government Post?" A voice from the pavement called.

"Not that I'm aware of!" John replied somewhat taken aback.

"You had a long conversation with the PM last night," The same voice insisted, "and we understand that you have been invited to meet him at Chequers. Can you give us some idea of the role that you are expected to play?"

Another voice piped in. "We understand that your area of expertise is in the field of transportation, are you being engaged to prepare at new Transport Policy?"

"I am currently the Chairman of Transport for the City of Hainton and that is all at the moment." Robertson stated.

"Then you do expect to be offered something in the near future!" The questioner persisted.

"I do not expect to be made any sort of offer at this time." John reiterated.

"Mrs Robertson, Kathryn!" Another voice questioned. "What did you and the PM talk about whilst you were dancing?"

Kathryn was taken completely by surprise. "It was

just small talk. We talked about dancing and my family, that's all."

"Mr Robertson another voice asked from the rear of the group. "I understand that the PM asked you for a copy of a Policy Document that you had prepared for your area, requesting that it be sent to Number Ten as soon as possible? Can you confirm or deny that this is the case."

"Yes the PM has asked me to send him a copy, but there should be no significance attached to that request." John answered, and then added, "If you would be good enough we do have a train to catch, and we are beginning to be pressed for time."

"Good Morning John and Hello Kathryn." It was Reevesby. "How are you both on this fine morning?" He walked towards them as he spoke. "My goodness you have attracted some attention haven't you?"

"Hello Reg." They both spoke in unison.

"I think that I should make some sort of statement just to cool the situation for you." Reg whispered, and then turned to the group of journalists. "My good friend John Robertson has been spotted as being one of the young men who will soon be embarking on a Parliamentary career. He's one of the people who we are looking too to frame the policy of the party towards the next century. He is currently the Chairman of Transport in his home city, and the member of a number of influential groups who define the operation of our National Transport System. He has prepared a policy in which the PM has shown an interest, and to that end a number of meetings have been arranged, some of which he himself is not yet aware, and when there is something of significance to report a press statement covering the details will be issued to you. Until that time we must ask for your cooperation. Now if you will let these people through, they must get to the station to catch their train home after what has been a hectic week for them."

Francis moved quickly to lead their way through to the car, and they were whisked away. But the same situation prevailed at the station. They were surrounded by a host of cameras and note books, but this time there was help at hand, in the form of uniformed policemen, who ushered them to the platform and the waiting train.

They boarded the London bound train, and settled at last into their seats.

"However do they get used to dealing with that sort of situation each and every day?" John asked Kath when they were settled. "They just will not accept what you are telling them even when it is the truth."

"The fact is that they all have a living to earn." Kath answered. "But just how you get used to it, I don't know. But Reg seemed to play them like a piano I think that you have to develop a technique that allows you to control them. Because we didn't expect them, we allowed them to have the upper hand. I suppose that we will learn, that's if you intend to go ahead in the way that everybody seems to want you to go."

"Well let's forget about it until we get home." He sighed. "I can't believe that they got hold of so much of the conversation from last night. I mean, most of what they were coming out with was simply private conversation, and they knew all about it."

"What surprised me was the fact that they placed a lot of significance on my having danced a couple of times with the PM." Kath remarked.

"Yes they certainly had you stumped for a few seconds." He laughed. "Do you think that you will be able to keep them at bay when you are at home and I'm away?"

"I think that I could get used to it." She laughed in return. "Fancy you being considered one of the nations bright young men. I bet my mother wouldn't agree with anything that they might have to say."

By the time that they reached Waterloo Station, all semblance of their last week had disappeared. There was no car to pick them up. There was no Inspector Francis to clear their way, and they finished up carrying their accumulated luggage across London themselves. John thought to himself, it's only the English who can change the whole of your existence, and then have it ripped away simply by taking a train journey.

They arrived at Hainton Station about mid-afternoon and carried their luggage to the front of the station to join the queue for a taxi. The short journey home was soon over, and they sighed with relief when they turned into Arundell Rise. What greeted them looked like something out of a movie!

There were cars blocking the narrow road, so that they couldn't get to their house. Both local TV stations had camera crews there, and the press had turn out in force. The children were watching the whole of the proceedings from the front bedroom window, and Kath's mother was shooing some of the reporters away from the front door. They decided that the best thing that they could do was to run the gauntlet carrying the cases themselves, so that is what they did.

"Here they are!" The cry was followed by a surge towards them.

"Now hold it right there for a minute." John shouted. "We have just arrived home after a long rail journey, and if you will give us just a few minutes to get rid of our luggage, and say 'Hello' to our family, we will come out and answer those questions that we can in about ten minutes. So move a little so that we can get through to the house."

They parted to let them through, and they reach the door to find Kath's mother almost in tears."They wouldn't believe that you weren't here." She sobbed. "They've been all over the garden, even round the back. It's been so bad that I've called the police."

At that point there was a knock at the door. "Mr Robertson?" The policeman asked.

"Yes, that's me!" John responded.

"I think that it would be best if you made a short statement. Sir" He suggested. "Then we can get rid of this wolf pack and get some semblance of peace back to this quiet road." He smiled in sympathy.

"Yes I've already told them that I will do that in about ten minutes. "But we have only been in the house about two minutes before you arrived, and my Mother-in -Law was just telling us that she'd phoned you."

"I understand Sir!" he said in a matter of fact sort of way, "but the sooner you get it done the quicker we can clear them away."

John asked them all to go into the sitting room at the back of the house, and they sat down quietly, and tried to calm themselves down. "Now this is what I will do, John spoke slowly. "I will go out and face the press, make a statement that will be short and sweet the we will all get ready and go out for a meal at 'Colly Mansion', where we can talk about all that has happened this week. So Anne, will you make us all some tea, while I straighten my tie, wipe the lipstick off my face, and decide what I'm going to say when I get out there.?"

Jason spoke next. "Dad, what are you going to be?" The question was a serious one.

"Well I haven't decided yet," John answered, "But whatever the answer is I will still be your Dad, and that's one of the most important things for you to remember. So if you will help me just a bit, by going out into the garden and fastening the side gate, that will be a good job done. Just make sure that it is locked and bolted. I think that we had better keep it that way for a while."

He took off his overcoat, and straightened his tie. Ran a comb through his hair and moved towards the door.

Kath followed him. "Do you want me to come with you love?" She asked him.

"No, I think that the sooner I get this done the better we will be too." John Smiled "I think that your mother could do with a little tender loving care at the moment, don't you?"

"I guess that you're right at that." She said smiling.

He stepped outside, and walked slowly to the garden gate.

"Are you ready Mr Robertson?" The policeman asked.

"Yes let's get on with it." He declared. They all settled down. "Now all that I have to say is this, my wife and I have just returned from the Conservative Party Conference, where, I'm sure you are all aware, we found ourselves in exalted circles. During the week I have discussed many things with Sir Reginald Reevesby, Sir Marius Clarke, Sir John Barker, and last night with the Prime Minister. As far as I am aware, there is no job for me in the Government, primarily because I am not a member of Parliament, and I have not yet decided whether or not I will even seek a seat at the next election. That is something that my wife and I will decide in good time.

The Prime Minister did ask me to send to him 'post haste' a copy of a report that I prepared for this area some weeks ago. What will be the outcome of that I do not know. My family and I have been invited to join the Prime Minister at Downing Street, and later at Chequers, one weekend that has yet to be decided. This has been a very momentous week for me and my family, and as yet there is really nothing that has changed. A copy of the report that the Prime Minister has requested was circulated to all media groups at the end of April this year, but if any of you do not have access to a copy, I will make arrangements for them to be redistributed on Monday. As soon as I have any knowledge of the outcome of these affairs I will issue a press statement to you all. Now , if you will excuse me, I would like to get back inside and have a cup of tea."

He turned to go back into the house. "Could you tell us Councillor Robertson if you intend to seek the vacant seat at Newton Forest? A Voice bellowed. "I can say without a doubt that I will not be attempting to fight that seat." John replied.

"Is you wife a special friend of the Prime Minister?" A female voice asked from the back.

"We are both friends of the Prime Minister, and he has been kind enough to ask us to visit his home." John stated without rancour.

"Will your involvement at National level, affect, in any way your position as Chairman Of Transport in this city?" A man from one of the local TV Stations asked.

"That is a fair question, but the answer is no!" John asserted. "As I said a few moments ago, there has been no offer of a position either at Central Office, or in the Departments of Government that would in any way affect my current position so now if you will excuse me, I'm tired and hungry, and I would like to spend some time with my family. Good afternoon!"

"Come on now lets get this road cleared" The police started to move towards the group. "You heard what the man said so let's have you all on your way. You're all causing an obstruction."

Within a matter of minutes they were gone, the road was clear, with the very distinct exception of a manned police car that was parked visibly under the trees at the end of the Cul-de-sac.

Was this really the start of how things were to be? Had their privacy disappeared in the welter of one week's dream of the future?

28

Work

Robertson's return to Convellium Engineering was one of trepidation. The fact that he had spent a week firmly fixed in the public eye was of little concern to Conrad Barnes. His sole objective was to get cleared the back-log of work that had accumulated during John's absence during the previous week. The fact that the week had been part of John's holiday entitlement was secondary to keeping the flow of work at a satisfactory level. John was into the office very early, knowing full-well what the situation would be, and by the time that Barnes arrived he was immersed in the day to day problems that he would normally have cleared in a matter of hours.

"John!" Barnes called as soon as he had settled himself in his office. "Can you spare me a few minutes?"

John had felt that this would be the case, and moved quickly to join him.

"We are running into trouble," He began, "Trouble with the simple day to day running of the office. The amount of time that you are spending away is hitting us quite significantly, and I must ask that you put more core time into what is after all, the means of supporting your family. I am not suggesting that you are taking unnecessary time away from your job to carry out your commitments to Council, but I feel that because of the volume of work that you have achieved in the past, your public life is having a significant affect here. I know that from reading the papers during the course of the past week that you will soon be leaving us, and for that reason I must start to consider employing someone who will be able to replace you when you are gone. I cannot emphasise enough my feeling of regret about all of this, but you must realise that Convellium Engineering will have to continue when you leave."

"Now hold on a minute Conrad," John was annoyed, "when I applied for promotion, you told me that, and I quote, 'I had the makings of a good engineer, but I needed a few more years of experience before I could be promoted beyond what I am now'. Now you are telling me that I play a pivotal role in the company, and that unless I spend more time doing the work of the company, then my position in the company is in doubt. That just does not make sense. On the one hand, I am not worth a higher position in the company, and on the other I am pivotal to the future well-being of the company. I cannot appreciate that my taking a weeks holiday, which was planned long in advance, can raise the problems that you have indicated. And before I finish I want to make my position absolutely clear, I have not been offered anything by anyone; I have not committed myself to do anything more than I have on at the moment, and when and if I do, you will be the first person with whom I will discuss it. Further to this, anything that has been in the press and on television during the past few days is and has been pure speculation, and I must ask you to remember this."

"Thank you for saying that." Conrad began, "But I don't think that you understand the problem here. The fact is that you have spent a lot of your time here, and I must admit that you have given of your time freely, and now, because of circumstances that have arisen over the course of the last few months, that time has been seriously reduced. Not, I hasten to add, that you haven't fulfilled your contractual obligation to the company, it's that people in your position have always provided services that fall outside the normally accepted terms and conditions of employment."

"What you are saying Conrad, is that you should be able to dictate to me how and when I spend, what is, when all is said and done, my free time." John responded. "That is really not on."

"That is not what I am saying at all." Conrad insisted. "What I am saying is that if you want to participate in local Government, and make up your time outside the normally accepted working hours, that is one thing. But if you intend to run for Parliament, and take some job in government, as the papers have been reporting, then that is an entirely different matter."

"As far as I'm concerned," John stated, "I have not taken a decision on any of these matters, and as I said a few minutes ago, when I take a decision on the matter I will discuss the process with you. In fact I will probably come and ask your advice on the matter before I take a decision."

"This really isn't getting us anywhere." Conrad concluded. "All I know is that if I were in your position I would jump at the offer. It isn't everyday that the Prime Minister asks one of my employees to send him a copy of a report, and the significant fact is that he has never asked me to provide him with anything, let alone invite me and my family to spend a weekend with him. My God I envy you John."

"To be frank Conrad" John confided. "I don't know whether I'm on my arse or my elbow, and that is a fact."

"What ever the outcome give me time to make some alternative arrangements if they are necessary, there's a good chap John!" He concluded.

John returned to his desk just as the rest of the crew were coming into start work.

Harry was the first through the door "Hello John I

didn't expect to find you here today, what with your new job, and all that!"

"There is no new job." John shot back at him. "All that crap in the papers was just hogwash. These journalists have nothing to fill their scandle-rags with, so they tend to make it up as they go along. I still work here, so there's no need to start moving your things across to my desk yet."

"Do I detect a sign of sour grapes?" Harry joked. " But joking aside, what's it like cavorting with the PM and Sir this and Sir that?"

"It's just like me talking to you Harry." John remarked. "They are no different, and as soon as they appear so then they have lost it."

"I didn't think for one moment that it would affect you John." Harry replied. "Nothing would change you from the bloke that you are."

"Thank you for that Harry, you don't know how much that simple remark means to me." John felt a great sympathy for this man he felt humble, and that was the way that it should be.

He tried to settle down for a normal days work, and soon the requirements of the shopfloor meant that he had to walk down through the bays of the assembly shop to sort out a problem. He stuck to his usual routine of stopping and asking all of those who he knew well how they were, and how they had spent their weekends. Nothing controversial; Nothing political but there was the inevitable ribbing, and coarse remarks, all of the things that he would expect from these down to earth individuals who he'd known for years. Nothing could phase them they called a spade a spade, and there was little that could pass them by without some form of comment. These were the people that he knew best, and they accepted him for what he was.

When he returned to the office there was the usual

Monday call from Germany, asking him to return the call when he was available. He called Doktor Linz.

"Ah! John, it is good to hear from you." He greeted him warmly. "I just wanted to let you know that I will be coming across to see Conrad next week, and wondered if you could arrange for me to go round your transport department whilst I am there?"

"That will be no problem at all." John assured him. "What is more, I will see if our Lord Mayor can see you for a few minutes. He is the same as your burgermeister."

"That would be excellent." Linz replied. "I will bring a letter of good wishes from our burgrmeister, who happens to be my brother. Who knows what that might lead to."

"We will make your usual reservation at 'The Millington Hotel'" John informed him. "What day and at what time will you arrive?"

"I will be flying in on the early morning the Lufthansa flight will arrive at Birmingham Airport at nine thirty in the morning of Tuesday." Linz responded. "Will you arrange for a car to pick us up as usual?"

"Yes that will be no problem." John answered.

"Then I will look forward to seeing you, and your new department." He sounded really interested in seeing how things were run in England. "Good bye until next Tuesday."

"Good bye Wolfgang" John concluded.

Robertson thought that at least there was one person in his working life who felt pleased that he was putting in some effort for the good of his community.

29

Forward Planning

It was getting close to the period of the year when all of the departments of Council started to prepare their budgets for the coming year, and to put together the projected plans for the next five years. The CityTransport department was no exception, and a whole range of committee meetings were needed to get agreement with the Treasury Department, and Finance Committee. As was predictable in any year the Party in power was seeking to reduce the rates and at the same time increase the range of services that they provided. Any housewife could have told them that what they had embarked on was 'Mission Impossible'. But still the leader of the party decided that the exercise required his personal attention to root out all of the Pet Projects that department heads had been trying to introduce to the system for years past.

The cost cutting exercise for the Transport Department was no exception, and out went all of the proposed Security cameras and video records that the Unions had so vehmently opposed at the out set. Out went all of the Garage improvement works. Out went all of the New Bus Shelters in exposed positions. Out went all of the new light controlled pedestrian crossings and the bus replacement programme was slowed down to increase the number of years that buses were required to be in service. John left the meeting in a state that was on the verge of explosion, because many of the things that he had bargained for in his election campaign were summilary deleted at the stroke of a pen, without discussion and without reference to the previous election manifesto. There was no justice in many of the actions, and why was it simply because the leader had agreed with the City Treasurer that they would cut the budget in line with Government Guidelines. That was hardly representing the wishes of the people. John had returned to his office in a steamng temper. His first caller was the Chief Engineer. "I wondered if I might come in and see you chairman" He had asked.

"Yes you may!" John had snarled. "But I give you fair warning that I am not in the best of moods."

"That I can understand Chairman, if what I hear is correct." He answered.

"Then you had better come up and tell me the sorry tale, Ian." He calmed a little.

The chief was not a happy man, and it was plain to see as he stepped into the room. "Well I have a serious problem at the Greenfields Depot, the Health and Safety Boys have just condemned as dangerous, all of the overhead lighting and all of the wiring in the Garage and Workshops. They have said that unles we present them with a programme for the gradual replacement of all the electrics by the end of this month, they will close the place as a hazard."

"Now tell me that the replacement program has just been scrapped at the budget review." John smiled for the first time that day.

"Yes Chairman!" He too smiled. "The rewiring of the place has been included and deleted from the Budget for the next financial year."

"Don't come round the desk Ian" John thumped the desk. "because if you do you will be in serious danger of being kissed."

"In that case I'd best stay in this side of the divide, if you don't mind Chairman." He replied ruefully. All of the details for the Budget had to be completed by the end of October, and at that time the Leader of the Council had to seek re-election as leader by his party. In normal circumstances there would have been no doubt about the existing leader being elected for another year in office, but this year there were many who would have liked to see a change to the Charles Browns leadership. He had ridden rough-shod over many of those in his own party, and there was a strong tide of opinion against him.

"The trouble with Charles," thought Robertson, "is that he thinks that everybody thinks exactly the same thought that he does. The truth is that they don't. But he does not ask the questions of the members of his party, he simply expects every one to follow like a herd of lost sheep."

John had no designs on the leadership, he was finding it quite enough to handle his own department, continuing to do his wage earning job, and travelling all over the place speaking. This had really taken off since the party conference, and there were two or three constituencies who were vying for him to become their prospective candidate. All things considered, it had not been a bad year.

John had now been a member of council for nearly eighteen months, and the Transport Undertaking was now breaking even, in purely financial terms. It had been his brief at the outset to make transport pay for itself, and initially it had been thought that it would take about four years to turn the two point five million pound deficit into a small profit. It had transpired that the policy was more effective than had been envisaged, and the Undertaking would be in profit for the start of the new financial year.

The fact that the Council was now being forced to take actions that had been included in the budget estimates for the past five years, and each year they had been deleted as an unnecessary expenditure, were in the set in the mind of John Robertson as a sort of poetic justice. Now all of the Officers and the Leader would have to admit that they had been wrong to remove the item from the Budget.

He phoned Charles Brown. "Leader I have a matter of some urgency to discuss with you." He said.

"I'm afraid that I'm in with the City Treasurer." He started to excuse himself. "We are in the process of finalising the budget. So I can't see you until tomorrow."

"This matter has serious implications for the Transport Budget for the next year." John pressed him. And I demand to be heard."

"Tell me about it now!" He demanded.

"This matter is so serious I am not prepared to discuss it over an open phone line." John replied.

"Are you sure about this John?" He tempered his tone.

"I am absolutely 100% certain" John stated bluntly.

"Then you had better get round here as quickly as you can." Brown decided.

John lost no time in getting round to the Town Hall and he took the Chief Engineer along with him to support his claim. He was shown straight into the Leaders office, where he found the Treasurer, the Chief Executive, and the City Secretary and Solicitor around the conference table.

"Well John now tell me what is so important that it can't wait!" He snapped.

"This!" John snapped back, and handed him the report from the Health and Safety Executive.

Brown read the summary of the document, and placed it on the table in front of him. "Is that all? They're always doing that sort of thing."

"No that is not all" John insisted. "If you had

bothered to read the Chief Engineers report on this garage you would be aware that this garage has been in operation since the end of First World War, and much of the over-head wiring is unprotected copper wire. That means that it has no insulation of any kind. We spray our bus bodies in this shop, and while that is underway the air becomes volatile. In layman language that means explosive. I am surprised that the HSE has allowed this to go on for as long as it has. We are asking people to work in highly dangerous conditions, and if the Unions get wind of this we will have the whole fleet out on strike."

The Chief Executive picked up the report and read it, and passed it to the City Secretary and Solicitor, and then said. "What Councillor Robertson says is correct, but more to the point they are telling us that if we have not rectified the problem before the end of this year, they will prosecute us. Our duty is clear, Councillor Robertson has included the refurbishment in his budget, and you Leader, have seen fit to remove it. The onus of responsibility is now with you, and in his wisdom, Councillor Robertson is now asking you to reconsider the decision. This is not a matter of political manipulation this is an attempt by a shrewd Chairman to give notice of the consequences of an action that has been taken by someone who was not in full possession of the facts when the decision was taken. My advice in this matter is that we should reinstate the refurbishment of this Garage and also ask that the Transport Department commence works before the start of the new financial year. I think that we have been saved from a potential disaster. Thank you Councillor for your vigilance in this matter"

"Then we have no alternative." Brown conceded. "I think that we should also survey all of the depots and have reports to the Finance and Transport

Committees." He added.

30

Red Herring

The first murmurings of discontent reached John via his Vice-Chairman. It was his habit to go into the Town Hall each Saturday morning to pick up any post that there was in his post-box, and to assist with any of the Parties of Visitors who wished to be shown around the building. The tour of the building took about an hour, and Robertson enjoyed meeting the people and showing them the inside of a building that they would not normally see.

On this particular Saturday there were no parties to be shown round, and having picked up his mail, Robertson made his way to the members Sitting Room, and started to sift through the envelopes.

"Ah John, I'm glad that I've managed to find you here," It was the Vice-Chairman of the Transport Committee.

"Hello Frank!" Robertson smiled "We don't usually see you in the Town Hall on a Saturday morning."

"No I usually spend the day down at the Golf Club." He was clearly uncomfortable. "But this morning I needed to speak to you on an urgent matter, but you had left home before I rang, and Kathryn told me that this is where I would find you."

"Come on Frank, there is something on your mind that you have to discuss with me." John could see that he was not sure of his ground. "You might just as well get it off your chest."

"Well it's like this John," He began, "It's nearly time to elect our new Party Officers for the coming year, and whether you are aware of it or not there is a great deal of discontent with the leadership of Charles Brown. Now before you reply, let me have my say. The problem with Charles is that he does not discuss the policy of the Conservative Group with the members of the Group. He simply announces a Policy when he has put together what he believes the Policy should be. There are about ten members of the Group who have raised this question with him, and he refuses to discuss the matter with any of us. We have held a couple of meetings, and we have decided that to make the process more democratic, we should oppose him in the election of the leader of the party in council when it is held at the Group Annual Meeting next week. I have been detailed to ask you the main question because it was the unanimous decision of our little group, that you should be asked to run against him when the time comes, and as it stands you would both stand a fifty-fifty chance of being elected leader."

"What the hell made you think that I wanted to be the Leader of Council?"

John was amazed at the proposal. "I am only just beginning to get the hang of running the Transport Department, how do you all think that I would manage to look after the whole Shooting Match?"

"Well the facts of the matter are simple." He started. "Charles Brown has had a year and six months to demonstrate to us his style of leadership, and what he has done is simply to show us that he cannot trust the rest of his party with his idea of how the business of Council should be conducted.

The group, that is our group of about ten members believe that you would make a better leader of Council than he has shown us he can be, and we are putting your name forward as a candidate to oppose him."

"Now hold on a minute!" Robertson was now beginning to see where this was leading. "If I don't want to be the Leader, then there is little point in putting my name forward."

"The whole point about this is that we can put your name forward as a candidate, and there is nothing in the rules of the group that says that we have to tell you what we are doing." It was clear that he was going ahead with this with or without John's agreement.

"This is hardly fair or democratic," John protested, "On the one hand you say that Charles Brown does not give you a democratic say in the running of the partys policies in Council, and on the other hand you are denying me the right not to be a candidate for the leader of the Group. Now I am truly flattered by the trust that you want to place in me, but do you really think that a man who has only been in politics for a few months, is qualified to lead a Council as big as Hainton?"

"The truth is that you are a high profile Politician, not only locally but nationally," Frank was persistent. "You are a friend of the Prime Minister, and are well known in the higher echelons of the National Party. The feeling is that before too long you will be off into Parliament, and the Local Group will not have had the benefit of your contacts or your expertise. Charles Brown is not at all helpful to us, and the general consensus is that you would be. The whole of the party has been amazed by your actions in the Transport Department. It was felt that when we came into office if there was one area where there could be serious problems is was in the field of Public Transport. That was because of the hold that the TGWU had in all of the depots. You have taken that all in your stride, your experience in the Trades Union Movement yourself, and as a voice of reason that will hear all of the problems in a quiet and non-confrontational way, has won them and the conservative management of the Undertaking over, in a way that nobody believed was possible. Well we believe that it is time that your sort of Political control was brought to the whole Council, and we will try to get you elected to lead, with or without your permission."

"Come on now please be reasonable Frank." John protested yet again. " I can't set up shop in opposition to Charles Brown, he is after all the man who brought me into politics in the first place. There has to be some elements of loyalty even in the mire of local Politics."

"That is not true and you know it John." Frank was adamant. "The trouble with you is that you believe in the concepts of service and support, well that doesn't wash in this sort of politics. Charles Brown would hang you out to dry given half an opportunity. He hates your natural ability to be able to get on with everybody, and what is more I'll bet there's some joyful little toad who is speaking to him in respect of this conversation right now."

"Oh come off it Frank." John laughed. "Don't you think that you're getting just a bit paranoid?"

"John, this is not a joke." He was deadly serious. "The whole place is filled with people who he pays to keep him informed. What is more, there are voice activated recorders in most of these rooms, and he spends time each day listening to them for items of interest from both sides of the chamber. My belief is that one of the Security Staff is on his payroll to keep all of the machines serviced, and to let him know when there is something that he should hear."

"It sounds like the blasted Kremlin." John responded. "I thought that we had progressed beyond all that sort of thing."

"That is why we want to get him away from the Leadership." Frank went back to the attack. "There is far too much wheeling and dealing, that has nothing to do with the running of Council. We are looking for a real politician to run this town, not someone who is there primarily for his own ends. We want you to run for Leadership, but I will not try to delude you, because if you fail, you will not retain the Chair of Transport or indeed any of your other committee attachments."

"I cannot give you an answer one way or the other." John answered. "I need time to think this matter out properly before I make a decision. I don't think that I will be able to afford the Leadership, because I rely on my full-time occupation for my total income. Un-like many of you others, I do not have private means to support me when I am not working. Charles Brown does. I will not be rushed into this matter, it must be a carefully considered process, and all that I will say at this time is that I will consider the proposition."

"That is all that we can ask John, but I must warn you that if you do not let us know within thew next two days we will look for another candidate and still put your name forward."

"That is the worst kind of blackmail Frank and you know it." John stated at Jamison and walked out of the Members Sitting Room without another word.

John sat in stunned silence, the 'Old Club' atmosphere of polished tables oak panelling and leather chairs, serving only to add to the shock of what he had just heard. Never again would he feel any element of peace or tranquillity in this lovely old place. Could it be that it was all facade, the building nothing but a receptacle for all of the schemes and distortions that people brought into it? Was there nothing in this world that anybody could hang their hat on without getting all of their preformed ideas mashed into fragments The idea of secret tape recorders astounded him, it was something that should only happen in spy novels and films, it reduced the value of what he believed he should be doing, and perhaps that was what Frank and his group were trying to get at.

He made his way back to the front of the building, and passed the Sergeant Major from the Messenger Corps, it did not seem possible that these trusted and revered former members of the armed services could be purchased for a few pounds. He did not have the time to ponder the problem longer, in order to justify his continued employment by Convellium Engineering he would have to spend the rest of the day working in his office. Perhaps there were elements of truth in what Frank had said, but could John be certain that he too was only trying to get John out of the way so that he could become the Chairman of Transport, just like his Grandfather had been before him. Could be that this was a sort of family status that was to achieved regardless of the cost to others?

He had to unlock the main gate when he arrived at the company, after all nobody in their right mind would be working on a fine Saturday in September. John felt no pangs of regret, he enjoyed his work, and it didn't really matter to him when and where he had to do it. He was not alone for long, Conrad Barnes arrived shortly after John, and after a short greeting they both settled down to work. One of the beauties of working on Saturdays is the fact that very few other people do so, inconsequence of which there are very few interruptions, so the volume of work that can be accomplished is very high. By two-thirty in the afternoon John had achieved his target, and was in the process of clearing his desk when Conrad came out of his office. "Do you fancy a pint and a natter for a few minutes?" He asked.

"Yes!" John replied. "That's a very good idea."

They ambled out to the Red Firkin, the pub at the end of the road, and settled themselves, each behind a cool pint of bitter.

"How are things going with you John?" Conrad could see that he had something on his mind.

"Not good Conrad." John sighed. "It's all basically as you told me that it would be. Rather like walking on quick-sand, and everybody waiting for you to make the slip that will finish you forever."

"The Political life has alway been a precarious one." Conrad spoke as if he knew what it was all about. "The trouble has always been that local politicians have always had a difficult job; the local population think that they can fit it all in and still do a full time job. So they have never thought that they needed paying for any of their duties, and when they did finally start paying them attendance allowances, the local press published their allowances like a list of money that had been stolen from the local old peoples home. The truth is that there are still many people who believe that Councils like this one here, can be run by amateurs who have either full-time jobs or run their own businesses. The truth is that with budgets of nearing £800M a year, many local Councils have more need for full time elected heads of department than some quoted companies."

"Yes that is my problem." John admitted. "I run, and I do mean that, run the City's Transport Department. It has a fleet of over Five Hundred Buses and it employs two thousand three hundred people in five different locations; it carries nearly a hundred million passengers a year, and its revenue/turnover exceeds £180M per year, and we are expected to deal with all of the problems, and all of the strategy for running this Undertaking in, our spare time. The thing that bugs me most is the fact there are people getting paid large salaries to administer these Undertakings, but most of them are like absent landlords, away either on Departmental business (and the definition of

285

Council Business is very, very broad), or on extended sick leave. Do you know that they can be away from work for 26 weeks sick on full pay, and then 26 weeks on half pay, and nobody can touch them. My General Manager has only been in his office for fifteen working days in the last six months, and the Deputy had been away on extended sick leave for more than four months, so the whole administrative burden has fallen on me and the Chief Engineer.

And to add to all of that the Chief has now given notice that he is leaving to take up a post with another authority. Which really doesn't help you Conrad, and it certainly doesn't help me, but I really had to have someone to unload it on, just to clear my mind."

"Then what I have to say to you is going pour oil on the wound." Conrad lowered his voice. "The facts of the matter are simple Convellium Engineering is slowly going bankrupt."

"It's what?" John exploded.

"Now just before you say things that you may regret," Conrad tried to calm him. "Let me finish what I was saying. We have had a good number of contracts in the past two years that have either just broken even or we have lost money on them. This years Results are going to be the worst we've had since I came to the company over twenty-five years ago. The losses are going to be in the order of about seven million pounds, and we cannot stand another year like this one. What is worse, things are not improving. If anything they are getting worse. The truth is that if we don't get a substantial order in the next two months I will have to start laying people off."

"I thought that when we got that order from Dr Linz it would give us a little breathing space." Robertson had now forgotten about his political problems. "Why has it not had the desired effect?"

"It really is the old story." Conrad explained. "To be able to quote the price that ensured that we would get the job, I had to have some of the more expensive units, made and assembled by our suppliers. We have had them done that way when we were too busy to do them ourselves, and the fact is that they can make the parts and assemble them much cheaper than we can do them in our own works. On this particular order price was critical, so I have had to bite the bullet, and have them made where they are cheapest. The result is simple, we have a large contract where the majority of the manufacture is being done by suppliers, and all that our workers will have to do is assemble the units when they are delivered. We have a satisfied customer, but we only need about half of the work force that we needed for a similar job in the past."

"So what you are saying is that if this trend continues, Convellium will become nothing more than a design office and assembly shop." John deduced. "so most of the Engineering Staff will have to go as well."

"That is not the real problem though." Conrad interrupted John's thoughts. "We are in a state of flux, changing from one form of manufacture to a completely new way of working. We have to buy all of our requirements and pay for them on the basis of payment after sixty-days following delivery. Some of our assemblies will be in our works for up to one hundred and twenty days before they are dispatched as part of a complex multi- machine manufacturing process so that the amount of money that we have tied up in inventory has increased about two-fold in the past three months. Our liquidity is becoming a critical factor, and despite my efforts the Banks will not increase the level of borrowing against either individual contracts or against the assets of the company as a whole. In short, whilst we have a pretty full order book, the facts are that we are gradually being squeezed out of business because we cannot finance the through-put of our orders."

"What about the Governments Export Credit System?" John was thinking out loud. "Wouldn't that help you over the hump, so to speak?"

"No not really." Conrad smiled to himself. "To be blunt, by the time that you've managed to get all of the documentation sorted out, the need for the credit requirement has passed. But the real reason for me being here today, is because that the situation is so difficult that the rest of the Board have asked me to find some immediate savings, and basically they've asked me to terminate your contract at the earliest possible convenience."

John was speechless. He tried to express his feelings, but words would just not come to his lips. He waved his hands, palms upper-most, as was his habit. But nothing would kick-start his sound system.

"I know that this must come as a great shock to you," Conrad started to say. "but..........

"But, Bloody nothing" John found his voice. "You mean to say that after all that guff about my having to make up all of the hours that I took off to carry out Council Business, that set of jerks still feel that I've been skiving off, and not doing my hours or job?" He was getting into full swing now. "Do you really want to know why you got the last order from Dr Linz? Well I will tell whether you want to know or not. Harry cocked the contract up, and he quoted them a price that was over 15% higher than it should have been. He phoned me in a panic thinking that he had lost the company the contract, and I recalculated the prices down to the correct level, and then spoke to Linz, who gave you the contract on my verbally revised figures. And now what do I find, I find that all of the hours that

I've spent slaving away here at night and at week-ends count for nothing. I find that all the years that I stayed here waiting on false promises, all that counts for nothing when it comes to a few insignificant and incompetent money grubbers who only believe what they see, and to whom there is no such thing as loyalty, I guess that I've said as much as I need to say."

"Well you have got every right to feel aggrieved." Conrad paused. "But how do you think that I feel, I've devoted nearly thirty-five years of my life to this company, and my dismissal came to me via a messenger on a motor bike about mid-afternoon yesterday."

Conrad was almost in tears, and it was only by a great effort that he did not break down in tears. John was bitterly ashamed of his outburst. It's strange how one reacts to personal bad news. The whole thing tends to blot out everything else, and the personal self becomes the only thing that can be affected by any sort of public announcement. The being becomes lost in a field of its own isolated grief, and it does not react to the plight of others caught in the same trap.

"My God" John's feet slammed into the magnitude of what Conrad had just related to him. "How the hell can they do that? After all that you've done for the company. Damn it all!" He slammed the table. "That is your company, and they've taken from you." He rested his head on his hands and his elbows on the table.

Conrad continued calmly. "We have both been given one week in which to clear out our personal equipment and papers. Our entitlements will be available to us on Tuesday of next week. Other than that, we are not required to attend as from yesterday at 17.00.hours. That is OK from my point of view because I have received an official notification, but you have not, as yet. You have not been dismissed, so you must have been made redundant and as such you are entitled to a formal notification telling you of your reason for dismissal, and the details of your redundancy package. You cannot receive that through the post, it has to be given to you by a competent manager, and explained in detail. If I were you I would make contact with your union branch chairman and tell him what is happening. If they cite your Council work as the reason for your being made redundant then they are in trouble via the tenets of the Employment Protection Act."

"Conrad, will you please stop worrying about me." John insisted. "They can't simply step in and take your Company away from you. You must put up a fight! I have a legacy that will comfortably see me through any of this outrageous action but you really must fight."

"I don't want to fight John." He smiled. "As far as I'm concerned they can all go and fry in Hell. All I want is my money pulled out of the firm, that is all of my money, and then all those self-righteous bastards can find out for themselves just how easy it is to make a profit in Engineering, year in year out. I'll do what they've been doing this past ten years. I'll sit back and chant 'give me the money, give me the money, give me the money, and see how they like it."

"Who is taking over the day to day running of the site?" John enquired. "That is until they appoint a new Managing Director."

"Now that is a stroke of great genius." Barnes laughed. "It was accidental that you mentioned Harold in your initial outburst, because he is now in charge at Convellium."

"That is a sick joke Conrad." John shook his finger at him. "That is a joke and it's not a funny one either. Now tell me who have they draughted in to be the acting MD."

"That wasn't a joke John." Conrad laughed. "I was

deadly serious." He paused for a moment. " I thought that it was best if you learned all of this from me, because if the News Hounds get hold of this today, it will be all over the National Newspapers tomorrow and this way you get to tell your family yourself, if you get my drift."

"God I hate to think of what my family are going to say!" John mused. "As it is I think that I will go and clear my desk now. It will save me the embarrassment of having to do it with all of my friends and colleagues watching me."

"I think that I will do like-wise." Conrad added. "Then I can drop you off with all of your things at home."

They both returned to their respective offices and began the process of clearing away the accumulated trappings of years of endeavour. John became more and more depressed as he packed items and papers in the boxes that he had collected from the dispatch department. Within an hour they had both completed the sorry task, and their sum total of a collective thirty-five years of working life, had been packed into five cardboard boxes.

"You wouldn't think that all of those memories could be condensed into this would you John?" Conrad commented. "Well I think that from here on I'll adopt the attitude of an old friend of mine, he said, 'that one should never accumulate anything in a place of work that you couldn't pick up and depart with in five minutes. I think that he has been right all of these years, and I've always argued against his thought."

"I suppose it's like being in the Navy really," John added. "Those chaps pick up their grips, and depart at a few minutes notice, but when they change ships all of their allegiances are transferred with their kit, and the never go back to their old ships do they?"

They both carried their boxes down to the car and piled them into the boot and on the back seats. They drove off knowing that this would be their penultimate visit to the place that had been their working life for so many years. That in it's self was bad enough, but now they had to go and' drop the bomb-shell' to their respective wives, and that would be even worse. As they drove Conrad admitted, "I haven't gathered the courage to tell my wife the news, even though I have known for more that twenty-four hours. I really don't know what to say to her, and I know that she will be really cut-up about how it will affect me."

"Ours will be a full family conference," John spoke almost to the air. "We will all sit around and discuss that cause and affect, along with a possible out -come. But it still won't really give us any idea of what the real outcome will be. In truth we can sit here and muse about it until the Day of Judgement and still be no wiser about the future than we are now."

"I suppose that you are right." Conrad agreed. "But we must keep in touch, no matter what happens."

"Of course we will keep in touch." John replied. "I've got to keep in touch with you, you are my Political Agent, and now that I have joined the ranks of those who are only Part-time workers, I will have the opportunity to further my Political Career."

"Do you really mean that John?" Barnes spoke earnestly. "Of course I mean it." John was surprised. "You don't think that I would trust an old reprobate like Charles Brown with my Political Future, do you?"

They had now arrived at the Robertson household, and Conrad followed John down the path carrying the second of John's two boxes. They were met at the side door by Kath. "Hello!" She smiled. "Moving house again?"

"In a manner of speaking" John answered.

"Why what's happened?" She looked from one to the other.

"We are both in the process of being ejected from our jobs." John replied, there being no easy way to soften the blow.

"Both of you" She asked quietly.

"Yes both of us." Conrad joined in the conversation. "The Board sent me my dismissal yesterday, by courier, and John's Redundancy Notice is to be given to him on Monday."

"Wow! That's a bit of a blow." Kath exploded. "I could understand John being high on the list of those whose services could be dispensed with, because of his heavy involvement in the City Council, but you Conrad, you have been the prime mover in the building of the Company. How can they justify dismissing you. I thought that you were the largest single share-holder in the Company."

"I am!" He admitted. "But the fact is that alone, I only hold about 15% of the total share-holding in the company, and I am also a paid employee. I am only being dismissed from the job, not from my holding. The real truth is that I have already asked my Stock Brokers to sell all of my holding in the company, and even at the currently depressed valuation there will be enough to see me through, and I will of course be entitled to a fairly large Redundancy Payment as indeed will John."

"When will you both be finished?" Kath enquired.

"I'm already finished." Conrad replied. "And I think that John will be formally notified on Monday. Unless they've done to him the same as they've done to me that is to send it through the post to you because they haven't got the bottle to tell you to your face."

"Just a minute, there's a stack of mail that I put in John's study." Kath murmured. She wandered off and then returned sorting absently through a pile of envelopes. "I can't see anything that's obvious." She spoke as to herself.

"There!" Conrad indicated over her shoulder. She stopped, and handed the envelope to John. He opened the letter and looked at the lead sheet of what appeared to be a lengthy document, and then began to read:-

'Dear John,

By the time that you get this letter you will probably know about the re-structuring of the Company, and the departure of Conrad Barnes, so I will get to the point. The company has not been performing well for the past two or three years, in line with much of the Manufacturing Sector. But this years results leave us no alternative but to make cuts in our overheads, and in the ways that we achieve our final product at a competetive price.

Of late your commitment to the Company has not been what we would expect from one of our senior engineers because of your move into the field of Politics. It is therefore, with great regret that I have to inform you that the position that you currently hold will cease to exist as from the 30th of September, and that accordingly, there being no equivalent job available in the company so you will be made Redundant as from that date.You will not be required to attend at the Company as from the date of your receiving this letter, and arrangements will be made for you to collect those personal belongings that you may have left in the Company.

May I take this opportunity of thanking you for your service to the company over the past ten years, and give you our very best wishes for the future.

Yours etc..

Well that put's it all in a nutshell doesn't it?" He paused reflectively. "I'm glad now that we stopped and collected all of this stuff. I think that I might have been inclined to bop somebody on the nose if I'd found out about this first thing on Monday morning."

"I think that I'd better leave you two young people to decide what you are going to do." Conrad made off towards the door. "I'll give you a call on Monday morning John."

"OK! Conrad." John waved, "I'll be down at the Transport Department from about nine onwards. I suppose that I can spend even more time down there now that I will be holding a Redundancy Certificate."

"We'll talk about that on Monday, after you've found out what your package is like." Barnes called from the garden path. "OK?"

"Yes! Right Ho". And he turned to face, a very straight-faced Kathryn. "What the hell has been going on?" She demanded to know. "Why has Barnes been sacked, and why have you been made redundant?"

"The truth is that I don't really know what has been going on." John offered.

"Now don't you start coming that little-boy lost routine with me" She countered. "This is Kathryn, your wife who you are talking to, not some innocent little old lady down by the Market. Companies like Convellium do not dismiss Share-Holding Managers of Barnes seniority at the drop of a hat. There has to be some sort of legal matter before they do that sort of thing."

"This is what I understand has happened" John explained. "The 'end of year results' have shown that the Company has lost £7M during the course of the last twelve months, and that unless a profit is shown in this current year then chances are that the company will be dissolved. The manufacturing costs are very high, and the decision has been taken to change the format of the company from an in-house make and assemble company, to a company that buys all of it's needs from suppliers, and becomes a build and test company. That being the case, and being a production engineer then I am surplus to their requirement. So they are making me redundant."

"John Robertson, you are without a doubt the most infuriating person who ever walked the face of this earth." Kath clenched her fists in frustration. "How can you stand there and analyse the situation, with such calm deliberation, and explain what is happening. It's your job that we are talking about. It's our house, our food, and they are taking it all away from us."

"But it is how I have earned my living for the past ten years." He explained. "I always knew that if I did my job properly, there would come a day when I would work myself out of a job. It looks as though that day has arrived, and there is nothing that I can do about it. In reality I cannot see Convellium surviving. The trend of the markets is away from manufacturing, and the cheaper labour costs in Eastren Europe and the far East will make it very difficult for people in this country and Western Europe generally to compete on price alone."

"Oh ! my God! He's at it again." Kath looked towards the heavens. "I think that we had better get used to the idea that you are going to be a full-time politician, and cut our cloth accordingly."

"I don't think that we can make spot decisions Kath luv," John stated solemnly, "We need to have a full family meeting so that we can decide which way we go. Without a full-time job for any length of time there will have to be some cuts in what we do and how much we spend. So it is essential that we discuss it with Anne and Jason before we make a final decision. We do have the buffer of the large sum of money that I was left so things are not too bad when you consider that I will also get quite a good redundancy payment."

"I don't think that you are being realistic about this at all John." Kath said calmly. "If you consider your employment prospects alone; who do you think is going to even consider employing you when half of the time you will be away on Council Business? The second point is this:- When will you get a better opportunity to make an entry into the real world of politics than you have now? Everything has been going your way. You have made some very good contacts, and the free time that you'll have for the next few months you can spend doing the rounds of Conservative Association Meetings, and buttering up all of those little old ladies who find you so attractive. You will have a fairly large Redundancy Settlement plus the money we have in reserve from the Catton bequest and we can use that to finance ourselves until after the next General Election. Then if you haven't got anywhere, you will have to withdraw from Politics and get yourself a Proper Job. In the meantime my news is that I have been asked to work full-time for the next year so at least the finances will not fall apart."

"When did you start planning all of this Mata Hari? John asked sternly.

"I don't understand the question Sir!" She responded coyly.

"You've been working on this for some time now, haven't you?" he persisted.

"In a way" She admitted. "You know since I had my operation I have felt really good, and at work they started talking about more hours, and then promotion. You know the things I mean, and when I asked if they would consider me for a full time position now that my problem had been sorted,they were all for it. So I've been training for a new job for the past two weeks. I thought that I would wait and see if I was going to be any good at before I said anything. But the people at work have said that I am getting on much more quickly than they thought I would and they have asked me to start the new job on Monday, And, and I'm really pleased with myself. So as things appear to be going well I thought it was time that you did what you really want to do as well. So let's give it a try!" She squeezed him conspiratorially, and smiled. "With a little gentle restraint on spending and with the attendance allowances that you get we should be able to manage for more than a couple of years or so. But I don't think that all of those little old ladies will be able to keep their hands off you for that long."

"You really are something else Kathryn Wilson!" John whispered as he kissed her. "And I thought that I was the planner and the politician."

"We all have our little uses." She purred gently.

"There is one matter that we should all be aware of." He suddenly voiced.

"And what might that be?" Kath asked.

"If the press get hold of this today, it might make the National Press to morrow." He replied.

"Yes I suppose that there is that to it." She added. "But it is nothing that we can't handle. After all we are experienced in these matters."

As it was the weekend passed without any problems. That is except for the meeting with Anne and Jason, both of whom baited John unmercifully about his being a 'kept man'. It surprised him the ease with which they accepted that he had been dismissed out of hand and that he would now be concentrating his efforts on his political career. If John's father had tried to do what he was doing then there would have been murder committed.

He was really lucky that he had a wife and family who were preparde to work things out together, took decisions and then supported each other to try to achieve the objective. John decided to telephone Charles Brown and let him know about the situation that had developed. He was fairly mute about the whole thing, but asked John to see him in his office at the Town Hall at 11.30 am. on Monday morning. John was a little put off by the lack of concern that Charles had shown for his predicament.

John spent the rest of the afternoon and early evening getting his diary up to date and making sure that he knew what free dates he had for the next few weeks. He sorted out a couple of free days, and then telephoned Horace Parker down in Handlebury.

"Hello Mr Parker." He replied when the phone was answered. "This is John Robertson speaking."

"Hello John!" Parker responded. "This is strange, I was just going to write to you to see if we could agree a couple of dates for you to come down here and learn a little about Handlebury."

"Well that is why I decided to phone you." John said. "I thought that you might have difficulty getting hold of me by phone, because we have moved home recently, and we have had to go ex directory because we are getting a few nuisance calls. How shall we approach this?"

"I think that it would be best if you tell me the days of the month that you will have to be at home," Parker suggested. "And then I will give you a few dates when we have events arranged, and then you can see if you can get the date to match."

They poured back and forth through their diaries and finally agreed two sets of dates where it would be possible for John and Kathryn to visit the Constituency and meet all of the people who were able to influence the selection of a Prospective Candidate, Having done that, Horace asked. "Have you completed the necessary documents to send to Central Office to allow your name to be put on the List of Approved Candidates?"

"Yes!" John replied. "The last set of necessary papers were put into the Post to Marius Clarke yesterday."

"Excellent John" Parker was clearly pleased. "I've spoken to the people down here about you, and they want to meet you and your family, if that is possible."

"Kathryn will be coming down with me." John told him. "But my daughter is swotting ready for her finals, and my son plays football for the local team and trains two nights each week. They might not be able to get down for the first visit but no doubt they will come down for the second."

"That's first class John." Parker responded. "The people here are eager to select a candidate who is married, with children who take a keen interest in political life. When I told them that you had children still at school, they were very enthusiastic. So we will make arrangements for you to stay at the local hotel, and we will see you in two weeks time. The main event that week-end is a garden fete that will be held in the grounds of Handlebury Manor, that's the home of Colonel Fortescue- Robertson. He's not any relation is he?"

"Not that I'm aware of." John laughed.

"There will be a dance in the Hall of the Manor House in the evening." Horace continued. They are rather boring affairs, but I'm sure that I don't have to tell you about them."

They tied up all of the details and said their farewells. On an impulse, when he had finished with Horace Parker, John telephoned Reg Reevesby, but he was not available. He worked at the pile of letters that he had waiting for reply until he suddenly realised that it was getting dark. When he looked at the clock it had moved round to nearly five-thirty. Where had the day gone, where had a lot of other things gone. He put on the light and strolled through into the lounge to find Kath asleep on the settee. Anne was up in her room, and Jason had gone round to visit a school friend at his house.

John returned to his correspondence, and Committee Papers for about an hour, and he then joined Kath in the lounge. She had just started setting out a light meal on the coffee table, when the phone rang, and being the nearest to it she picked it up.

"Guten Arbend, Herr Doctor Linz!" She trilled. "Sehr gute Danke und ihnen? Ja! Bitte warten."

"Hello Wolfgang!" John took up the phone. "It's good to hear from you again. I didn't know that you had my home number."

"I was speaking to Conrad about today's developments, and I asked him for your contact details." Dr Linz replied. "All of the details in our records are for your old address, so it took me a little time to find you. Conrad tells me that both of you have been discharged by your Company, as part of their rationalisation. Had I known that, I would not have signed the contract when Harry Richards was here two months ago. I am very disturbed by the situation that has developed at Convellium. That was the initial reason for my firstly calling Conrad, and secondly calling you."

"Well I can assure you that neither I nor Conrad had been made aware of any change in the emphasis of the company." John informed him.

"There is not the slightest of doubt in my mind, that had you known anything of the changes you would have informed us, so that we could make a 'Gericht'. How do you say this?"

"It is a 'judgement' Wolfgang." John stated.

"Ja! Das is it." Linz accepted. "So that we could make a sound judgement in the matter, but that is all over and done with now, and it is time to move on to new and more exciting things. Conrad says that he will be a wealthy man once the 'Aufsichtsrat' er! The board of directors of the Company have bought his portion of the company from him."

"Yes!" John agreed, "If they pay him the current market value, the need for him to work will have disappeared."

"The reason for my calling you and your wife this evening is that whilst I was talking to Conrad, he said that he was concerned for your future."

"He really has no cause to be Kathryn and I have been discussing that very problem during the course of the day." John explained. "We have made a decision that I will concentrate my efforts on the political portion of my life, in the hope that I will be able to get a Parliamentary Seat at the next election we have sufficient funds to be able to see us through until then and should I be unsuccessful I will then search for a full time job."

"Yes I can understand that you would make such a decision." The Doctor understood. "But during our talk Conrad expressed his concerns about your being able to finance yourself for long enough to obtain a good constituency, and it is for that reason that I wished to have a serious talk with you about the prospect of you coming to work for us here in Germany. Now before you start raising objections let me explain to you what we want you to do. You have been a good friend to this company, and we do not like to see our friends treated in the way that both you and Conrad have been treated.

You are a good Engineer, who has worked well with members of our team, and you have gained the respect of many of our designers over the past six or seven years. For a young man you have developed quickly, and you have gathered a large store of information about our machines, and the machines of other manufacturers whose equipment works together with ours in many production plants all over the world. Some of those machines you designed, and supplied to us, others you have repaired when their suppliers appeared not to have a way of doing it themselves. You have worked for many hours, un-paid, when others would have walked away and left us to get on with our problem. You have travelled to help us when your company refused to pay your Air Fares and you have taken holiday to come and get us out of a difficulty. My fellow directors and I would have offered you a job some years ago if it had not been for the good relationship that existed between us and Convellium. But now that relationship has gone, for the two most important men in that relationship have been dismissed. So I can now tell you that our board have instructed me to make you an offer. They have asked me to retain your services as 'ein Berater'r, I think that you call them advisors. They asked me to offer you a Salary of 40,000 Euros per year, and for purposes of taxation they asked if you would accept ten payments of 4,000 euros. I have spent most of the afternoon on the telephone making all of the necessary arrangements, so what do you think?"

"I'm overwhelmed Wolfgang!" John gasped. "But I could not possibly accept the offer, generous as it is. I have far too many commitments here in Hainton to be able to justify the salary that you are offering, and as I have said already, we have taken a family decision that I will spend the next two years looking for a suitable

Parliamentary Seat to contest at the next election. This alone will make it very difficult for me to be of any use to you."

"You think that we are not taking a decision too, John." He laughed. "And if I read you correctly a decision that you believe is a bad one. But you forget what hard task-masters we Germans are. We do not take these type of decisions lightly, nor do we pay large salaries to people who cannot justify them. You will earn your money, and you will be able to continue with your political career. Even though we do think that your idea of having 'part-time' politicians is a little out-of-date. We think that you are an asset to be retained by our company, and you will have all of the benefits of the Social Security System as well. I think that you should understand that your salary is after all of the Taxes have been taken out, and there will be a necessity for you to come to Germany to sign the contracts and to register as a worker in Germany. All of the Permits and papers that you will need are being assembled by our lawyers, and as soon as they are available I will let you know so that you and your wife can come to Germany and see where you work." The doctor chuckled down the phone. "you see we are not going to let you slip through our fingers. Anyway with all of the developments across the European Union, it will be good for a German Company to have an English Member of Parliament as an Adviser and Designer Engineer."

"There are far too many things that can go wrong here." John protested. "There are many points where interests will conflict."

"Think that you are wrong John." The doctor interrupted. "One of your most strong points, and this has been mentioned on a number of occasions, is your 'Redlichkeit' , your honesty and your integrity. When the time comes for integrity, I think that you will make the right decision and that is why I am not going to take No!, for an answer."

All right then, I will accept your very generous offer." John relented. "When do you think that the necessary papers will be ready?"

"Herr Valentin our company lawyer says that he will have the papers and a copy of your contract, in the Post to you on Monday. I am really pleased that you have decided to join us John, you cannot know what a relief it is for my company to know that you are prepared to put your knowledge and expertise at our disposal. We will try not to be too much of a burden on your time, but of course we will have to justify your existence on our company strength. There is one other point that we must clear up before we go any further, we must have better communications, so it is essential that you get a Handiphone, I think that you call them Mobile Phones, so that we can contact you at any time. Of course we do not expect you to have it with you when you are in meetings, but it would be of great assistance to us if we wanted to get hold of you in a crisis."

"Yes! I can understand that, and I will make the necessary arrangements to get one on Monday." John agreed.

"I think that covers all of the points that we need to discuss at the moment." Wolfgang concluded. "So unless there are any points that you need to be clarified, I'll say Good Night."

"Well thank you again Wolfgang, and Good Night." The call was ended.

"What was that all about Lover Boy?" Kath smiled over her cup of tea.

"Well not to put too finer point on it." John whispered smugly, "They have just offered me a job as an adviser to their company at an annual salary of 40,000 euros, after stoppages, and after much soul searching I have reluctantly accepted. You heard how I tried to talk them out of employing me, but they insisted."

"Well that decides the whole thing" Kathryn smiled. "The move to get you elected to Parliament is now officially underway. You're a bit of a clever old thing on the quiet, aren't you John Robertson?. I never realised until now, just how many people have a call on your services."

The door bell rang, and John made his way to see who it was. Even before he opened the door he knew that it was Martin. "Come on in my old friend! How are you?"

"I'm fine thanks John" He said seriously. "I had to come round and see you, because there is a rumour going round the Depot that you have been made redundant from Convellium. Is it true?"

Yes I'm afraid that it is, although I won't be officially notified until Monday." John admitted.

"Is it true about Conrad Barnes as well?" He added. "Yes they have decided that they are going to change the nature of the business that they're in, they no longer require our services." John continued. "So we've decided that I will devote all of time to the political business, but I will be doing a little bit of consultancy work on the side from now on."

"You've been with them for a long time." Martin remarked. "So there will be a sizeable redundancy payment due to you, do you mean that you are going to invest all of that into getting a Parliamentary Seat for the next election?"

"Yes, that's about the size of it." John said as they strolled into the lounge.

"Hi Kath" Martin bent down and kissed her cheek.

"The rumour boys have been at work down at the depot, about John being made redundant."

He explained. "They are all pretty despondent, because they know that it is almost impossible for a member of Council to get a job anywhere, and the feeling was that you would resign so that you would stand a better chance of getting another position."

"Well they are all wrong" Kathy boasted. "For not only will he remain as a member of council, but he already has a new job, and he will be able to devote most of his time to finding himself a seat for the Parliamentary Elections."

"You have got yourself another job already John?" Martin was astounded.

"Yes!" John smiled. I will be working for a company in the Rhineland in Germany."

"But I thought that you said you would be staying as a member of Council?" He puzzled.

"That is also true." John explained. "The company is one of Convellium's customers, and I have done work for them in the past. Their MD phoned me about an hour ago and made me an offer that I willingly accepted. So I start as an adviser to the company as soon as they can get a contract drawn up, and across to me."

"Jesus! How lucky can you get?" He whistled. "So you only have to sort out problems that they can't sort out themselves, and the rest of the time is your own. I wish that my lot would allow that sort of thing, and that I was qualified to carry out specialist work. But that's what education does for you." He gazed wistfully into the distance."

"Come on old friend let's have a beer and a natter." John tried to change the subject.

"That's what I like about you John." Martin reflected. "It doesn't matter what happens you will

307

always be the same bloke, and that's what makes you such a good bloke to have as the Chairman of Transport, they all know that if you say you will try to do something, you will pull out all of the stops to get it done, and even if you fail, they know that you have tried your best." He paused. "Listen at me, if the rest of my Party heard me saying what I've just said they would throw me out."

"Tell me who it is who's been making all of the noise at the Depot?" John asked.

"Well there's a certain loud-mouthed Branch Chairman, who thinks that you will run at the first opportunity, and I don't need to tell you his name."

Martin stated. "It was Harry who wanted me to find out what the situation was, because he's at an area meeting tomorrow, and he wanted to know the full impact of the case."

"Are you going to be in the 'Red Firkin' at lunch tomorrow?" John asked.

"I usually drop in after the half-day shift on Sunday, for a quick pint." He admitted. "But don't tell the wife will you governor?" He aped.

"I'll be in there for a pint myself about twelve-thirty." He informed him.

"But only if the wife will sign my pass."

"I don't believe you two!" Kath exploded. "Anybody would think that the two of you were at our beck and call. When the truth of the situation is that we hardly ever see you."

"I think that I'd better be on my way." Martin said making a strategic withdrawal towards the front door. "I'll see you tomorrow John.

John followed him to the front door, and as he closed the door after him the telephone rang again. This time it was Peter Church the General Manager.

"I'm sorry to bother you at this time of night

Chairman, but I've just heard a rather disturbing rumour, and I wondered if you could let me know the truth of the matter, just in case the press get onto the department. He explained. "I've just heard from the Unions that there is a rumour afoot that you have been made redundant from your job."

"Yes Peter, it is true, and the MD has been removed as well as part of what the Holding Group have chosen to call a 're-structuring of the company' John continued. "It is also true that I have agreed to work for one of our former customers, as a consultant, and the result will be that I will have greater flexibility in respect of my political life."

"So there will be no change as far as the Transport Department is concerned Chairman? He enquired.

"Oh! Yes there will Peter." John added. "It means that I will have more time to carry out my duties as Chairman, and in addition to that I will be seeking a Parliamentary Seat to Contest at the next election."

"So you will not be resigning as Chairman then?" He enquired.

"I have no intention of leaving Hainton City Council during this term." John answered. "I will be in my office at nine-thirty on Monday morning, fit and ready to do business."

"You cannot imagine what a relief that is to me." Church admitted. "Since you came into the Department and started to take an interest in the staff and what they were trying to achieve, the whole spirit of the Department has changed. We now have someone who is prepared to listen to us, and even though you may not be able to implement all of our ideas, at least we can now express them. Ever since I joined the City Transport Undertaking I have not had a Chairman who actually came into the Offices and used the office that is set aside for them. We were amazed that you asked where your office was, because nobody had ever used it before, except for the odd meeting when there was no other room available. The staff and the Unions feel that if you should leave now there would be a return to the old idea where politicians set policies without regard for what the professionals thought or wanted. We are all routing for you in your attempts to bring better, more efficient services to the City, and I want you to know that both the deputy and myself will do all that we can to assist you in your endeavours. You told me when you first visited my office that you wanted me to tell you situations as they are, not what I thought they should be, well now you are getting it straight from the shoulder. If you leave now, within a few weeks everything will be return to as it was before you took over. I'm sorry if I'm sounding a bit dramatic but that is how we all feel, and I'm delighted that you will be staying with us."

"Thank you for your vote of confidence," John remarked. "Frankly I do not know what it is that I've done to illicit such support from such a wide spectrum of opinion. But I am aware only of a great feeling of achievement, in as much as there is now a feeling of belonging to a team of people who are willing to try all manner of ideas in the search for better ways to get a difficult job done. I feel that this is due to the fact that the reasonable men in the Undertaking now believe that they have as much say as the peddlar's of rumour and despondency. Thank you again Peter and I will see you first thing on Monday morning."

"Just before you ring off Chairman!" Church interrupted. "There is to be the Annual Conference of the Confederation of Passenger Transport that is to be held at Bowness on Windermere, starting on the 1st of March next year, and lasting until 4th of March. Normally I attend as a representative of the City, but the invitation always includes the Chairman, and I wondered if this time we could have a full representation at the AGM. You see no one from the political side of the City has ever attended, and as you will now be getting a rather full diary, I thought that I would get a date pencilled in for you to attend with me."

"I don't see why not Peter, it will give me an opportunity to meet people from all sides of the transport industry." John paused for a moment. "Yes that is a definite date."

"Right Chairman, I will notify the General Secretary that you have marked the date in your diary." He uttered joyously. "They will be so amazed that you are going I wouldn't be surprised if they didn't ask you to make the main speech at the Annual Dinner."

"Hey!" John riposted. "I didn't expect to have to sing for my supper."

"But Chairman," Church replied seriously. "The speech is always reported Nationally on TV and in the Newspapers. It would do no harm at all to your chances of getting a Candidacy for the next election. That's all Chairman Good Night!" He put the phone down leaving John smiling at the now purring hand set he was holding.

"You crafty old Bastard" he said out loud, "you led me right up the garden path into that one."

"It's a sign of madness when you start to talk to yourself." Kath called from the kitchen.

"Only if you start answering "He responded.

"Who was that then?" She asked.

"It was Peter Church asking about first of all the redundancy, and then inviting me to a Conference at Bowness on Windermere in March." He giggled. "He led me right up the garden path, and then told me that I would probably have to make the keynote speech at the

Annual Dinner."

"Is he a quiet insignificant little man?" She asked with a knowing look on her face.

"As a matter of fact he is!" John answered. "What makes you ask the question in that way?"

"Well!" She smiled. "My mother always told me that quiet, insignificant little men were the ones that young women always had to watch 'Still waters run deep' and all that kind of hog-wash."

"Oh! So we've got to resort to witchcraft now have we?" John had always called Kath's mother 'The Witch', a good humoured gibe that took the place of all of the 'Mother-in-law' jokes that had ever been told. The fact was that they got on like a house on fire, and she thought that he was wonderful. This rather made any idea that the two women were ganging up on him, a bit of a misnomer.

"You know that she would be terribly hurt if she heard you calling her names behind her back." Kath responded. "She thinks that you're the best thing that has happened since they invented sliced bread. Anyway, enough of all of that, what will they expect you to speak about when you go to this conference?"

"The usual thing is to wait and see what's in the News, and then speak on an up to the minute subject." John replied. "I think that I've got a firm supporter in old Church, he seems to think that the speech will get national coverage, and that the whole process will do my chances of getting a Parliamentary seat no harm at all."

"I thought that Local Government Officers weren't supposed to get involved in politics". Kathy said thoughtfully.

"They spend the whole of their time involved in internal Politics," John added. "So when it comes to the small problem of setting some innocent up to make a speech that will help his political aspiration, its all a matter of child's play to them. I bet that he fixed up this Conference on the spur of the moment, perhaps even before he had heard that I was trying to find a Parliamentary seat. It would be second nature to turn it to make it look as though he was doing his Chairman a political favour. But you are right Kathryn Wilson, Local Government Officers are not supposed to indulge themselves in Party Politics. Although I can say with some degree of confidence, that my General Manager is a staunch, but dormant Conservative."

"How can you say that?" Kath asked with a harsh ring to her voice. "How do you know that for sure?"

"Because the man told me, in an indirect sort of way" John replied."Not a straight forward admission, but almost a confession that he had a leaning towards the party that I represented. He was really more concerned about the fact that I might be leaving before the next council elections, and when I told him that I would be seeing my elected term through he was over-joyed."

31

Handlebury

They drove down on the Friday afternoon, as a family, and arrived in the small market town just after five-o'clock in the evening. 'The Boar's Head' is a fine Georgian Coaching House that stands at the southern end of the Market Place, and is a four star hotel that provides fine ales and good English cuisine. There was ample parking space for the car at this time in the afternoon, and their rooms were ready for them.

"It's very 'Olde Worlde'," Kathy said as they were shown into their suites. "It's rather like being on our honeymoon again, but this time with the children along." She giggled. "The porter brought in their cases, and asked of they would require a valet service to unpack and hang their clothes. Even the Metropole hadn't provided that luxury. They declined. But Anne and Jason held no such qualms they opted for the full service as they informed their parents when the burst into their suite after about ten minutes in their own.

The porter returned, this time carrying a dispatch case.

"Your Despatches from the Department of Transport Mr Robertson" He announced. "Would you and Mrs Robertson require some tea Sir?" He enquired. "Dinner will not be served until about seven." He informed them.

"In that case we had better have some tea and biscuits." John declared. "Better make it for four." He added.

"Did you wish me to tell the younger Robertson's that it will be served in here Sir?" He asked.

"If you would be so kind" John answered. "Would you tell me what your name is please?"

"I am Hartley Sir!" The young man replied. "And I will be looking after you during you stay here. Would you be using the Dining Room for you meals Sir? Or perhaps you would prefer them to be served in your rooms?"

"I think that the Dining Room would be fine." John answered. "Yes that will be fine thank you Hartley!" The porter departed.

"He did say that he was a porter didn't he?" Kathy asked. "Only he was behaving more like a Butler."

He's perhaps in the market for a new position." John laughed. "It's rather like a time warp here, isn't it?" He added.

The phone rang. "Colonel Parker for you Mr Robertson" The reception desk announced. "Hello Horace! How are you?"

"I'm fine thank you John!" He seemed very happy. "Have you had time to see around our small town yet?"

"No! Horace we have only been here for about thirty minutes." John replied. "We were just going to have some tea, and then we were going to stretch our legs a little."

"If you give me about ten minutes I'll come round and give you the grand tour." He laughed.

"All right" Robertson answered "We'll wait for you." He turned to Kathy. "Horace is coming round to give us a short tour of the town, before we have dinner. He says that he will be here in about ten minutes."

There was a knock on the door. "Come in!" Kathy called and in strolled Sir Reginald and Bella Reevesby.

"Bella, Reg! This is a pleasant surprise!" Kathy and Bella hugged each other, and Reg pecked her on the cheek."We didn't expect to see you this week end."

John strolled in from the bathroom. "Reg, Bella! Its

315

really nice to see you both again. What are you doing here?"

"Well it's like this old friend," He smiled. "Horace thought that with the bit of bother that there has been up there in Hainton, you might like a bit of support, just to let everybody here see that you still have the support of the senior members of the party. So we are just like we were down in Brighton, except of course that this is about a century behind everybody else, but don't tell anybody that I said that." He laughed out loud. "Kathryn my dear girl, you are looking as gorgeous as ever."

"There is one slight difference between here and Brighton Reg." Bella introduced a note of caution. "The two children are here."

"Ah! Yes!" He smiled as they walked through the door. "Anne and Jason I believe."

"Anne and Jason I want you to meet Sir Reginald and Lady Bella Reevesby." John said formally. "Reg and Bella these are our children Anne and Jason."

The two youngsters walked in and shook hands like veterans, but Jason asked, "What do we call you?"

There was a short but pregnant silence that was broken by Bella who said. "Call us Uncle Reg, and Aunty Bella it will be a lot easier that way."

"All right Aunt Bella." Jason stated in a matter of fact sort of voice. "Just so long as we know what's right!"

Kath and John were speechless, but everybody else saw how funny it was.

Horace Parker arrived looking as fit and spry as when they had last seen him. There were greetings all the way round, and introductions for Anne and Jason. They set off on their tour of the small town with Anne wanting to see what it was like, but Jason had attached himself to Bella and had decided to stay with her while the rest of them took the air. The town was fairly typical of small market towns, an even mixture of Elizabethan and Georgian Architecture built round a church that was considerably older than the buildings that were built around it. They were back at the hotel after about half an hour and opted for an early dinner prior to going off to the first event of the weekend.

Hartley attended to all of their needs, fetching drinks serving at table, running around after the young people, so by about seven-thirty they were finished in the dining room and thinking about leaving to attend the meeting of the local party. It all turned out to be a fairly routine sort of party week end. Just the sort of thing that they would have at home but here the people were clearly much wealthier, and the standard of living much higher than they were accustomed to.

The average age of the people that they met seemed to be much higher than they expected, but when they raised the matter with Horace Parker he explained that it was quite usual for the 'Stock-Broker Belt', and that in the surrounding Constituencies the average age was usually considerably higher.

The Friday evening meeting was one of their Constituency Executive Meetings and it was usual for there to be a Guest Speaker. No one had warned John that he would be expected to speak so he had not prepared any notes. So when it came to the last item on the agenda and Horace announced. "So now we come to our guest speaker for this evening. Ladies and Gentlemen I would like to present to you Mr John Robertson who is currently the Chairman of the Hainton Transport Undertaking and is a leading member of the City Council. He is also a Member of the Executive of the Federation of District Councils, a Member of the Confederation of Passenger Transport, and is a special adviser to a number of Committees run

317

by the National Union. John has worked for a number of years in Europe in his capacity as a Design Engineer and is retained as an advisor to a number of Companies in the Rhineland. He is a member of the National Executive of the Conservative Party, and is the Chairman of a Regional Trades Union Advisory Committee. John speaks fluent German and French and he is married with two children.

Ladies and Gentlemen Mr John Robertson" John made his way to the front of the hall and waited for the applause to die down. He was racking his brain for a subject on which to speak and inwardly swearing at Horace Parker for not warning him about the necessity to have a speech ticked into his inside pocket. "Thank you Ladies and Gentlemen, for your warm welcome. Thank you too Horace for tripping out all of my credentials, I hope that I will be able to live up to your expectations. As I drove down to Handlebury I thought about what I could speak to you about this evening, and I thought that everybody has a need for communication, everybody has a need for being able to get around in our beautiful country. Most of us are fortunate we have ready access to one form of transport or another in the normal run of everyday life, but what happens if the driver or vehicle that we use becomes unavailable. In that respect we all have a need for some form of public transport at some time in our lives. So what if that Transport is not available, because it has not been utilised and scrapped. Where does the non-driving widow turn? Who provides the old or infirmed with the means to be able to continue to live in their rural landscape? And who ensures that there will be adequate services to maintain our standards of life?" He paused and took a sip of the water that was provided for him. There was silence. He had them, now all that he had to do was hold them. "In an age when the motor car has become almost a necessary tool for living, there are still many who did not and could not afford to run a car, and there was a significant minority who were physically incapable of driving a vehicle of any kind. It was part of the responsibility of any Government to ensure that everybody was able to get adequate transport to maintain the basic requirements of life, regardless of their location or the constraints placed upon them by dint of handicap or finance. The Rural Transport Initiative, proposed via the Secretary of State for the Environment, had selected seven rural areas for experimental services to be tried, and so far the results had been encouraging." John went on to explain the pro's and con's of the Scheme, and then applied an idea that would led itself to the situation in Handlebury, where the Cottage Hospital had been closed, and hospital services were now over twenty miles away, in the county town. John illustrated verbally what the current Government were doing to try to eliminate some of the short sighted schemes of the previous Government. He finished by saying, "Thank you for listening to me, I hope that what I have said gives you food for thought, Are there any questions?" There were, and many of them, but the whole tenure of the meeting was that John had hit on a sore point, and the answers that he gave did much to answer the doubts. It was after ten when Reg and John finally got away.

As they walked away towards the hotel Reg said. "You didn't expect to have to speak there did you?"

"To be honest about it, when Horace started to introduce me" John laughed nervously. "I thought that I was going to wet myself. But once I got underway I didn't feel all that bad really."

"So all of that was off the cuff?" Reevesby asked

"Yes!" John replied. "I thought the real point was that this is was a community with a high ratio of retired

319

and elderly people who could find themselves isolated if their cars were in some way removed from them. The rest just followed from what I have read in papers that are circulated from the various bodies that I sit on as a representative of the city."

"Well I wish that I could remember, off the cuff, all of the statistics that you've just reeled off." Reg remarked. "All of that without a single note!

I don't think that we need worry about you young man!" He said to the night.They made their way back to the hotel and found Bella with Kath in the small snug just off the lounge. They sat there like two ladies in waiting.

"What was it like Reg?" Bella asked eagerly.

"Not a problem!" Reg remarked.

"Not a problem!" Bella shrugged. "His wife tells me that he has gone out to meet the dragons, without a note or any preparation of any kind, and you tell me that it was 'Not a problem'. I have been sitting in here like an expectant father, drinking more gin than is good for me, and Kath has been pacing up and down for the last hour in a frenzy of doubt and a fever of fear, and all you can say is that it was 'not a problem'."

"Well it is true!" Reg said calmly. "Horace announced that John was the guest speaker, and John got up and spoke for about twenty five minutes on the Problems of Rural Transport. He answered questions, and explained some of the finer points for another fifteen or so, and then we came here for a couple of drinks, and that is all there was to it!"

John came from the bar with the drinks on a tray. "Have you had a good night Bella?" He asked.

"No I have not!" She snapped indignantly and turned away from him.

"Was it something that I said?" John asked.

"I think that Bella has been worrying for you." Reg

explained. "Kath must have told her that you hadn't prepared anything for tonights meeting, and the two of them have been sitting here worrying about you."

"Come on ladies and I will tell you a funny story." John started.

"Oh! No! you won't." Reg interrupted. "This is one story that I am definitely going to tell myself. So ladies, are you sitting comfortably?

Good, then I will begin. Once upon a time, there was a young man called John, who went out into the wide world to seek his fortune. In many ways John was an innocent in the wild until the night that he arrived in Canetown. Here the black magician lived, and being a fair man he set a test to find out if John was made of the right sort of stuff to make his own way in the world, but more to the point he wanted to see if John could adapt himself to an awkward situation without anybody being aware that the test had been set. The magician invited John to a meeting at which all of the townsfolk would expect some great piece of wisdom would be expounded. But no one told John that he was the one who was expected to produce a new plan for the advancement of the town. So John set off to the meeting expecting to listen to all of the great local men speaking about what they wanted to happen in the town. When the magician asked who would speak nobody wanted to be heard, and John being the only stranger there was asked to speak to the meeting about the plight of the town. So he stood up, and started to speak about things that he had heard of, in other parts of the country, and the people of Canetown liked what he had to say. They thought that he was very wise for one so young, and all of the little old ladies thought that he was a very handsome young man, who might well represent the town at the countries Parliament, and they all went away happy in the knowledge that they had found such a man to look after their affairs. And if that young man ever goes to a meeting like that again, without so much as a few notes in his pocket I will personally strangle him." Reg turned towards John and said. "Don't ever do that again, or I will tear up my Membership Card of the John Robertson Fan Club."

"Sorry Reg!" John blushed. "Sorry Bella! Kath!, but I really did not expect to speak to night, I thought that it would be a round of gentle introductions, and a few questions. When Horace started to introduce me as the Guest Speaker I nearly died."

"God you should have seen his face!" Reevesby laughed. "I don't think that I have ever seen anybody look so shocked, but it only lasted for about two seconds, and then he was on his feet and speaking as though he had been doing it all of his life. He slayed them, he had that room full of old dears eating out of the palm of his hand."

"I say John that was very good!" Horace Parker steamed into the snug. "They are already asking if you are on the list of prospective candidates.

Who told you that you would be speaking tonight?" He smiled.

"Oh! Nobody" John replied.

"So all of that was off the cuff, so-to-speak?" He asked.

"Yes." John replied.

"Astounding" He uttered and he turned to the others and said,"He spoke for thirty five minutes, and then answered questions for fifteen more all without any warning at all. My report to Marius Clarke will be very good reading. Well I must be off. I'll see you all in the morning about eleven I think." He scurried off, and their laughter followed him out to the road.

"I'll tell you all something right now." said Reevesby as he looked after Parker disappearing into the night. "There goes a Constituency Chairman who believes that he has found their next MP"

"Do you really think so Reggie?" Bella smiled.

"I'm absolutely convinced of it." Reevesby replied thoughtfully. "Unless our friend here makes some awful gaff this weekend, I would say that were are home and dry. Friend Horace will be on the phone to Marius on Monday staking his claim to our friend John."

Once they were back in their rooms, having checked to see that the two children were all right, John and Kath relaxed for the first time since they had arrived in Handlebury.

"You have two very good friends in Reg and Bella." Kath remarked to John.

"Yes I didn't appreciate quite how good until tonight." John answered. "I think that Reg was more nervous than I was. He was absolutely livid when he discovered that I had not prepared a speech for tonight. I really hadn't given it a thought, my idea of this weekend was to see if we liked them, but it seems to be the other way round, that is to say we are here to see if they like us. So I'd better be a good boy scout, and be prepared for almost anything."

"When I told Bella that you had nothing prepared, "Kath grinned. "I thought that she was going to have kittens. She almost admitted that you had blown it!"

"Did she really?" John said quietly. "I will admit to having been a little surprised by being asked to be the Guest Speaker without any warning, but once I got underway there was no real problem. I simply stuck to things that I knew about and fortunately the question of access to Transport here is becoming a key problem. All things considered it wasn't too bad."

Bella was saying that Reg used to spend hours preparing before he spoke to an audience." Kath told him seriously. "She said that he felt it very important to have a record of what you had said, so that if people quoted you in the future you were able to rectify from the text, any error that they made."

"Ah! That us why he was so annoyed" John appreciated.

"You do know that the local MP is seriously ill. Kath told him.

"No! Nobody has bothered to tell me that!" John emphasised.

"Apparently he has Cancer and is not expected to live until the General Election." Kath said. "But he had already told Central Office that he would not be seeking another term because of his heath problems. He has not been a very popular MP that is why they were looking for a young married man to take over. They do not think that an elderly bachelor is the right sort of man for this type of constituency"

"I'm not sure that I like the sound of that much." John commented.

"Why ever not Love!" Kath asked.

"Well it is all a question of the man." John answered. "I don't think that it has much to do with his marital status."

"Having a family does change ones perspective. You must admit that?" Kathy said seriously. "Michael Brabbant has been around a long time, he's been the MP here for nearly thirty years."

"Yes and that leads me to conclude a number of things."John replied. "The least of which is the fact that he was very young when he was elected and that probably had an effect on his ability to be able to find a wife."

"I hadn't really considered it in that light." Kath admitted. "I suppose that most MP's don't really start to get anywhere until after they are married. So if one is elected while they are single, then the prospects of being able to find a suitable partner is some-what limited" She thought for a moment. "It must be a very lonely sort of existence for anyone who doesn't find a partner with whom they can share their life and their work.

I think that I will find out where he is, and go and visit him either tomorrow or Sunday morning."

"That's a very nice thought." John hugged her and kissed her neck. "You really are something else Kathryn Wilson."

They decided to delay breakfast, and walked out into the fine frosty air of a country market town. The whole place was alive and buzzing with the activity of setting up stalls in a market place that was clearly small, but very popular with both stall holders and customers alike. They had not gone more than twenty steps when Reg shouted them to join him in the middle of the melee. "John, Kath!" He called. "Come over here and see who is here." They walked into the centre of the market place to find Reg talking to Sir John Barker. "Hello Sir John!" Kathy greeted him. "How are you and Lady Barker."

"We are both very well thank you." He replied. "How are the two of you keeping?"

"We are both very well John. Thank you." John smiled. "I didn't know that you lived down here."

Oh I don't!" Barker stated. "We have come down to visit my sister and her husband who live about five miles away. They run a small holding, so we volunteered to help them on their stall this morning. We often do this it is a very pleasant change from being couped up in Central Office all week."

I was just trying to tell Barker about the meeting last night." Reevesby related. "But he all ready knew the most of it. His sister was one of your audience last night, and she has given you ten out of ten for performance."

"It's true," Sir John told them. "She told me when I arrived last night that she had seen a future Minister, and asked me to make a note of his name, because he was going to be in Parliament at the next election. When I told her that I knew you, she was quite disappointed. But she does think that the people here will want you to be their MP when the time comes."

They left John Barker lifting boxes of vegetables from a barrow and onto the stall, and the three of them wandered around speaking to some of the people who were at the previous nights meeting, asking and answering questions about trade and farming in general as they went. At about eight thirty they returned to find that Bella, Anne and Jason had already started their breakfasts, so they joined the family group to assuage the appetites fuelled by their early morning walk around town.

The afternoons event was a fund raising 'bring and buy' sale in the local community centre, and by the time that the Robertson's and Reevesbys arrived the place was packed. Many of the towns folk who were not Party Members poured through the doors in the hope that they could find a bargain of some description. It proved to be a very short affair mainly because all of the items that were available were snapped up in quick order. Kathryn was called on to announce the prize winners in the raffle, much to her surprise, and this time it was her turn to be unprepared. Anne and Jason enjoyed the fact that Kathryn was in the 'Hot Seat' and teased her unmercifully until they got back to the Hotel.

The evening was taken up entirely by the Constituency Annual Dinner and Dance, which was held at Handlebury Manor the home of Colonel and Mrs Fortescue-Robertson. Both John and Reg were due to speak after dinner and on this occasion John was very well prepared, as indeed was Reg.

Handlebury Manor had been in the Robertson family since they came rampaging down from the north in the times of Edward the Confessor.

He greeted John like a long lost brother, and would have monopolised his time if Parker had given him the opportunity. As it was the Colonel did not believe in standing on ceremony, and he moved all of his 'important' guests into his library to get them away from the rest of the crowd. Mrs Fortescue-Robertson turned out to be a very wispy kind of lady, who didn't seem to know what day it was, and she wandered round asking the visitors all sorts of silly questions. But nobody took any notice of her much, and she seemed happy just being there. The Colonel looked after everything, and that included his wife, in great detail. The event was run with military precision, and the raffles raised large sums of money from the County Set who were out in force. The Colonel was a Jack of all Trades and acted as Master of Ceremonies despite the fact that his wife was constantly interrupting him with pointless and sometimes derogatory remarks. He soldiered on, and treated her with great care and affection.

The whole evening was a great success, and despite the fact that she did not see much of John once dinner was over, Kathy had a good night dancing with members of the local party and talking to Bella. It was after midnight when they returned to the hotel, both absolutely shattered. The children had left the Manor just after dinner to watch TV and by the time that the Robertson's returned they were both in bed fast asleep.

They all said their farewells just after nine o'clock on Sunday the Robertson's to drive the 250 miles to the north, and the Reevesbys to drive 150 miles to the south west. They were all satisfied that it had been a weekend well spent.

32

Confrontation

Charles Brown was not a happy man and he was still brooding when at 11-30 on Monday morning he was kept waiting. His thoughts circulated around John Robertson who was due to be in his office in the next few minutes. Robertson was proving to be a great disappointment to him, he was not the pliable, self thinking, money-grabber that he had perceived he was. Brown was annoyed with himself for being wrong about someone he had placed in a strong position in the belief that he would be able to easily manipulate him when the time arrived.

"How could I have got him so wrong?" He said to himself. "He is far too self-sufficient to be of use to me in the future." He heard John enter the secretary's office, and he was shown in straight away. "What the Devil is going on at Convellium?" He blasted off as soon as John was round the office door."I expect my Chairmen to keep me informed of this type of trouble!"

"Hey! Just you hold on a minute." John responded. "You hadn't got time to speak to me when I rang you on Saturday. So don't start giving me any hassle, because I won't stand for it. The weekend has been bad enough without you trying to add to it."

Brown was speechless he sat there with his fists clenched trying to calm down enough to give a reasonable response. "Don't speak to me like that." He bleated some-what belatedly. "I'm the leader of Council."

"I don't give a damn whether you're the Leader of Council or God Almighty." John persisted. "Don't blame me for things that are beyond my area of control."

"I think that we had better start again." Brown relented. "I understand that both you and Conrad Barnes have been fired from Convellium."

"No!" John interrupted. "Conrad Barnes has been fired, and I have been made redundant."

"Then it amounts to the same thing!" Brown inferred.

"No it does not!" John persisted. "Because of the changes that they are making in the way they produce things, the job that I was employed to do is no longer required. So I am being paid off. Conrad has been ousted from the company. There is a distinct difference. Conrad's job is still there, my job isn't."

"So I suppose that this will make a difference to your position on Council?" Brown was just a little too quick to respond.

"I don't see why it should be." John answered quietly, feeding the air with sufficient doubt to trigger another question.

"What are you going to do for money now that you don't have a regular income?" Brown posed the question as a ' fait accompli'

"It will might be a little tight, but we have sufficient funds to survive for a couple of years or so." John answered without a pause.

"Then you are not here to offer your resignation?" Brown raised his eyebrows.

"Whatever leads you to make that assumption?" John could play this game as well. "I merely came to tell you that the matter was under control. Why did you expect to hear differently?"

"I thought that you were dependent upon your income." Brown stated arrogantly. "That is that you have to live off your earnings. I know that you will be hard pressed to continue as a Member of Council, let alone as Chairman of Transport, and that is an embarrassment to us. Of course if you had taken that little present that I set up for you with Straw, none of this would have been necessary."

"Just let me get this right." Robertson suddenly felt very calm, and spoke very quietly. "So it was you who set me up for that bribe! And it was you who thought that I was desperate enough to accept it. Now for your information, there is no necessity for me to resign either from Council or as Chairman, What is more to the point is the fact that I will not resign from either position, and you will not ask me to, because if you do I will raise such a cloud over your head that all the winds in hell will not clear the stench. If you concluded that I was weak enough to fall for your simple schemes before this affair, I now dare you to sack me, and I dare you to prevent me from challenging your leadership when the time comes. Charles I want you to hear this and hear it well 'John Robertson is a very good friend but he is an implacable enemy', and you have just got yourself an enemy. What is more to the point is that John Robertson has independent means directly available to him and has had for a number of months your bush telegraph is not working Charles."

"What do you mean that you have no problems in being able to stay on Council?" He demanded having completely ignored Johns warning.

"I mean that I have both a capital sum from the will of a close personal friend and an income from a source that is beyond your scope to be able to manipulate, an income and capital sum that will allow me to pursue my political career without having to look over my shoulder to see if you are there waiting to twist your way into a position of control." Robertson turned to leave.

"Wait!" Brown demanded. "I think that I might have been a bit hasty."

"In a pigs eye you have!" John laughed. "I bet Frank Jamieson is on his way over here with his eyes glowing on a promise that you are going to make him Chairman of Transport."

"As a matter of fact he is in the outer office now!" He slurred the admission and smiled.

"Well just in case you haven't changed you mind about getting rid of me." John sneered. "I will guarantee that within thirty minutes of your announcing that Jamieson is your new Chairman of Transport, you will not have a bus running in this City. You will close all of the depots and you will have no official cars available to either you or the Lord Mayor."

"You would not dare!" Brown spluttered.

"I would not have to do a thing." John stated. "I think that you should learn a thing or two about your supposed 'network', all of the city's employees know all about them. They know who your informants are, and they feed them anything that they like. So that you are aware of how good the Jungle Telegraph is, they all knew about my meeting with Straw before it took place, and they were running a book on the outcome. So don't tell me what I dare or dare not do."

"You do not expect me to believe all of that, do you?" He laughed nervously.

"You can believe what you like!" John smirked confidently. "It's true though. It is also true that they all know about the voice activated recorders that you have strategically placed in the Town Hall. Do I need to go further? I would get them removed, if you don't want the opposition to reveal them to the world. They are only waiting for a chance to make political capital out of showing them to everyone."

"What are you going to do now?" Brown asked

rather as a prisoner asking about his fate.

"I'm going to do nothing." John answered. "As far as I'm concerned you are the Leader of Council, and that is all that there is to it. I don't want to be leader. In truth I do not wish to be a member of this council for any longer than is necessary to do the job that was set for me eighteen months ago. When that is done I will go!" John made to leave the office but paused and turned to face Charles "And just so you don't think that I am playing games, within twelve hours of my being made redundant, I was offered, and I accepted an appointment with an International Company that will pay twice as much as Convellium did simply to be retained as an adviser. That will take care of my financial needs for the next five years. So you can forget any idea about trying force me out."

"That would be the German Company would it?" Brown slid to question in to see if John was really listening.

"You think that you are a real whizz don't you Charles?" John sneered, "But I've been wise to your manipulative little games right from the start. You didn't expect a man with my back-ground to fall for that sort of crap did you? It's time you got yourself up to date. And just to save us all a lot of time and explanations, I think that it falls to you to tell Frank Jamieson the sad news about both of your projects."

"Both projects, I don't know what you mean." Brown looked puzzled.

"The fact that I will not be leaving the Transport Department," John smiled. "And the fact that he can now cut out the pretence and openly weild your wooden spoon. You didn't really think that I would swallow that story about a group of agitators inside the Party, least of all coming from some one as dumb as Frank. He couldn't think of any thing as complicated as that."

John strolled out with the air of a man who has just established his credentials, and as he walked through the secretaries office, for the first time in weeks he felt in control of the situation. He didn't even notice that Jamieson was sitting on the chair outside waiting to go in to see Charles

Charles secretary asked "Is there anything for me to type Councillor?" as he walked by.

"No!" He laughed. "Not from me there isn't. Were you expecting something?"

"I was told by the Leader that you would beneeding me to type a letter for you." She smiled.

"Now you know full well that I type all of my personal letters myself." He teased. "But as it stands, I don't have any need to write a letter of any description. Thank You!"

33

The Seat of Power

The visit to Downing Street was not quite what Kathryn had expected. First of all the notice that the visit was to take place was very short. She was told at four o'clock on the Friday afternoon, and the car would arrive to collect them all at seven in that evening. Contacting John had been a problem, and when she did he already knew all of the details, and this infuriated her because she had spent precious time trying to find out exactly where he was to tell him.

The call from PM's Private Secretary was quite unexpected. John Robertson was in a meeting with the Garage representatives discussing various aspect of how the department operarted it's Tyre Replacement, and General Maintenance Programmes. In normal circumstances meetings were not interrupted, but on this occasion The GM's secretary broke the rule and entered the room. "Chairman" She called. "The Prime Ministers Private Secretary Sir Jocelyn Pike is on the line for you, and I thought that you should know straight away."

"Thank you Mary!" He replied. "I'll take in my office if you would be good enough to have the call put through."

He walked casually out of the office and down the corridor into his office, and seated himself comfortably before lifting the reciever.

"Robertson here" He spoke without haste. "Ah! There you are Councillor I was beginning to think that they had forgotten me."

I'm sorry for the delay," John responded. "But I was

in a meeting with the Trade Union Representatives, and it is not normal for meeting to be interrupted."

"I see!" He said with an air of boredom. And quite clearly he did not see.

"I have been instructed to tell you that the Prime Minister has arranged for you to visit Downing Street this week end. He tells me that you made an arrangement to do so whilst you were at the Party Conference. He apologises for the short notice, but subject to your approval he will arrange for an offocial car to collect you and drive you down to London this evening, along with your wife Kathryn, and your two children Anne and Jason. The car will be at your home at seven o'clock this evening. All of the necessary security checks have been carried out. I trust that this will be satisfactory!"

"That is OK by me, but I'm sure that my wife will need a little more notice than when I arrive home." He was quite flustered.

"Have no fear Mr Robertson." The man laughed. "We have already spoken to your wife, and explained what is happening. She informed us that she would be delighted to visit the PM at any time."

Will we need anything other than general everyday clothing?" John asked.

"Well there is a small dinner party at Number ten tomorrow evening." He replied. "So you will require a dinner suit and other than that a couple of lounge suits will suffice. You will be staying over night at the PM's City house, and a car has been ordered to return you to your home, departing from the City at around five o'clock on Sunday afternoon."

"Thank you for you help, Sir Jocelyn." John stated. "I look forward to seeing you tomorrow."

"Thank you Councillor." He replied. "I wish that everybody whom I contacted in this way was as easy to deal with as yourself and your charming wife. I hope that you and your family have a pleasant weekend with us." He ended the conversation by putting down the phone abruptly.

Robertson returned to the meeting, and as he re-enterred the Meeting Room thewas a sudden silence.

Peter Chirch was the first to break the silence. "Are we to conclude that you will be leaving us Chairman?"

"Only for the weekend Mr Church" He smiled. "Just so that there will be no ugly rumours, my wife, my children, and I, will be spending the week end with the Prime Minister, a date that was fixed at the Party Conference, and which has been well publicised. I will be back in the office on Monday. So I would be obliged if we could press on with the meeting, because I haven't had time to pack yet."

They all laughed at the idea that someone who was going to spend the next two days with the Prime Minister at No. 10.Downing Street needed to get off home to pack his own case.

"Thank you for letting us know Chairman." Church informed him. "While you were out of the room we continued the meeting, and the question of Garage security has now been agreed subject to your approval. Of course"

The meeting broke up, and the members of the group gradually drifted off to return to their working lcations. John collected his papers and Peter Church joined him in thoughtful mood.

"I suppose that this is nothing more than a visit for you to meet some of the people who are high up in the Party John?" He asked.

"I really don't know much about what the purpose of the visit is!" He admitted. "But I don't see it as being much more than a social affair. The PM arranged all of this with Kathryn, while they were dancing together, and he expressed the desire to be able to spend a family weekend with the children playing the central role. I think that he likes the idea of showing young people around Number Ten, primarily because he has no family of his own."

"In that case it does seem as though he is the lonely man at the top." Peter commented.

"Yes!" John mused."I think that you may be right there Peter!"

It was nearly six o'clock before John arrived home. But as he expected Kath and the children had everything under control. Sir Jocelyn had explained all of the planned details, and quite unexpectedly Anne and Jason were invited to the Saturday evening dinner. By the time that the car arrived they were ready, and anything that was forgotten would now have to remain so. The response of the two children was not the one that either John or Kath had expected, they had both thought that they would be rather against having to spend a weeekend in the company of a lot of 'old fogey's' But the appear to be quite excited by the whole thing, and when the knock came on the door, they raced to be the first to answer it.

They were met by a rather dour looking man in the uniform of an official chauffeur who was accompanied by a police officer. "Is this the residence of Mr John Robertson?" He asked in a dull monotone.

"Yes it is!" said Jason who had won the race to the door. "Are you the driver?"

Before the man had time to answer the question John arrived on the scene.

"We are ready to leave straight away." He informed him. "That is unless you would like a hot drink and something to eat before we leave?"

"No, that will not be necessary Sir!" He answered. "I had a sandwich and some coffee on the way up here.

Thank You! I have been asked to get you down to the Bloomsbury house by nine thirty, so the sooner we can be back on the road the better."

The car was a large six-seater Daimler with ample room for all of them to sit in comfort, Their luggage was stored in the huge boot, and they all clambered in to the rear seats, with the exception of Jason who on impluse opened the front passenger door, and seated himself next to the drivers seat. "I think that you'd better sit with the rest of us at the back, Jason!" Kath told him.

"No that's quite all right Madam." The driver declared. "He'll be fine up there with me. He can be the navigator."

"Strewth we'll never get there." John whispered to the others.

They set off at a stately gaite, that is until they turned into the Hainton Road, where they were joined by a Police escort, and from then onwards the speed rarely dropped below seventy miles per hour until they hit the traffic in North London.

Unlike other Prime Ministers Calvert Handsworth did not reside in Downing Street preferring to use his own family home in Bloomsbury as an escape from the tedium of full-time interference from the permanent Civil Service. He used Number Ten as a day office that was but a few minutes from Downing Street should the need arise for him to be there. It also suited the Chancellor of the Exchequer who was able to use some of the bedrooms in number ten when all of his tribe were assembled at one time. There were, of course, times when it was essential for Handsworth to stay over night, but generally speaking he preferred the comforts of his own home to that of the Official Residence.

The Bloomsbury House proved to be in Russell Square one of those fine houses that were built by the

Dukes of Bedford in the Grand Georgian Style, set around a well maintained central garden, By the time that they had turned into the Square, their single escort had increased to a Police Car leading the way and a Specioal Branch Car bringing up the rear. All of the details of their movements had been relayed to them by Jason via the intercom, which he had been instructed to use by the Chauffeur. He was also being gradually indoctrinated into the art of driving by the chauffeur who clearly enjoyed the company of an inquisitive young man.

It was just striking nine as the car doors were opened by the young footman, who had scampered down the front steps of the house to become the reception party,as soon as the car entered the Square. Jason offered to carry some of the cases, but the chauffeur said "No Master Jason, you'd best leave those to young Charles here. He will know which room to take each item of luggage to, and anyway the Prime Minister, has asked to see you all as soon as you arrive."

"What is a Prime Minister, Harry?" Jason asked him innocently.

"He is the man who is in charge of our country, Master Jason." Harry Laughed

"I thought that the Queen did all of that stuff." Jason remarked.

"Well she does in a way." Harry thought that he was on dangerous ground here. "But there is far too much for the Queen to do by herself, so she asks the Prime Minister and his Cabinet to help her."He smiled thinking that these were the sort of questions that the boy should be asking of his father.

"Anyway that is the man who you are going to spend your weekend with at least until Sunday Night. He has been planning your visit for weeks, so I think that you will have a good time. So get a move on young Sir, and catch the rest up." Jason ambled after the others and into the house. He was surprised at how large it was, and how different it was to theirown house. There were lots of people there, and they all seemed too busy working to even notice him. The Robertsons were shown into their rooms, where they made ready to be presented to the PM, the most important man in England.

At about nine thirty they were escorted down to the sitting room and shown in and there they found the PM sitting talking to Sir Marius, and Lady Clarke.

He turned and said. "Ah! Here are my House guests for the weekend." He stood up and walked to meet them. "John and Kathryn, you both already know the Clarkes but Anne and Jason will not. So come over here the pair of you and let us get to know you a little before the rest of the guests arrive"

The two chiuldren went shyly forward and introduced themselves to Calvert Handsworth and the Clarkes. Their ordeal was cut short by the arrival of Reg and Bella Reevesby, and Jason peeled away to go and talk to his friend Bella. Dinner was a surprise in more way than one; firstly because the children were there and secondly because the main course was fish and chips in their honour. But this was not your normal or in any way normal Fish and Chips, there were all sort of dips and sauces for them to try with the meal. And to top all of this there was a huge trifle that was presented to the children by the chef. In truth the adults also enjoyed the meal, it being a change from their normal run of evenng meals. The conversation at table was of favourite foods from their childhoods. The whole idea was a tremendous success, and Calvert was delighted with the results and was almost childlike in his enthusiasm.

Saturday was a whirl of activity, Calvert Handsworth acted as guide while they toured the austere rooms of Number Ten Downing Street and he had collected reams of information for the chuldren to take home and read up at their leisure. He clearly liked the idea of having young people around the place, and when two of the Chancellors children burst through one of the dividing doors between numbers Ten and Eleven, he cheerfully greeeted then both by name and without batting an eye.

At about eleven o'clock Handsworth took them both back to the front door and asked the duty driver to take them to the Tower of London where a Yeoman Warder took them on a pre-arranged tour of the place and explain some of the history that surrounded it.

Handsworth himself went off on an Official welcome for a delegation from the European Union, and arranged to meet Anne and Jason at a later time. Kath and John had three glorious hours to themselves, simply strolling round like a pair of honeymooners through the streets of the Capital. They were carefree hours of the sort that they had not known since John had become involved with Politics.

They returned to Russell Square at about four in the afternoon to find that Handsworth had just arrived back from the formal meeting with the delegation form Brussels. He had left a message for John asking of he could spare him a few minutes, so he made his way to the PM's study and knocked on the door.

"Come in!" He heard from the inside, and he entered.

"Ah there you are John," He greeted him. "Come over here and sit down.

There are a couple of things that I want to discuss with you and get your feelings about. As you know I have just been with a group of delegates from the EU."

He paused. "Would you care for a drink of any description John? I find this whole process rather thirsty work. I suppose it has something to do with never keeping the mouth shut for more than twenty seconds at a time." He laughed.

"I think that I will have a whisky and dry please." John replied. "We do tend to go on a bit once we get the bit between our teeth don't we?"

Calvert moved across to the small drinks server, and the presented John with his drink, and then sat down to resume the conversation.

"Whilst I was with this EU Group one of them asked me if we had any young Engineers who were fluent in either French or German or perhaps both. I answered that I had a young man who would be in the House of Commons after the next Election, who was not only an Engineer, but spoke German like a native of the country, and was also fluent in French and Spanish. This man, who was a German said "That he knew of a young man from Hainton who could be a great asset to us all, It was very important that we should all be able to speak and understand each others language and culture.

"Can you remember this mans name Prime Minister?" John asked.

"Yes! I think it was Lint." He replied.

"Could the name have been Lintz?" John enquired.

"Yes that's the fellow." The PM recalled. "Doctor Conrad Lintz. Why do you know him?"

"Yes!" John informed the PM. I've met him on two or three occasions before, but I have known his brother Wolfgang Lintz for about eight or nine years, in fact I currently do work for his company. To be fair, he is the man who allows me the time to pursue a political career."

"Well would you believe that?" The PM laughed.

343

"We were both talking about the same man. It's good to know that the party have their finger on the pulse of things when it comes to future commitment, but it is especially good when it comes to the position where the Germans are trying to tell something about one of our own. The point about all of this is that I have invited Conrad Lintz to join us for dinner tonight, and I have taken the liberty of placing you and Kathryn on either side of him at table.

Will that be all right?"

"Yes! That will not be a problem. Sir" John replied. "Kathryn can carry on a conversation in German too. But she does not understand Technical German in the same way that I do, but that stems from having worked in the country for a number of years."

"You are really quite a talented pair." Handsworth remarked. "And you have two very nice children too. They don't tear around the place like the Chancellers children do. You are really very fortunate."

"We are very happy in what we do Prime Minister." John told him. We talk together about most things with the children so that they can see how we arrived at where we are. All decisions are arrived at after a family discussion in which we all have an equal say, and then we have a vote on the issue in that way we hope that our offspring will have an appreciation of what it is that we are trying to do. Of course it is necessary at times to go against the wishes of the rest of the family, through lack of knowledge or experience they can make a decision that is fundamentally wrong and we then have to explain in detail why what they wanted was not attainable."

That sounds like the right approach to me," Calvert remarked, "but I can't see the majority of men allowing that sort of thing they might get far too much sound common sense for them to believe that it would be practicable." He laughed. "Tonight might be a little high-brow for the youngsters don't you think?"

"No!" John replied. "My view of it is that they are dying to see what it is like to have dinner with the Prime Minister in the company of a load of foreign visitors. They have both brought their dinner clothes and are looking forward to the event with interest. From my point of view it will be an educational exercise, as well as a memorable event in their lives so far."

"That sounds pretty good to me John" Handsworth stated. "Just one final point, Marius and Reg have informed me that you have been accepted on to the Approved List of Official Candidates for the Party. Now I want you to accept their guidance on this matter, and whilst I am not asking you to act in blind faith on all that they have to say, listen to them for they both have great experience in politics. Then when you get elected you and I will discuss your place in the general scheme of things."

"I understand and hear what you are saying Prime Minister." John informed him.

"Finally, there will be a car to take you all round to Number Ten at seven-thirty," Handsworth told him. "Dinner will be at eight-thirty, and I hope that you will all enjoy the night."

The evening was a very grand affair, all dinner suits and diamonds, but John Robertson seemed unperturbed by all of the wealth and power that surrounded him. The youngsters were not alone for there were four of the Chancellors children in attendance. Anne was seated between Marius and Reg whilst Jason sat between Bella and Mary Clarke. For John it was not an easy night as he was pressed into service to act as an interpretor on four occasions during the course of the night, and of course having discovered that there was someone who could carry out transaltions in both directions every time a problem of understanding arose he was sent to try to sort it out.

By the time that they were seated at the table to eat John was beginning to feel the strain. The process of switching from one lanuage to another is tiring at the best of time, but during the course of the reception he had used all three of his language skills, and really wanted to sit and enjoy the meal. But this was not to be, Conrad Lintz clearly wanted to talk about a whole raft of things, and he chose his own language in which to speak. He and his brother Wolfgang had clearly discussed matters in detail, and Conrad had been chosen as the spokesman. In being introduced to John and Kathryn he said. "Ah! Yes! John and I are well known to each other, he and my brother have been friends for many years, but I have never had the opportunity to meet his charming wife, but now we will rectify that omission." He was delighted to be placed between the two of them, and asked of they had any children.

Kathryn replied. "We have a son and a daughter, my son is over there between the two ladies, and my daughter is sitting six chairs down the table between Sir Marius Clarke and Sir Reginald Reevesby."

"Do you always include them in your Political Functions?" Lintz asked.

"Not in the normal run of daily affairs." John informed him. "But we are the house guests of the Prime Minister this weekend and they were invited by him to spend the weekend here."

"That is a wonderful idea." He laughed. "What ever will they tell their friends at school when they return."

"To be frank," Kath replied. "I do not know how they will get round that problem. They will probably just say that they went away for the weekend to stay

346

with friends."

"I see," He smiled. "Just visiting? That is typical of the English. A natural instinct for understatement, learned at an early age. But if you would excuse me Kathryn, I must talk for a few minutes with John on matters that relate to our company and to his blossoming political career." He turned to John. "I have spoken to Calvert about you, and wanted you to know that we are trying to assist you in your endeavours."

"Yes!" John replied. "He has told me as much."

"Well the truth is that we are short of people who are in the professions who have linguistic abilities, and your abilities have been abundantly displayed here tonight. You have assisted at least three different groups of people with your language skills, and I can tell you now that they are very impressed with your knowledge and ability. There are very few English men who are fluent in four languages, but you are one of them, and I am pleased that our company is promoting your move into your Parliament."

"I have only done what I have always done." John informed him. "And that is to try to help people with the knowledge that I have."

"That is not strictly true John." He interrupted. "When our company was struggling you gave us many hours of help and advice. You did this without any sort of payment, working through the night on numerous occasions to make sure that the machines that we were learning to make were of the best quality and design. When it came to watching the market for changes, you were the first person to let us know which direction the market was taking, and you assisted, without asking the price, in the redesign of our products and our methods of production. In Germany we do not forget this type of friendship and commitment."

"But I enjoyed the work and the company of

Wolfgang and his team of engineers." John protested.

"I will not hear of it." Conrad laughed. "You will not put me off what I have to say. Your latest design, only slightly modified, is now in production, and the Board of Directors have asked that you be in attendance at their next full board meeting. You will be informed of the date and location when they have been set. I think that you will know what this means. So Congratulations, and welcome to the Board."

"I am astounded!" John spluttered. "I don't know what to say."

"Then wait for the letter and say nothing." He answered lifting his glass in salute. "Now we are hosting a conference at the EU in Brussels later on in the year, and I have ask that Bristish Delegation should include yourself primarily so that you can more fully explain to your Industrialists the finer points of some of the Plans that we are making. Calvert Handsworth has agreed that you will be in attendance, subject to it not interfering with your election progamme."

"I'm sure that he will inform me when he thinks that it's appropriate." John replied.

"Well having got the business out of the way we can now concentrate in the food." So he tackled the meal with gusto.

The PM spoke of the move towards a more integrated Europe with Britain playing a full role in the expansion of the European Community. Conrad Lintz, much to John's surprise, spoke in response to the Prime Minister.

He emphasised the need for joint ventures between Companies and individuals with new ideas across the breadth of Europe, much in the same way that his brother and John Robertson had been promoting for the past five years. They were the leaders in the new Europe, and now others should take up the challenge, and reap the rewards that were there for all of to take. The whole affair lasted for about five hours, but the youngsters were shipped back to Russell Square just before midnight both full of the events that surrounded the evening.

Many of those to whom John had spoken to before the meeting returned to apologise to him, they had thought that he was the duty interpreter and had not known that he was an aspiring politician.

At about two thirty in the morning they returned to Russell Square, tired but happy.

As they lay in bed relaxing Kath said proudly "I did not appreciate just what you did until this evening. I watched as you went from group to group, changing the language each time you moved, and thought is this really the man I have known for all of these years? Not only are you a good engineer, you can speak to laymen in language that they can understand, and that is a gift."

"It wasn't very easy this evening." He mumbled. "I'm absolutely knackered."

"And I've just come down to earth with a bump." She wheezed.

They all went to St Martins in the Field for morning service, and had a light lunch in the dining room at Russell Square. The PM had been called to Downing Street on some matters of State, and had not returned before the time for departure had arrived.

The drive back to Hainton was a stately affair, with Harry instructing Jason on some of the finer points of driving large cars. The escort left them as they turned into Arundell Rise, and after bringing in the luggage Harry came into the kitchen, where Kath made him a cup of tea and a sandwich before he set off to drive all of the way back.

34

A Major Incident

It was three days before Christmas, and the centre of town was dressed up for the occasion. a huge Norwegian Pine tree stood in the centre of the Market Place decked in all manner of electric Christmas decoration, and the children from all of the local school choirs were taking it in turns to sing a varied selection of Carols. It was bitterly cold, and there had been flurries of snow during the day, but never sufficient to add that final touch to the stereotyped Christmas scene.

As evening fell the sense of occasion was increased by the effect of the lighting that covered the Tree, and the lighted decorations that were attached to each lamp post and flag post. This was the evening when all of the children and grandchildren of the Members of Council attended a traditional Pre-Christmas Party. At about seven in the evening all of those attending the party began to arrive by car and taxi in the car park reserved for all who had business at the Town Hall.

The hosts for the evening were Lord Mayor and Lady Mayoress, and in terms of Civic entertainment, nothing was spared. One of the difficulties of this type of affair is always the vast age range of those who are entitled to attend. In many cases whole families turned up, particularly where there were two generations of the same family represented in Council. This was one of the few times in the Civic year when all of the family could be together at a Civic Event, it was also looked upon as a way of thanking the children of Councillors for their support during the year. Few people outside the sphere of local politics appreciate just how much the children of active councillors have to carry on with one of their parents unavailable for much of the year. The number of time that John had given an apology at the last minute to either Anne or Jason, because some unavoidable duty had cropped up at short notice, that made it impossible for him to attend a parents night or a school play, so all of the members spared no effort in making this the party of the year.

Each family group was greeted by the Lord Mayor in his full regalia, and the children chatted to for a few minutes. Great care was taken to make sure that the Mayor knew the names of all of the children so that he could speak to them as individuals and they each presented with a gift from the Members of Council by the Lady Mayoress. This formality over every one was directed to the Dining room where a massive buffet was set out on tables, and staff from the catering department assisted the children to get what they wanted when they wanted it.

This was not a political occasion, and all of the party factions mingledwith each other in a display of friendship and humour. John, Kath, Anne and Jason arrived along with Martin and Sheila Smith who had three children who were all known to each other. But as so often happens on these occasions Charles Brown wanted to see all of his Chairmen in his office to have a quiet drink before the proceeding got under way. So it was that John strolled along the well worn corridors into the Leaders office. There were three of the other chairmen there when he arrived, all standing around, glasses in hand, and talking the usual sort of pseudo jargon that is the lot of local politicians.

Charles Brown stood there, red faced and obviously well into the spirit of the season. "Come on in John" he called. "And get yourself a drink, I just thought that it would be the right thing to get all of us together and have a drink to celebrate the first full year of our administration, and to thank you all for a job well done."

"Thank you for the vote of confidence Charles." John responded. "And I would like to take this opportunity to thank you all for the support and assistance that you have all offered to me in the past few months."

"You're too modest" Charles replied. "We haven't really had to give you much assistance at all." There was a murmur of agreement from the others. Little did John appreciate the amount of time that Charles had been forced to spend on other chairmen who had not the ability to run affairs for themselves. The talk as was inevitable drifted around the various problems that had beset the city during the past year. Others came and went so after about ten minutes John judged that he had spent sufficient time among the clan, and he departed to find that the Party was now in fill swing in the main ballroom. He joined Kath and they strolled round the buffet collecting their choice of the vast array of food that was available.

There were clowns and conjurers to entertain the young children, and there was modern music from a disco that was set up in one of the main committee rooms, for the older people.

At about seven fifteen the Deputy General Manager of the Transport Department entered the ballroom in an obvious state of agitation. He looked around clearly trying ti locate an individual, and when he spotted John, it was clear the he had found who he was looking for.

He rushed across towards him. "Chairman," He gasped. "I think that you had better come outside for a moment."

"Why? What is the problem?" John was not amused at being interrupted at this particular time.

"We have a serious problem, Chairman." He insisted as he started towards the main door of the Ballroom. John followed and when they were outside in the corridor the DGM continued. "I'm really sorry that I have had to call on you now, but I'm afraid that the Central Depot is on fire, and it is not a small fire. The roof is ablaze, and at the last count it looks as though about thirty of our best vehicles are burnt out. Mr Church is on his way from home, but he has been caught up in the traffic jam that has been caused by us having to close some of the roads around the depot. The Chief Executive has asked me to notify you and to ask you to attend at the scene."

"Just hold on a moment, John." John muttered. "I'd better get my coat and let my wife know what is happening." He returned to the Ballroom and said to Kath. "I'm afraid that I'm going to have to leave you for the moment, the Central Depot is on fire, and I have been called to the scene."

"Is it serious?" She enquired.

"Very serious, it looks as though we have lost quite a large number of vehicles in the blaze so far, and they have not yet managed to get it under control." He added. "I'm sorry but I must go."

It was not possible for them to drive there because the whole of the centre of the city was jammed with rush hour traffic, so as they walked the DGM briefed John on the events as he saw them."The fire appears to have started in a line of buses that were parked inside the depot for the night. Early indications are that this is the work of an arsonist. The three vehicles were well alight before the fire was spotted, and because of the close proximity of other vehicle it rapidly spread to them and into the roof. We have cleared as many of the buses as possible, and have parked them where ever we could in the surrounding streets and if it had not been for the prompt action of the drivers, we would have been looking at the loss of around a hundred buses. The police and all of the emergency services are in attendance, and there are three fire services fighting the blaze. You will be able to judge for yourself once we are at the depot. All of the offices are filled with black smoke, and when I left the Fire Chief informed me that there was a distinct possibility that they would not be able to prevent the fire from penetrating the main building. That is all that I have to report at this time Chairman."

"Have we got all of our people out of the offices and the garages?" John asked.

"Yes we have all of the people clear of the offices and accounted for. But the garage is a different matter. We have a large store of fuel, and tyres inside the garage and the garage staff have remained inside to assist the Fire Brigades in their attempts to prevent the fire from reaching the fuel tanks. There are also some drivers still trying to clear vehicles away from the main seat of the blaze." He concluded as they turned the corner and John saw for the first time the extent of the fire.The roof of the main depot was ablaze across the four bays closest to the main office complex, and thick cloud of dense black smoke was being whipped away by the breeze. The whole area around the buildings was ringed by fire appliances close and an outer ring of police vehicles were preventing any traffic from entering the adjacent roads.

They could see that the surrounding streets were packed with buses that had been driven away from the fire. As they walked down the hill they were stopped by the police.

"I'm afraid that you can't enter this area at the moment Sir!" An officer stated. "There is a major fire in the bus depot and all of the roads are closed to the public."

"Yes we are aware of that constable." John stated as he took out hisidentification, and showed it to him. "I am the Chairman of the Bus Undertaking, and I have been asked to attend. This gentleman here is the Deputy General Manager, and we both need to see the Chief Fire Officer as soon as it is possible."

"What is your name please?" He asked.

"I'm Councillor John Robertson." John replied.

"If you would wait here for a moment please Councillor" He stated calmly. "I will see if it is in order for you to enter the area."

They both waited whilst he returned to his car to use the radio, and after a few moments he returned. "There is a mobile control centre in Craton Street on the right hand side of the building at the bottom of the hill." He informed them. "I have been instructed to take you there. So if you will follow me, I will take you past all of the controls between here and there."

They continued their short walk in silence, and arrived at the control room without any further delay. As they waited outside they could see the vast clouds of thick smoke billowing out of the depot from just under the roof and there were Transport employees who were assisting the fire brigade running in and out of the building through the smoke.

They did not have to wait many minutes before they were asked to enter the Control Room.

Inside was a hive of industry, there four radio operators constantly contacting their crews in all areas of the buildings and yards.

From the outside the building did not look very big, but they were deceptive, in reality they covered an area that allowed for the over-night parking of about four hundred vehicles, plus an area where the routine maintenance of buses was carried out. In addition to this there were three bays of automatic washing machines, tyre changing facilities, and refuelling pumps. All things considered the whole place covered an area in excess of seventy acres in area, all under cover, and all flammable.

They entered the Control Room to find that the General Manager had parked his car and walked to the depot. He was in discussion with both the Assistant Chief Constable and the Chief Fire Officer.

"Ah! There you are Chairman." Peter Church greeted John. "This is a terrible blow to us. Gentlemen this is our Chairman Councillor John Robertson, and I think that we had better put you in the picture, but first of all let me introduce you to the officers here. This is Robin Calderwood the traffic manager who was on duty at the time of the outbreak the Assistant Chief Constable Mr Bolton, and Chief Fire Officer Harrison. Let's all take a seat, and we can then listen to all of the reports in sequence of events." He concluded.

They retired to a small meeting room that was part of the Mobile Unit, but was hardly made to house six rather large people.

"We had better make it brief" Harrison stated firmly. "I am here to control the fire not to participate in a discussion of 'why's and what if's'.

"That is clearly understood Mr Harrison." John agreed. "So we will make this as brief as possible, and I suggest that we dispense with the idea of trying to run reports in sequence, and hear those who have important jobs to do first. Mr Harrison would you please give us an idea of how things are progressing?"

"Thank you Chairman." He cleared his throat. "We have now contained the fire in the three bays that form the Castle Road end of the Depot, and whilst the fire has penetrated the Main offices, the damage there will be minimal. There will, of course, be substantial smoke damage in the whole of the building but there is no water damage in the Administration Block as far as I can tell. The garage is a different matter. There are twenty six buses that are burnt out, and five others that are substantially damaged. In addition there are a further fifteen that are damaged to a lesser extent. The prompt action of the drivers and garage staff has prevented what could have been a major disaster. Some of the actions taken by the employees of the Department were carried out at great risk to themselves, and their actions should not go un-noticed. The fire is contained, but we still have a dangerous situation, currently my crews, assisted by garage staff are trying to prevent the large volume of fuel in the main tanks, from igniting. The roof is still well alight above the main tanks, but we are keeping a constant flow of water spraying over them to prevent the temperature from rising further. There are no casualties as far as we know. One or two people have been affected by inhaling the dense smoke, and two of them have been sent to the Hospital as a purely precautionary measure. The damage to Bays 1, 2 & 3 is severe and worsening by the minute, So far the steel structure has stood up well to the temperatures. Bay 4 is slightly damaged along the whole of its length. The final point is that all of the people on duty have been accounted for, and we have been very fortunate in that the outbreak took place at the change-over of shifts so there was double the normal number of drivers available to clear the garage of buses. That is all that I can say at the moment, so if there aren't any questions to which you need answers at this time I will get back to the job in hand."

"Thank you for your detailed report Mr Harrison" The GM stated. "I think that is all for now!" The CFO left to continue the attack on the fire.

"Mr Bolton, have you anything that you can add to

that report?" John asked.

"From our initial enquiries," He started. "We have ascertained that the fire appears to have started almost simultaneously in five or six vehicles, all at the rear, and all in the downstairs portion of the buses. From that we would concluded that the fire was started deliberately. Of course this is only a matter of the observations of those members of staff who were here in the initial stages of the fire. Our investigations will continue once the main fire is out and our forensic teams can get into the buses to establish the truth of the matter. I will add, for information only, at this stage, that we have recovered one small incendiary device, from one vehicle, that appears not to have functioned. My officers are currently examining all of the buses in the surrounding streets to see if any other devices were put in place. The whole of this area of the city is at a stand still, and will remain so, until the Fire Boys declare that it is safe for traffic to resume. I do not think that this will be possible for a number of hours. That is all that I can say at this time."

"I think that I would like to see the problems close up." John stated. "So think that if we have a walk around the Depot, and view the problem in close-up then we will have a better appreciation of what is being done and what will need to be done in the future."

They clambered out of the Mobile Control Unit, and set off towards the Canning Street entrance of the Depot. Through the huge access door the inside of the Depot could be seen, but only to a height of three or four feet above the ground, the rest of the door space consisted of a billowing cloud of thick black smoke, that curled through the door and was then dissipated into the atmosphere above the city.

The group ducked under the smoke and entered the garage, with its long trenches of inspection and repair pits. There were about ten buses that had been reduced to blacken chassis, and a further six or seven that were badly damaged. The rest of the Garage was empty up to bay ten. The Firemen and garage staff were still engrossed in fighting the roof fire, and the fire that was threatening the fuel store. The group made their way into the Main Office Block, to find that there were still groups of firemen damping down' those areas of the offices that had been most threatened by the fire in the garage roof.

Having seen what they thought was necessary they made their way back through the smoke filled garage and out into the freezing night air. Charles Brown and the Chief Executive had by this time arrived at the scene, and John briefed them on the current situation.

"Why didn't you inform me of the situation before you left the Town Hall?" Charles Brown demanded.

"When I left the Town Hall" John explained. "I was not aware of the severity of the fire, and you, along with the Lord Mayor, were playing host to a group of people. My initial idea was to cause as little disruption to the Christmas Party as possible, and it was not until I arrived here and saw for myself the serious nature of the fire that I deemed it necessary for you and the Chief Executive to be called. I was about to carry out that function when I saw that you had already arrived."

"I just didn't want you to feel that you had to carry the whole burden yourself John." Charles stated defensively. "You are a young man, in a very senior position, and I didn't want you to feel that you were isolated."

"As it is Charles" The Chief Executive interrupted. "John has done a very good job here. All of the services are well represented. He has called a meeting of the Chief Officers of the Utilities involved, and even The Salvation Army has turned out to provide the workers with food and drink. I couldn't have done better myself."

"I don't think that we can do much here now." Charles steamed into the night air. "The best we can do is go back to the Town Hall, and get a couple of stiff Whisky's below our belts, and then get off home, because tomorrow morning we'll all be bogged down."

35

Seen from a Different Perspective

In normal circumstances Kath Robertson would have stayed at the Town Hall and waited for John to return, she did not like becoming too involved with the political side if his life. She was after all, a full partner in the family business, and while she looked after the family end, John tried to establish himself in his chosen profession. It was not easy, because whatever the party, the life was subject to whim and fancy of the electorate, if indeed you ever got the chance to ask for their support.

This time John was being harangued, by some member of the opposition, this time it was a physical danger, and she was aware that John was not a stand-by and watch sort of person. On this one occasion she felt a need to be there. By the time that she had decided that she was going to the Bus Depot, John had been gone for about half an hour, and the party was beginning to fall to pieces. Nearly all of the members of Council who were at the party had now gone to stand out in the cold and watch their Main Bus Depot go up in flames. She felt a need to be near John.

Jason and Anne had decided that they would go home rather than hang around waiting for their dad to tear himself free from his buses, and they strolled off into the night to make their own way home.

Kath strolled down the hill to the depot, away of the billowing smoke and the flames pouring from the burning building. She reached the outer control point, and was stopped by a uniformed police man. "I'm sorry madam, but because of the intensity of the fire

361

we're having to keep people away from the buildings."

"Yes! I do understand the problem." Kath sympathised. "But I am trying to reach my husband. He is Councillor John Robertson, who is the Chairman of Transport, and he's been called to the Depot because of the fire."

"Just a moment Mrs Robertson I'll check to see if it is all right for you to go through." He turned to his car and radioed through to control, and they answered in the affirmative. "OK Madam, would you go down to the Control Unit against the Castle Road entrance to the depot. They will be able to put you in touch with your husband there."

"Thank you officer" She smiled, and carried on walking towards the fire.

Close to the depot the scene was a hive of industry. She could see John moving around the outside of the building along with transport, police, and fire officers. Everybody seemed to have a job to do or a place to go.

It was a cold night, and there were flurries of snow borne on a stiff easterly wind. It really wasn't a night to be standing about doing nothing.

She first saw him standing against the Castle Road doors to the garage. Just standing, watching the funnels of smoke billowing out from just under the roof trusses. He seemed to be mesmerised by the movement of the smoke. Unaware that he was being observed he moved closer, until he could see the glow of the roof burning.

Kath could see the excitement in his eyes. He was enraptured, totally absorbed by the fire, but not by the action that was going on around him.

Such was his concentration that he did not observe the fact that he too was being watched.

Kath was watching the boy, because that is all that he was, a boy. Not through any idea of having seen anything that related to fire-raising or arson, but simply

362

because he looked out of place. Like her, he had nothing to do but watch, and every body else had a job to do; or had a task to perform. He was slim in away that young men are slim between being boys and filling out to be mature adults. He was well wrapped up against the cold, and the affects of the wind and the snow flurries on him were minimal.

He was excited. His eyes were bright, and his hands kept coming together in an involuntary clapping motion rather like an excited child at a Christmas Party, Strange that the call to the fire had summarily terminated theirs. He move, almost furtively, off towards the other main doors where the wind was drawn inwards to feed the requirement of the fire, and was then expelled through the doors at the Castle Road end of the Depot. Here he had a full length view of the bays of the Garage and smoke did notdisguise the beauty of the scene. The boy was mesmerised Kathy thought at a later time that this was of almost sexual significance to him. As the intensity of the fire subsided so did his attention and excitement, and by the time that the first fire appliances were beginning to leave his interest had gone, and he began to move off.

Kathy took the decision to follow him before he had started to move off, because he was not acting normally, and there had been a crime committed here. His made his way from the area of the garage and towards the City Centre total oblivious to the fact that he was being followed. Much to Kathy s surprise he boarded a bus to New Park and went upstairs, this was the bus that Kathy herself would normally have boarded to go home so there was nothing unusual about her taking this one to night. The driver nodded recognition as she boarded the bus and when she took a seat near the door he chatted to her as the bus filled up. They travelled until two stops before her normal stop when the boy came back down stairs and alighted. There was no problem in Kath being able to follow him, she being strategically placed against the door. The boy only walked about thirty yards from the bus stop, and promptly turned into a gate, and walked up to the front door of the house. He produced a key and entered. Kathy paused on the pretext of looking for something in her hand bag under the nearest street light. She turned and walked off towards her home after the boy had entered the house. The actions of this young man were not those of a normal boy his age. He had actually enjoyed seeing the Garage burn.

36

Meanwhile back at the Office

"Now don't you refuse me like the rest of these house-husbands John" Charles insisted. "I think that you are in dire need of a stiff Whisky before you get off home, so I'll see you at the Town Hall in about half an hour."

"That's a good idea, but I must see Mr Church before I leave." said John "What is all of this, 'Mr Church' routine John?" Laughed Charles "It always seems to me that if I say Church, some people may construe it as being something that relates to the Church of England, but if I say Mr Church' it cannot." John explained.

"I see what you mean now." Charles bellowed "I though for one minute that he was being held in some sort of reverence. Any way let's get off and warm ourselves up a bit, this is supposed to be a party night"

"OK I'll see you back at the Town Hall I really must see the GM before he leaves for home." John called as he moved back toward the Depot. John was immediately surrounded by the media.

"What are the initial findings about how the fire started?" Called one reporter "What are you going to do about Garage security?" Asked another."I think that it would be best if I made a general statement and then I will take a couple of questions afterwards but it must be done quickly because I have to be in a meeting with the leader of Council and the Chief Executive in about fifteen minutes time. So if you are ready this is the statement. ' At around seven-thirty this evening I was called, from a reception in the Town Hall, to attend at a fire in the City Councils Main Bus Depot. Four bays of the depot have been seriously damaged by the fire which is now under control, and the main fuel tanks were saved from the blaze. The damage to the four service bays is extensive, and the fire has penetrated the walls to the Main Offices, but the damage here has been minimal. It is known that ten buses have been reduced to charred rubble and a further twelve are seriously damaged. Fortunately due to the bravery of the drivers who were in the depot at the time of the outbreak a lot of buses were driven out of the garage, and the fire did not reach as many as it could have.

The Police and the Fire Brigade are working together to try to find out how the fire started, and until their investigations are complete it would not be right to speculate on the nature of the fire. I have a series of meeting to attend both tonight and tomorrow morning, and as soon as I have any more information I will release it to you. That is all that I have to say at this time"

"Chairman! Could you tell us whether there will be a change in the functioning of the Depot to improve security" The reporter from the Gazette asked.

"It has always been difficult to make vast bus depots secure," John explained. "By their very nature they are large open spaces that will allow buses easy access. If one makes the access easy for buses, then the access for people is significantly easier. Tight security would mean delays in getting buses onto the roads to pick-up passengers. It is not easy, no matter how one looks at the problem."

"Can you confirm or deny that the fire was deliberately started?" The reporter from the Star asked. "I will not be drawn on this matter all of you will have to wait until the investigations have been completed. That is all. Good-night" John strode off towards the Cheddar Road Entrance of the Garage leaving them all to the cold night. The firemen were still damping down, and some of the staff called out 'Good-night!' as he walked past. He returned their calls knowing that like him they felt that there was someone out there who was jeopardising the jobs, and they needed to find them fast. He walked up the incline, his hands thrust deep into his coat pockets, there were a few snowflakes drifting about in the wind and the temperature was falling. He did not feel as though he was alone. He paused and looked back down the hill, but the road was clear. He moved on. But it was there again, a faint sort of echo every time he moved forward. He stopped, looked back again, and there was still nothing to see. There was definitely some one tracking him. He dodged down a small alley, and ran as fast as his legs would carry him to the end, and turned back towards the depot on the back road, and then slipped into a hotel car park, entered the bar via the back door, and walked through the front door out onto the road that he had left a few minutes before, but about sixty metres further away from the Town Hall than he had started. There was a young man, about eighteen years old looking about as though he had lost someone. John approached him."I think that it's me you're looking for young man."

"In your dreams Sailor" He slurred and off he went into the night.

"A Nice try!" John whispered to himself. "But I've got your number young man." And he continued his journey.

He left his coat in the Cloak room at the entrance to the Town Hall and went up the stairs towards the main Ballroom. The lights were all on but there was no one there. The Party was over, and all of the children had gone off to their respective homes. John made his way to the Leader of Councils Office, where he found Charles Brown sitting alone, deeply morose, and clutching a glass of iced whisky.

"They are trying sabotage us John." Brown muttered. "The bastards are trying to ruin our policies."

"I don't think that this is a political problem Charles!" John commented.

"Get yourself a drink, and come and sit here" He slurred.

'The old bastard's as high as a kite', John thought as he helped himself to a large whisky and dry. He had never seen Charles in this sort of state before normally he held his drink very well.

"I think that the Unions have had something to do with this." He continued his tirade. "They don't want us to show them up for what they are, so the are sabotaging our efforts. Well the Bastards are not going to beat me."

"I think that you are very tired Charles" John tried to sooth him. "And the best thing that you can do is to get home to bed so that we can start tomorrow fresh and full of fight."

"They really are trying to beat us into the ground, you know John." He continued as though John had not spoken. "They don't understand that their day is over, and that Socialism has been shown up for what it is, a sham, a damned sham?"

"We all know what they are Charles that is why we are fighting against them." John declared with great patience. "What we both need to do is to get off home and get a good night's sleep doing that will give us a chance to face them tomorrow with a clear head and a sound mind.

So come on. let me get you off home."

There were always a string of taxis in the rank outside the Town Hall, and tonight was no exception. John helped Charles down to the lift at the end of the corridor, and they emerged in the main entrance where the member of the Messenger Corp was Staff Sergeant Johnson who was widely known locally as Johnnie.

"Johnnie can you get me a cab up to the front door for the Leader of Council" Robertson asked as he struggled to support him. "I could get one of the duty drivers from the garage to take him home if you like Councillor Robertson." He suggested.

"No I think that would not be a good idea in his current state." John responded. "I think that an anonymous cab might be the better of the two evils."

"Perhaps you're right at that Councillor." He winked, and walked off into the night to get a cab round. He returned in a matter of a minute or so, and between them they managed to get Charles Brown through the rear doors and into the back seat. John went round to tell the driver where he wanted to go, and then the driver climbed into the car and drove off into the night. leaving Councillor Robertson, and Staff Sgt. Johnson standing on the steps of the Town Hall waving him Good-night, and Charles Brown swaying and waving to the empty taxi, through which he had past whilst the others were contemplating his fate.

John looked at the Messenger and said with a straight face, "On second thoughts, perhaps it might be a good idea to ring the garage for the duty driver to take him home."

"I think that might be the best thing in the circumstance Sir!" The old soldier smiled tapping the side of his nose.

The duty car arrived in a matter of minutes, and the driver, who was clearly used to this sort of thing said, "I thought that you had more sense than to get lumbered with the sweep-up run Councillor Robertson."

"Well there is a first time for everything." He observed. "But I don't intend to make a habit of it

369

either."

"No!" The driver commented. "This is becoming quite the regular thing, and it won't be long before the matter is raised in committee if it goes on like this." They drove in silence out to Charles Browns house, and having woken him from his drunken slumber assisted him to the front door of his house.

"Well now that we are here," The driver smiled. "I might as well take my boss home."

"Am I your boss Bill?" John asked him in surprise.

"Yes! You are Chairman." He laughed. "All of the duty cars and drivers are paid for out of the Transport Budget."

When John arrived home he was surprised to find that Kathy was still out of bed and as bright as a button. She was full of the fire and all this things that surrounded it.

"I had a bit of an experience down by the bus depot tonight!" She stated.

"I didn't know that you had been down there!" John replied, "No body said a word to me. Did the children come home on their own then?"

"Yes!" She added. "But there is something that I want to tell you. It's something that I saw down there. But first of all answer me a question.

"Was the fire down at the depot started deliberately?"

"Well were almost certain that it was." John said. "Why do you ask?"

He was surprised that she was taking so much interest.

"It's just that I saw somebody acting very strangely outside the depot>" She answered. "It was not so much what he was doing it was just the way he looked."

"We can't go round accusing people because of the look in his face."

"If you'd have seen him, I think that you'd have been suspicious too. Whole everybody else was moving around with specific jobs to do this young man was getting into positions where he could view the fire, rather like a child at a football match. He was enjoying the fact that the place was on fire."

"Did you see him do anything at all?" John asked now sure that Kathy was in earnest about this.

"No! But as soon as the fire brigades started to move out he lost interest and left." Kath told John.

"So he walked away, and that is all that there is to it!" John concluded. "We don't know anything about him, and now we will have to wait and see."

"No we don't!" Kathy laughed. "I followed him to where he lives."

"You did what?" John exploded. "I've never heard anything so stupid in my life. You could have been in all sorts if trouble if he'd spotted you."

"Well he didn't." She responded indignantly. "As it was he caught the same bus that I did coming home. So when he got off so did I, and as luck would have it, he lives in a house near the end of Cider Road. I don't know the number but I can show you what house it is."

"Now listen to me Kathy." John was now sitting up and taking notice. "I want you to go over the whole episode in detail and tell me everything that you can remember."

Kathy explained that she had wanted to meet up with John, and that she had gone along to the depot in the hope of finding him there. She described the boy and what he was doing and how she had followed him round the depot to get better views of the fire and the damage. When she was finished John wiped the sweat from his forehead. "Just promise me one thing." He begged. "Don't ever go after anybody like that again."

"Well only if you insist!" She laughed.

"It looks as though this might be a long night." John explained. "You realise that I will now have to call the police and report this matter."

So it was, that a little after midnight Inspector Thompson, and Sergeant Weatherall, arrived at the house, by the time that they had taken Kathy's statement, and they had ridden up the City Road to establish the number of the house that the boy went into, and had returned it was well after two in the morning.

37

The Morning After.......

At nine o'clock the following morning when John called at the Town Hall to collect his mail from the reception area, there was a message for him to see the Leader. He went up stairs and went into his secretary's office.

"I understand that Charles wants to see me Sheila." He said to the secretary.

"Yes he does but be very careful I think that he is a bit fragile this morning." She smiled. "But perhaps you know more about that than I do."

"Not really, I am not surprised that he is feeling a bit fragile." He admitted "but why? I'm not too certain aboutthat either."

"You'd better go in," She stated positively. "He's been phoning your wife to find out where you were since nine o'clock this morning.

"Ah well, in that case we'd better go in and put him out of his misery!" He smiled as he made his way to the door.

"Good morning Charles!" He boomed as he entered the office. "How are you to day?"

"Clearly not as well as you are." He spoke softly. "But where did you get to after the fire last Night?" He asked quizzically.

"You really don't remember, do you?" John poured out as he walked boldly around his desk. "Who do you think organised your trip home last night Charles?"

"I don't recall you coming in here after the Chief Executive left." He said without any indication that he could recall what had happened after John had finished at the Transport Depot.

"Well I did come here after dealing with the Press at the Depot last Night." He related. "And I came here to have a drink with you, as you had asked me to do. But you were 'well out of it' by the time that I got here and the Chief Executive was long gone. Which was just as well I suppose."

"What do you mean by that?" He demanded.

"Well to put it bluntly, you were pissed last night." John informed him. "And Johnnie and I tried to get you into a cab to take you home, but you'd have none of it. So in the end we called the Garage and had the Duty Driver take you home."

"I can't remember any of that." Charles murmured apologetically. "It must have been the affect of cold and lack of food that caused that. I can't remember the last time that I was like that I can usually drink until the cows come home without any effect. I can't understand it really."

"Well it has been a hard year for all of us." John tried to pacify him. "It might be a good idea for you to get yourself checked by your doctor. if you are feeling a bit below par. Perhaps you need a few days complete rest."

Don't talk nonsense, John. I never get ill." He protested.

"It is not a question of being ill," John tried to explain, "It's a question of getting over tired, and then reaching a point at which the most innocuous of illnesses can cause you a major problem."

"Stuff and nonsense" Charles protested.

"Suit yourself Charles." John was openly outspoken."Well what was it you really wanted to see me about. Perhaps it had something to do with the reason you asked me to come back to the Town Hall last Night instead of going home to my wife and family."

"Yes there was something but I can't remember what it was." He admitted. "I read the details of your statement to the media, and thought that it was a proficient stalling routine. I don't think that I could have done better myself off the cuff. You want to be careful when you do things like that. You got away with it last night, but it pays to take your time, perhaps write a few notes down just to make certain that you don't drop yourself, the department or the City Council in the mire. It pays to be careful in this sort of situation."

John was surprised by this approach from Charles Brown. He had expected him to be blasting away in all directions, laying blame on anybody but himself. and generally creating mayhem. But here he was handing out advice.

"Was I really bad, last night?" He was suddenly very serious.

"You were well oiled, as the saying goes." John explained.

"I'm glad that it was you who found me." Charles admitted. "But I do wish that I had not been sent home in the duty car. The drivers leak stories to the press at a drop of the hat."

"Well we tried the Taxi method of getting you out of here and we failed abysmally." John answered. "So I was left with no alternative really."

"Yes I understand. I really do." Charles reflected. "That must not be allowed to happen again."

They both fell into fits of laughter as John retold the episode about putting him into a cab, waving him good bye, only to discover that he had gone straight across the back seat of the car and clambered out of the other side before the driver had chance to drive away. But the funny part of it was that the driver didn't notice that

Charles wasn't in the car until he tried to get the fare at the other end, and had then driven slowly back to the Town Hall in the belief that he had fallen out at some point along the route. It was only when he went back to Johnnie in the reception of the Town Hall that he discovered the truth.

They had been together for about thirty minutes when they were interrupted by a phone call from Peter Church. Charles passed the phone to John. "Chairman, I think that you should get down here as soon as possible there has been a significant development in respect of the fire last night and you should be on hand before anything leaks out." He added.

"Why what is being said?" John asked.

"I think that is best for me to say nothing further until you arrive at the offices Chairman." Church insisted.

"OK Peter, I'll be there in about twenty minutes." John informed him

"What's the matter with him?" Charles demanded.

"He's playing cloak and dagger over the fire." John told him. "And I think that what he has to say is going to cause a few ruffled feathers around here."

"Why?" Is there something that I should know? Charles was all attention.

"Well the fact is that last night, the Chief Fire Officer indicated that there were some 'devices' found in the rear downstairs seats of two buses that had not ignited, and by this morning they would most certainly be able to confirm the truth of the matter. So I think that Church is going to tell me that they have found that the fires in the Depot were deliberately started by someone who gained access to the garage whilst the shifts were changing over."

"Do you think that it was started by an employee John?" Charles enquired.

"No! I think that it was set by someone, who is either sick, or has a grudge that they think can be settled by their burning down the Transport Departments main depot. What ever the case, I think that we have an arsonist on our hands".

"Then I think that the police had better catch him fairly quickly." Charles demanded.

"I don't think that there will be any bother on that score." John smiled.

"They have already got someone in custody in that matter."

"Bloody Hell That was quick." Charles laughed. "It must be Christmas, where did they get the information from for that then."

"A member of the General Public saw somebody acting suspiciously down near the depot last night." John related. "And when they left, this lady followed them, and reported the matter to the police early this morning.

They made an arrest at just after six a. m. this morning and a fourteen year old boy has been charged with arson and criminal damage this morning."

"God I'm impressed." Charles looked distinctly better since John first arrived. "Who is this doyen of city society? Have you got her name and address?"

"Yes! I most certainly have John replied.

"Well come on man!" He screeched. "Tell me what it is I want to write a letter to her on behalf of the City."

"OK! If you insist" John wound in the reel. Her name is Kathryn Robertson, and she lives at eleven Arundel Rise, New Park,..........

"Hold on a minute." Charles interrupted. "Are you telling me that it was Kathy who followed this maniac?"

"Yes!" John answered.

"My God she was taking a bit of a risk." Charles

gasped. "So while we here drinking, she was out there following this bloke then?"

"That is about the size of it." John agreed.

"Tell her from me never to do that again." Charles demanded

"Anyway you'd better get off to your office to find out what the score is. Some Christmas Party that's turned out to be."

John strolled round to the Transport offices where he found Peter Church waiting for him in the Main Entrance. He was in a state of agitation.

"What's the matter Peter?" John enquired.

"We have had the preliminary report from the Chief Fire Office this Morning," He whispered. "And he has confirmed that at least five of the buses that were burned out last night were deliberately ignited. They all had crude, but very effective fuses placed in the back seats. The seat covering had been slit using something like a Stanley Knife, and then who ever it was inserted a fuse that would ignite about ten or twelve minutes after they had been set. Two of them failed to ignite, and so we have ample evidence to support what was a theory last night."

"Have we got any information on known trouble makers?" John asked. "Is there any body who would be likely to want to cause the Department problems."

"We have never had cause to keep a record of potential arsonists." Church looked mystified by the whole thing. "Suppose that we could look at the possibility of some disgruntled former employee, but I think that it is a long shot."

"Well until we have carried out a full security assessment I think that we must keep watch on all of the access doors." John informed him. "If that means getting in extra staff, then I will have to meet the City Treasurer to get finance for it. Perhaps we can use some of our recently retired crews for a couple of hours a day to do this for us. Leave that one with me Philip!"

"We have had a large volume of support from other Transport Departments offering to loan us buses to replace those that have been burnt out." Philip informed John. "It is normal in these circumstances for other operators to rally round to assist each other in this sort of situation."

They strolled round to John's office, and by the time that they arrived there the Chief Fire Officer, and The assistant Chief Constable were there to start their meeting. It was not a long or drawn out meeting, all of those in attendance were accustomed to keeping their statement as brief as possible. The Fire Officer was the first to speak, "I can now confirm that the fires were started deliberately, and that all of the buses that were destroyed had fires that started at the rear, downstairs, and in roughly the same position each time. The person who had placed the devices knew or had been told where to place the fuses for them to do maximum damage in the shortest time. This infers that they were either experienced or had been instructed by some one with wide experience of this type of bus engine. The Assistant Chief Constable said "The outlook did not good the police had no leads, or suspects, until a few minutes ago when a member of the public came forward with some useful information. The items used for the fuses are so common that it would be almost impossible to trace a criminal through that route. But this is not the real point in our being here this morning, the real bombshell is that this garage is not the only one to have been entered and damaged last night. Whilst the Fire brigade were engaged in fighting your fire, they were also in attendance at a fire in the Whitham Bus Garage which is less that four hundred yards away. They had four buses damaged, and had it not been for

379

the sprinkler system in their new garage they would have been in the same position as you this morning. We are at a loss to explain all of this, at this time, and we must ask you and your staff to think over the time that they spent here last night, and try to recall anything that might have seemed out of them ordinary. That is all that I can say at the moment."

John left the Office after the meeting in a state of confusion, nothing it seemed would make it possible to tie the boy that Kathy had followed, to the person who wanted to destroy the transport services in the area..The holiday period would soon be upon them, and with a bit of luck the arsonist would not fade into insignificance. He walked along the roads that ran along-side the depot on its four sides deep in thought, and looking for ways in which the security of the garage could be improved. The area surrounding the garage on its Northern side was a very old part of the city, and the housing reflected this age. It was a poor area, and the people were in constant conflict with the City Council over their living conditions, but John did not subscribe to the belief that it was poverty that caused people to turn to crime as a means of alleviating their conditions. Rather he believed that there were millions of people who were poor, and law abiding, and those who thought that being poor was an excuse for turning to crime, offered the greatest possible insult to those who were poor and despised crime. It was the weak, in any level of society, who turned to crime to feed themselves on the efforts of others, and to attribute this to a specific portion of society was as insulting as it was inaccurate.

John was not the only person touring the perimeters of his garages, so was the Chairman of the Whitham Bus Company, one William Whitham, and their paths coincided at the furthest point from the City Transports Main Office. Both men were deep in thought, both men were alone, and both men nearly walked into each other.

"Oops Sorry" John called moving deftly to one side to avoid a collision.

"I don't think that either of us can afford another incident after last night's" Whitham responded. "You are John Robertson aren't you?" He added.

"Yes I am, but you have me at a disadvantage I'm afraid." John replied.

"I'm Bill Whitham of the Whitham Bus Company, and like you, I lost buses last night." He presented his hand to John and they shook hands like long lost brothers. "I'll bet you are doing just what I'm doing, that is strolling round trying to fathom what made that bastard try to put us out of business last night."

"Yes, it's something like that." John paused. "What I'm really trying to do is to figure out why! But what I started out to look at was the question of how we could improve the security of the garages."

"Who ever did this, must have hit your place first." Whitham thought aloud. "I think that he probably walked into your garage at the Castle Road end, placed his incendiary devices down the line of vehicles, and then exited using the Cheddar Road doors made his way to our Garage, nipped in through the trap hit the four first buses in the line and then beat a rapid retreat before the night service crews came on duty."

"Yes that seems reasonable." John added thoughtfully. "By the way, have the police and Fire Brigade told you officially that the fires were started deliberately?"

"Oh yes!" He smiled. "They told me last night."

They walked in silence towards the Whitham Garage and stood outside looking at the access. "We really don't have a hope of increasing the security of our places do we?" John asked.

"No, short of having a man at each door all of the time, there is little that we can do." Whitham admitted. "But we are introducing a policy of locking all of the bus doors when they are parked in the garages and each driver must sign for the keys and then return them at the end of his shift.

We hope that it will reduce the chances of strangers gaining access without impairing the rate at which we can get buses on the road."

"We certainly have to do something, here and at two of our other garages." John mused. "In all three cases the garages are wide open to the public. It's a nightmare really."

"Your right there John" Whitham agreed. "But we must stand together in this, so if you come across some scheme that helps, let me know so that I can have a look at it, and I will do likewise for you."

They parted each to their own world of buses and passengers. It was clear to them both that this was the work of an individual, but was he really trying to kill the movement of people in the city, or did he just like fires?

That was the real question that needed to be answered.

John returned to his office and sat there deep in thought. The more that he thought about it the more he believed that Kath had taken a grave risk in following that young man from the fire.

His thoughts were shattered by the phone ringing. "The Assistant Chief Constable for you Chairman" The Operator informed him.

"Please put him through." He asked. "Good Morning Alan!" John greeted him. "How are you this morning?"

"Good Morning John!" He Replied. "I'm fine thanks. Have you recovered from last night?"

"Is that before the fire or after the fire?" John laughed.

"What I really rang about was this young fellow that your wife saw last night. It would appear that he is a real contender for fire- raising, and to be frank we have him coming down to the Central Police Station in a Police Car under arrest. It looks as though your wife has an eye for a trouble maker. I want her to come and see if she can pick him out in an identification parade."

"Well you wouldn't find her at home today." John told him.

"No we've already tried that. The ACC replied. "That's why I was ringing you. We can only hold him for about four hours, because he's a juvenile, and we would like to get the question of identity cleared up as soon as possible."

"Kath is at work at the moment, but she will be finished at three o'clock."

John explained. "I dare say that she would come straight to Central. if you gave her a call and set it all up."

"We don't have her works number." He informed me. So I gave it to him.

"Between you and me, the whole thing rests on Kath's identification we have found all of the ingredients to make the fuses in his bedroom. All that we need to do is to place him at the scene of the crime."

"I think that both Bill Whitham and I will be exceedingly relieved if he is the one." John growled. "But with a little bit of luck you might be able to fix him in their garage. They have video surveillance cameras in their depot in the same way that we do, but theirs were not burned out because their sprinkler system prevented the fire from reaching their roof."

"Then we had better get on to them to see if they captured him on film." He was quite happy all of a sudden. "Thanks for that John it could be that between the two of you this case is moving in the right direction."

Kath picked the young man out at the line up, and despite his protestations the video evidence from the Whitham's Garage cameras was overwhelming.

John picked up the phone and dialled Bill Whitham's direct number.

"I just thought that I'd let you know that the Police have arrested a young lad aged about fourteen in respect of the fires last night." John told him.

"Good God!" He laughed. That's a bit fast for our lot isn't it?"

John explained the situation, and told him about Kath's bit of detective work, and how she'd followed him to find out where he lived.

"Jesus Christ!" He exclaimed. "That was a bit risky to say the least. Your wife sounds as if she's a bit of a Miss Marple to me. That took quite a bit of nerve, to do that on her own after dark. I can't see my wife doing that sort of thing."

"When I looked into your garage last night I saw that you had video surveillance cameras in you garage. Would they have been in operation at the time that the fires were set?" I asked.

"Bloody hell" He snorted. "I completely forget about them. They were only fitted about three weeks ago. But I'll tell you what if they weren't operating heads will roll. God I feel better already. I'll call you back on about twenty minutes John." He rang off.

In ten minutes he was back. "Hey we've got the little bastard, full face, John." He was ecstatic. The police say that even if your wife does not pick him out, there is enough evidence here to get a conviction always assuming that this is the same guy as the one who is under arrest. I am really pleased that you and I ran into each other this morning."

It was decided that there would be no public announcement about who gave the information about the arsonist, but a huge bouquet of flowers arrived at the office where Kath worked with a card that read 'With Best Wishes to Kathryn for Christmas and the New Year from the Directors and Staff of the Whitham Bus Company' a factor that caused some merriment, because John was the boss of their main opposition.

38

Christmas

There are those in our society who believe that at a certain point on Christmas Eve, the whole outside world comes to a grinding stand-still. For those who work in the Health Services, and Public Utilities this certainly is not the case, for them it is a case of carrying on as normal, or in most cases as near to normal as the outside world situation allows. Most City Transport Undertaking offer a 'restricted service' on Christmas Day, and Hainton was no exception.

For John Robertson it was a nice change to be able to lay in bed a little longer than usual and talk to Kathryn whilst they exchanged their personal gifts to each other.

"I've managed to get you a copy of that Richard Carpenter book that you have been going on about." Kathryn smiled as she handed John a gift-wrapped item that certainly was not a book. "But that is downstairs under the tree and you can open that when we are all together."

"In that case you will have to wait until we get downstairs for all of your bits and pieces." John giggled boyishly. "There is nothing this year that the rest of the family can't see."

"Well that does nothing for a girl's ego." Kath muttered as she rolled out of bed.

It had always been the custom in the Robertson household to put all of the presents under the ChristmasTree that was downstairs. The whole family then opened their presents together at a leisurely pace whilst a cold buffet style breakfast was self served.

This had been set out in the lounge because both Grand Mothers had stayed over-night, and would remain until late on Boxing Day. It was only eight-o'clock when they sat down in the chairs around the fire-place and started to hand round the vast pile of presents that were stored under the tree. The food for breakfast was set out in the kitchen, and there was coffee and tea already on a series of trays on the table in the dining room. They were all still in their dressing gowns, laughing and joking about some of the gifts they had been given when there was a knock on the door.

John shuffled his way to see who it was and opened the door to be greeted by Peter Church. "A Happy Christmas to you John." He beamed. "I see that you are not ready for the tour of the depots."

"A Happy Christmas to you too Peter" John returned the greeting. "Do come inside. It is only Nine-o'clock Peter and I rather thought that we had arranged to meet at ten-thirty."

"Yes that is so Chairman," He laughed, "But I thought that you might like to get the visits over and done with so that you could spend the rest of the day with your family. Didn't Mrs Robertson senior tell you that I phone last night?"

"The swift answer to that is No she didn't." John answered as all was explained. "If you would wait for just a few minutes I'll get ready to go with you"

"What's the problem darling?" Kath asked coming into the hall." Oh! Hello Mr Church" She was surprised. "Whatever are you doing here at this time, I thought that you were getting together later?"

"A Happy Christmas Mrs Robertson" He seemed quite unperturbed. "It would seem that the message that I left last night has not been passed on to the Chairman."

"A Happy Christmas to you too Mr Church" She

replied. "I can't remember taking a message from you last night." She was clearly not aware that a message had been received.

"It's all right." John explained. "Peter spoke to my mother, and she hasn't passed the message on. So it looks as though I will have to do a quick change, so if you can entertain Peter for a few minutes I'll go upstairs and get washed and dressed."

"There is yesterdays dispatch case for you as well Chairman, just so you don't get then idea that anything stops just because it's Christmas." Peter tried to make a joke.

When John returned Peter was in deep conversation with Jason on the subject of fuel taxation, and how the use of taxes could influence the amount of pollution that was emitted by motor vehicles. a matter that amazed John mainly due to then fact that he didn't think that Jason was into that sort of thing.

It was a cold crispy sort of morning, where the sun was attempting to break through the haze, and not quite managing to do it. There was a sharp frost, and all of the branches of the trees were white with Hoare, and the grass areas were tinged with white. The sky was clear, and it was very cold as Peter Church drove down towards the centre of the city. The roads were very quiet and John thought that the very idea of people wanting to move about on this the most peaceful day of the year was a bit peculiar. But not everybody observed the Christian Festivals, as John was to discover when he met the drivers who had volunteered to work, for most of them were from the Indian Communities within the City.

It was traditional for the Chairman to go out on Christmas Day to tour the Depots and Termini, simply to meet those who were working, and to wish them the compliments of the season, and to thank them for their service to the community. The whole thing took about an hour, and when they were done they returned to the Robertson Household for coffee and mince pies.

John and Peter brought into the house a draught of freezing air into a house that was warm and filled with the smells of cooking. They removed their coats and went into the lounge to find the whole place full of people.

"Whatever's going on here?" John shouted above the noise of people talking. Martin Smith, his wife, and family had driven from the Colly Farm Estate, and Sarah Beecham from number seven had come in to wish every one a 'Merry Christmas' and they were all standing round drinking Sherry and talking.

"You appear to have a very full house Chairman." Peter Church began. "Perhaps it would be better if I shot off home and left you to your family party."

"You will do nothing of the sort, I hope." John protested. "You must at least stop for a drink and a mince pie. This is traditional. Where are you having your Christmas Dinner Philip?"

"I have it all arranged back at home." He smiled. "So I must not stay too long or I won't have it cooked before this evening."

John turned, "Kathy! Have you got a minute Love?" She made her way from the kitchen. "Can we set another place in the dining room Peter is alone this Christmas and I've only just found out."

"Oh! No he's not." Kathy stated firmly "He is here for the rest of today as our guest, and I will not take no for an answer."

"Oh! No! I could not possibly intrude on your family celebration." Church protested.

"You heard what the lady said, Peter." John spread his hands in a gesture of acceptance. "And what the lady says, in this house, is the Law. It looks as though you will be staying at least for dinner. You know most of the people here anyway."

"There is just one thing Martin, Peter, and John." Kathryn called above the chatter. "The rule today is that there will be no talk of Transport or Politics. Anybody guilty of this heinous offence will be banished to the kitchen to do the washing-up"

And so it was that the Robertson family and friends, thirteen people in all, settled down to spend Christmas Day together. Sarah Beecham as the neighbour without relatives, and Peter Church as the lonely man whose family were spread far and wide, joined in the celebrations with a gusto that only those who are alone can raise when they suddenly find that they have somewhere to go, something to do. They played all of the Party games, shared all of the party prizes and left at about ten in the evening to go to their respective homes.

Boxing Day was a day of rest and recuperation for the Robertson's, they did not get out of bed until after ten o'clock, and even then they sat around in pajamas and bath-robes until after mid day. After a light lunch they all went for a walk in the local park, the first time that they had done this since they moved home. In the evening they watched TV, played cards, and as the evening drew to a close they all sat reading some of the books that they had received as presents. And so the brief interlude that was Christmas slipped swiftly by.

39

The New Year

It was surprising how a change of date could instill in an individual a feeling of renewal, of rebirth. On New Years Eve, John Robertson felt that things were really beginning to happen for him and his family. He was now a full-time Politician who was seeking to enter the Houses of Parliament at the next Election (Which could be held in the coming year), and his wife had been promoted and was now recovered sufficiently from her surgery to be able to assist in helping John to achieve his political ambitions.

The Robertson family had spent a quiet Christmas Holiday wallowing in their own company. The house had been full on a number of occasions and the flow of details from the City Transport Undertaking continued unabaiting in the holiday period. Transport, like the medical services and the public utilities had a duty to continue when all other forms of work had been shed like unwanted skins. The daily dispatch box arrived with monotonous regularity, at about four thirty in the afternoons, and the morning post, swollen to enormous proportions, was now being delivered by a van because the postman found that it was too heavy to include in the general delivery.

It had become a regular habit between the Smith and Robertson families to spend Christmas at the Robertson's, and New Year at the Smiths, and this year was to be no exception. Just before lunch they set off to return to the Colly Farm Estate, which was the first time that they had been back since leaving the previous April. They had been friends of Martin and Jenny

Smith since the day that they had moved into their first house in Colly Farm, and they have stuck together through all sorts of difficulties helping each other in spite of their political differences.

They arrived at the house to find that the New Years Eve party was just beginning to get under way, so Jenny and Kath disappeared into the kitchen to continue the preparation that was required for a party that would last until the small hours of New Years Day. It was a tried and tested routine that Jenny and Kath had developed over the years, as the party grew in size, and the families grew in stature. The difference this year was that there would be fewer people from the Estate, and more people from the wider sections of the community. The members of the family disappeared upstairs, to test each others skills on the computers, and Martin passed a drink to John and said, "Well what do you think about the past couple of years?"

"Well! When it all started I thought that we would still be living here today." John admitted. "I did not think for a moment that we would be living in a private house, or for that matter, that I would be a full time politician looking for a seat in the House of Commons. But I don't know what the future holds, only that I am going for broke, in an attempt to get into the top level. How do you see things Martin?"

Martin thought for a moment. "I will be leaving the Transport Department at the end of January, to go to a training school for Full-time Union Officials. So like you things are a little unclear for me."

"I will be very sorry to see you go, my old friend." John told him, "I thought that we would at least have a few years of chipping at each other across the floor of the Council Chamber."

"Well! It's a paid position," He smiled. "And I know that it will allow me to gain more political experience than I'm gaining at this time. As it is I was planning to make a move, but I hadn't really fixed on where I really wanted to go, so when this came up I applied and was surprised to get selected. Anyway I hadn't planned on being a bus driver all of my life. I was going to tell you on Christmas Day, but you invited the boss to stay for dinner and it blew my surprise right out of the window."

John raised his glass, "Good luck to you and all of your family on your new career. Will it mean that you will have to move home?" The potential for change suddenly hit John.

"No! Not at the moment." He smiled. "But when I have completed the course, I could be sent anywhere in the UK."

"Just changing the subject for a minute" John was serious. "Have you had any contact with Molly Bacon since she was elected to Council? I have been unable to get any response from her. If I phone, she hangs up as soon as she recognizes my voice. If I write she will not reply, and as one of the two Liberals on Council she must be very isolated."

"No! I've had no response either." Martin replied. "And to be perfectly frank I've stopped trying. She has resigned from the Tenants Association, and has refused to take-up any of the Local School Governorships that have been offered to her. For her part Jenny has tried to contact her, and all that she has in return for trying to continue their friendship has been a load of abuse. So in the end we all stopped trying and left her to it."

"The death of her niece seems to have affected her deeply." John stated.

"But she has hardly attended a meeting of Council or Committee, and all that she seems to be capable of is criticism."

"That's true." Martin confirmed. "But she is the

main source of all the invective that has been published about you and I. Frankly I'm surprised that you haven't sued her for defamation."

"What do you mean?" John enquired

"Don't tell me that you haven't seen some of the letters that she's been putting in the local papers." Martin Laughed.

"Well the truth is that there is so much reading to do, just to keep up with events here and on the National Committees" John admitted. "I've had very little time available to read the local papers. What's she been saying?"

"The gist of it is that both you and I have betrayed the people of the Colly Farm Estate." Martin relayed to him. "That we both used the Tenants Association to make our way in Politics, and that despite all of our promises we have done nothing to improve conditions here on the estate.

But most of all we have not installed the Road Safety Measures that we were committed to providing following our Surveys and that is causing the unnecessary deaths of children on the roads in the area."

"It just goes to show what people will do when they get a bee under their bonnets." John smiled. "I think that the best we can do is to ignore her, and she'll soon get fed up."

"I'm not so sure John." Martin was annoyed. "I've been told by the party to kill off the arguments. But I will need you to carry out a similar attack to make it stick."

"OK!" said John. "This is what I will do. One of Mollies main grouses is that we have let the people of this area down, by going to another ward for a City Council seat. Molly Bacon has stayed here, and the people of this area elected her to be their representative on the Council, and not us. We have continued with our campaign for better road safety measures to be applied, you through the Planning committee, and me through Transport Committee in the City and the Transport Planning Committee at County Council. What has Molly done?" Before Martin could answer John continued. "Molly Bacon has done nothing. She does not attend Council or Committees. She does not look after the problems of her Wards Electorate. In fact all she does is accuse others of doing exactly what she is doing herself. The fact is that through her inactivity, the people on this estate have had little or no representation since the City Council Elections, and I think that a letter to that effect will shut her up once and for all."

"Don't you think that might be a bit drastic?" Martin started to back-off.

"Personally I think that we might have let her go on a bit too long," John responded. "We must now show her that she cannot be like a local gossip and back-bite as she has been doing without some fairly solid response."

"I think that if we both write letters to the press." Martin compromised. "and let the people know just how they are not being heard in Council, that would be enough to stop her from shooting her mouth off."

"OK!" John agreed. "That's how we will approach it."

By mid-afternoon the house was a heaving mass of people, most of whom were from either the Labour Party or from The Transport and General Workers Union. John was like a Blue Button in a sea of Red Roses. He lost count of the number of times he was asked "What the Bloody hell are you doing here?" by surprised socialists who recognised him and thought that he had gate-crashed their party. He had his stock answer, "I'm drinking Whisky. My Whisky, why whose ale are you drinking?" Even so that becomes over-used after a while. Fortunately it was a mobile crowd that moved around from party to party, on a day that was a feast of parties.

The best thing to do in this sort of situation is to find a comfortable chair, and then armed with a glass and a bottle of your favourite tipple, sit down and hold court for anyone who wants to come and visit you. And if no one comes then you can sit there and get quietly drunk without offending anybody.

The food was distributed via a running buffet that Jenny and Kath kept supplied, with the children collecting plates and glasses in relays through-out the day. There was a lull in proceeding at about seven in the evening, but as the day drew to a close more people arrived and the whole thing became a seething mass of people in various states of inebriation. The more that they had to drink the funnier the stories became. They danced and sung the New Year in, much as they had done for almost ten years past, but when at last it came round to the time for going home, it was not just a short walk round the corner for John, Kathy and the children, and they had to wait for almost two hours before they could get a taxi to take them back to New Park.

40

A Change in Direction

It was almost ten-thirty before John surfaced from a deep sleep. There was something hammering away in the back-ground that stirred him.

The door bell was being pressed and the letter-box was being rattled, but the rest of the house was in deep sleep. John heaved himself out of bed and pull on his bath-robe, and staggered bare-foot down the stairs to open the door.

John opened the door to find a young man standing there.

"Good Morning Sir!" He began "I wonder if I can speak to Councillor John Robertson Please?"

"Good Morning !" John replied. "I'm John Robertson, how can I help you?"

He produced a warrant card, and said. "I am Detective Constable Parker Sir! There are a number of questions that I wish to ask you so perhaps it would be better if we went into the house for a few minutes."

"By all means," John agreed. "It would certainly be warmer than standing out here on the doorstep in this cold wind. We'd better go into my office."

John pointed to the study door and they went in. "Would you like some coffee before we get started?"

"That would be very welcome." The young officer replied.

"Kath can we have some more coffee please?" John called out.

"This is all very nice." The young DC said looking around the room. "Have you lived here very long Sir?"

"Is this the start of the questioning?" John asked

more as a joke than a response. But the young man was very serious and turned to look at him.

"In a casual sort of way Councillor" He replied. "But I suppose that we had better get down to business. This is just a preliminary interview, just to establish the 'Why's and Wherefores's' of a number of things leading up to your departure from Convellium Engineering. Can you tell me the reason for your leaving the Company?"

"Yes the reason was very simple, the Company was brought out by one of our main competitors, and I was made redundant." John replied openly.

"Did you have any share holding in either of the companies involved?" The young detective asked.

"No!" John was suddenly alert. "I have never held shares in any companies in my whole life. Like most people today I have lived what is basically a 'Hand to Mouth' existence, and have only recently had any surplus money that I couldhave invested anywhere."

"What about Conrad Barnes," He moved on. "Did he have any shares holding in the company?"

"Oh yes!" John quickly replied. "Conrad initially owned about 40% of the company. That was reduced to about 15% when ity became a public company, and when the take-over was completed he was due to get a fairly substantial amount. At least that is how he described it."

"Have you any idea how much that sum would have been Sir?" He enquired.

"I have no idea at all," John told him. "But surely those details will be part of the contract documents that were exchanged when the acquisition was completed and will be part of the public record."

"That's just the point that I am trying to establish," The young man confirmed. "because we don't appear to have any record of the details anywhere."

"Can you tell me where all this leading?" John asked. "There seems to be some ulterior motive here, and until I am made aware of that I think that it would be unwise for me to continue to answer this type of questioning without having my solicitor present."

"There is no ulterior motive here as far as you are concerned." He explained. "But you do have a lot of ties with and to Conrad Barnes. He is your former employer, he is now your political agent, and he is the Chairman of the Ward Party of the Conservative Association."

"What has that to do with the questions that you are asking me today?" John asked forcefully.

"We are currently holding Conrad Barnes in custody on a charge rising out of the sale of Convellium, and certain irregularities that have been found since the date of the sale." He admitted. "I merely wished to establish because of your association with him in your private, working, and political life, whether or not you had any knowledge that would be of help to us in finding out if indeed an offence has been committed."

"Why have you come to me? I have known Conrad for about ten years as my boss at work. I am a Design Engineer, I am a novice in the matter of company accounts and how the systems work. Politically I have been involved with Conrad for about one year, and as far as his private life is concern, well I know nothing other than where his house is."

"Would you consider him to be a friend of your's." The question was flat and without apparent rancour.

"Yes!" John responded quickly. "He was my mentor when I first came to this city from university, and he spent a lot of time showing me how to prepare documentation for tender and contract. I respected him, because he was free and open with his advice. a lot of people of his generation held back people of my generation because they thought that we would use their knowledge to undermine their jobs. And I suppose that in some respects they were right."

"Outside of your working life have you ever, at any time, taken large sums of money from him to banks in Europe?" This was getting serious.

"The answer to that is an emphatic No!" John was now out of his chair and pacing the floor. "I have spent a large amount of time travelling to and from Germany, and have lived there for months on end. But I have never been involved in any smuggling of funds into Germany or France. Why do you ask that question?"

"Well one of your former colleagues, err. Harry"

"Harry Richards?" John prompted him..

"Yes that's the name." Parker agreed. "Well he say's that he was instructed to take a route to Dusseldorf that involved a night's stay in Zurich, and he was also asked to deliver a parcel to a bank there and give them a number in which the parcel was to be deposited."

"All of my flights were direct to Dusseldorf, and I still have all of the details because I retained all of the stubs. I always stay at the same hotel so that will be easily traceable. Here is a card for you to contact them."

"I think that we had better stop here." Parker said. "I did not come to cast any doubt on your integrity Councillor."

"Like hell you didn't." John blasted back at him. "I think that you are the softener, and I will not give you or any other officers any interviews without my solicitor being present, and I want you to make that clear to your superiors."

"I did not intend infer that you were in any way implicated in any offence that had been committed at Convellium." The young detective was now trying to retrieve the situation.

"I have found your approach most offensive." John now had the bit between his teeth. "You come here, to my home, early in the morning on a Bank Holiday, when you think that I cannot get access to legal representation, and you think that I will be at my least resistant; you make accusations against me, and one of my friends that you cannot substantiate and you think, just because you are the law, and that you are beyond reproach. Well I can tell you now that the accusations that you have made against me, by inference, are incorrect, and I will pursue you, and any of your forces officers who imply otherwise. Now you will leave my house. You will leave my property, and if you or any other member of the County force wish to interview me on any matter, and I do mean any matter. You will make an appointment through my solicitor's office. My solicitor is Mike Parkin. I'm sure that you will know what his office address is."

"I think that you have got the wrong end of the stick, Councillor Robertson." The DC protested.

"And I am equally sure that you are making a bigger mistake than the one you think that I am making." John replied. The trouble is that you and your superiors are concluding that because my boss is alleged to have committed an offence, by implication it could be construed that I have committed an offence too." John was furious. "There is no way in which you can tie me into the process of committing an offence, because I have not committed one, either alone, or in conjunction with another person."

"Councillor Robertson we are not implying that you have committed an offence" The DC was now almost in a state of panic. "Perhaps it would be better if a more senior officer was to interview you?" He was now trying to diffuse the situation.

401

"Do what you will!" He replied. "If your higher ranks are anything like you young man, you had better tell them to get some armour. Now get out."

Councillor Robertson, would you please hear me out." The young man was aware that he had exceeded his authority. "I have made an error here, and I hope that you will give me a chance to redeem the situation."

"I think that we should terminate this conversation now Constable Parker." John was adamant. "The whole tenor of this conversation has gone wrong, and perhaps it would be better if we made an appointment at a time and place that is mutually agreeable, then perhaps we will be more amicable than we are at this time."

"I think that you are probably right." The DC agreed. They said their good-byes and Parker left the house.

As soon as he had left Kathryn was into the office. "What ever was all that about?" She asked with a worried look on her face.

"Well it seems that Conrad has been arrested on a charge arising out of the sale of Convellium, and some sort of errors in the keeping of company accounts and records. Harry is also implicated, because when he did some of the runs to Germany, he did a detour into Switzerland, and deposited something for Conrad on the way."

"Oh my God!" Kath's hands covered her face. "What's he done?"

"Well it looks as though the Fraud Squad think that Conrad has been syphoning money out of the company, and placing into a numbered account in Zurich. The Detective Constable who has just been here came to ask me a series of question about my relationship with both Convellium in general and with Conrad in particular. He asked me some very offensive question with the result that I told him to leave, and make arrangements for a formal meeting when I could have my solicitor present."

"My God John" She was horrified. "What have you been doing?"

"I haven't been doing anything." He protested.

"My mother always said 'that there was no smoke without fire, and the police don't go around questioning people if they don't think that they have something to hide." She had a set expression on her face. "So I want to know what you have been up to"

John was amazed, this was his wife taking the part of the police against her own husband. "Look at me Kath," He spoke quietly. "The police came here to ask me some questions."

"Yes and you got on your high-horse and refused to answer them." She replied.

"No that is not true" He tried to remain calm. "I answered the officer's questions until he started to infer that I was part of an alleged fraud. When he did that, to protect myself I told him that if he continued to imply that I had played a part in the as yet unsubstantiated offence then I would have to postpone the meeting until my solicitor was present."

"To me that mean's that you have something to hide." She responded.

"I can't believe that you are doing this to me Kath." John was astounded at her reaction, if there was one person in the world on whom he thought he could rely, it was Kath. "I have no idea what they are talking about. I have not done anything that could be twisted into a fraudulent act. I am being questioned because they think that there may be a slight chance that I participated in this act. I did not. And what I find most disturbing about the whole thing is that if you're prepared to consider me guilty by association, then when it comes to the general public and police, I do not stand a chance."

It had been a number of years since John and Kathryn had argued in the way that they had. Kath retired to the lounge and John went up stairs to shower and dress. Having done this he returned to the office and locked the door.

It looked as though there was going to be a period of silent running.

41

The Rising Storm

If New Years day had been a difficult day, then on a scale of 1 to 10 the 2nd January was a catastrophe. The early morning Newspapers were full of it. 'Leading Tory Held on Fraud Charges' and 'Up and Coming Tory Quizzed in Company Scandle'. But no body had asked Robertson whether or not he had been a party to the alleged fraud.

Just after eight a.m. Charles rang him. "Is all of this true about Barnes?" He asked.

"If it is then it is news to me." John answered. "I had a detective constable round here yesterday asking all sorts of questions, and implying that I was involved, but I sent him away with a flea in his ear, and told him to make an appointment to see me through my solicitor."

"You're not involved are you John?" Charles asked tentatively, "If you are, you had better consider resigning."

"Until the Police arrived at my house yesterday, I knew nothing about it all." John was getting annoyed about the fact that all of his friends and some of his family didn't know him well enough to know that fraud and embezzlement were not part of his style. "I'll tell you this as well Charles, the next one of my 'so-called friends', who has to ask me whether or not I am involved, is in severe danger of getting his or her nose punched through the back of their head."

"Well that takes care of that problem, applying as you do your usual round of tact and diplomacy John." Charles was clearly pleased that there would be no scandle in the ranks of his Committee Chairmen. "I would appreciate it if you could spare me some time during the day, just to bring me up to speed on the situation." With that he rang off.

It was too early to call Mike Parkin at his office, but John was spared the problem of having to contact him, because he was the next caller.

"I've just read about Conrad Barnes, and the various snide remarks about you in the Press, and wondered if there was anything that I could do to help?" As usual Mike was very quick to assess the implications of what appeared to be a gathering scandle.

"I had a visit from the police here at home yesterday." John explained. "They sent a young DC round to ask me a few fairly straight forward questions, but he made some fairly pointed comments, and I asked him to leave. I also informed him that as I believed that he had gone beyond the point where he was seeking information, and had moved to a position where he was implying complicity on my behalf, that I was not prepared to answer any more questions without my solicitor being present. I gave them your name as my solicitor, and said that any further meetings between me and the Police would now have to be made through your office. Did I do the right thing?"

"It just depends what you told him before you decudeed that this was the case." Mike answered.

"Oh! It was all fairly innocuous really. He asked me if I knew that Conrad had been arrested, and if I had been involved with any movement of funds between here and Zurich. He wanted to know if I knew Harry Richards, and of course I did. He asked if I could prove the routes by which I travelled to and from Dusseldorf, and I said that I could because I always keep my flight papers and boarding cards. He thought that is was a strange thing to do, but I've always kept them, ever since I first went on school trips abroad."

"I think that you are all right really, it sounds to me as if this young copper has over-stepped the mark really." Mike seemed relieved. "But leave all of this to me, I'll see what I can find out. But before I go, I thought that I should let you know that Conrad has Sir Charles Hilton QC acting for him, and in my experience that is an indication that he has something to hide. The greater the degree of guilt, the more expensive the defence council they tend to employ. So leave all of this to me, and let me handle all of the details. If anyone approaches you, all you have to do is refer them to me. The other point is that I will contact the DCS at Central, and arrange for the two of us to go in and make a statement, that covers all of the points that they want clarified. Don't talk to the press, but most of all don't talk to any of your political friends either. You know as well as I do that some of them are rather like actors, they will do and say almost anything simply to get their names in the papers."

"Thank you Mike" John replied. "You cannot imagine what a weight that has taken from my mind. You say that I should not talk to anyone, but Charles Brown has all ready asked me to see him in his office, to bring him up to speed in this matter."

"My advice is to tell him as little as possible without incurring his wrath." Mike giggled down the phone. "This is just the point that I was trying to put across to you. You see, it is important to Charles Brown that every one knows that he has his finger on the pulse of the party and the city. All he wants to be able to do is to tell everybody who walks into his office, in the strictest confidence of course, what the latest information is. He really doesn't give two hoots whether the snippets of information he gleans from you, plus the other pieces of information that he gleaned from elsewhere, will condemn Conrad to a life in prison, or ruin your chances of getting a Parliamentary Seat for the next Election. All he wants is to give the impression that he is the font of all knowledge. So take my warning, tell no one anything unless you have run it past me first."

"Are we being a little paranoid about this Mike?" John asked.

"Let me put it like this," Mike explained. "You do not have a paid, full-time job. Your wife has just spent the best part of three months recovering from major surgery. You are a Member of the City Council with a strong recommendation from Conservative Central Office to be adopted as a Candidate for the party at the next general election in a very safe Conservative Seat. You have just moved into a very big House in one of the best suburbs of the city. You formerly lived in a Council House on a not very suitable city council estate. All of which has happened since you were made redundant from Convellium Limited a company whose former main shareholder, former employer, personal friend, political agent etc. is now under investigation for whatever. Need I carry on? As for you the majority of people would assume, purely on the basis of Association that you would have been aware of what he was doing, albeit legal or otherwise.

"I am telling you to keep your head down. But that does not mean that you have to go into hiding, all you need to do is what you would normally do.

Be so normal that you bore the pants off the following tribe, because I do think that you will have a following tribe for the next few days. Simply refer everybody to me. Tell nobody anything. Got that?"

"Yes I hear what you are saying Mike!" John stated. "Can I go and see Conrad?"

"No!" Mike snapped. "Send him a 'Get well soon card', and leave it at that. I don't want you to go anywhere near him. The best thing you can do for yourself is forget that you knew him as a friend, all you did was use his political expertise, and that is all."

"I am going down to the Town Hall to try to tell Charles Brown nothing at all." He laughed. "That should be a set exercise for anyone who is considering entering the political arena."

I think that at last you might be getting the gist of all this political stuff John." Mike stated sarcastically as he put the phone down.

But it was clearly going to be one of those days when the phone demanded all of your attention. No sooner had John replaced the receiver and the phone rang again. This time it was Harry Richards.

"What are we going to do about Conrad?" He screeched down the phone.

"What do you mean?" John lobbed the question right back at him.

"Well he's been arrested." The clown stated the obvious. "He's being charged with fraud, but it was me who took the money out of the country."

"Look here Harry, I don't really want to know any of the details, at least I don't want to know them now." John protested.

"But they've been here asking me all sorts of questions." He bleated "So I told them to come and ask you, because if any one knew about you would."

"You did what? Why you blithering idiot" John almost screamed. "So it's you who's put me in the mess that I'm in. Well let me tell you, I know nothing about what Conrad did with the companies money, and as I understand it, it was you who took it to the Bank in Zurich. For your information I have never been to Switzerland, and what's more I have no intention of going there. Your stupidity has caused me a considerable amount of trouble, and as far as I am concerned you are a walking disaster area, and if you ever try to contact me again, or put other people in contact with me,or in any other way try to communicate with me, I will take out an injunction to prevent you from doing so."

"I have only done was I was told to do." Harry whined. "And Conrad told me that if anything went wrong, I was to contact you. Well things have gone wrong, and Conrad has been arrested, but I suppose that as you have done in all other cases, when the chips are down, you run for cover."

"I will tell for once and for all." John was being as patient as he could be with the man he called a 'disaster area'. "This is the score sheet, when Conrad told you that if anything went wrong you were to contact me, it related to the Engineering content of the work that you were doing for Dr Linz. In that context I was the person to contact. As for the private travelling arrangements that you made with him, well that is your affair. The deliveries to addresses in Zurich, I cannot help you with. I know nothing about them or their origin. The only person that you can ask is Conrad, and it is pointless your directing anyone to me in relation to those deliveries that you made. I know nothing about them, and while we are about it I want to tell you in no uncertain terms that when I decided to enter politics and was told that I could expect no further promotion in the company, you were the person who relished the chance to jump into my shoes. You were the person who made great play of your increased pay and your additional perks. Even when you cocked up a contract it wasn't Conrad you called to get you off the hook, it was me. All because you didn't want Conrad to know that you weren't up to the job. Well for your records Conrad knew what a failure you were, and asked me to keep an eye on you, but even that wasn't enough to save the company from the inevitable shut down. And now you are bleating all over the place, trying to blacken every body else, and ensure that you are pure white. Well you can forget about me, because I have nothing to say to you, or for you, and as far as I'm concerned you have ceased to exist. I have no desire to see you or hear from you again. Is that clear?" That said John slammed down the receiver.

42

The Nature of the Beast

"That was rather a fraught conversation." Kathy had surfaced.

"Yes it was rather, wasn't it?" John murmured. "It was Harry Richards, apparently he made a number of deliveries to banks in Zurich for Conrad, while he travelling backwards and forwards to Germany."

"That sounds a bit of a problem in the light of what has been revealed over the holiday period." Kathy agreed.

"Well what it means in real terms is that Harry undertook an additional 700 miles round trip, so that he could deliver a parcel to a bank in Zurich for Conrad." John thought aloud. "Now if I had been asked to do that, I would have asked questions. But Harry is a naive sort of soul and he would be dazzled by the intrigue of it all. But not intrigued by the mystery of it all. The trouble from my point of view is that Conrad Barnes told Harry that if anything went wrong he was to contact me. Conrad would have meant that if anything went wrong from an engineering business point of view, Harry should contact me. As indeed he has done nearly every time that he has been to Germany. The simple truth is that he was not up to the job, and Conrad knew that I could solve any problems probably quicker than he could do himself, simply because all of the basic design work for their style of machines was mine. But Harry now thinks that what Conrad told him (i.e. That if anything went wrong he should contact me.) infers that I was party to what Conrad was doing, and I could get Harry off the hook. By telling the police all of this, he has dropped me right in the soup, and the simple truth is that the way that Harry, in retrospect, has selected to interpret this, is the reason for the police coming to see me just after they had arrested Conrad."

"So you really don't know anything about this?" Kathy stated.

"No! I don't." John retorted. "If I had done, I would have told you in the first place. But I can't help thinking that Barnes must have thought that his luck had changed, when I was elected to Council, because at last he had an idiot who he could even use as a courier. He could never have used the likes of me because I would have seen through his little scheme right from the beginning."

"Johnnie, I feel such a fool." Kathy had taken on the air of a little girl lost, as she always did, when she needed to get a positive response from John.

"Yes! I know all about it." He replied sternly. "You actually thought that I had been involved in this scam, and were prepared to believe that just because the police had been here to question me, that was proof enough of my guilt. Well for your information, if some one told me that you had been on the fiddle, whether you had or not, you would have had my total support. You have really hurt me, because you were prepared to believe somebody else, and not me. That is what I cannot understand. There is also the fact that the police are not infallible, they have been known to make mistakes and I can assure you that in this occasion they are totally out of order."

Kathy was shocked by what John had said. She had never seen him so annoyed and so sad about the whole thing. She had jumped to a wrong conclusion, and she had seriously damaged the relationship between herself and her husband. "I'm so sorry John it must have been like being punched in the face. But I could see all of our hopes being run down the drain because of this alleged fraud. All that we had planned seemed to be on the brink of collapse, and I didn't know what to do or say. What I did was wrong and I'm sorry." She put her arms round him but he did not respond, and she knew then that she had hurt him deeply.

"I have got to go into the Department, and to see both Mike Parkin and Charles Brown." His mind was racing. "I think that it is only fair to tell you that this thing is only just beginning and that the flak is likely to be flying around for a number of months. That stupid little prat has probably ruined our chances of getting a seat for the next election, so we could be in for some lean times."

"You don't think that it's as bad as that do you?" She enquired.

"Oh! Yes I do." He replied. "It could not have occurred at a worse time, and it has space in all of the National Newspapers. There are many people on holiday, and when they are the do tend to read more of a paper than they do in a normal working week. So all of those little old ladies that you are always talking about will have read the articles, and will have had the seeds of doubt sown in the minds."

"You've already had a fair number of calls this morning." Kathy commented. "And it's not nine-o'clock yet."

"It doesn't need to be," John headed towards the bathroom. "I need to be in the office before the bells start ringing." He ran up the stairs and made to bathroom door just in front of his half awake daughter.

He got to the Town Hall in time to see Charles Brown before his first meeting of the day.

"What's the score on this Conrad Barnes thing then, John?" He demanded.

"The score frorm my point of view is simple." John

replied. "I don't know anything about the financial side of Convellium. I was not a director, nor even a departmental head, so apart from looking after the budget for specific contracts none of the financial affairs of the company were my responsibility."

"What's this Harry Richards fellow blabbing about then?" Brown knew more than he was letting on.

"He was the errand boy, who took the loot across to Zurich." John informed him. "But he was told by Conrad, that if anything went wrong then he was to contact me because I would know the answers."

"What exactly does that mean?" Brown demanded.

"I think that it means that if anything goes wrong with the Engineering side of things, then Harry Richards was to contact me. And that is the way that he saw it until he started thinking about it. Now he has jumped to the conclusion that Conrad meant all things and everything, because he believes that I know the answers to the questions that the police are asking him, but I don't."

"Yes! I can see why the police have come running to you," He laughed."if that's what this fool is running around saying. Have you seen Mike Parkin about it yet?"

"No! I'm due to see him at about two-thirty." John omitted to tell him that he had already spoken to him.

"The best thing that you can do is to make a statement to the media. You know the sort of thing, a full and frank revelation." He loved this sort of theatre. "Kill them all stone dead in one beautiful movement."

"Perhaps it might be better if I see my solicitor first." John concluded.

Peter Church was into his office before John could get his behind on the seat. "What has been going on Chairman?" He asked, "The switchboard has had difficulty coping with the volume of calls."

"I don't know too much Peter." He spoke calmly. "It would appear that my election agent and former employer, Conrad Barnes has been arrested and charged with some offences under the Companies Act. One of the former employees at Convellium Limited has gone to the press and has made certain statements that imply that I am implicated in some sort of company fraud. All of this is based on one statement made by Conrad Barnes in which he told the person concerned that if anything went wrong he was to contact me because I would know what to do. This, the person has interpreted, very late in the day, to mean that if this 'thing' became known, I would know what to do. But the fact is that I don't, I know nothing of what the two of them have been involved in, and I have told the person that I do not wish to see or hear from him ever again. He, through his sheer stupidity, is causing me untold damage, my belief is that it is quite deliberate."

"If you can tell me this mans name I will instruct the switchboard to block his calls." Peter was quite indignant about it. "We cannot have people attacking our Chairman without due cause."

"I will probably be making a statement to the media later on in the day," John told him. "That will be after I have discussed this matter with my solicitor. Just so that you are aware, the police have already been to visit me at home, and although that meeting was unsatisfactory, I don't think that there will be anything to bother either my position or the running of the department. I will try as far as possible to keep the two matters apart."

"Rest assured Chairman the people in the department will do all that they can to help you through this irritation." He smiled. "After all we are all friends and colleagues here."

The afternoon saw Robertson calling at his solicitor's office, and being kept waiting for a rather long time. It must have been close on half an hour before he finally got into see Mike. But it had occurred to John that since he had been a member of Council waiting, for even a short time, caused his blood pressure to rise rapidly, and he could feel his temper beginning to get the better of him. He made a mental note to get a grip on this, just because he was a politician it did not mean that everybody else should drop what ever they are doing just to pander to his needs.

Mike came to the door of the waiting room. "I'm sorry about that John, but I simply could not avoid it." He apologised. They walked through into his office, and it was rather like stepping back into the time of Heap and Micawber. Old leather chairs and beautifully polished oak desks, floor to ceiling books, and the smell of wax polish. There was little wonder that Mike had resisted moving away from this haven in the midst of a bustling city. It had been his fathers and grandfathers office before he took up the reigns of the family practice.

"Well!" He started. "I have had a look at the charges that are being filed against Conrad, and things are looking fairly grim for him. In real terms it doesn't look as though he has been very clever about the whole thing. But our concern is what have they got on you?" He paused and turned over some papers. "It appears that the only reference to you has been made by this fellow Richards, who was the courier for Conrad, and all that he has said is that Conrad told him that if anything went wrong , he should contact you because you would know the answers. That is vague to say the least, do you know what it means John?"

"Yes this is not what it appears to be in the light of

417

the irregularities on the financial side of the business." John explained. "When Harry Richards first took over the German Engineering Contracts from me, because he was not a German speaker it presented him with some difficulties. As an addition to the fact that he lacked the engineering experience to effectively cope with the purely engineering nature of the business the fact that he did not understand what the people around him were saying for most of the time caused him serious problems. Most of the designs that he handled were designs that I had put together specifically for German Industry, and I had worked with many of the staff in the German works. Add to that the fact that I spoke fluent German and the puzzle no longer exists. So when Conrad told Richards that if anything went wrong he should contact me, he was referring to the Engineering content of the business, because that was the only part of the business that I knew. When Harry tells people that Conrad told him to contact me if there was any trouble, and relates that to this current situation he is way off beam. I think that Harry is trying to clear himself, and he doesn't care who he hurts in the process. He was the courier, a fact that I did not know until the police informed me yesterday."

"You were right about the young DC." Mike smiled. "He was asked to come and see you, and try to establish if you knew anything about the trips to Zurich. I spoke to his DCI this morning and he told me that the fellow had been put back on the beat. But he did add that he would like to see you just to clear up a few details that Harry Richards had passed on to them, that did not appear to make sense."

"Have you made an appointment for us to see them?" John asked

"As a matter of fact I have arranged for Detective Chief Inspector Gallaway of Central Division, who is handling the inquiry to come here today and he should be here any time now." Mike concluded.

Just as Mike was about to get up and find out if he was on his way DCI Gallaway knocked and walked through the door.

"Hello Archie!" Mike greeted him. "How are you?"

"I'm fine thank you Mike." The tall officer replied. "How are you in yourself?"

"I'm fine thanks. Archie this is John Robertson." Mike lost no time in getting down to business. "John this is Archie Gallaway who is going to ask you a few questions concerning the disposal of Convellium Engineering, and the part you played in it, if any. This is not a formal interview, and there will be no notes taken at this time."

John and the DCI acknowledged each other, and Mike passed the mantle to Gallaway. "Can we first of all establish what I am trying to do here." He spoke slowly and deliberately, at a pace that could lead a person who did not know him, to believe that he was a bit simple and had to choose his word very carefully. "What I want to do is to try and find out what you did in Convellium." He drawled. "Why you went to Germany so often. What you did while you were there and who your associates were. What was the state of your relationship with Conrad Barnes? How and why Harry Richards took over your contracts in Germany? I don't think that there s much that is contentious in that. Well at least I hope that there isn't. So if we can make a start! Now Councillor Robertson, can you tell me what was your Job in Convellium Engineering in the years leading up to it's disposal by Conrad Barnes?"

"I was initially employed by the company as a Design Engineer that was approximately ten years ago." John started. "I stayed in that position for about two and a half years, and then I was promoted to

Contracts Engineer, and I took over all of the contracts that related to work in Germany. At the time of the disposal I was the Production Engineer, and it was only in the last year that I had to pass the control of the German Contracts to Harry Richards. This was made necessary by the fact that I was elected as a City Councillor, and became the Chairman of Transport."

"Can you tell me if you resented the fact that Richards would be getting all of the trips, and you would be office bound?" Gallaway enquired.

"I understood the reasoning behind Richards being given the German work." John explained. "But could not work out why it had been given to him in particular. He was not a brilliant engineer, and as a linguist he struggled to make himself understood in his native language, so he hadn't got a word of German in him. On every trip that he made, at least once he had to phone for me to clarify points that he should have been well aware of. On one occasion he came close to loosing all of the German Business because he had used the wrong conversion factor in converting the prices from Pounds to euros. On that occasion Dr Linz our German customers Managing Director phoned me to to help to clarify the situation, and had it not been for my long association with the MD of that company we would have certainly lost most of our European Business at that time."

"That is clear!" Gallaway said very slowly. "Now when you were dealing with the German business, why was it necessary for you to spend so much time over there?"

"When we first started manufacturing for the European Market we assembled complete machines here in England and shipped them unto Europe complete. The machines, which were nearly all based on designs that I had drawn or were original designs that I had modified, so when we began shipping out components and sub-assemblies, that were to be assembled and tested in Germany, I was sent to demonstrate the machines, show them how to carry-out the assembly, and test, calibrate and commission the machines.." John paused for a moment and then continued. "When it came round to further developing the machines by improving the design, and efficiency of them, I was employed by the German Company for nearly two years, simply to work with their designers and test engineers. So I spent a lot of time there, and I have many friends there."

"If I was to contact Dr Linz, do you think that he would confirm your story about Richards?" The DCI asked.

"I think that he would." John replied. "Wolfgang was not very happy about Harry becoming the link man in the first place, and to be frank he tried to lure me to Germany with the offer of a full-time job over there. As it is the German Company retain me as a consultant, in their direct employ and from time to time I carry out work for them."

"Now let's get round to Conrad Barnes." Gallaway leaned forward, in a way that could have been interpreted as being menacing, but John was aware of the thinking behind it, and ignored the attempt to put him under pressure. "Conrad Barnes was your friend and mentor? Your words not mine." Gallaway remarked.

"Yes! That is true." John confirmed.

"So how long had you known him?" He asked.

"In all, about twelve years" John replied. That could be split into two periods; the first being my placement at Convellium as an under graduate, plus my final year at University, the completion of my Dissertation, and then for a period of about ten years after I graduated until the time that I was made redundant."

"Why did Convellium employ you after you had Graduated" Gallaway was persistent.

"I had based my final year's dissertation on the use of modules in the production of ranges of standard machines." John responded.

"Can you explain that for the layman?" Gallaway asked.

"Certainly" John answered. "Many basic functions in the production of machines for individual industrys are the same. Consider a mixer, a weigher, a bagging machine, etc. If you then consider that there are many similarities in components that make up the machines, then by making a slight modification, one component could carry out a number of functions. To make that a more practical proposition I divided machines into modules that were 'Stand Alone Assemblies'. So that not only were the components interchangeable, so were the modules. It then became possible for a whole range of modules to be manufactured, rather than having to produce single items for each order. This significantly reduced costs and made our machines more competitive on the open market"

"But it was not enough to save the company from sinking into a state where it allowed another company to force its sale?" Gallaway deduced.

"That is not strictly true." John answered. "Bear in mind that my initial designs are now about ten years old. But they were sufficiently good to keep Convellium afloat until a few months ago."

"Had you tried to further develop your ideas?" Gallaway shot the question back at him.

"Oh! yes!" John admitted. "But each time I was given the answer that whilst the current machines were selling, we did not need to develope new styles of machines."

"Was this a sound policy? He asked.

"Definitely not" John responded. "At least in my opinion it wasn't. In reality it was a recipe for disaster."

"Did you, at any time, raise this as an argument with Conrad Barnes or any other member of the board?" The DCI was now getting to the crunch.

"Yes! There should be enough documentary evidence to indicate the concerns that I expressed over the course of about five years." John informed him.

"So you were at odds with your MD over a matter that was of prime importance to the future of the company?" Gallaway slammed his hand against the arm of the chair.

"I would not put it quite like that." John replied. "It was true that I was frustrated by the fact that we were not developing machines that could take the place of our existing machines when they became obsolete. The advances in control technology were not being incorporated into our systems at the rate that I thought they should be. But I was only in a position where I could make proposals, and it was up to the Board of the Company to accept or reject my proposals."

"I see!" Gallaway drawled. "When you decided to enter the political arena, what was Barnes reaction?"

"He called me a Bloody Fool!" Robertson snapped. "He said that it was a stupid bloody waste of my talent as a design engineer."

"And yet he agreed to become your Election Agent, isn't that a bit of a contradiction in terms some-where along the line?"

"Yes I suppose that it is!" John smiled. "But that is how Conrad is. He will do all that he can to try to prevent you from making a decision that he thinks is ill-founded, but once you have decided the course of action that you will take, then he gives you all of the help that he can to achieve your target. That is what he did when I decided that I would stand for City Council."

"So you saw nothing strange in the fact that he thought you were wasting you talents, and his deciding that he would be your Agent? Gallaway reiterated.

"No! That is the way that Conrad is!" John reiterated.

"Did he ever ask you to add a diversion to you trips to German?" The policeman asked very slowly.

"No!" John replied. "I have always flown directly to Dusseldorf. What is more, I can prove that in all of my journeys abroad, I have never been to Switzerland. My passport has not been stamped, and I have every boarding card that has ever been issued to me. I decided as a young man that I would save them, and I have all of them from my first flight as a school boy to the last journey II made to Dusseldorf as an engineer almost eleven months ago."

Gallaway must have decided that was not a fruitful line of questioning. He suddenly changed tack. "Did Conrad Barnes ever discuss with you, the financial status of Convellium?"

"No!" John was blunt.

"Is that all there is to say on the matter?" He persisted.

"Yes!" John answered in equally clipped fashion.

"What you are saying is that here we have a man, who you obviously admire, who was your mentor in both you engineering and political career, and yet when it came to the point where his world was about to collapse about he ears," He paused for effect. "He did not mention it to you, not even in passing?"

"That's right!" John declared. "I don't think that I could have summed that up more succinctly myself."

"I find that very difficult to believe Mr Robertson!" Gallaway responded belligerently. "I find that very difficult to believe indeed."

"My client has answered the question." Mike stated, entering the round of questions and answers for the first time. "I think that it is time for me to say that Councillor Robertson has volunteered to try to help you with your inquiries, and my understanding was that this would be a straightforward question and answer session. If we are going to move away from that format then I must advise my client to reserve his information."

"I'm sorry!" Gallaway apologised. "I did not mean to imply that there was anything significant in that, merely that I thought it strange that two people who were rather like father and son, had not discussed the approaching collapse of the Company. I only have one additional question to ask, and that is 'How long do you think that you would have continued to work for Convellium, if the sell-out had not taken place?"

"It was getting very difficult for me to do my job properly, and it was presenting problems all-round." John admitted. "The amount of time that I had to devote to City Council work was increasing, and my search for a Constituency to represent as a Member of Parliament was going to almost double my working day. I don't think that I would have lasted more than a couple of months or so."

"How did the redundancy affect you?" He asked.

"After the initial shock, all it did was to focus our minds onto what we wanted to do. My wife had been promoted, and had a significant rise in salary, and I had benefited from the will of an old friend I had a lump-sum redundancy payment, and my attendance allowances. As a family we decided that I would spend a couple of years trying to obtain a seat in Parliament. It would be not be tight, but we would need a strict control on the finances and we could just about make it.

If I failed then, that would be that, and I would go back to a day job."

"Thank you John. and you too Mike." Gallaway dropped his Policeman act. "I don't think that there will be any need for you to worry about this matter. Barnes seems to have kept the whole thing very close to his chest and even Richards didn't know what he was carrying. There is just one point that I missed. In his statement Richards said that Barnes had told him that if anything went wrong, he was to contact you, because you would know all of the answers. Can you elaborate a little?"

"I'm not sure now, what Conrad meant by that." John explained. "I had believed that Conrad was talking about the Engineering content of the German side of the business. Richards seems to interpret this as his 'get out of jail free' card, but that was not so. My belief is that Richards thought about all of this, after Conrad was discharged from the company, and thought that he could get his hands on some of the loot that he mistakenly believed that Conrad and I had hidden away."

"Yes that is the way that I read it too!" He added. "We will be making a statement to the press in about twenty minutes, and if you care to join us we can effectively put this matter to rest from your point of view. So if we amble across to the central Police Station we should just about have time to prepare what we are going to say."

The press room at the Central Police Station was awash with reporters from all sections of the media. TV cameras were prominent, and clearly they were expecting something approaching a sensation.

Archie Gallaway led the team out into the room, and there was a surge of comment when they were followed by Mike Parkin and John Robertson.

It was Archies show, so he was the first to speak. "I know that many of you have received information regarding the financial management of Convellium Limited that is currently under investigation by this force.During the course of our investigation certain allegations were made against Councillor John Robertson, by an employee of the company. We can now confirm that those allegations are totally without foundation. Throughout this investigation we have been assisted by a number of the former employees of the company, but none have been more cooperative than John Robertson himself. We have made inquiries in three European Countries, and there is no evidence to tie Councillor Robertson to the Convellium investigation. That is all that I have to say on the matter."

It had been decided that Mike Parkin would make the statement on John's behalf. "John Robertson is a man who thrives on sorting out problems that other people find difficult. That is what attracted him to politics, and that was the root cause of him being here today. A simple statement that said 'If anything goes wrong contact John Robertson he will know all of the answers.'was all that tied him to the Investigations here, But the facts are that the questions were not on the same subject, and far from asking John to solve the problem, this person chose to ask questions via the National Press on a series of matters that were out of the scope of John Robertson's function as a Design and Production Engineer. To me this indicates a certain amount of malice, and a degree of envy or hatred that defies explanation. John Robertson is an Honourable man, who has nothing to try to hide and as is the case in most of these situations, right has prevailed. That is all. Thank you!"

"Is Mr Robertson prepared to answer questions?"

The BBC journalist asked.

"Not at this time." Mike answered before John volunteered. "The investigation is still on-going, and because there may be a need to use some of the information at a later date, should any proceedings arise, we have been asked not to enter into detail at this time."

John and Mike, along with the rest of the group filed out, and they departed through the yards at the rear of the Magistrates Courts to avoid any further contact with the media. The two of them returned to Mike Parkin's office to discover when they arrived, that Charles Brown was already waiting for them.

"I thought that it would be better for all of us, if I came and got the picture from the two of you, before I contacted Conservative Central Office." He seemed strangely smug.

"Why would you need to contact them?" Mike asked frowning.

"Well we have a serious case of fraud here with a number of prominent Conservatives involved, and this could do untold damage to the Parties chances at the next election." He appeared to be acting as Judge and Jury here. He was condemning John and Conrad and implying that there as no form of defence available to a man who was not even part of the crime.

"Charles!" Mike asked carefully. "Are you saying that you believe that John is to be condemned for assisting the police in their enquiries?"

"Well we all know what that means!" He spluttered. "They only say that when they don't know the extent of the crimes, and it gives them time to consult with the Crown Prosecution Service."

"We have just come from a News Briefing," Mike intoned. "At which the Police have stated clearly that they have no reason to charge John Robertson with any offence, either now or in the future, in respect of the activities surrounding the disposal of the Assets of Convellium Limited. They have publicly thanked him for his help in the matter, and they have received a signed statement from John, and as far as we are concerned that is the end of the matter."

"So there are to be no charges?" He blushed

"No!" they both answered in unison.

"Then why am I here?" Brown asked the question as if they had invited him.

"You tell me Charles!" John placed the ball firmly back in his court. "Perhaps you did not expect me to return from the Central Police Station with Mike? You wouldn't happen to have Frank Jamieson sitting in your office in the Town Hall waiting to take over the Chair of Transport, now would you?"

"Nothing of the sort" He was blustering again. "But we do have to be ready for all problems. My information came from an anonymous caller who said that you had been 'taken' to the Central Police Station. This implied to me that you were under arrest."

"The facts are that we were invited to join in a Police Press Conference to announce that John Robertson was not implicated in the any of the current investigations surrounding Convellium Limited." Mike intervened.

"In that case there is nothing to be done!" Charles concluded and he made a hurried departure.

"What is all of that about?" Mike asked.

"Charles is trying to get me to hand over Transport to Jamieson." John informed him. "He wants to get rid of me because I will not play ball on some of his more under-hand schemes."

"I had heard that you were going to oppose him as leader." Mike stated openly. "And to be perfectly honest you would get a lot of support. He really is a bit of a 'has-been' and is out of touch with much of the detail that is necessary to run a Council of this size."

"I was approached last October." John admitted. "But I have come to the conclusion that local authorities are not the place for me, and I will leave at the end of this term, if I don't get a Parliamentary Seat."

"That is a real shame, John!" Mike replied. "I thought that you were going to be the first of a new breed of Councillor who would take us into the new Millennium."

"The real problem is that there are too many people around in local politics like Charles Brown, who believe that they can manipulate things to their own liking." John confessed. "And I for one will not be subjected to the type of stupidity that places personality above the needs of the community. I am therefore trying to move on before I get caught up in their web of juvenile intrigues."

"I see what you mean." Mike declared. "And I will be sorry to see you go!"

43

On the Road Again

John walked back to the Transport Offices to be greeted with a host of messages. The first was from the PM's press secretary, whom John called back straight away.

Alistair Craig was not known to John, but he clearly knew of John's contact with the PM. "Councillor Robertson," He began. "The PM is a little concerned about some of the details that have been circulating with reference to a company called Convellium, and has asked me to speak to you on the matter."

"There has been a statement issued by the local police in the past hour, concerning this matter" John informed him.

"And what was the substance of the statement." Craig demanded.

"The facts were announced." John stated. "That is to say that the Police told the Press that I had been assisting them with their enquiries, and that the outcome was that I was in no way connected with the problems concerning the disposal of Convellium Limited, and that they did not expect to have to carry out any further interviews with me. They did however say that I may have to give evidence for the Crown."

"That sounds very satisfactory." Alistair Craig sounded relieved. "The PM has asked the local police to send a copy of their findings to the Home Secretary. You will of course appreciate that he has to be very careful in these matters particularly when it concerns some-one whom the PM wishes to become part of his Government in the near future. Now if you would just hold the line, I'll see if the PM is free to speak to you."

"Hello Mr Robertson." It was the PM speaking.

"Good Morning Prime Minister!" John knew that there would be ears pressed to phones all over the place. "How are you this morning?"

"I'm very well! Thank you John!" He answered. "And how are Kathryn and the Children?"

"They are all very well thank you Sir!" He replied

"I just wanted you to know that Alistair has told me the details of the Press release, and I wanted to let you know that the party have never doubted you for a moment." He sounded sincere. "But certain people, who will remain nameless, have been stirring the pot for you. I'm sure that you know what I mean. Sir Marius Clarke will be in touch with you in the next few days to let you know about your application, and I look forward to seeing you and Kathryn again in the near future. So Good-bye"

He was gone. The Phone was replaced, and he sat there a little bemused.

Why had the PM phoned him? But he had no time to answer himself.

"Chairman there's Sir Reginald Reevesby on the line for you!" The switchboard operator was having a field day,

"Reg how are you?" John felt pleased to be speaking to a friend.

"I think that it is me who should be asking that question young man!"

Reg was in good form. "What's that bastard Brown trying to do to you?"

"I don't think that it's Brown who's the problem." John countered.

"In a pig's ear it's not." Reg blasted back. "He is one of the Consortium that has put Convellium out of business."

"Are you sure about that Reg?" John was visibly

shocked.

"I can see that you are not aware of what has been going off John. My department are in the process of gathering information on the whole sorry mess. The real truth of this matter is that a few unscrupulous individuals have plotted the down fall of this company, and have tried, by various means, to implicate you in their schemes. Fortunately it hasn't worked. But rest assured I will provide you with all of the information that I can without making it obvious where it has come from."

"Thanks Reg." John answered. "It has felt rather like being in the middle of somebody else's war for the last few days."

"I can imagine your feelings." Reevesby sympathised. "The sooner we get you out of that nest of thieves, the better." He concluded.

"The PM's been on to me today, on the same matter." John informed him.

"Yes! I think that he feels a little responsible for your current situation." Reg related. "All of the publicity you and Kath received following the Conference, raised a few heckles in your neck of the woods and he feels that he is partly responsible for what has happened. They will all start to back off now that the DTI have become involved."

"Do you think so?" John asked. "There has already been two attempts to oust me from the Chair of Transport here in the past two weeks. Brown is in full cry, but I've managed to block his attempts on both occasions."

"Good for you young man" Reevesby laughed. "That's better than most when Charles starts trying to put the skids under what he thinks might be a young pretender to his throne. Well I must be off. No peace for the wicked is there?"

433

"Thanks for calling Reg. Give our regards to Bella. All the best." He was gone.

"The phone went straight away again. "There's Sir Marius Clarke down in reception waiting to see you Chairman."

"He's where?" John exploded.

"Down here in reception. Chairman." The receptionist replied. "When I told him that you were speaking to the Prime Minister, he said that he would wait. So he's here reading your copy of the FT."

"I'm on my way down." John scrambled for the door. He made his way as calmly as possible down to the reception area to find Marius sitting reading the paper. "Hello Marius!" John extended his hand. "It's good to see you again, but some-what surprising."

"Hello John!" Marius shook his hand warmly. "I was in the City so I thought that I might drop in and see how you were."

"Come along to my office, and we can arrange some coffee and the like." John advised.

"No! I think that we should stay here for a few minutes and meet some of your people." Marius responded.

The reason soon became obvious, as the local press came through the outer door, and cameras started to whirl as the two men held a mock conversation. They talked about their wives and the good time that they had at the conference, and when the Press had their pictures Marius turned and spoke to them. "I would like to make a brief statement regarding the discussions that I have had with John Robertson over the course of the past few days. And what is more they are nothing to do with Convellium Limited. As you are all no doubt aware John is highly regarded in the party at the highest level, and subject to the necessary arrangements being made he will be fighting the Handlebury Constituency at the coming General Election. At a Special General Meeting of the Constituency Party last night he was formally adopted as their candidate. But because of other matters he was unable to travel down to Handlebury so I attended the meeting as his proxy and accepted the nomination on his behalf. The Prime Minister has asked for John to attend a special conference in Germany along with representatives of the DTI and CBI. It is felt that his knowledge of the German language and the many friends that he has in German Industry will be of great assistance to our delegation. Thank You! That is all!"

"Councillor Robertson can you tell us how this will affect your position here in Hainton?" The Local BBC reporter asked.

"As I see it," John replied. "The immediate affect will be minimal all that I have been asked to do is to spend a few days helping to oil the wheels of British and European Industry. In the longer term, and subject to my winning a seat in the next election, I will hopefully be moving away from local politics and into the broader stream. As I have previously stated, I intend to complete my term as Chairman of Transport here in Hainton. Thank you! If you would excuse us Sir Marius and I have a few other points that we need to discuss before he sets off to London."

The two of them went up to John's office where there was already a tray of tea and coffee available.

"I'm sorry that we didn't have a chance to talk before that John." Marius laughed. "But you handled it as if you had been doing it all your life."

"Is all of what you said down there true?" John asked.

Oh! Yes! Young man The PM telephoned Horace Parker two weeks ago and told him that the Parliamentary Party would be obliged if the Party in

Handlebury could assist them by adopting you as their candidate at the earliest possible convenience. This would enable the PM to send you to Germany as part of our delegation. They called an emergency General Meeting, and you were adopted in your absence."

"This all a bit of a shock to my system" John gasped. "I spoke to Horace only yesterday, and he never said a word about it."

"That is because the PM told them not to bother you too much at this time, because you were handling a very difficult situation here and it was essential to the Parties interests that you should be here." Marius smiled. "We hadn't counted upon my old adversary Charles Brown taking up the flag against you quite this early. We knew that he would, because he wanted to be able to manipulate you into a position that would be advantageous to him. This thing about Convellium came right out of the blue, so the PM ordered a DTI investigation straight away. But by some means you had already stopped Brown in his tracks."

"That was easy." John smiled. "I found that he had bugged many of the committee rooms and interview rooms with voice activated tape recorders and I let him know that all of the council employees knew about them. I threatened to leak the details to the press and he backed down."

"You're a wylie bastard John Robertson," Marius laughed. "And the more I see of you, the more I know that we are right in pushing you forward.

The PM will love that one." He said shaking his head.

John called all of the Senior Staff into his office to meet Sir Marius, and having done all of the things that a visiting politician is supposed to do, he went on his way.

By the time that John arrived home he had appeared

on both local and National TV, as had statements by Marius Clarke, and Reg Reevesby.

Horace Parker had announced to the world that the Conservative Party Candidate for the Handlebury Constituency at the Next Election would be John Robertson the current Chairman of Hainton City Transport, who had been unanimously adopted at a Special Meeting of the Parties Executive Committee last night.

All reference to the Convellium Affair had been swept away. Now there was a clear run up to the next General Election and the Robertson Family were truly on their way

Epilogue

On the 8th of May later that year, in the General Election, John Robertson was duly elected Member of Parliament for the Handlebury Constituency and took his seat in the House of Commons. He had a majority of over twenty thousand and became a Junior Minister at the Department for Trade and Industry. The Robertsons moved down to Handlebury about twelve months after the election, and are still living there. Kathryn has a small shop in the town that specialises in Porcelain and China. Anne Robertson is training to be a nurse, and Jason is waiting to go up to Cambridge to read Politics and Economics.

At the same election Martin Smith contested the seat in the Hainton West Constituency and was defeated by the Liberal Democrat. He now leads the Opposition on Hainton City Council. The Smiths and the Robertsons are still good friends and visit each other when their various political commitments allow.

Charles Brown died of a heart attack in June just four weeks after the Election and Frank Jamieson became Leader of Hainton City Council. He never really managed to understand all that was going on around him but he had always had difficulty in grasping the fundamentals of political life. He died following a stroke about twelve months after becoming Leader.

Conrad Barnes was found guilty of Company Fraud and was sentenced to a term of five years imprisonment. He served a little less than two years and lives in retirement in the Cotswolds.

Harry Richards was found guilty of aiding and abetting Conrad Barnes and was sentenced to three years imprisonment. However he was transfered to a mental hospital within two months having suffered a complete mental breakdown.

The End?